# a surfeit of guns

*A Surfeit of Guns*
◇◇◇

Also by P. F. Chisholm
*A Famine of Horses*
*A Season of Knives*
*A Plague of Angels*

Writing as Patricia Finney
*Firedrake's Eye*
*Unicorn's Blood*

# a surfeit of guns

## a sir robert carey mystery

P. F. CHISHOLM

Poisoned Pen Press

Copyright © 1996
Reprinted with permission from Walker & Company.

First Trade Paperback Edition 2000

10 9 8 7 6 5 4 3

Library of Congress Catalog Card Number: 99-068848

ISBN: 1-890208-35-3

Poisoned Pen Press
6962 E. First Ave. Ste 103
Scottsdale, AZ 85251
www.poisonedpenpress.com
info@poisonedpenpress.com

Printed in the United States of America

To Rosie, with thanks

*Historical Note*

Anyone who wants to know the true history of the Anglo-Scottish Borders in the Sixteenth Century should read George MacDonald Fraser's superbly lucid and entertaining account: "The Steel Bonnets" (1971). Those who wish to meet the real Sir Robert Carey can read his Memoirs (edited by F.H. Mares, 1972) and some of his letters in the Calendar of Border Papers.

# R IS FOR....EXTRAORDINARY

The number of "R" words that come to mind when describing P.F. Chisholm's rousing Elizabethan detections is remarkable. Filled with rakish, ruthless, reckless, rapacious, rough-riding, ruffianly, rascally, reprobative, roguish, occasionally rueful rapscallions, raiders, and reivers, they are rich, ribald, rowdy, riveting, riotous, robust, rollicking, rambunctious, randy, roistering, racy, and rattling good reads. What makes them so?

It is, of course, their blend of those basic components of fiction—plot, characters, setting—plus content, all washed with the sort of prose that turns such elements into literary gold. Rare is the novel in which the reader finds each building block to be of high quality, rarer still when a real balance is achieved. In my book, the Robert Carey novels, *A Famine of Horses, A Season of Knives, A Surfeit of Guns,* and *A Plague of Angels*, reach that plateau.

As P.F. Chisholm, *nom de plume* of author Patricia Finney, notes in her Introduction, to each Poisoned Pen Press edition, Carey is a real historical character whose life was itself the stuff of fiction. He's a natural to be the hero of a book, or books, that flesh out the bones of the historical record and embrace not only what we actually know of Carey, but imagine what could have been the truth of his life and character.

Elizabeth Widdrington, too, is a real woman and I think it's especially to Chisholm's credit that she gives us Elizabeth's character and behavior in a manner consistent with her time and not as rendered through the lens of today's sensibility. An Elizabethan woman would not have carelessly abandoned her marriage but endured its vicissitudes, although many took such comfort as there was along the way, nor would she have shown disrespect to her husband in public, nor been heedless of her reputation. Nor would she have risked a breach with the Queen which, in the case of a relationship with Robert, the Queen's blood kin, would have been likely. The rocky course of the Carey/Widdrington romance is, of course, the very stuff of good fiction. Interesting, too, is its unlikely nature, for Elizabeth was no beauteous maiden but a mature woman who'd acceded to an arranged marriage with her elderly husband. She had, thus, family obligation to honor along with personal and political considerations. I think Chisholm captures her dilemma movingly in the closing pages of *A Season of Knives*.

Other historical personages appear such as Philadelphia, Carey's sister, and her ineffectual husband Lord Scrope, and Lord Hunsdon, Carey's father, met finally in the flesh in *A Plague of Angels*. But *A Surfeit of Guns* belongs, in great part, to that difficult monarch James VI of Scotland, son of the beheaded Mary, cousin and perhaps heir to Elizabeth, husband of Anne, and progenitor of those unlucky and ill-judging Stuart kings who ruled England and Scotland during the 17th Century. James it is who eventually gave Carey his break in life, and James it is who really rules these pages as the story moves back and forth from Carlisle to Dumfries. With James comes his court, the powerful Earl of Mar, the quarreling and scheming nobles and their henchmen, foreign agents, and the nasty boy, Lord Spynie, who has captured the wayward king's heart. With James, the role of Favorite, usually filled by female forms, went to men, some of whom, like Lord Spynie, played power games of their own.

Chisholm has a dazzling ability to plunge her readers straight into the late 16th Century, straight into the Debateable Lands, the most dangerous part of Elizabeth's kingdom, that border country so porous that blood relations took arms against each other and posses rode back and forth on legitimate hot trods and illegitimate raids. So well transported are we that any interruption becomes unwelcome and we must follow the twists and turns of the plots to the end. In *A Surfeit of Guns* we are led to Dumfries, "the centre of gunmaking for the whole of Scotland, being placed in the area of highest demand," and thus onto an enlarged stage. Its sequel, *A Plague of Angels*, then carries the action to London.

*A Surfeit of Guns* is arguably the bleakest of the Carey stories, filled with doubts, duplicity, double dealings, and death. It is of the novels the most political, centering around the machinations of the Scottish court, and it is the most venal. While in part a police procedural, consonant with Carey's official post as a sort of Sheriff, the plot is built upon power politics and espionage. Its hook lies in armaments, in the valuable guns shipped into—and out of—the Carlisle garrison. To what purpose? the author asks, and challenges us to work out the answer.

As a plotter, Chisholm is inventive and does not repeat herself. In her third Carey novel she is, I think, more interested in character than in story. And it is somewhat dour. Let's face it, there is less to like in James and his court than in Elizabeth's, and less *joie de vivre*, less electricity. It was, for the Stuart monarch, a waiting time and a waiting game. But, in the overreaching arc of the Carey series—and I, for one, hope for many more novels as we build up to the events of 1603—it's as important to establish the anchor end in Scotland as it is the other anchor in London, though we spend much time on the grounds where Carey filled his post as Deputy Warden. Thus we need to meet up with James and firm the connection between him and Carey.

To me, the real joy of the Careys lies less in the real life figures than in the glorious secondary characters, as ruthless, charming, and complex a bunch of survivors of what Chisholm spares no pains to reveal as a harsh, unforgiving, real minimalist life, as ever you will meet. From stalwart Sergeant Dodd to the randy servant Barnabus to the unfortunate Long George and his Little family to the imp Young Hutchin, you meet them and you know them, just as you learn to wander familiarly among the Grahams and the other Border clans. You could as easily be in our American Wild West, caught up in Tombstone territory with rustlers, outlaws, hired hands, and a few guys sporting badges, the whole bunch operating under the umbrella of shifting alliances or clan loyalties—or just for the paycheck.

I've paid tribute to the characters, the setting, the plot, and the historical content of Chisholm's work. In the end, however, what makes me a True Fan and completes that sense that "You Are THERE!" —noted by Sharon Kay Penman in her Introduction to

*A Famine of Horses*, Dana Stabenow in her Introduction to *A Season of Knives*, and Diana Gabaldon in her Introduction to *A Plague of Angels*—is the language. It is through her lively dialogue and unfailingly canny sense of the Right Word that Chisholm conveys the rags and riches of the period and the in and outs of character. There is no question her research has been prodigious, though it is never flaunted nor allowed to take over the narrative. But somehow, perhaps as a consequence, she has simply stepped into a pattern of speech as into a time warp and sucked us right along with her. It is the web of language she weaves that holds us, once transported to Carey's world, and leaves us reluctant to travel back when the end of the tale is reached.

As the editor of Poisoned Pen Press, my enthusiasm for our publications is unbounded. A joy of working within a small press is that we can publish what we like, not what will sell, although one hopes for a successful marriage between the two. It is a privilege as well as a pleasure to bring you the novels of an author as talented as P.F. Chisholm in the hope that you will share both in the joy of discovery and in the journey each affords.

To bolster my recommendation, let me end with a statement from a reader. "P.F. Chisholm's strength lies in her ability to write a dialogue which is natural and not preciously 'period' and she certainly seems to understand the mind of the borderer. I speak as a borderer myself, albeit from the East, not the West March. I would strongly recommend this book to lovers of both historical and mystery fiction."

—Barbara Peters
The Poisoned Pen Mystery Bookstore
www.poisonedpen.com
www.poisonedpenpress.com

# fRiday 7th july 1592, late afternoon

Sir Robert Carey woke up to a knock on the door, feeling sticky-mouthed and bad-tempered and uncertain what time of day it was. He was in his clothes with his doublet buttons undone, his boots by the side of the bed. Through the window the diamond mosaic of sky had greyed over. Barnabus Cooke his man-servant came stumping in carrying a bowl of cold water, a towel over one arm, a leather bottle of small beer under the other.

"Afternoon, sir," he said in his familiar adenoidal whine. "Sergeant Dodd wants to know where you was thinking of patrolling tonight."

Ah. Night patrol, therefore an afternoon nap.

"I haven't decided yet," Carey answered.

He sat up and swung his legs over the side of the bed, hearing the elderly strapping creak beneath the mattress. Although the bed had once been honoured by the sleeping body of Her Majesty the Queen of Scots while she was briefly an uneasy guest in Carlisle, that was nearly thirty years before and it had had a hard life since then. He honestly thought a straw pallet on the floor might be more comfortable and certainly less noisy.

While he splashed his face with cold water and drank some of the beer, Carey gathered his thoughts and tried to wake up properly. Barnabus fastened his many buttons, helped him on with his jack. As always there was a depressing moment when the padded, double-layered leather coat, with its metal plates in between, weighed him down like original sin. Then, once it was laced and his belt buckled so the weight was evenly distributed between his shoulders and hips, his body adjusted and he no longer felt it. As armour went, it was very comfortable, much better than his tilting plate that was in pawn down in London. He had his new broadsword, the best the Dumfries armourers could produce, and Barnabus had oiled it well, though the hilt still felt rough and odd against his hand after he had strapped it on. His helmet was a fine piece, a blued-steel morion, with elaborate chasing on its peaks and curves, well-padded inside. He knew it made him conspicuous, but that was the idea after all—his men needed to know where he was in a fight.

Fully-dressed, he caught sight of himself in the mirror, saw the martial reflection and unconsciously smiled back at it. Barnabus knelt to put his spurs on, tutting at the state of the riding boots which Barnabus's nephew had forgotten to clean. Finally accoutred, Carey clattered down the stairs, his handguns in their case under his arm, weighing perhaps sixty pounds more than he had when he got up.

Sergeant Dodd and the men were waiting with their horses in the courtyard. Carey did a quick headcount, found they were all there and went over to ask Dodd what Long George had to say for himself.

Long George Little was the man standing next to Dodd. He was showing a pistol to him, a new one by the gleam of its powderpan, and Dodd was sighting down the barrel and squeezing the trigger.

"Dumfries work, is it?" Dodd was asking.

"Ay," said Long George, who was actually no taller than Dodd and an inch or two shorter than Carey himself, but gave the impression of even greater height because he had long bony legs and arms.

"What did ye pay for it?"

Long George coughed. "Twenty-five shillings, English."

"Mphm," said Dodd noncommittally.

"Good evening, gentlemen," said Carey with some sarcasm. "I'm delighted to see you, Long George. Where have you been since Wednesday?"

Long George's face was round and his beard a straggling decoration that refused to grow around his mouth but flourished all the way down his neck and into his chest hairs. The face suddenly became childlike in its innocence.

"It were family business, sir," he said. "One of the weans was sick and the wife thought it might be the smallpox."

"Ah. And was it?"

"Was what, sir?"

"Was it smallpox?"

"Nay, it was chickenpox."

Had he had that, Carey wondered, and decided he had. He remembered his mother putting him in a camomile bath to soothe the itching and cutting his nails down short.

"I might have needed you as a witness at the Atkinson inquest."

Long George shrugged and wouldn't meet his eye. Clearly he had made himself scarce precisely in order to avoid being a witness. "I'm here for the patrol, sir, amn't I?" he said truculently. "That's all ye want, is it not?"

Carey gave him a considering stare. "It will do for the present," he said coldly. Long George gazed into space, put a helmet on, knuckled his forehead and went to find his horse.

They were a little late going out, but the watch at the city gates had waited for them. They crossed Eden Bridge and struck north and east, heading for Askerton Castle and Bewcastle beyond that.

As the sun set behind its grey blanket of cloud, and the night closed in, they slowed down, letting their horses feel their way. It was a black night, blacker than mourning velvet, the sky robbed of diamonds and the countryside full of hushed noise. Most of the cattle were still up at the shielings but the small farms announced themselves with the snoring of pigs and occasionally sheep would wander abstractedly across the path they were using. The men were quiet behind him apart from the occasional clatter of a lance against stirrup or the jingle of a bridle.

Now he was properly awake and his nightsight had come in so he could see the world in subtle shades of grey, Carey couldn't help feeling happy. He knew it was ridiculous when he was theoretically supposed to stop multiple mayhem and feud on the lawless West March of England, with a grand total of nine patrolmen including himself, but still he never felt better than when he was on horseback wondering what might happen. His sister said he was quite mad to enjoy himself so much when at any time he might meet raiders who could kill him, but then she was a woman and would never understand.

However, most of the night passed in jingling boredom. And then at last they were passing by an outpost of forest not far from the Border and Carey was about to order them to turn for home, when they heard a crashing and clattering from between the trees. The men immediately began to spread themselves along the path and tighten their helmet laces. Carey put his hand up for caution. Long George was pouring powder into the pan of his new gun. But whatever was coming was four-legged and certainly not horses…

The deer burst from the wood, tightly bunched, a group of young staggards and other rascals from what he could see of their antlers, their nostrils flaring and their white rumps flashing. They came suddenly, blindly, upon a line of men downwind of them and dodged in their panic from place to place. Long George lifted his pistol two-handed, screwed up his face thoughtfully and fired. The boom of the shot caused the deer to leap and double their speed, but one of them was turned into a still-moving fountain of blood, with most of its neck destroyed by the bullet. Gradually catching up with the disaster its legs stopped running and its body slumped into the ground, flopping about until it lay still.

"Good shot!" shouted Carey, delighted at the prospect of fresh venison. Long George grinned with pleasure and blew the remnants of powder off his pan.

Carey and Dodd dismounted, waited for the blood to stop and then inspected the beast. It was nicely fat and at least a stag, so although there was no particular honour in killing it, at least there would be good eating.

"We'll gralloch it and drain it for half an hour," said Carey. "The butcher can do the rest when we get it home."

Dodd nodded. "We're not poaching, are we?"

Carey thought for a moment. "I don't think so, we're on English land and anyway, Long George only hit the animal by accident, isn't that right, Long George?"

"Ay, sir. Me gun went off wi'out warning, sir."

The other men sniggered quietly.

"Exactly. And it would be a pity to waste the meat." Carey did not have his set of hunting knives with him, but Dodd passed him a long heavy knife with a wicked edge that was suspiciously apt to the purpose. Stepping around to the back of the beast, Carey leaned over the carcass and made the belly-cut with a flourish, thinking of the many times he had broken a beast with full ceremony to the music of drums and trumpets in front of Queen Elizabeth at one of her various courtly hunts.

"By God, he does it prettily," one of the men remarked in a mutter to Dodd, who happened to be standing next to him. "Will ye look at him, not a drop on him?"

"Ah've seen it done faster," sniffed Dodd.

"Ay well, so've I, but that's with one ear out for the keeper..." He paused, cocking his head thoughtfully. Far in the distance, there was more crashing in the deer's wake through the forest.

"That's a man running," said Dodd, swinging up onto his horse again and taking his lance back from Red Sandy. Carey looked up, stopped, wiped his hands and blade sketchily on the grass and vaulted up onto his own horse's back just as the sound of feet burst out of the undergrowth and shaped itself into the blur of a human being, head down, arms pumping. He saw them waiting in the darkness and skidded to a halt, mouth open in dismay.

Carey knew prey when he saw it; the man's oddly-cut doublet was flapping open and his fine shirt ripped and stained, his hose were in tatters and his boots broken. He had pale hair plastered to his face with sweat, a flushed face, a pale beard and a square jaw.

"Hilfe, hilf mir," he gasped. "Freunde, helft mir..." His legs buckled and he went to his knees involuntarily, chest shuddering for air. "Um Gottes willen."

"He's a bastard Frenchman," said Red Sandy excitedly, aiming his lance at the man and riding forward.

"Nay, he's that Spanish agent..." someone else shouted. Long George was reloading his pistol as fast as he could.

"*Nein, nein...*"

"Wait!" roared Carey. "God damn your eyes, WAIT!"

In the distance, they could hear dogs giving tongue. The man heard it too, his eyes whitened, he tried to stand, but he was utterly spent and he pitched forward on his face, retching drily.

Carey dismounted and went over to the man.

"He's a French foreigner," said Red Sandy again. "Did ye no' hear him speaking French, sir? Can I get his tail for a trophy, sir?"

"It wasn't French," said Carey. "It was something else, High or Low Dutch, I think. He's a German."

Red Sandy subsided, mystified at the thought of a foreigner who wasn't French.

"Like one of them foreign miners down by Derwentwater," put in Sim's Will Croser helpfully. "Ye mind 'em, Red Sandy? They speak like that, ay, with all splutters and coughs and the like."

"Qu'est vostre nom, monsieur? Parlez-vous français?" Carey asked as he approached the man who was lifting himself feebly on his elbows. Behind him he could hear the men muttering between themselves. They were arguing over whether the German miners had tails like Frenchmen.

"Hans Schmidt, mein Herr, aus Augsburg. Ich spreche ein bischen…je parle un peu de Français."

"Well, that's French, any road," said Dodd dubiously as the hounds in the distance gave tongue again, musical and haunting. The German winced at the sound and tried to climb to his feet, but his knees gave way. His fear was pitiful.

"I know, Sergeant," said Carey, coming to a decision, "Have the men move off the road into the undergrowth over there, spread them out. Not much we can do about the venison seeing they've got dogs, so leave it. Red Sandy, you set the men and don't move until we know what's coming after this man. If I shoot, hit them hard. Dodd, you stay here with me."

This they understood. Red Sandy swung his horse back the way they had come and the other six melted briskly into the bushes with their mounts. As the leaves hid them, Long George had the slowmatch lit for his pistol and was cupping it with his hand to hide it. Sim's Will Croser was taking his bow out of the quiver and stringing it. It was ridiculous that in this day and age most of his men had no modern firearms but must still rely on the longbows of their great-grandfathers, Carey thought to himself. They were waiting the devil of a long time for the ordnance carts from Newcastle.

Dodd loosened his sword, took a grip on his lance and slouched down in the saddle, sighing in a martyred fashion as he stayed out in plain view to back up his Deputy Warden. Heart beating hard, Carey could hear the other horses now, crashing through the undergrowth behind the hounds.

The German, Hans Schmidt, had got to his feet, swaying with exhaustion, jabbering away desperately in High Dutch, not one word of which Carey could make out. He could talk to a whore or an innkeeper in Low Dutch, but that was the size of his ability. French came easier to him.

"Nicht verstehe," he said. "Je ne comprends pas. Plus lentement, s'il vous plaist."

For answer the man put his face in his hands and moaned. There was no time left, the hoofbeats were too close. The German began wobbling away, across the field. Carey shook his head, remounted his horse and pulled both his dags out of their cases. They were already shotted and he wound them up ready to fire, but from the sound of it two shots would not be enough.

The dogs broke from the woods in a yelping tide, making his horse snort and sidle. Lymers and sleuth-hounds flowed around them, yelping excitedly, sniffing ground, hooves, bellies. The fugitive at least had sense enough not to run, or perhaps he could not. He had fallen and was curled into a ball with his hands over his face. The dogs gathered round, tails wagging furiously, sniffed curiously at the man, then caught scent of the partly-gralloched deer and gave tongue. They entirely lost interest in their original quarry and gathered about the deer. Some began pulling guiltily at the entrails.

"Off, off. Allez!" shouted Carey, riding over to protect his kill, looking around for the huntsmen.

For a moment it was hounds only, the horses heralded by sound. Then, like the elven-folk from a poet's imagination, they cantered out of the tree shadows, three, four, eight, twelve of them, and more behind, some carrying torches, their white leather jacks pristine and lace complicating the hems of their falling bands and cuffs, flowing beards and glittering jewelled fingers, with the plump flash of brocade above their long boots. Carey was surprised: he had expected one of the Border headmen and his kin, like Scott of Buccleuch or Kerr of Ferniehurst, perhaps even Lord Maxwell. Certainly not these fine courtiers.

The Master of the Hunt whipped the hounds off, and the highest ranking among them rode forward on a horse far too good for the rough ground. Carey recognised him immediately.

"My lord Earl of Mar," he said in astonishment, looking from the dishevelled panting German to the King of Scotland's most trusted advisor.

"Eh?" said the earl, squinting through the mirk. "Who's that?"

"Sir Robert Carey, my lord, Deputy Warden of the English West March."

"Eh? Speak oot, mon."

Carey repeated himself in Scots. Behind him he could feel Dodd sitting quiet and watchful, his lance pointed upwards, managing expertly to project a combination of relaxation and menace without actually doing anything.

The Earl of Mar was glaring at Carey's dags. Rather pointedly, he did not put them away. Out of the corners of his eyes he could see a further six or eight riders milling about in the forest, rounding up stray dogs, while three of the other huntsmen tried to reassert discipline over the hounds who felt they had a right to the deer's innards after their run.

"What are ye doing here?"

"Well, my lord, I could ask you the same question since we're on English land."

"We're on a lawful hot trod."

"Oh?" said Carey neutrally.

"Ay, we are. My lord Spynie, where the devil's that bit of turf?"

A young round-faced man with a velvet bonnet tipped over his ear rode forward. Some crumbs of turf still stuck to the point of his lance, and he was frowning at it in irritation. He was a handsome young man, of whom Carey had heard but had never met, known variously as Alexander Lindsay, Lord Spynie, King James's favourite and the King's bloody bum-boy.

"I see," said Carey, relaxing slightly and putting his dags away but leaving the case open. "Well, my lord, in that case, as Deputy Warden of the English West March, I am a proper person for you to tell the cause of the trod to, and if necessary, I will render you what assistance I can."

The Earl of Mar glared at him. Two of his men had dismounted and were lifting the German to his feet, not very gently.

Knowing he was well within his rights, but feeling a bit of oil might be appropriate in the circumstances, Carey bowed lavishly in the saddle and added, "If my lord will be so very kind."

The Earl of Mar harrumphed. He either ignored or did not understand the edge to Carey's obsequity. "Ay, well," he said. "Ye've already assisted me, by stopping this traitor here, so I'll thank ye kindly and we'll be awa' again."

"Ich bin nicht…" the German began yelling. His arm slipped out of one of his helpers' hands, he swung a wild punch at the other which connected by sheer chance. Hands plucking at the empty scabbard on his belt, he shouldered past another would-be helper, running at a desperate stagger for the forest, only to be knocked off his feet by a kick in the face from one of the other horsemen. He was hefted up again and his hands tied briskly behind him. Carey had tensed when he made his break, every instinct telling him to help one against so many, but intelligence and self-preservation ordering him not to be such a fool. He had eight men—the Scottish courtiers had at least thirty plus the law of the Borders on their side. And the man was a foreigner.

"I see," he said, looking away as the German was hauled to a riderless horse, still half-stunned and bleeding from the nose, and slung across it like dead game. "May I ask what form his treason took? Is there anything likely to be a threat to Her Majesty the Queen?"

"Nay," said the Earl of Mar, backing his horse with a rather showy curvette. "Tis a private matter between yon loon and our King. We'll be off now."

With great difficulty the hounds where whipped off the stag, some of them still trailing bits of entrail from their mouths as they lolloped unwillingly away. The whole cavalcade plunged back into the forest, heading north again, with the unfortunate German occasionally visible, like a feebly struggling sack of flour across his horse's back. Cheekily the Earl of Mar winded his horn as they disappeared from sight.

◇◇◇

Dodd said nothing as Carey dismounted and went back to the stag to see what could be salvaged. The stag was quite a bit the worse for wear but much of the gralloching had been done. The skin would not be useable though. The men reappeared and, unasked, hung the stag up on a tree branch by its back legs to drain.

They waited by the tree while the most part of the deer's remaining blood trickled out. With suspicious efficiency the men constructed a travois out of hazel branches and argued quietly over whose horse should pull it.

Dodd was still saying nothing, and cocking his head northwards occasionally with an abstracted expression.

"What's the problem, Sergeant?" asked Carey.

Dodd coughed. "It's the trod, sir."

"The Earl of Mar's taken his captive back into Scotland by now, I should think."

"Ay, sir."

"So?"

"Sir, did ye never follow on behind a hot trod so ye could claim the beasts ye took were part of it?"

"You mean there might be a Scots raiding party following the Earl of Mar's trail so they can claim they're legally coming into England as part of the pursuit?" Carey asked carefully.

Dodd clearly wondered why he was belabouring something so obvious. "Ay, after about an hour or so," he agreed. "To let the...excitement die down, see."

"I do see, Sergeant. Do you think they'll come by here?"

Dodd's wooden expression told Carey he had asked another stupid question.

"Only, ye can mix the trails about, sir."

"Fine. What would you suggest, Sergeant?"

Dodd's suggestion took shape: they took the deer carcass down from the tree and lashed it to its travois, which Long George and Croser hauled into the branches of an oak to keep it away from foxes.

"We can't actually stop them coming south," Carey said while the others cleared the ground of their own tracks. "They haven't committed any crime and they're following a lawful hot trod, so..."

Dodd and his brother Red Sandy exchanged patient glances.

"No, see, sir, if we stop them before they've lifted aught, then we'll get nae fee for it, will we? We'll stop 'em after."

"I see. Very interesting. Do you ever…*arrange* for raids, so you can stop them and get the fees for them?"

"Ay, sir," said Sandy. "Why, last year the Sergeant and…"

Dodd coughed loudly.

"…ay, well, Lowther's done it," his brother finished, managing to look virtuously indignant. "But *we* wouldnae, would we, Sergeant?"

Even in the darkness, Dodd's glare could have withered a field of wheat.

"One of us must track them on foot," he said judiciously. "Sandy's the best man for that job, seeing he's the fastest runner and he knows the land." Red Sandy made a wry face. "Then when he's seen them find the beasts they're after, he comes back to us and we stop them on their way home, red-handed."

"What if they take a different route?"

Dodd rubbed his chin with his thumb. "They might," he allowed. "But I doubt it. They'll keep to the trail the Earl of Mar made with a' his fine men to confuse us from following."

Carey nodded.

"I rely on your judgement, Sergeant. Shall we take cover now?"

"Ay, sir, it'd be best. Though it might be a long wait."

Dodd and Red Sandy had a quiet conversation as all of them carefully pushed in among the undergrowth. Carey watched in fascination as each man of his troop then took his horse's head and forced the animal to lie down with great rustling surges in the bracken and leaves. Long George swore because he'd found a patch of nettles, a couple of the horses snorted and resisted. Carey found that the right pressure on his own animal's neck and head laid the rough body down with a great lurch and grunting and splaying of legs. They were completely out of sight. He copied Dodd, lying down as well, with one arm over his horse's head, the other arm supporting his own head.

Red Sandy was nowhere to be seen. Carey realised then that he was already outside the woodland, where it met the rough pasture of the hillside, and inspecting them all for concealment.

"There's a man wi' a shiny helmet moving," Red Sandy said accusingly. Carey turned his head to see who was revealing them. "Ay, there he goes again."

Luckily the dark hid his flush as he realised that he was the guilty man. Dodd reached over with some leafy twigs and stuck them in Carey's plume-tube.

"Tha's better," called Red Sandy. "Tell the silly get to stay still, Henry."

Dodd grunted softly and didn't look at Carey. Red Sandy hardly rustled the bushes as he took cover himself.

The silence clamped down around them, like the forest and the night. Not even the horses moved, though Carey could see the wide eyes of his own mount, alert but very well trained and not moving a hoof.

Time passed. The damp coolness of the earth began working its way through the layers of leather and cloth to his stomach, the warmth of a sultry summer night was weight on his back. Little trickles of sweat began seeking water's own level down the muscles of his shoulders. There was an ant's nest under his knee. Perhaps the ants wouldn't mind.

Strain his ears though he might, he could hear absolutely nothing of the eight other men hiding only a few feet away from him. Not a snort, not a rustle. He could swear they were even breathing quieter than him.

The back of his head was itching where the leather padding of his helmet was making his scalp sweat. Also he was convinced there were ants running up his legs. Also he had a cramp starting in one foot. Where the hell were these theoretical raiders?

There was a loud rustling and crunching sound. For a moment Carey wondered which idiot could be making it, when he saw a small bundle of spines wander into his field of vision. It stopped short, stared at him out of little black eyes. He stared back. Never before in his life had he been nose to nose with a hedgehog, though he had once eaten one, baked in clay.

The hedgehog snuffled out a slug and began eating it noisily with every sign of enjoyment. Carey was irresistibly reminded of one of the Queen's councillors eating a bag pudding and had to swallow hard not to laugh. He swallowed too loudly. Disdainfully, the hedgehog finished the slug and trundled off into the leaves like a small battering ram.

The cramp in his foot was getting worse. And the ants were exploring dangerously high up his thigh. And he desperately wanted to scratch his scalp. Where were the raiders?

Without moving his head, Carey looked for Dodd. Between the leaves the Sergeant seemed quite at ease, his long limbs sprawled and relaxed, peering over his horse's neck. He wasn't like a statue, more along the lines of a bolster on a bed. Blast him.

Nothing happened. Carey wondered what a German from Augsburg was doing in the Scottish Borders and why King James wanted him and what for: he wove several wonderful webs of possibility, but the facts would have to wait until he got back to Carlisle and even then he might never know unless he went into Scotland. The ants seemed to be excited about the discovery of his boot-top. Perhaps they were planning a new nest. Would they have time to build it? Probably the itch in his hair was a louse. Perhaps the ants would form an alliance with whatever other vermin he had picked up in Carlisle...

Wondering how much longer he would have to stand this torture, Carey began trying to distract his mind. Inevitably he thought of Elizabeth Widdrington. The last he heard, she had been at Hexham on her way home to the East March. The smile dropped off his face. Her husband, Sir Henry Widdrington, had met her there. She had sent Carey a letter breaking off their friendship, and a verbal message continuing it. God knew what Sir Henry had done to her, to make her write the letter, might even be doing to her now.

He thought of the Latin poem he had recited for her a few days before, one of the muckier ones by Catullus that every schoolboy found easy to remember.

His tutor had translated it, disapprovingly, "Give me a thousand kisses, then a hundred, then another thousand..." It was pleasant to imagine kissing Elizabeth Widdrington, breaking through all her honourable propriety, her entirely misguided faithfulness to her elderly husband, lifting her skirts and petticoat and the hoops of her farthingale and her smock and...

No, it wasn't only his heartbeat. Hooves pointed the metre: soft unshod hooves on the turf. Carey peered through leaves cautiously and saw horses pass like shadows nearby. There was a pause and another shadow departed, on foot, loping like a wolf in their tracks.

"Sir!" That was Dodd's scandalised hiss. "Sir, wake up!"

"I wasn't asleep," he hissed back quickly. "I was thinking."

"Oh aye. Well, they've come and gone whilst ye was thinking and Red Sandy's gone off after them. Ye can let your hobby up to stamp about a bit now."

Knowing he was bright red and still hindered by the effects of thinking about Elizabeth, not to mention the cramp in his instep, Carey staggered to his feet. The horse lurched up and shook out its mane, Carey brushed astonished ants off his boots and got bitten half a dozen times.

They stayed in the bushes, for what seemed like another hour while Carey tried to keep his mind on his job and off his fantasies. Girls he had known at Court flitted irritatingly to and fro before his mind's eye—he surely was in desperate need of a woman. Sorrel nuzzled at him with his broad low-bred nose, and Carey patted him absently.

At last they heard pelting feet, a single man, sprinting down the hill towards them. Dodd cocked his head, led his horse out of the bushes.

Red Sandy himself arrived, breathing hard.

"Bastard Elliots, about seven of them, all mounted," he whispered triumphantly. "Wee Colin Elliot's wi' them. They've taken twelve sheep off one of the Routledges an' they're on their way."

In the distance the sound of protesting baas floated to them, and horses.

Dodd's mouth thinned and his face lengthened, which meant he was delighted. He and Carey swung up into the saddle together and Carey opened his guncase again. Behind them, he heard Long George cursing as he burnt his fingers trying to relight a slow match from the little clay pot of coals he carried on his saddle bow.

"Keep the light hidden," Carey said and got a protesting "Ah know that, sir."

His heart settling to a steady fast thumping, Carey came up close to Dodd.

"This wasn't done by any arrangement, was it?"

"With Elliots, sir?" Dodd was scandalised and Carey remembered that the Sergeant's surname had a fifty-year-old blood-feud running with the Elliots.

"No, obviously not. Well then, let's see if we can catch a few to hang."

Dodd nodded dourly. Clearly, taking the trouble to capture Elliots was not his highest priority. Carey grinned at him, the prospect of a fight raising his spirits as always.

"One or two will do," he amended.

Was that the faintest flicker of an answering smile at the edge of Dodd's mouth? Probably not.

The sheep arrived first, milling about confusedly and baaing. Dodd and he rode between them, straight at the reivers, while the rest came around from both sides of the flock. For a moment there was confused shouting; the reivers weren't sure what was happening: Carey fired both his dags, missed both times. A couple of arrows whipped into the ground, Sim's Will rode past with his lance in rest and his horse tripped over a sheep.

"A Tynedale, a Tynedale, Out, Out!" roared Dodd happily, barrelling lance first at the widest mounted shadow.

Carey hauled his sword out, felt rather than saw something coming at him through the night, turned his horse and struck sideways. The sword went into something, there was a splash of hot blood and the blade stuck. He twisted and wrenched it out. Then a horse cantered past on his other side, its rider jumped onto his back and hauled him to the ground, giving him a headful of spinning lights and a nasty twinge from the ribs he had cracked two weeks before. A snarling face was lit up briefly by a bright red flash; dimly somewhere in the distance he heard a very loud bang and a sound of shrieking, but he was too busy to wonder who had been hit.

He elbowed his enemy in the face while neither of them had any nightsight, rolled to loosen the man's grip and brought his sword hilt down on the white patch of face he could just see under the helmet. He tried to get to his feet, there was a blow on his side, the man was trying to grapple his neck, he managed to pull his dagger free with his left hand as he twisted away and stabbed under the man's arm, heard the grating of metal and a gasp. This time he could get his legs under him, he raised his broadsword up and swung down, there was a satisfying meaty thunk and the man's head came off. He hopped backwards quickly to be away from the blood.

Somebody still mounted came riding towards him with a lance, black shadow on a bigger shadow, the shadow of a lance. Carey's world focused down to its point and time slowed. He waited until the last possible minute, then threw himself sideways into the horse's path. The hobby reared, frightened of the movement, one of the hooves caught him a glancing blow on the helmet, he caught the nearest stirrup, reached up, hefted the man out of the saddle and onto the ground. They both tangled in the lance-haft and fell down together and just as Carey got on top of the man, and was preparing to stab him lefthanded in the throat, he realised it was Sim's Will Croser.

For a moment he simply knelt there stupidly as his sight cleared. Then he got up.

"Are you hurt?" he demanded.

"Nay," said Sim's Will. "Sorry, sir, Ah mistook ye."

Both of them were on their feet, Carey picked his sword off the turf, looking around for enemies but none were left. Hooves thudded off in the distance. He wiped his blade down with handfuls of grass and sheathed it. The body of the man Carey had killed was still bleeding into the ground, four horses were trotting around shaking their heads. Further off the shrieking was fading to gasps. Carey went over to the source of the sounds where two others of his men were standing by helplessly. Dodd cantered up and dismounted.

"They've run," he snarled. "We got two of them, I think, but it seems my brother canna count. There were at least ten. And Long George is hurt bad."

That was an understatement. Long George Little was kneeling on the ground, hunched over and making short gasping moans. He looked up at Carey like a wounded dog, his face spattered with black mud. With a lurch under his breastbone of sympathy,

Carey saw George was cradling the rags of his right hand against his chest. All the fingers were gone, the thumb hanging by a piece of flesh with the splintered bone sticking out of the meat. Long George had his other hand gripped round the wrist, trying to slow his bleeding.

"Anybody else hurt?" Carey asked.

"Nay," they all answered.

"Who's got the bandages?"

All of them shrugged. Carey suppressed a sigh. "There's a dead man over there," he snapped, pointing. "Go and cut long strips from his shirt."

Red Sandy trotted off with his dagger and came back a few minutes later with some strips of grey canvas in his hand. Carey tied up what was left of Long George's hand and made a tourniquet with the rest of the strips. Long George gasped and whimpered as he did it, but managed to hold still with his eyes shut, while Dodd patted his shoulder. A trickle of blood came from his mouth.

"Well, we rescued the sheep," said Red Sandy brightly. "That's something."

"Thank you, Red Sandy," said Carey repressively. "Can you ride your horse, Long George?"

"Ay, sir, if ye give me a leg up," whispered George.

Red Sandy and Dodd helped him over to his horse, lifted him on, while the rest caught the other loose horses and linked them together. Long George was already starting to shiver, something Carey had seen before: when large quantities of the sanguine humour were lost, a Jewish Court physician had told him once, then the furnace of the heart began to cool and might cool to death. Warmth and wine were a good answer, but they could give him neither until they got to Carlisle.

Carey rode up close to the shaking Long George. His face was badly hurt too, he realised now: what he had taken for mud on the right side of it was a mess of cuts and burns that had laid his face open to the gleaming white bone.

"Can you ride as far as Carlisle?"

"Nay, sir, take me home. My farm's by the Wall, not far fra Lanercost."

"Of course. Red Sandy, do you know where?"

"I know," he said sombrely.

"Good. Red Sandy, you take the Elliots' horses and help Long George get to his home."

"Ah wantae go home, sir." George didn't seem able to register anything except his injury. Tears were running down his face as he spoke.

"Of course you do."

"Only, there'll be the harvest to get in and all…"

"Don't worry about it. Here." Carey found his flask of mixed wine and water and helped Long George to drink it. He choked and his teeth rattled on the bottlemouth. "Red Sandy, a word with you."

"Ay, sir."

Carey drew him a little aside. "If his wife's got her hands full with sick children, stay and help. When it's getting on for morning, take the horses into Carlisle castle, find the surgeon and send him back to George's place. Tell him I'll pay his fee."

Red Sandy looked alarmed at that but only nodded.

"You're in charge."

Something very cynical crossed Red Sandy's face and disappeared, though he nodded again.

"Ay, sir. Dinna be concerned, I'll see him right. I'll bring my own wife to nurse him if need be."

"Good man."

They rode off at a sedate pace southwards. Carey noted that the other men were letting the deer down from its tree. Dodd had seen to the rounding up of the sheep and, no doubt, the stripping of the two dead bodies. Carey had no intention of burying them: let Wee Colin Elliot see to it, if he wanted.

# saturday 8th july 1592, early morning

It was an enraging business, taking the sheep back to the Routledge farm they had been raided from. Carey was an innocent about sheep and was astonished at how stupid they were, wiry and rough-coated creatures though these were, in contrast to the smug rotund animals that milled their way through London to Smithfield market every week. Dodd and the others worked around them making odd yipping and barking noises, like sheepdogs, and the whole process took hours. It was past dawn when the sheep poured over another hill and began baaing excitedly at the smell of home and at last moved sensibly in a flock in one direction.

The farmer, who owned his own small rough two-storey peletower, already had a group of men around him, all talking excitedly, while the women saddled the horses.

Carey, who had left the experts to their business, said to Dodd, "Looks like we're just in time to stop a reprisal raid."

"Ay," grunted Dodd. "It's a pity."

"Not if you have to deal with the resulting paperwork, it isn't. This is simpler."

It was, but not much. Jock Routledge seemed very offended that Carey had caught his sheep for him, no doubt because he had been planning to lift a few extra when he retrieved his own from the Elliots. He was also scandalised at the thought of paying the Wardenry fee.

"Ye canna take one sheep in twelve, ye'll ruin me," he shouted.

"I can in fact take one sheep for every ten, so you owe me an extra lamb," Carey said. "I might remit the lamb if I get my rights quickly."

"Oh ay, yer rights," sneered Routledge. "Why did ye not stop them at the Border then, eh? Dinnae trouble to tell me, I know well enough. Well, ye'll not..."

"Sir," called Dodd from a few paces away. Carey looked round and saw he was slouching on his horse which was eating its way methodically through the pea-vines of a vegetable garden. In his hand was a lit torch. "Will I fire the thatch?"

Carey held up his hand in acknowledgement.

"Good man," said Carey through gritted teeth. While messing about with the sheep he had had time to notice the burning ache in his side from the knifecut he had got the day before yesterday. Furthermore, his head hurt, his eyes were sandy, the ant bites were itching his leg and he'd bruised his half-healed ribs being thrown to the ground twice. "I've no intention of arguing. That animal there is mine and I'm taking her. Sim's Will, get that...that... sheep."

"The fat four-year ewe, ay, sir," said Sim's Will riding over stolidly and nipping a nearby animal from the herd, although not the one Carey had pointed to. It bleated piteously at being separated from its mates.

"Ye bastard," growled Jock Routledge. Carey heard a crackling and saw that there were flames licking through the thatch of the house. He glared at Dodd who looked blankly back at him and moved away from the roof he had just set fire to. Luckily it was still too damp to burn well.

Carey growled and turned his horse, led his men away from the farmstead, followed by shouts of anger and the hissing of water on the flames.

As they continued south, following the course of the Eden towards Carlisle, Carey rode beside Dodd.

"Sergeant, why did you fire their thatch before I asked you to?"

Dodd blinked at him. "I thought that was what ye wanted."

"I was trying to get what I wanted without burning first."

Dodd was a picture of blank incomprehension. "Whatever for, sir?" he asked. "He's only Jock Routledge. He pays blackrent to everybody, he might as well pay a bit to you."

"That was our fee for the night's work."

"Ay, sir, like I said. And he'll be more civil next time."

Carey growled but decided not to pursue the matter. While he rode he examined his side cautiously and found that something must have hit him there. He had a mark on his jack the width of his hand, but the metal plates inside had turned the blow. Unfortunately that was just where the knife slash was and from the tenderness he thought it was bleeding. It was only shallow, but it was scabbing into the bandages Philadelphia had wrapped round it and it pulled whenever he turned.

Their fee was unwilling to be taken from kith and kin and was as much trouble to drive as the full twelve had been. It was well into the morning before they came to Long George's small farm. As expected, Red Sandy was gone but the barber-surgeon's pony was cropping the grass outside. Four children were sitting in a row on the wall, and not one of them had any kind of rash or fever. The three boys were muttering together, and the littlest, a fair-haired girl, had her hands clamped tight over her ears.

"Now then, Cuddy," called Dodd as they rode up.

"Good morning, Sergeant," said the eldest boy, politely, sliding down off the wall. His breeches were filthy and his feet were bare, his shirt had a long rip in it and his cap was over one ear. "Who's that?"

"The new Deputy Warden," said Dodd sternly. "So mind your manners."

Cuddy pulled his cap off and made something of a bow.

A strangulated howl broke from the farmhouse. The little girl winced, hunched and stuck her fingers deeper in her ears. Her eyes were red from crying.

"They're cutting me dad's arm off," said Cuddy matter-of-factly.

"Will it grow back?" asked the youngest boy, fascinated.

The howling rose to a shriek, bubbled down again. Cuddy unwillingly stole a glance over his shoulder, looked back at Carey who was staring at the farmhouse, waiting.

Another scream which at last faded down to a sequence of gasps.

"It's over now," he said, mostly to the little girl.

She shook her head, screwed up her face and dug her fingers in deeper. Her bare feet under her muddy homespun kirtle twisted together.

All of them listened but there was no more noise.

"How did ye know, sir?" asked Cuddy.

Carey coughed, looked at the ground. Somehow he felt the boy should know, that imagination would be worse than the facts.

"The first cry is when the surgeon begins to cut. Then you can't get your breath for a bit, but just as he finishes you can get out another yell, and then the final one is when they put pitch on the end."

"Oh," said the boy, inspecting him for missing limbs. "Ye've watched before then?"

"Yes," said Carey.

"Who was it? Did he live?"

"Oh yes. He's got a hook instead of a hand now."

"Will it no' grow back?" asked the smallest boy anxiously. "Will it no' get better again?"

"Ye're soft," sneered the middle boy. "It's no' like a cut."

"It will get better, but it won't grow again," Carey explained. The little girl had taken one finger out of her ear and was blinking at him with the tears still wet on her cheeks. "He should be well enough by harvest time, there's no need to cry."

"If he doesnae die of the rot," said Cuddy brutally.

The girl nodded. "Ay, that's what me mam said."

"Anyway," Cuddy added, "she's only crying because mam wouldna let her watch."

"Me mam said it's your fault, if ye're the Deputy," accused the middle boy.

"Call him sir," snarled Dodd.

"Is it yer fault, *sir*?"

Carey took a deep breath and began to stride to the house.

"Nay, ye soft bairns," Dodd said. "It were the Elliots, that's who we were fighting."

Cuddy nodded fiercely. "When I'm big enough I'll find the man that did it and cut his hand off."

"That's the spirit lad," said Dodd approvingly.

Long George's farmhouse was one of those built quickly after a raid, out of wattle and daub, with turves for a roof and pounded dirt bound with oxblood and eggwhite for a floor. George was lying in a corner on a straw pallet covered over with bracken, gasping for breath and moaning. One man who looked like his brother and another older one who seemed to be his father, were standing next to him talking in low voices, while Long George's wife tended the fire on the hearth in the middle of the floor to keep the broth boiling. Smoke shimmered upwards into the hooded hole in the roof. She stood up and wiped her hands on her apron and blinked at Carey as he stood hesitating in the doorway, his morion making a monster out of him.

The father stepped forward protectively, while Long George's brother moved unobtrusively for an axe hanging on the wall.

"Who're ye?"

"I'm the Deputy Warden."

There was a sequence of grunts from the men and a sniff from the wife. Carey saw that the barber-surgeon was squatting beside his patient, tending the stump. Finally he wrapped the remains of George's hand in a bloody cloth and rinsed his arms in water from one of the three buckets. George's tightly bandaged stump was partly hidden by a cage of withies that the surgeon had bound around it. It lay stiffly inert beside George, not seeming to be part of him.

"Did ye kill the man that did it?" demanded George's father with his eyes narrowed. "What family was he, sir?"

"I killed one Elliot myself, I don't know who killed the other."

"Did ye not hang the rest?"

"They escaped."

George's brother spat eloquently into the bucket of blood by the bed. The surgeon stood up, nodded to Carey, handed the gory package to George's wife.

"Bury that with a live rat tied to it to draw out any morbidus," he prescribed reassuringly. "Give him as much to drink of small beer as he'll take but no food till tomorrow and I'll come the day after to see to him. My fee…"

Carey caught the man's eye and shook his head. The man looked puzzled, then caught on, and nodded happily, no doubt tripling his fee on the instant. He began wiping, oiling and packing his tools away in his leather satchel, whistling between his teeth.

Long George's family stared at him and Carey went over to the bed, squatted down beside it. Carey had visited wounded men of his before; he knew there was not much he could say that would make anything better, but he was very curious about the cause of Long George's maiming.

"Long George," he said softly. "Can you hear me?"

"Ay, Courtier." The voice was down to a croak and Long George's face had the grey inward-turned look of someone in too much pain to think of anything else. He was panting softly like an overheated hound. It was a pity he had been too tough to faint while the surgeon did his work.

"I'm sorry to see you like this, Long George," Carey said inadequately.

"Ay." Long George tried to lick his grey lips. "What about ma place?"

For a moment, Carey was nonplussed.

"Ah canna fight now, see ye."

"Oh for God's sake, don't worry about it. I'll look into a pension for you."

"Ay." Long George sounded unconvinced.

"What happened to your new pistol?"

A long long pause for thought. "I dinna ken."

"Did it blow up in your hand? Is that what happened?"

One of the men behind him sucked in a breath suddenly, but said nothing.

Another long pause. "Ay. Must've."

"Did you load it twice?"

Long George couldn't understand this, the unbandaged bits of his face drew together in a puzzled frown.

"Why would he do that?" demanded his father. "He wouldnae waste the powder."

"It might happen, in the excitement."

"Nay," whispered Long George. "Once."

Carey sighed. "Where did you get the pistol?"

No answer.

"He canna talk," said the woman sharply. "He's sick and hurt, sir. Can ye no' wait till he's better?"

Carey straightened up, nearly hitting his head on a roofbeam, and turned to her.

"Do you know where Long George got his pistol, goodwife?" he asked.

Her thin lips tightened and she folded her arms. "Nay, sir, it's nae business of mine."

"Or either of you?" Both the other men shook their heads, faces impenetrably blank.

Carey sighed again. Almost certainly the pistol was stolen goods from somewhere and completely untraceable now it was in bits on the Scottish border. Trying to swallow the coughing caused by woodsmoke and a foul mosaic of other smells, Carey moved to the doorway, bent ready to duck under the half-tanned cowhide they had pegged up out of the way so that the surgeon could see to cut.

On an afterthought he felt in his belt pouch and found a couple of shillings which he put into the hard dirty hand of Goodwife Little. From the smell of it, the pot on the fire had nothing in it except oatmeal.

"I'll ask the surgeon if he has any laudanum," he said. "If he hasn't, I'll talk to my sister about it."

Oppressed by the hostility of their stares and the smells of blood and sickness in the little hut, Carey went out to where the surgeon was waiting and told him to come for his fee to the castle in Carlisle, and come to him personally. The surgeon did not carry laudanum, since that was verra expensive, and an apothecary's trade foreby. Carey returned to Dodd, mounted and they continued wearily back to Carlisle. Behind them the children stood in a hesitant row outside their hut, arguing over whether they should ask to be let back in again.

They went into Carlisle Castle by the sally-port in the north-east wall and led their horses between the buttery and the Queen Mary Tower to the castle yard which was bare save for two empty wagons parked in the corner. Carey handed Sorrel's bridle to Red Sandy and told Dodd to see to the horses and put their rebellious fee in the pen by the kitchens and then try and make sure all of them got some sleep and food before evening. There was no chance any of his men would go prudently to bed early that night, when the taverns would be full of their friends and relatives come in for the Sunday muster. In the meantime, if he could get his report to Lord Burghley written and ciphered quickly he might catch the regular Newcastle courier before he left at noon.

He climbed the stairs to his chambers in the Queen Mary Tower, found nobody there at all. Damn it, where were the two servants he paid exorbitantly to look after him? Feeling hard done by, he stripped off his filthy helmet and jack and left them on the stand. He opened his doublet buttons to take the pressure off his side, then answered the heavy door himself to a timid knock.

Surgeon's fee paid, he decided he could stay awake until the evening. Sleeping during the day always made him feel frowsty and ill-tempered, and he was surprised to find himself so soggy and weary after only one night's lost sleep. He stamped into his office, rubbing his itchy face, his head aching but the memory of the night's doings clear. One of the many things he had learned when he attended Sir Francis Walsingham on an embassy to Scotland in the early eighties had been the vital importance of timeliness in intelligence. Burghley was not the spymaster that

Sir Francis had been, but he needed to know about James VI's mysterious German as soon as possible—which meant by Tuesday, with luck. Carey took a sheet of paper, dipped his pen and began to write, hoping that what he was writing was reasonably comprehensible.

An hour later Philadelphia came hurrying up the stairs, knocked and entered her brother's bedchamber and found it empty. She heard snoring from the office, went through and found Carey with his head on his arms fast asleep at his desk.

"Oh, for goodness' sake," she sniffed, and shook his shoulder gently. "Robin, if that's a letter to Lord Burghley, you'll drool on it and smear the ink…"

Robin grunted. Philly saw his doublet was open, pulled it back and saw blood on his shirt. Her lips tightened.

Moments later she was in the castle courtyard, sending every available boy scurrying to find Barnabus. The small ferret-faced London servant eventually arrived looking hungover and even uglier than usual.

"Good day, Barnabus," she said with freezing civility. "Did you have a pleasant evening?"

"Er…" said Barnabus.

"I'm delighted to hear it. Are you free to do your job now?"

"I didn't know 'e was…"

"When I want to hear your excuses, I'll ask for them. Now get up there and help me put your master to bed, you lazy, idle, good-for-nothing…"

"What's wrong with him?" muttered Barnabus resentfully as they climbed the stairs. "'E drunk then…?"

A tremendous backhanded buffet over his ears from Philadelphia almost knocked him over. Barnabus shook his ringing head and blinked at her in astonishment. Seeing her fury, and remembering whose sister she was, he decided not to say the various things he thought of, and carried on up the stairs.

Carey was extremely unwilling to be woken, but finally came groaning to consciousness and let his doublet and shirt be taken off him so that Philadelphia could attack the re-opened cut with rosewater, aqua vitae and hot water. She peeled the bandages off, making him wince.

"God damn it, Philly..."

"Don't swear, and hold still. You've another bad lump on your head, what did that?"

Carey thought for a moment. "Sim's Will Croser's horse kicked me," he said. "My helmet's dented."

"I'm not surprised. What was he thinking of?"

Carey blinked and said with dignity, "Insofar as Sim's Will is capable of thought, I should think he was thinking I was an Elliot."

"Hmf. I wish you wouldn't get into fights."

Carey began laughing. "Philadelphia, my sweet, it's my job."

"Hah! Hold still while I..."

"Ouch!"

"I told you to hold still. Barnabus, where are you going?"

"I was only getting a fresh shirt from the laundry."

"Bring bandages and the St John's wort ointment from the stillroom and small beer and some bread and cheese too."

"I'm not hungry, Philly." She bit her lip worriedly and felt his forehead, her gesture exactly like their mother. "No, I'm not sickening. I'm not as delicate as you think me. It's Long George. He had to have his right hand cut off this morning. His pistol exploded and took most of the fingers from it."

"I don't see what Long George's hand has got to do with you not eating," said Philly, with deliberate obtuseness, getting out her hussif from the pouch hanging on her belt and cutting a length of silk. "Are you feeling dizzy, seeing double?"

"No, no," said Carey. "I'm perfectly all right, Philadelphia." She stepped back and stared at him consideringly. In truth he looked mainly embarrassed at having fallen asleep over his work, like some nightowl schoolboy. "Can you send out some laudanum to Long George's farm? And some food?"

Her face softened a little. "Of course." Carey nodded, not looking at her and she frowned again.

"I think you should be in bed so your cut can heal," she said.

"Don't be ridiculous."

"Well, anyway, I'm going to sew the edges up and then bandage it again to try and stop it from taking sick and don't argue with me. Don't you know you can die from a little cut on your finger, if it goes bad, never mind a great long slash like that? Go on. Sit on the bed and lean over sideways so I can get at it."

She looked a great deal like her mother when she was determined, despite her inevitable crooked ruff. Sighing, her brother did what he was told. Barnabus shambled back with supplies from the stillroom and then went away again to fetch food. Philadelphia threaded her needle and put an imperious hand on his ribcage.

"Now stay still. This is going to hurt, which is no more than you deserve."

It did, a peculiarly sore and irritating sharp prickle and pull as the needle passed through. Carey tried to think of something else to stop himself from flinching, but wasn't given the chance.

"You couldn't have picked a worse time to get yourself hurt, you know," Philadelphia said accusingly as she stitched. "What with the muster tomorrow and King James coming to Dumfries and all. Don't twitch."

Before he could protest at this unfairness, Barnabus came limping back with a tray and a fresh shirt. Philadelphia knotted and snipped.

"About time," she sniffed, putting her needle carefully away and picking up the pot of ointment and the bandages. "Up with your arms, Robin."

Trying not to wince while she dabbed the cut with more green ointment, Carey asked, "What did you come to see me about, Philly?"

For answer she tapped irritably at a scar on his shoulder. "When did this happen?"

"In France. A musketball grazed me. It got better by itself."

"You were lucky. Why didn't you tell me?"

"What for? So that you and mother could worry about it?"

"Hah. Hold this."

Holding the end of the bandage with his elbow raised and his other arm up, Carey said again, patiently, "What did you want me for?"

She blinked at him for a moment and then her face cleared with recall, and switched instantly to an expression of thunder. "I assume you know that my lord Scrope has appointed an acting armoury clerk to replace Atkinson?"

"WHAT?"

"And the guns from London came in at dawn this morning while you were prancing about poaching deer on the Border and they've been unpacked and stored already and Lowther's changed the lock on the armoury door again... *Will* you stay still or must I slap you?"

"God's blood, what the Devil does your God-damned husband think he's playing at...?"

"Don't swear."

"But Philly...OUCH."

"Stay still then."

"But what's Scrope up to? Does he want me out? What is he *doing*?"

"You weren't here when the guns came in. Lowther was. Scrope was panicking about who was going to keep the armoury books and Lowther said his cousin could do it for the moment and Scrope agreed. He must have forgotten that the office should be one of the Deputy Warden's perks."

"The man's a complete half-witted..."

"And as far as I know, Lowther's cousin didn't even pay anything."

Carey was now tucking his shirt tails into the tops of his trunkhose and he winced when he moved incautiously. "Atkinson paid fifty pounds for it, damn it."

"I know. And the armoury clerkship has always been in the gift of the Deputy Warden. I checked with Richard Bell and he agreed with me, but when I talked to my lord Scrope all he would say was that the appointment was only temporary and you could have the sale of it later."

Carey shrugged into his old green doublet and snapped his fingers impatiently at Barnabus to do up the points to his hose at the back.

"God damn it," he muttered. "I was relying on selling the clerkship to pay the men next month."

For once Philadelphia did not tell him off for swearing. Her small heartshaped face was bunched into a worried frown. "It's worse that Lowther has the keys to the new lock and you haven't," she pointed out. "I'm sure he'll find reasons not to let you have any of the new weapons."

Carey went into his little office and sat down at his desk again, ignoring the bread and cheese Barnabus had laid out for him. He propped his chin on his fist and stared into space.

"Has the Newcastle courier gone yet?"

Philadelphia looked blank at the sudden change of subject. Barnabus coughed modestly. "No, sir," he said. "He was in Bessie's, last I saw."

"And where the Devil were you, Barnabus?"

"Well, I…"

"I don't ask much of my servants, just that they occasionally be present to serve me. Nothing elaborate."

"Yes, sir. Sorry, sir. Shall I fetch the courier for you, sir?"

"If it isn't too much trouble, Barnabus."

Barnabus limped out the door muttering under his breath about his water being sore and his master being sarcastic and life in the north being even worse than he expected. Carey continued to stare into space for a moment and then shrugged, took a fresh sheet of paper and a small leather notebook out of a locked drawer in his desk.

"What are you going to do, Robin?"

"Finish writing to London. I'll ask Burghley to try and persuade the Queen to pay my salary direct to me, and to do it quickly, and try to find me some funds for paying informers as well. I'm deaf and blind round here at the moment."

"Are you going to tell him about my lord Scrope and the clerkship?"

Carey looked at her seriously. "Do you want me to?" he asked. "The Queen thinks little enough of your husband as it is, and she hasn't sent his warrant yet. He's not even officially Lord Warden. Do you want to give her excuse for delay?"

Philadelphia scowled and shook her head. She watched as Carey's long fingers took up the pen and began the tedious business of ciphering his letter.

"Will you go to bed when the courier's gone?" she asked after a few minutes.

"Well, I…"

"Only I want you fresh for this evening." Carey stopped writing and glanced at her warily.

"Why?"

"I want you to come to the dinner party I'm giving for Sir Simon Musgrave, who brought the convoy in, and some of the other local gentlemen who have come for the muster."

"Must I?"

"Yes. If the Deputy Warden isn't there, people will begin to wonder if my lord is planning to take your office away, especially when they hear about the armoury clerkship."

"Damn."

"And besides everyone in the country wants to meet the dashing knight who solved Atkinson's murder, never mind what he was up to the week before last—of which I have heard at least five different versions, and none of them as ridiculous as the truth."

Carey rolled his eyes at the sarcasm in her voice.

"I have nothing fit to wear."

Philly looked withering. "This isn't London, you know. The only people who dress fine around here are the headmen of the big blackrenting surnames, like Richie Graham of Brackenhill. I'll make sure Barnabus has mended your velvet suit by then; but your cramoisie would do well enough."

Carey grunted and continued counting letters under his breath. Philly came and kissed him on the ear.

"Do say you'll come, Robin."

"Oh, very well. So long as you don't expect me to do anything except feed my face and smile sweetly at people."

"That would be perfect."

The boom of gunfire woke him up. Carey found himself halfway to the window with a dagger in his hand before he was fully awake. He peered out into the castle yard and saw a small crowd of garrison folk gathered around a cleared space. He smiled at himself, thinking back to his time in France the year before when he had been similarly on a hairtrigger. As he watched, a thickset middle-aged man in a worn velvet suit and Scottish hat lined up a caliver with a well-earthed target and squeezed the trigger. Carey nodded. Typical. Not only had they unloaded the weapons without him, now they were testing them while he had a much-needed rest.

Muttering to himself he went back to bed, drew the curtains and tried to go back to sleep in the stuffy dimness. Eventually he did.

Awakened once more by Barnabus, Carey decided to dress early and go and talk some sense into Lord Scrope.

The Lord Warden of the English West March was nowhere to be found, however, until Carey thought to go round to the stables to see how Thunder his black tournament horse was faring. There he ran Scrope to earth, deep in conference with four local gentlemen.

"Ahah," said Scrope, raising a bony arm in salute as Carey wandered round the dungheap which was being raked and trimmed by three of the garrison boys. "Here he is. Sir Robert, come and give us some advice, would you?"

Carey coughed and with difficulty, managed a politic smile at his brother in law.

The gentlemen were debating horse-races. Specifically, they were insistent that a muster of the West March could not possibly be held without a horse race or three and were even willing to chip in for the prize money. They had already decided on one race for three year olds and two for any age, and a ten pound prize for each.

"No," said Carey in answer to one of the gentlemen. "Thunder's not a racehorse, he's a tournament charger."

"Might be useful in the finish," said the gentleman. "Twice the leg length of a hobby and good bones. Be interesting to see how he ran. How does he do in the rough country hereabouts?"

Carey raised eyebrows at that. "I never use him on patrol, he's too valuable."

"Oh quite so, quite so," said the gentleman. "Still. Got a mare might come into season, you know."

"I wouldn't put Thunder to a hobby," Carey said. "The foal might be too big."

"Well, she's a bit of a mixture, not a hobby really, got hobby blood so does well on rough ground, but still…"

"Sir Robert couldn't ride him in the race," put in Scrope. "He's the Deputy Warden, he has to maintain order at the muster. Can't have him breaking his neck in the race as well."

"Put someone else up," suggested another gentleman with a florid face, who had been feeding the horses carrots.

"That's an idea," said Carey, warming to the notion. If Thunder won a race, it would at least put the stallion's covering fees up. "Who would you suggest? He's not an easy animal to ride."

"Find one of the local lads," said a third gentleman. "Little bastards can ride anything with four legs, practically born in the saddle."

There was a flurry on the top of the dungheap, fists swung and then a sweaty mucky boy scrambled down to land in front of Carey.

"Me, sir!" he was shouting. "I'll ride him, let me ride him, I'll bear the bell away for ye, sir!"

Carey squinted at the boy, and finally recognised Young Hutchin Graham under the dung.

Another boy, one of the steward's many sons, leaned down from the top of the heap, holding a puffy lip and sneered, "Ay, ye'll bear it away on ycr bier, ye bastard, ye canna ride better than a Scotch pig wi' piles…"

Young Hutchin ignored this with some dignity, and stood up, brushing at himself ineffectually.

"I can so," he said to Carey. "I've rid him at exercise and he…"

Carey stared fixedly at the boy as the gentlemen listened with interest.

"…he's a strong nag, an' willing," Hutchin finished after an imperceptible change of course. "And I'd be willing, sir, it'd be good practice."

"I wouldn't want you to be disappointed if he proved slower than you expected," said Carey gravely.

"Och, nay, sir, I wouldnae expect him to win, not wi' Mr Salkeld's bonny mare in the race and all," said Young Hutchin, all wide blue eyes and innocence.

Mr Salkeld was standing beside Carey and gave a modest snort.

"Well, she shapes prettily enough," he admitted. "Prettily enough, certainly."

"Hm," temporised Carey artfully. "I'm not sure it would be worth it."

Mr Salkeld took out his purse.

"Sir Robert," he said with a friendly smile, "I can see ye're too modest for your own good. How about a little bet to make it worth your while?"

"Well..."

"I'll do better than that. I'll give ye odds of two to one that my pretty little mare can beat your great Thunder."

"Now I think *you're* being modest, Mr Salkeld."

"Three to one, and my hand on it. Shall we say five pounds?"

They shook gravely while Carey wondered where he could find five pounds at short notice if he had to.

After that nothing would do but that Scrope must show the gentlemen his lymer bitch who had pupped on the Deputy Warden's bed at the beginning of the week. There was little to see at the back of the pupping kennel, beyond yellow fur and an occasional sprawling paw, while the bitch lifted her lip at them and growled softly. Carey waited while the rest of them went off to examine some sleuth-dog puppies, then put his hand near her muzzle. She sniffed, whined, thumped her tail and let him pat her head.

"I should think so," said Carey, pleased. "Where's your gratitude, eh? I want that big son of yours, my girl, and don't forget it."

"Sir Robert," hissed a young voice behind him and Carey turned to see Young Hutchin slouching there. He smiled at the boy who smiled back and transformed his truculent face into something much younger and more pleasant.

"Now then," Carey said warily.

Hutchin drew a deep breath. "When I take Thunder out for his evening run, will I let anybody see him?"

"Certainly," said Carey. "Let them see he's no miracle."

Young Hutchin nodded and grinned in perfect understanding.

Scrope and his party returned and Carey tagged along while they wandered down to the Captain's gate to look at the alterations and refurbishments being done to the Warden's Lodgings in the gate-house. Finally the gentlemen went off into Carlisle town which was already getting noisy and Carey at last had Scrope to himself.

Scrope, however, did not want to talk about the armoury clerkship or the weapons. He chatted about horses, he held forth on Buttercup the lymer bitch's ancestry and talents, he spoke hopefully that some of the falcons might be out of moult soon, he congratulated Carey on the venison his patrol had brought in and the sheep which was being butchered even now, and he regretted at length the sad news about Long George.

At last Carey's patience cracked. "My lord," he said, breaking into a long reminiscence about a tiercel bird Scrope had hunted with five years before. "Will you be issuing the new weapons for the muster?"

"Oh ah, no, no, Robin, not at all, never done for a muster, you know."

"But for God's sake, my lord, even the Graham women have bloody pistols and my men are only armed with longbows."

"Never done, my dear chap, simply never done. Now don't huff at me…"

"I would have taken it very kindly if you had waited to consult me over the temporary clerk to the…"

"Quite so, quite so, I'm sure you would." Scrope beamed densely. "Very patient of you, bit of a mix up over the armoury clerkship, and once it's all sorted out, we'll look into the matter, of course, but in the meantime, if you could…ah…be kind enough to leave it with me? Eh?"

Carey took breath to say that he was not patient and was in fact highly displeased, but Scrope beamed again, patted his shoulder with irritating familiarity and said, "I would love to carry on chatting, Robin, but I simply must go up to the keep and change or Philadelphia will skin me, bless her heart."

Carey could do no more than growl at the Lord Warden's departing back.

"Ay," said a doleful voice behind him and Carey turned to see Sergeant Dodd standing there. "Valuable things, guns. So I heard."

Carey's lips tightened with frustration. "Well, Sergeant, thanks to my Lord Warden. I've lost the sale of a fifty pound office and you've lost about ten pounds in bribes from hopeful candidates trying to get you to put in a good word for them."

It hardly seemed possible but Dodd's face became even longer and more mournful, which gave Carey some satisfaction.

"Och," said Dodd, sounding stricken, "I hadnae thought of that."

Carey snorted and turned to go back to the Queen Mary Tower to see how much money he could raise for backing Thunder the next day. Dodd fell into step beside him.

"Lowther'll gi' us none of them," Dodd predicted.

Carey snorted again.

"If they're there at all," added Dodd thoughtfully.

"What?"

"If they're there…"

"Are you saying the guns might not have been delivered?"

"Och, I heard tell there were barrels full o' something heavy delivered this morning and barrels of gunpowder and all, but I never heard anyone had seen the guns broken out of the barrels."

There was a short thoughtful silence.

"I saw Sir Simon Musgrave testing a caliver in the yard."

"I heard him too, the bastard."

Strictly speaking Carey should have reprimanded Dodd for talking about one of the Queen's knights so rudely, but he didn't like Musgrave either.

"You know he's one o' Sir Henry Widdrington's best allies," Dodd added.

"Hmm."

"And I know he proved two calivers, but naebody saw any of the other guns save Sir Richard Lowther and his cousin, the new armoury clerk. And they was mighty quick to change the locks again, so ye couldnae see them yourself, sir."

"Hmm."

Carey said nothing more because he was thinking. At the foot of the Queen Mary Tower he turned and smiled at Dodd.

"Could you manage to stay moderately sober tonight, Sergeant?"

"I might." Dodd was watching him cautiously.

"Good. Meet me by the armoury an hour after the midnight guard-change."

"Sir, I didnae mean…"

"Excellent. I'll see you there, then."

Dodd shut his mouth since Carey had already trotted up the spiral stairs and out of sight. "Och, Jesus," Dodd said to himself sadly. "What the Devil's he up to now?"

## saturday, 8th july 1592, evening

Philadelphia sat at her table in the dining room that presently doubled as a council chamber and stewed with mixed rage and hilarity. This supper party was clearly not going to be an unqualified success. All down the table were ranged the higher ranking of the local gentlemen who had come in for the muster, and some of the hardier wives and women-folk. They were talking well, their faces flushed with spiced wine and the joys of gossip, hardly tasting their food as they thrashed out the two most recent excitements: the inquest into the previous armoury clerk's death and the raid on Falkland Palace the previous week. Seated with infinite care according to rank and known blood-feuds between them, they were settled in and looked like being no trouble.

However there was trouble brewing right next to her where her husband sat, his long bony face struggling to appear politely interested. At his right sat Sir Simon Musgrave, and facing Sir Simon was Scrope's younger brother Harry, who had brought his young wife. The silly girl was tricked out to the nines in Edinburgh fashion, halfway between the German and the French styles, bright green satin stomacher clashing horribly with tawny velvet bodice and a yellow-starched ruff. She was also flirting outrageously with Robin who was next to her and courteously swallowing a yawn.

Sir Simon was booming away to Scrope about some tedious argument between the Marshal of Berwick and the Berwick town council. Sir Simon was firmly on the side of the town council. This was tactless of him because the Marshal of Berwick was Sir John Carey, elder brother of Robin and herself.

"It's ridiculous," opined Sir Simon for the fourth time. "Yet cannot let your garrison troops run wild in the town and then expect the mayor and corporation to pay for them…"

Scrope nodded sagely, while young Harry Scrope, who was even less bright than his brother, but had the sense to know it, kept his mouth shut.

Meanwhile Harry's wife Mary cooed at Philly's favourite brother, "Oh, Sir Robert, tell me more, it must be so exciting to serve the Queen at Court."

"It certainly can be," said Robin, being courageously polite. Philadelphia felt sorry for him. It was essential that he be seen there, but he looked more than ready for his bed and there was the cut in his side which must be hurting. Perhaps she could think of some excuse for him to leave. Then she saw him smile and lost all sympathy. Weary or not, he simply could not help being scandalously conspiratorial with Mary Scrope, who clearly thrilled to it. "It's particularly exciting when the Queen takes against something you've done and throws her slippers at you," he said.

Mary Scrope gasped and her breasts threatened to pop loose. She tilted a little so Robin could get the full benefit of them.

"Oh! What do you do then, Sir Robert?"

"Duck," said Carey, picking up his goblet and drinking.

Philly noticed he had eaten practically nothing but that the page had refilled his drink three times. The continuing drone from beside her caught her ear briefly.

"...Sir John's never been any good as Marshal, you know, my lord, he hasn't got the grasp of Border affairs. I'd niver say nothing against his father, mind, but the..."

Mary Scrope batted her eyelashes: she was a sandy sort of girl, Philly thought unkindly, sandy hair, sandy eyebrows, sandy complexion and whoever had recommended tawny had done her no favours.

"I can't think what *you* could do to offend her."

Carey smiled with a slightly sardonic turn. "It depends on your sex and your activities," he said, letting his gaze wander all over Mary's willing chest. His voice dropped. "A woman might offend her by dressing too well or misplacing a gem."

Good God, Robin, thought Philadelphia, you're not going to allow yourself to be seduced by Mary Scrope of all people, are you?

Robin cut a choice piece from the dish of mutton in front of him, placed it delicately on Mary Scrope's plate with the tip of his knife, smiled winningly again with his eyes half-hooded.

"And a man might offend her by marrying or sed..."

Philly kicked her brother.

"Or not knowing what he was talking about," she said brightly with a warm smile at Mary "That sort of thing offends her seriously."

"Oh," said Mary Scrope coolly. "Have you been at Court, Lady Scrope?"

"She's one of Her Majesty's favourite ladies in waiting," said Robin, a reproachful glance on the oblique to Philly. "So much so that the Queen even forgave her when she married my lord Scrope."

"So it's true Her Majesty doesn't like her courtiers to marry," breathed Mary Scrope, with her breasts in desperate danger now as she leaned sideways. "Have *you* ever had that trouble, Sir Robert?"

Robin swallowed and smiled. "Not yet."

On impulse Philly dropped her napkin and took a peep under the table: Robin had now tucked his long elegant legs awkwardly to the side, while Mary had one foot at full stretch trying to find his knee to touch. Philadelphia wondered where the various limbs had been before she kicked him. Honestly, men were impossible creatures. Imagine flirting with Scrope's sister-in-law, as if his position weren't delicate enough as it was. There was also a small lapdog, who had crept in somehow and was snuffling about on the rushmat for droppages.

Pink with suppressed emotion, Philadelphia took her seat again. Carey gave her a knowing look, but Mary Scrope hadn't noticed, still being intent upon her prey.

"What else do you do at Court, Sir Robert?" she was asking.

"Oh, we dance and we stand around in antechambers playing cards and waiting to be sent on errands and we..."

"Seduce the maids of honour," boomed Sir Simon who had finally noticed that nobody except Lord Scrope was listening to his stories about the politics of Berwick. "Isn't that right, Sir Robert?"

Nobody could escape the edge of hostility in his voice. It was also the first time he had actually spoken directly to Carey.

"Not all of us, Sir Simon," said Robin mildly. "Some of us have better things to do."

Lord, thought Philly admiringly, that was a good barefaced lie, Robin.

"Ay," sniffed Sir Simon. "I'll be bound. Run around Netherby tower in disguise and borrow horses from other people's wives, eh? That have no business lending 'em, poor silly woman."

"You've heard about Robin's little adventure, then?" said Lord Scrope, reedily trying to deflect Sir Simon.

"Oh, ay. Widdrington's not best pleased by it, I can tell you. The nags were exhausted by the time she got them back to Hexham, and one of them gone lame. The fool woman'll no' make that mistake again if I know Sir Henry."

Interesting, thought Philadelphia, feeling sorry for Elizabeth and the nape of her neck prickling at the sudden sense of boiling rage coming from her brother. Robin's gone white. He has got it badly, I wonder what he'll do?

To everyone's astonishment, the unregarded Harry Scrope spoke up.

"But in the process didn't Sir Robert manage to persuade the Borderers on Bothwell's raid to steal the King's horses at Falkland Palace, rather than kidnap the King himself?" he said nervously. "That's what I heard."

"Maybe," grunted Sir Simon. "But that's not *all* that I heard, eh, Sir Robert?"

Robin sat for half a heartbeat, as if considering something very seriously. Then he finished his wine, stood up and made his most courtierly bow to Lord and Lady Scrope.

"I can't imagine what you're talking about, Sir Simon," he said with freezing civility in a voice loud enough for the rest of the table to hear, "but I'm afraid I'm thick-headed at the moment. I was fighting reivers most of yesterday night and so if you will forgive me, my lord, my dear sister, I'll go to my bed." Philadelphia managed a gracious nod and a bright smile. "Good night, Mr Scrope, Mrs Scrope. God speed you back to Berwick, Sir Simon."

Mary watched him stalk out of the council chamber with regret written all over her face: it was perfectly true, Philly thought affectionately, her brother was a fine figure of a man in his (as yet unpaid-for) black velvet suit, though his hair was presently shaded between black and dark red from the dye he had used for his Netherby disguise. Who could blame Mary Scrope if she wanted a spot of dash and romance to liven her life in the dull and practical north?

## satuRday 8th july 1592, night

It was Sir Richard Lowther's turn to patrol and he had long gone. Once again the night was sultry and dark with cloud, though the rain still refused to fall. Solomon the gate guard was sitting and knitting a sock with his one arm, one needle thrust into a case on his belt to hold it steady, a second ticking away hypnotically between his fingers and the other two dangling. He was away from his usual lookout on the Captain's Gate, sitting quietly by the north-western sally-port where he could see into the castle yard. There was a stealthy sound to his left and he turned to look.

Two men crept out of the Queen Mary Tower, one tall and leggy, the other short and squat. The tall one was carrying a dark lantern, fully shuttered so only occasional sparkles of light escaped. His face made a patch of white against darkness as he looked up at Solomon, who lifted his shortened upper arm and nodded.

Carey hadn't felt it necessary to explain why he had paid Solomon to keep watch, but it was no surprise that he and his short henchman padded quietly to the Armoury door. Carey was trying a key in the lock, but it seemingly no longer fitted. He stepped aside and the smaller man took something in his hand and jiggled it into the keyhole. Shortly afterwards there was a stealthy sequence of clicks and the door opened.

There was a sound from the barracks. The taller man tensed, touched his companion on the shoulder. Out of the barracks door came the unmistakable slouching rangy form of Sergeant Dodd. He padded across the courtyard, there was a low conversation and then they all disappeared inside the armoury.

Solomon nodded to himself. He had served under the new Deputy's father, Lord Hunsdon, during the revolt of the Northern Earls, and he remembered Carey as a boy of about nine, perpetually in trouble, normally hanging about the stables and kennels while his tutor searched for him. The boy was father to the man there, no doubt about it. He grinned reminiscently. On a famous occasion, the young Robin had decided to try reiving for himself, along with his half-brother Daniel. The thing had ended unhappily, with Lord Hunsdon having to pay for the beast and the boys eating their dinners standing up for days afterwards.

Down in the armoury, Carey carefully unshuttered the horn-paned lantern and looked about at the racks.

"Well, they're here at least," he said to Dodd softly, as dull greased metal gleamed back at him from all around.

"Ay, sir," whispered Dodd. "Shall we go now?"

"Not yet, Sergeant."

Carey nodded at Barnabus who carefully took down the nearest caliver and handed it to him. "We're going to mark them, carve a cross at the base of the stocks."

"All of them, sir?"

"That's right."

"But it'll take a' night…"

"Not if we get started now."

"Ay, sir," said Dodd with a sigh.

There was quiet for a while, with the occasional clatter of a dropped weapon and a curse when somebody's hand slipped. At the end of an hour and a half, Dodd put his knife away.

"Will that be all, sir?"

"Hm? Yes, I think so. Barnabus, did you bring those calivers I gave you?"

"Yes, sir."

"Give them here then."

Carey took two guns at random from the middle of the rack and replaced them with Barnabus's weapons. He held up the lantern and although the replacements had darker-coloured stocks, they would likely not be noticed by someone who was simply counting weapons.

From outside came a low significant sound of an owl hooting. Carey shuttered the lantern immediately, put his fingers to his lips. Feet crunched past the armoury in the yard, someone yawned loudly outside. They stood like statues.

There was the sound of muttered conversation, a scraping and clattering of firewood bundles and then the heavier, laden footsteps walking away again. Moments later came another owl hoot.

"The baker, of course," said Carey to himself and yawned. "We're finished here, gentlemen." Dodd surreptitiously mopped some sweat off his forehead while Carey slipped the lantern shutters closed and went to the door, peered out cautiously. A cat was sitting in the middle of the empty yard, watching something invisible. It too yawned and trotted away as the three men slipped out of the armoury.

"I'll meet you an hour before dawn, then, Sergeant."

"Ay, sir," said Dodd on another martyred sigh.

Solomon was turning the heel of his sock when he heard the lock snick shut, and then one set of soft footsteps approaching. The once amateur reiver turned Deputy Warden loomed over him in the darkness, smelling of black velvet, metal and gunoil.

A small purse made a pleasant chink on the ground beside him.

"Are ye satisfied, sir?" asked Solomon when he was safely past the tricky bit in his knitting.

"Hm? Yes, for the moment. Will you be at the muster tomorrow?"

"Ay, sir, I'm on the strength after all. Garrison, non-combatant."

"Anything or anyone I should watch out for?"

Solomon's sniff was eloquent. "Where should I start?"

Carey laughed softly. "I know I'm not popular."

"Ay. Ye can say that. What was ye at wi' the guns, sir?"

There was a long silence while Carey considered this. After a moment Solomon realised why and chuckled again.

"Och, sir, ye've no need to fear my tongue. Who was it opened the gate for ye when ye and yer half brother brought back that cow?"

Carey coughed. "Lord," he said, "I'd forgotten that."

"Had ye? Yer dad failed his purpose then, which wouldnae be like him."

Apart from a reminiscent snort, Carey didn't say anything for a moment. "I've marked the guns so that if I ever capture a reiver carrying one of them, I'll know where it came from."

Solomon almost dropped a stitch as he choked with laughter. "Ay," he said. "Ay, ye'll know."

Carey thought this was tribute to his ingenuity. There was smugness in his voice as he went back to the ladder.

"Good night, Solomon."

"Ay, sir," wheezed the gate guard, shaking his head.

## sunday 9th july 1562, before dawn

Dodd found Carey was either up before him, or more likely hadn't bothered to try and snatch an extra two hours' sleep at all. Probably very sensible of him, Dodd thought sadly to himself as he tottered over to the well to slake his thirst in the dark blue predawn. He hated drinking water in the morning, especially from a bucket, but it was too early for the buttery in the Keep to be open and he was desperate. One of the stable lads was waiting in the courtyard, holding two of the horses from the stables, who were stamping and shaking their heads unco-operatively. The boy was yawning enough to split his face.

"Now then," croaked Dodd.

"Morning, Sergeant," said the boy with a cheeky grin.

Dodd grunted and washed his face, shivering at the coldness and slimy taste of the water, dried himself on his shirt-tails. He had slept in his hose after their midnight raid on the armoury, which always left him feeling ugly, quite apart from his sorely-missed rest.

"Ahah," said Carey, appearing at the door of the Queen Mary Tower with his dags in their case and Barnabus behind him with a heavy bag no doubt containing the borrowed calivers. "Good morning, Dodd. If you can get yourself dressed in time, you can come with us."

He strapped the firearms onto the hobby in front of the saddle, and checked the girth. There were already ten leather flasks of gunpowder slung over the pony's back. Dodd went back into the new barracks for his clothes, wondering what demon it was that got into the Courtier early in the morning and how he could kill it. Carey jumped into the saddle, just as Dodd slouched out of the barracks once more with his blue woollen statute cap pulled down to protect his eyes, lacing up his jerkin and hating people who were happy at dawn.

"How long will this take, sir?" moaned Dodd.

"Only an hour or so," Carey explained, blowing on the glowing end of the coil of slowmatch he had slung over his shoulder. "I'm doing some target shooting. Are you coming or not?"

Dodd supposed he had to now. "Ay, sir."

"Well, hurry up, I don't want a mob going with me."

They went out through the sally-port to which Carey had the key and rode round to the fenced-off racecourse. Dodd had lost more money there than he cared to think about.

They left their horses at the other end of the course, securely tied. Then they went down to the end where the archery butts and the new shooting range were set up.

It turned out that what Carey really wanted was to see how well Dodd could shoot with the Courtier's own wheel-lock dags. Dodd thoroughly disliked firearms, and once he had warmed a little to the argument was a stout defender of longbows.

"See ye, sir," he said, as Carey demonstrated how to wind up the lock which spun a wheel against the iron pyrites in the clamp, making the sparks that supposedly lit the fine powder in the pan and thus fired the gun. "See ye, an arrow kills ye just as deid as a bullet and I can put a dozen in the air while ye're fiddling about with yer keys and all, sir."

"Well, try it anyway, Sergeant."

"Och, God," said Dodd under his breath, who hated loud noises in the morning. He took the dag, sighted along the barrel to the target and fired. The kick was not as brutal as a caliver, but the boom and the smell of gunpowder made his eyes water. Carey had the armoury caliver and was loading it briskly, lit the match in the lock, put the stock on his shoulder, took a sideways stance and aimed the gun. The roar nearly blew the top of Dodd's head off and a hole appeared in the target, irritatingly close to the bull. Dodd's bullet had puffed sand and sawdust a yard below the target.

Behind them the market traders from the city were setting up their stalls ready for the muster, being chivvied into their proper pitches by harassed aldermen's servants. They had looked up at the sound of guns, but turned back to their own affairs once they saw that nobody was attacking.

"Firearms are the future, Sergeant," said Carey didactically, while Dodd carefully swabbed, charged, loaded and wound up the dag again. "Anyone who's fought on the Continent knows that."

"The future?" repeated Dodd, thoroughly confused.

"It takes five years to make a longbowman and six weeks to make an arquebusier, it's as simple as that. This time remember it isn't a bow, you don't need to aim low at this distance. Think of a straight line from the muzzle to the bull."

While he talked he was reloading the caliver, each movement precise, identical and rhythmic. Dodd watched, recognising something new in the way he did it. Carey smiled.

"Dutch drill," he explained as he finished. "I'm planning to teach it to you and the men once we get hold of the guns." He stood square to the target, lifted and lowered the caliver to his shoulder and squinted as he aimed.

"*Christ!*" yelled Dodd and made a wild swipe with his arm which knocked the weapon out of Carey's hands. It clattered to the ground and the match fizzed on the spilled powder.

"What the Devil do you think you're doing...?" Carey demanded, cold and furious.

Dodd stamped on the match end with the toe of his boot and then picked up the caliver gingerly. He could feel his knees shaking and his stomach turning.

"Look, sir," he said, trying not to stammer. "There's a crack in the barrel."

Carey looked and his face went white. He took the caliver out of Dodd's hands, and turned it, traced the death-dealing weakness all along the underside of the gun.

"Thank you, Henry," he said at last, in the whisper of someone whose mouth has gone completely dry. "I see it."

Dodd turned, aimed the dag he was still holding and discharged it, this time at least hitting the target now he wasn't trying. Carey was staring at the caliver which had nearly blown his hands and face to shreds. It was still charged. Dodd put the dags back in their case on Carey's horse, as Carey began very carefully using the ramrod to scrape out the wad and bullet and shake the gunpowder onto the ground. When it was empty he blew out his breath gustily and small blame to him if he had been holding it in.

"And that's something else ye have nae fear of wi' longbows," Dodd added, unable to resist making the point.

"True," admitted Carey very softly. "True enough."

Dodd met the piercing blue eyes and knew that both of them were thinking of Long George and his mysterious pistol.

They rode back to the castle in silence. Carey went straight up to the Queen Mary Tower, still holding the caliver and also taking the one that hadn't been fired. When Dodd came up to fetch him, ready for duty at the muster, he found the Deputy Warden still in his doublet and bent over his desk.

"What are ye doing, sir?" asked Dodd cautiously, wondering if Carey had gone mad. The desk was covered over with bits of metal and various tools.

Carey was muttering to himself. "Look at this," he said eventually. "The barrel metal's not thick enough and it's not been hammered out straight. And the forge-welding of the underseam is appalling. Look, it's got a hairline crack along its length, see, where the wood can hide it."

"Is that the one that was faulty, sir?"

"No. This has never been fired."

Never mind Carey, Henry Dodd himself might have pulled its trigger and ended up worse off than Long George. He felt queasy again.

"Ay."

Carey was peering squint-eyed at another piece of metal. "This is very cheap and nasty," he said, prodding it with one of his little tools. "See how it scratches. I doubt it was case-hardened at all. I can't believe they ever came from the Tower. Nor even Newcastle."

"Nor Dumfries, sir," added Dodd, puzzling his poor aching head.

"Eh?" said Carey.

"Dumfries," Dodd repeated for him. "Where the best guns in all Scotland are made, though ye'll pay through the nose for them."

Carey was staring into the middle distance, at the painted hanging of a siege which warmed the stone wall of his chambers.

"Interesting," was all he said as he piled the bits into a cloth and wrapped it up, put it in a drawer of the desk.

"Are ye coming to the muster at all, sir?" asked Dodd hintingly.

"Hm? Oh yes. *Barnabus!*"

Dodd went to wait at the foot of the tower while Carey speedily changed out of his black velvet and into his second best cramoisie suit, plus his newly cleaned jack and straightened morion helmet. He came down the stairs two at a time and Dodd fell in beside him as he strode across the yard to where their troop was lining up.

"Do ye think they're all alike, sir?" Dodd asked in a mutter.

"Almost certainly. I didn't even look at which calivers I was taking."

"The pistols too?"

"I think so."

"But who could have done it?"

"I've no idea. Never my brother, nor anyone at court. Maybe not Lowther either."

"Why not, sir, seeing how he'd laugh if ye was maimed?"

"Because he was so quick to put his man in as acting armoury clerk. If it was him got at the guns, he would have made sure I appointed the clerk."

"Your man might have spotted the difference."

"I doubt it. I didn't. On the outside they look fine."

"What shall we do?"

"Nothing for the moment, since we'll be late for church if we don't move ourselves."

Most of the men were hungover but relatively clean, their horses groomed and their lances and helmets polished. Dodd still didn't see what the connection was between good soldiering and the state of your jack, providing it kept off swords, but had to admit it pleased him to see that his troop easily outshone Lowther's and Carleton's men who were dingy by comparison. Carey had them line up, checked them over, told one that his tack was a disgrace and so were his boots, complimented their latest recruit on the fact that he already had a morion and a jack and led them down early to the cathedral for Sunday service.

# sunday 9th july 1592, morning

The young King of Scotland rode into the West March town of Dumfries by the Lochmaben Gate at about eight in the morning, to be met by the old Warden, the mayor, the corporation and both major local headmen, Lord Maxwell and young James Johnstone. There was tension in the air between the headmen that would have given good resistance to a battleaxe, mainly because their two families had been at feud for generations and both their fathers had been murdered by the other's relatives. At the moment, the Maxwells were ahead in the feud, the most powerful and wealthy Surname in the West March of Scotland. For this reason, the Maxwell was wearing a brocade doublet slashed with bright red taffeta, a lace-trimmed falling band and a shining back-and-breast-plate, chased with gold. Behind him were a hundred of his largest men, in their jacks, mounted in two rows of fifty, their highly businesslike lances tricked out with blue pennants.

The young laird of Johnstone was wearing a pale buff jack, a plain red woollen suit, and an anxious expression on his face, mainly because he had only fifty men behind him. The white pennants on their lances fluttered merrily enough, but fifty against a hundred is poor odds at the best of times, never mind what Maxwell could call on from his friends and followers in Dumfries, a town that he owned. At least, thought the Johnstone, most of my lads have good handguns and balls and powder to go with them. And surely even a Maxwell will not plan trickery when he's to be made March Warden and the King is about, though God help us when the King is gone back to Edinburgh.

Naturally, neither of the two surname-headmen had admitted to knowing anything about the Earl of Bothwell's raid on Falkland Palace which was the main reason for their sovereign's sudden arrival with three thousand soldiers behind him. However, both had come in and composed with him, promising in writing to behave themselves, not raid, not feud and not intrigue. Both of them were hoping very much that King James would not find out what they had really been up to.

Trumpets rang out a fanfare for the third time as the cavalcade came up to the gate, led by five hundred footmen from Edinburgh. Behind them on a prime white French-bred horse, came the King. As to his dress, he was not at all a martial sight, wearing a high-crowned black hat with a feather and a multiply slashed and embroidered purple doublet. His linen was somewhat grey. Hats and caps came off raggedly as he passed, a few sorry souls actually bent their knees as if he were the Queen of England. Most bowed dourly.

James Stuart, sixth of that name, was twenty-nine years old, a small man the shape of a tadpole, with powerful shoulders and short, very bandy legs. Luckily he was an excellent horseman. His face had never looked anything other than cautious, canny and slightly self-satisfied. He was the son of Mary Queen of Scots, but had last seen his mother when he was a baby. Certainly he had not remembered her well enough to intervene when Queen Elizabeth of England had decided to execute her five years back. Having been a king since babyhood he was accustomed to deference; having been a king of Scotland, he was well-inured to powerlessness, poverty, kidnapping, ferocious court faction fights and the suicidal lunacy of many of his most prominent nobles.

Everyone in the cavalcade was sweating freely into their fine linen, since the day was dull and heavy with moisture. Ever since the king's harbingers had arrived in Dumfries in search of lodging, provisioning and entertainment for the King, his court and the three thousand men, the town had been in a ferment, wagons and packtrains of provisions arriving every day, barns being cleared, pretty sons, daughters and cattle being driven up into the hills round about. Food prices had become farcical, what with the bad harvest weather and the press of people into the area.

The desperate trumpeters excelled themselves as the King stopped at the Lochmaben gate, escorted by the outgoing Warden, Sir John Carmichael. The King was feeling the heat as well, the sweat making runnels down the grease on his face. All his clothes were heavily padded because he was, rightly, afraid of daggers. Behind him his courtiers affected the same portly, soft-edged style, not because they themselves were in the least afraid of daggers, but because he was the King.

The King's heavy-lidded eyes flickered from the Johnstone to the Maxwell and back again. He was waiting, very patiently, for something.

Lord Maxwell came to himself with a start, dismounted, stepped to the King's stirrup and kissed the long heavily-ringed hand that was stretched down to him.

"Welcome to the West March, Your Highness," he said.

King James suppressed a sigh. No doubt it was foolish to wish that his subjects would address their monarch with the more respectful 'Your Majesty' introduced by the Tudors in England. 'Your Highness' would have to do.

"Ay," said the King. "My lord Maxwell, have ye heard anything of the outlaw Hepburn?"

This was the erratic Earl of Bothwell, nephew of that dashing Border earl who had raped the King's mother (according to her story) in the tumultuous year after James's birth. The younger Bothwell had been an outlaw for over a year, but his latest outrage had taken place only a week before when he had raided the King's hunting lodge three hundred miles away at Falkland, trying to kidnap James.

"No, your highness," said Lord Maxwell. "Naebody kens where he is."

"Playing at the football on the Esk in England, last I heard," said the King drily. "Well, let's go in."

## sunday 9th july 1592, morning

Standing at the back of the cathedral while the Bishop of Carlisle battered his way through the Communion service before the serried rows of gentlemen and their attendants, Dodd watched the Courtier out of the corner of his eye. Somewhat to his surprise, he realised Carey was paying full attention to the words he was following in a little black-bound prayerbook.

Dodd was shocked. He hadn't taken Carey for a religious man and yet here he was, clearly praying. Then obscurely he found the thing reassuring.

After all, if the Courtier had some pull in heaven, that might be no bad thing. And there was no question he was a lucky man, the way he kept giving death the slip: he should have been hanged by the Grahams two weeks before, never mind the knife fight at the inquest and the caliver that morning.

The Bishop began to preach on the text "Vengeance is mine, saith the Lord, I will repay." Dodd listened for a few words in case the Bishop had any new ideas on how to take revenge and then lost track amongst the Latin and Hebrew.

They slipped out early to be ahead of the rush to mount up. The people of Carlisle were streaming towards the Rickersgate, lines of packponies shouldering through the bedlam with barrels and parcels on their backs, storeholders with handcarts shouting at each other and the women with their baskets worse than the rest of them put together.

Scrope had ordered the garrison and townbands to muster in the open space before the Keep, by the orchard. They were first there, and lined up by the fence. Carey watched critically as the rest of the men who were supposed to keep the peace arrived and settled themselves. When Lowther arrived, high coloured and wearing a serviceable back-and-breast-plate, Carey actually put his heels to his horse's flank and rode over before Dodd could stop him. For all Carey's elegant bow, Lowther cut him dead and after a couple of attempts Carey rode back again, his lips compressed.

"I could have told ye he wouldnae speak to ye," said Dodd in an undertone. "What did ye want him for? Ye could likely talk to Carleton just as well."

"I wanted to discuss firearms with him."

Dodd's mouth fell open. "Ye werenae hoping to tell Lowther the guns are rotten, were ye, sir?"

Carey raised his eyebrows. "Why not?"

"Well, but if it's right he doesnae ken about the guns, all ye need to do is keep your gob shut about it and ye could get yer ain back on Lowther and a' the trouble he's caused you…"

Something about Carey's look made a dew pop out on Dodd's forehead.

"I'll pretend I didn't hear that witless suggestion, Sergeant."

It was such a lovely opportunity, it was awful to see the Courtier missing a way of paying back Lowther that was neater than anything Dodd had ever seen.

"But, sir…"

Carey turned in the saddle. "Dodd, shut up. I'm not making more cripples like Long George for the sake of scoring off Lowther," he said.

Offended, Dodd fell sullenly silent. That's what religion did for you, he thought, made you sentimental. Who the hell cared if Lowther or any one of his kin had his hand blown off? Serve him right for being a bastard.

A group of wives from the castle hurried past them, carrying bundles and baskets, surrounded by squealing running flocks of children. Everyone was in their finery with even the babes in arms wearing ribbons on their swaddling clothes, all treking out to the muster, ready to watch the fine gentlemen and horses in hopes of some major disaster.

"It looks like a fair," Carey commented to Dodd. He was being pleasant again: Lord, the man's moods were like a weathercock.

"Ay, sir," growled Dodd.

"Poor old Barnabus won't be coming, says he's too sore and he'd rather have the day off in bed."

Dodd, who knew that Barnabus had picked up a dose at the bawdyhouse, grunted. That was what venery and immorality got you, he thought, and tried not to speculate on which of the six whores in Carlisle Barnabus had been bedding. It must have been Maria, she was the youngest and juiciest and…

There was the sound of a single trumpet from the Keep and the two drums following. Scrope appeared, Philadelphia behind him, mounted and followed by her women. Carey's sister looked well on a horse, Dodd had to admit, in black satin and pink velvet, with a pretty beaver hat set perkily on her cap and finished with a long curled feather. Behind them came the Keep servants, all in their best liveries, and at the end an excited looking Young Hutchin Graham in the suit he had been given for the old Lord's funeral, leading Thunder, Carey's tournament charger. So it was true the Courtier was entering him in a race to show off his paces. Dodd narrowed his eyes and looked carefully at the gleaming black animal.

Scrope himself was resplendent in his shining back-and-breast, with a plumed morion and a brocade cloak—he had attended church in the Keep chapel. He trotted down under the Queen's banner and took up position facing the lines of garrison men.

Carey spurred his horse across the green, made his bow lavishly from the saddle and spoke quickly under his breath to Scrope. Scrope smiled reassuringly, patted Carey's shoulder and shook his head. Carey's eyebrows did their usual dubious dance, but he bowed again and trotted back elegantly across the cobbles.

"If ye'd asked me, sir," droned Dodd. "I would ha' tellt ye we dinnae take the armoury guns out on a muster."

"Just making sure," said Carey. "Though isn't that what a muster's for, to reckon up the strength of the countryside?"

"Ay, sir," said Dodd, still as tonelessly as a preacher at bier. "But we ken very well how many guns is in the armoury, sir, we want tae know what's out in the countryside, and we dinnae want any of our guns…"

"Going absent without leave," said Carey.

"Ay, sir."

Carey nodded in silence. "I keep forgetting to use the peculiar logic of the Borders," he said to no one in particular.

Scrope was making the remarks his father had made last year and the year before that: they were to watch for outlaws but only to take note of their associates; they were to be tactful and alert to stop any trouble before it got out of hand. They were not to get drunk, on pain of the pillory.

He called Carey to go behind him with his men and led the way down Castle Street and out through the eastern gate. There were still a few people in town, holding packponies or leaning on lances giving desultory cheers as they went by.

The racecourse was heaving with men, already sorting themselves out into long lines, ready to be called. Carey had seen far more chaotic musters in the Armada summer, when numbers of excited peasants had turned out in their clogs with a touching faith that their billhooks, English blood and love for the Queen would shortly see them trampling down the veteran Spanish tercieros and scattering them like chaff. At the time he had agreed with them, but that was before he had done any serious fighting himself and found it to be as addictive as hunting, but much more dangerous for the undisciplined.

These, as he looked up and down straggling lines of footmen and bunches of mounted men, were better furnished than he had expected. Scrope's father had always given miserable accounts of the musters, as his predecessor had done before him: there were no horses, there were no swords, nobody had proper armour...

Carey started to laugh. "You cunning old devils," he said under his breath. "Look at them." It was true that none but the richest headmen and gentry had back-and-breast-plates; almost everybody was in the pale elaborately quilted leather of their traditional jacks. But everybody had something hard on their head, even if it was only a clumsy cap of iron hidden under a hat. Not a single man there was without a weapon of some sort, a lance at the least, and often a sword as well, though few of them had firearms.

Dodd was watching him suspiciously and Carey swallowed his hilarity. So much for his oath faithfully to report to his Queen: Carey knew he would infallibly lie as much as any of the Wardens and no doubt his own father and brother in Berwick had done before him. If anyone had presumed to report the true level of general battleworthiness on the Marches to the Queen, two things would have happened: she would instantly have stopped sending arms and munitions north to Berwick and Carlisle; worse, she would have become suspicious of the power wielded by her three March Wardens and started moving them in and out of office as her cousin monarch, King James, did with his.

The morning was taken up with the main business of the muster, a very tedious matter. In the centre of the racecourse sat Scrope on his horse and in front of him Richard Bell with the muster books laid out on a folding table. There were two sets, Carey noted, and grinned.

Every half hour or so, a trumpet would sound and Richard Bell would call out a headman or a gentleman's name. The Carlisle town crier repeated it at three times the volume, the cry was carried back through the crowd. After some confusion the worthy who had been called paraded before the March Warden with all his tenants or the men of his surname. Then each of the men came up to the table, repeated his name, landholding and his weapons for marking in the book, then stepped back among his kin. There was a considerable skill even to the business of calling the surnames, because it would be a sad mistake to call out two headmen who were at feud, especially when they had their riders behind them.

Once each surname had been mustered, the headman dismissed them and they fell to the real business of the day of eating, drinking, gossiping, listening to the educated among them reading out the handbills of the horses running in the races, argument and ferocious betting.

As the day wore on, the alewives and piesellers made stunning profits and the crowd grew ever less orderly and more genial. There would be occasional sporadic outbreaks of shouting and confused running about. At that moment, Carey, Dodd and his men rode over and physically pushed the combatants apart, leaving them to glare at each other and call names, but giving them a face-saving way out.

Later, when all but a few unimportant families had been called, the crowds drifted over to the racecourse fences and the stewards began lining up the horses that had been brought for the races. Carey was over in the paddock, patting Thunder's neck and giving Young Hutchin Graham advice at length while the boy grinned piratically up at him.

Dodd saved his money in the first race, which was won by a Carleton filly, just as a long line of pack ponies trailed into Carlisle by the Rickersgate. The second race took a while to start because there was argument over who should be by the rail. Dodd had two shillings riding on a likely-looking unshod gelding which trailed in at the end, second to last, puffing, blowing and looking ashamed of itself, as well it might.

For the third race, Carey came over to him munching on a meat pie, having finally finished advising Young Hutchin. At the line up Thunder looked like a crow among starlings, towering over the mixed rough-coated hobbies and in particular an ugly little mare with a roman nose. Carey shouldered his way to the rail with a ruthlessness that belied his courtly nickname, with Dodd in his wake.

The gun fired, the horses charged forwards and bedlam broke out, Carey no different from any other man watching his horse run, bellowing and pounding the rail with his fist.

The first time the horses swept past, Thunder was up at the front, Young Hutchin's tow head bobbing away above all the other riders. The second time he was still there and Dodd started yelling as well, in hopes of mending his fortunes a little. The big animal looked too big to be fast, but length of leg does no harm and he was pounding away willingly. By the third lap, many of the other horses had fallen behind and there was only Thunder, a brown gelding and the ugly little mare who swarmed along the ground like a caterpillar and yet stayed up at the front. They were close packed as they swept past, the riders laying on with their whips for the finish.

The disaster happened between there and the finishing line, with Young Hutchin's head down close by Thunder's neck. The brown gelding moved in close, there was a flurry of arms and legs and then Young Hutchin was pitched off over Thunder's shoulder, hit the ground and rolled fast away from the other horses's hooves, while the ugly little mare ran past the finish to ecstatic cheers from the Salkelds.

"God damn it to hell!" roared Carey and kicked a hole in the fencing beside him. "Did you see what that bastard did, did you see it, Dodd?"

"Ay," said Dodd mournfully, thinking of all the garrison food he would be eating until whenever his next payday happened to be. "I saw."

Carey was cursing as he vaulted the fence and went over to where Young Hutchin was picking himself up, flushed with fury and a knife in his hand. It took some argument from the Courtier to bring the lad over to Dodd, instead of going to wreak vengeance on the brown gelding's rider and Dodd had every sympathy. It didn't surprise him at all to see Sir Richard Lowther in the distance patting the brown gelding and its rider on the back and shaking Mr Salkeld's hand. Carey saw it too and his eyes narrowed to wintry blue slits.

"Hell's teeth," he muttered. "I've been had."

"Ay, sir," said Dodd.

"Let me go, Deputy, I willnae kill the bastard until this evening, Ah swear it. There'll be nae witnesses, or none that'll make trouble…"

"Will you hold your tongue, Young Hutchin Graham?"

Ay, lad, thought Dodd, but didn't say, do it quietly and keep your mouth shut.

"Ah wisnae expecting to be shoved like that, Ah wisnae, sir, if…"

"Be quiet. Did you take any hurt when you fell?"

"Nay, sir, but I cannae let that Lowther bastard…"

"He's a Lowther, is he?"

"Ay, sir, he's a cousin or similar, will ye no' let me go and talk to him, just? Please, sir?"

"Absolutely not. Stay away from him."

"But I lost the race because of him, for Christ's sake, sir, will ye no' let me…hurt him, at least, sir?"

"It was only a horserace," said Carey, distantly, clearly doing some mental arithmetic of his own, "I'm sorry, but you don't murder or assault people over a horserace."

Hutchin's young face was miserable with disappointment and uncomprehending resentment.

"But, sir…"

"And besides, he's bigger than you are and he'll be ready for you. I wouldn't be surprised if he had some others of his kin waiting for you, so you stay by me."

Young Hutchin's face took on an evil look of cunning at this and he calmed at once.

"Ay," he said thoughtfully. "Ay, ye've the right of it, sir, he will. Ay. Me dad allus says there's time to take yer vengeance, all the time in the world." Carey either wasn't listening or tactfully pretended not to hear.

"Whit about Thunder, sir?" Hutchin asked after a moment.

"One of the boys has already caught him, don't worry about it. You should have won and it wasn't your fault you didn't; just don't get yourself hanged over it, understand?"

"Ay, sir," said Young Hutchin ominously.

Carey smiled faintly. "Keep an eye on him, Dodd."

He sighed, squared his shoulders and marched briskly over to the triumphantly grinning knot of Salkelds, taking his purse out from under his jack and doublet.

Even Dodd had to admit that there was more style in bowing graciously to Salkeld as he patted his mare's nose and personally led her up and down to cool her off. Carey paid his losses with a negligent flourish, smiling and laughing good-humouredly with Salkeld and ignoring Lowther. You could see that it took the edge off the bastards' pleasure that the Courtier didn't seem to care about his losses.

Philadelphia Scrope was less suave as she presented the silver bells for prizes. She glowered ferociously at Mr Salkeld as well as at Sir Richard Lowther, from which Dodd guessed she was hurting in her purse as well. It couldn't have helped that Sir Simon Musgrave had been sitting beside her and was looking as happy as Lowther. Dodd saw her hand a small fat purse to him and sighed. God damn it, if Carey and his sister had lost their shirts on the race, where were Dodd's wages to come from?

The savour had gone out of the day for him, and it only confirmed his mood when his wife caught up with him and demanded briskly to know exactly how much he had lost on the Courtier's big charger and didn't he know better than to think a Salkeld would lose so easily?

He heard his name called and turned eagerly to see who it was. Red Sandy was standing on one of the marker stones of the race track gesturing over by the rail, where a crowd swirled around a knot of shouting men.

Dodd mumbled an excuse to his wife and arrived at the outskirts in time to see two Lowthers piling into a Salkeld with their fists. The Salkeld bucked and heaved and slipped away, started shouting for his kin, three more Salkelds attacked the Lowthers and then it seemed half the crowd was at it, swinging fists, shouting and roaring and pulling up hurdles from the fencing to use as weapons.

Dodd had more sense than to dive into that lot, even if Carey had not given them strict orders on no account to get into any fights on their own. He blew the horn he had on his baldric, dodged somebody with a club and heard hoofbeats behind him.

Carey was riding up with four of the men, leading a horse for Dodd which the Sergeant took gratefully and vaulted into the saddle.

"Reverse lances," Carey called. "Don't stick them."

In the early moments of a fight they could push the combatants apart; once it had got to this stage, the only thing they could do was stop it from spreading by using their horses as barriers and try and push the fighters over and away from the main crowd. The shouting swirled and spread, more of the garrison horse came over, Carleton with his troop and the rest of their own. There were knives flashing now, ugly and bright, someone was puking his guts up by the fence and the horses were whinnying as they objected to being used as mobile fences. Then Sir Richard Lowther rode over with Mr Salkeld behind him and instead of joining the line of garrison men, he rode straight into the middle of the mêlée and began laying about him with the flat of his sword. Evidently, thought Dodd, he had gone mad. There he was, bellowing that as God was his witness, he would shoot one of them—ay, Ritchie's Clem, you too—if the fighting didn't stop.

Astonishingly, it did. Men who had been at each others' throats let go of each other, the knives disappeared, the fence posts were dropped. A few seconds later all of them had dispersed into the crowd.

Lowther sheathed his sword and rode over to where Carey was sitting with his fist on his hip, looking contemplative.

"That's how ye keep order at a muster," said Sir Richard, swelling like a turkey. "Ye know the men because ye've been ruling 'em for years and ye call them by name."

Carey ignored him pointedly.

Lowther's jowls purpled above the tight ruff while Dodd gazed busily into the distance. Away in the hills to the north was a long line of animals, small as ants, no doubt heading for Dumfries where King James would be in need of supplies. Eventually Lowther rode away.

The muster of the West March didn't come to an end so much as tail off. Those who lived less than ten miles away went home, those who lived further out went to their exorbitantly-priced, shared beds in the inns and taverns of Carlisle, or lit camp fires and prepared to doss down for the night, each surname forming its own small armed camp in the meadows and gardens around Carlisle. The competing smells of bacon pottage and salt fish rose here and there.

Carey caught up with Scrope at last and found him deep in conference with Sir Simon. He waited politely for a while and finding himself to be somehow invisible, turned his horse away to go and seek out Thunder and give him some carrots. You couldn't blame the horse: he had been doing his best to win and it wasn't his fault that he had mislaid his rider.

Carey had got as far as the paddock when he heard a shrill cry behind him.

"Deputy, Deputy!"

He realised that a woman had been chasing after him and shouting for some time, so he turned his horse to look down at her. It was a skinny whippet of a woman, with her blue homespun kirtle held up and her feet bare.

"Goodwife Little," Carey said courteously. "What can I do for you?"

She came up to him, skidded to a halt and dropped a sketchy curtsey which he acknowledged.

"Deputy, I want Long George's back wages and a pension."

"I'm sorry?"

"How am I to look after his bairns? We havenae land of our own, he was a younger son, and now I must pay the blackrent we owe the Graham and…"

"Goodwife, wait a minute," Carey dismounted and stepped towards her. "Are you saying Long George is dead?"

She blinked up at him, bewildered that he didn't yet know of her world-shattering disaster.

"He died in the night," she said bleakly. "The surgeon said if he saw the dawn, he'd likely be well enough. But he didnae. He went to sleep and he died. He were stiff as a board this morning."

Carey shut his eyes briefly. "I'm very sorry to hear of it," he said. "My condolences, goodwife."

"Whit about his wages?"

"I haven't the money on me now."

"Well, what do I do about getting it?"

Carey struggled to make his thoughts behave themselves. He kept thinking how the little girl's feet had twisted themselves together under her kirtle.

"I'm not sure I can help you myself at the moment," he said. "Do you need shroud-money for the burial?"

Goodwife Little sniffed. "He's in the ground already, his dad did it this morning. I need the money for the blackrent to Richie Graham of Brackenhill, or they'll burn us out again."

For a moment Carey stood still, thinking of Long George being buried in unconsecrated ground like a dog or a suicide, wondering if his ghost would walk. He shook himself, felt inside his doublet and shirt and found his purse which had a couple of shillings in it, his entire fortune.

"That's all I have, goodwife," he said, handing it to her. "I've troubles of my own at the moment, but I'll try and see what I can do for you."

She curtseyed again, muttered her thanks as she took the purse and ran off into the crowd. Hitching Sorrel to the fence and ducking under the poles, Carey found Thunder in the middle of an admiring circle of boys and men, mainly English Grahams, with Young Hutchin holding his bridle and enlarging on the wickedness of that poxed pig of a Lowther that tipped him out of the saddle. Thunder whickered and nuzzled Carey. There was no question that Hutchin had kept him in beautiful condition, his coat gleamed and felt like warm damask, and he hardly seemed tired by his race. Nor was it Hutchin's fault that his uncle was one of the worst gangsters on the Border. Carey gave him the rest of the day off.

It was soothing to Carey to ride Thunder back to the castle at the head of his troop, patting his withers while the big animal shook his head and pranced a little. Dodd, who had drunk enough at the end of the day to be imaginative, could have sworn the animal looked embarrassed and puzzled not to be wearing the victor's bell. Dodd himself was weary and miserable and his stomach queasy with the after-effects of four meat pies, a strawberry turnover and a gallon or two of beer.

However there was no rest in prospect once they got back to the Keep. Something was happening in the courtyard when they rode in through the golden evening. It was full of shouting men carrying lanterns and torches, with Lord Scrope standing wringing his hands in the middle.

Carey frowned and looked in the same direction as the Lord Warden. Then he checked his horse and sat completely still, his lips parted as if he was about to say something and had forgotten what.

Dodd followed his gaze and thought, that armoury door is a mess, will ye look at it, bust apart and off its hinges...Je-esus Christ!

Somebody had raided the armoury while the Carlisle garrison was at the muster. In broad daylight, under the noses of the Warden, Deputy Warden and all the defensible men of the March, they had raided it and emptied it of every single caliver and pistol that it contained.

## sunday 9th july 1592, evening

The meeting took place in the Council Room that doubled as a dining room, Scrope presiding, Lowther, Carleton, Richard Bell and Carey all present. Carleton's best jack was still dirty from his hurried ride out with his men to try and catch up with the guns or at least find some kind of trial. He had returned empty-handed, complaining that the number of feet that had trampled round the area made it completely impossible to find a trace.

Barnabus Cooke was holding the floor, answering Scrope's questions.

"I was asleep, my lord," he whined. "I'm sick wiv a fever and I was in my bed in Sir Robert's chambers, sleeping. I din't see nothing, din't hear nothing." That was all he would say with such monotonous regret that it was hard not to believe him.

There had only been six people in the Keep altogether, two of whom had been drunk and still were. The other two had been prisoners in the dungeon who hadn't seen daylight for days and certainly couldn't be suspected. And Barnabus had been asleep.

Scrope dismissed Barnabus and turned to his wife who was standing at his right hand.

"Walter Ridley?"

Walter Ridley was Lowther's cousin, the acting armoury clerk whom Carey had never met and now probably never would. He had been found at the back of one of the stables, knocked out cold.

"He's more deeply asleep than anyone I've ever seen in my life," Philadelphia answered rather quietly. "He's snoring and his colour's bad. There's a dent in his skull: I think he's going to die, my lord, so if you will excuse me I'll go back to him now."

She shut the door behind her softly.

"Why would they kill him if he was helping them?" asked Scrope in a frustrated voice.

"To stop him telling who paid him?" said Thomas Carleton significantly, swivelling his barrel body to look at Sir Richard Lowther.

"There's no reason to suppose he was helping them," Lowther sniffed. "No doubt they hit him on the head to prevent him raising the alarm."

"What was he doing up at the Keep in any case?" asked Scrope.

"Perhaps counting the weapons to be sure naebody had got at them."

"Of course, it's possible the thieves didn't intend to kill him," said Carey. "Perhaps they just wanted to give him an alibi."

All of them knew they were avoiding the main issue. Scrope had pressed his fingers very tightly together.

"I need hardly tell you that this is a very serious matter," he said pedantically. "All of the new weapons in the armoury have disappeared while we were mustering. And most of the ammunition and most of the fine-grain priming powder. How it could have happened is of less importance than finding and returning them...If the Queen got to hear of it..." His voice trailed off.

There was a moment of dispirited silence while Lowther and Carleton, who had never met her, wondered if all they had heard was true. Carey and Scrope, who knew that the legend was only the half of it, tried not to think of her rage.

"She simply must not be allowed...she must not be troubled with this," said Scrope at last. "We must retrieve the weapons and that's all there is to it. In any case, we can't possibly ask for more weapons and munitions, so we must get them back. And we must also not let it be generally known what has happened, how weak we are. Or we shall have every reiver in the Scots West March riding south to take advantage."

Scrope was looking upset, thought Carey, which was understandable. Carleton seemed quietly amused by the whole thing and Lowther…Now Lowther's attitude was odd.

Carey coughed behind his hand. Scrope turned to him.

"Do you have something to say, Sir Robert?" he demanded rather pettishly.

"No," Carey said blandly. "Although I think it's going to be difficult to keep quiet. I also think there's more to all these goings-on in the armoury than meets the eye."

It seemed that Scrope didn't want to hear it. He made an abstracted smile and spoke at large.

"We are agreed then that the Queen must not be allowed to hear of this and we must therefore make sure that our ambassador in Edinburgh doesn't hear of it either. We will have to make very discreet enquiries as to what exactly happened and who stole the weapons…"

Carey continued to look bland. "My lord," he said smoothly, "I shall of course bend every effort to finding the guns. But in the meantime—have you informed His Majesty of Scotland?"

"What?" Scrope looked more obtuse than seemed possible.

"Why the Devil should he do that?" demanded Lowther.

"King James is in Dumfries with an army to catch the Earl of Bothwell. That was the reason for the muster, if you recall, Sir Richard," Carey lifted his eyebrows insolently at Lowther.

"I recall it, ay."

"Surely the likeliest thief of the weapons is Bothwell or one of his friends, since they'd have need of them. They could be planning another attack on the King while he's in the area."

"I thought you said that Bothwell had gone to the Highlands," Scrope protested.

Carey spread his hands. "I heard that, my lord. I don't know if it's true. He could be in the Hermitage in Liddesdale, raising an army to meet King James."

There was a short silence while they all considered what could be done to the delicate balance of chaos on the Border and in the Debateable Lands by a couple of hundred handguns and barrels

of gunpowder. Scrope rubbed his eyes with his fingers and then
knitted his knuckles again.

"I must say, I hadn't considered that," Scrope admitted. "Puts a
different complexion on the raid, rather. High treason and so on."

"Precisely, my lord," murmured Carey deferentially.

"Perhaps we had better tell the King, better to keep…ah…to
show him respect."

Very carefully, Carey did not smile. Scrope was as interested in
keeping sweet the King of Scotland and likely future King of
England as the Cecils or anyone else for that matter. As was Carey
himself. King James in Dumfries, only a day's ride over the Border,
was an opportunity not to be missed, even if he had certain
personal reasons for caution at the Scottish court.

"What? Send a messenger into Scotland wi' news of the guns
being reived?" demanded Lowther with a sneer. "Why not print it
up in a pamphlet and sell it at the Edinburgh Tolbooth—it would
have more chance of keeping quiet?"

Scrope was looking round the room in the way he had, his
fingers fluttering on the table unconsciously as his gaze roamed
past the covered virginals in the corner. Carey forced himself to
sit still and keep his mouth shut. Would Scrope do it? It was an
obvious course of action, but Carey had a strong suspicion that if he
showed himself too eager, Scrope would shy away from the idea.

"We should send someone to the King with a verbal message
for him alone," Scrope pronounced at last. "Someone discreet that
the King would be certain to receive." His restless froggy eyes
rested on Carey. "Whom the King already knows, perhaps?"

Lowther frowned. "My lord, I see no necessity…"

"Then you do know who stole the weapons, Sir Richard?" Carey
snapped at him.

"No, I do not."

"Enough, gentlemen," put in Scrope with unwonted firmness.
"I will have no…no disputes. Sir Robert, would you be willing to
ride to Dumfries and speak to the King?"

Carey inclined his head. "Of course, my lord."

Even Scrope's face was cynical. "You could start tonight…"

"No, my lord," Carey said. "Not tonight. I don't know the area and I might be mistaken for a reiving party crossing into Scotland. I would want to take three men with me..."

"What for?" sneered Lowther. "To protect ye?"

"Yes, Sir Richard," said Carey sneering back. "I know the Scottish court and a man with no followers there is of no account at all. Three men is enough for respect."

"You could take your whole troop."

"No need, my lord, and in any case, I doubt I could find them anywhere to sleep. Also we will need to take supplies for us and the horses..."

"Ye sound like ye're going on campaign," Lowther put in again.

Carey sighed. "Clearly," he said, "Sir Richard has never seen a Royal court on progress, as I have, many times." Scrope nodded anxiously.

"I might have known ye'd be drooling after the chance to meet the King," said Lowther. Carey stared at him and wished he could find an honourable excuse to punch the man. The words were bad enough but Lowther's tone twisted them into an implication of sodomy.

"I have met the King of Scotland," Carey said with cold patience. "Nearly ten years ago on Walsingham's embassy." Lowther sniffed.

"What about the weapons?" Scrope asked, swerving back to the problem at hand. "If you leave tonight you could be sure of telling the King before they can be used against him."

"Either they are on packponies or they have been moved to wagons. Ponies, I would imagine, they move faster in this part of the world. But the quickest a pony train could go so heavily laden would be about fifteen miles a day, and it's thirty-five at least to Dumfries. I can get a good night's sleep and still talk to the King before the guns are likely to get near him."

"It's not nearly so far to the Debateable Land."

"True. But if that's where they're going, they're there already and nothing we can do about it." Scrope nodded. "I'll need some kind of excuse for going to the Scottish court as well."

"Hm? Oh, no problem, Sir Robert. You can take a letter of congratulations to my lord Maxwell on his forthcoming appointment as Warden of the West March of Scotland. It would be polite of me to send one and I want to ask for a Day of Truce, do some justice. That will do, won't it?"

"Perfectly, my lord."

"I'll send the water-bailiff with you, he's a Graham and he knows the way."

Lowther scraped his chair back as he stood up. "Ay, it's a pretty sight," he sneered heavily. "Ye'll keep it from Her Majesty the Queen what happened to her own weapons, but ye'll tell it to the Scotch King to keep him sweet."

Scrope coughed and tapped his fingers on the table as Lowther marched out. "And now, unless any of you has any useful suggestion on retrieving our weapons..."

There was a pregnant silence. Not even Carey spoke.

"...I think we will end this meeting. No, Mr Bell, I do not require a record of it. Good evening, gentlemen."

Carey was the last to leave, rapidly totting up what he would need to take with him by way of clothes and supplies and money. He drew Scrope aside once the others had clattered down the stairs and told him that Long George was dead.

"Dear me," said Scrope, looking concerned. "Was that the man who lost his hand when you ambushed Wee Colin Elliot?"

"Yes. He leaves a wife and four children and they need a pension."

"Er...well, I'm not at all sure if..."

"My lord, without one they will either starve or turn to theft."

"Well, yes, but there's no obligation for us to provide a pension to..."

Carey looked around at the hangings, the wax candles, the softly shining rosewood of the virginals and the silver flagon of wine in the corner. Bad wine, true, but wine.

"Not only an obligation, my lord, but a necessity," he said through his teeth, something old-fashioned and feudal rising in him at Scrope's modern stinginess. "If other men see that their families might starve should they be killed in the Queen's service, how the Devil do you think we shall find men to garrison the Keep?"

"Er...yes. True."

"Whereas if Goody Little receives a pension, even a small one, the word will get round that we look after our own at least as well as the Grahams."

That was a hit. Scrope flushed slightly and his jaw set. "Well…if you put it like that, Robin…Yes. Of course, Goody Little must have a pension."

"Thank you, my lord. I'll talk to Richard Bell before I go. There is also the matter of money that I need to take with me into Scotland. I shall need a minimum of ten pounds for bribes, possibly more, some good silver plate and another five pounds sterling for rooms and stabling."

"Haven't you got it?"

"No, my lord. To be bald, I haven't a penny at the moment."

Scrope blinked at him. "But you brought a large loan from the Queen with you. And you won a considerable amount from Lowther only last week."

Carey coughed self-deprecatingly. "And I've spent it, my lord," he said. "And…er…lost it."

"On the horse-racing? On Thunder?"

Carey shrugged. "Not having the sale of the armoury clerkship in prospect, my lord, I felt I needed to raise cash to pay the men next month."

Scrope wandered over to his beloved virginals, sat down in front of it and began stroking the lid. "Well, er…Robin, I'm very sorry, but I'm in a few difficulties that way myself."

"But, my lord, your estates yield…"

"Oh, to be sure, to be sure, theoretically. Do you have any idea how much it costs to be March Warden? Especially if I'm to pay pensions to the families of men killed in my service? Let alone burying my father properly? The funeral cost me more than two thousand pounds, most of it cash which I had to borrow. And the Queen has not yet seen fit to send my warrant, nor any of my fees."

Carey stared at his brother-in-law, half-thinking of Long George being put in the ground by his father as cheaply as a dead dog. Though a peer of the realm was not to be compared with a Border tenant farmer, of course, still the worms would find them equally tasty…

"But, my lord, can you not at least advance me something against my own fees, for travelling expenses?"

Scrope began playing with a faraway expression on his face, something pretty and tinkling, making Carey want to slam the virginals lid shut on his spidery fingers. He shook his head.

"Your sister was...ah...as hopeful of Thunder's prospects as you were yourself. I'm afraid I have no actual money at all at the moment."

The perky little tune tweedled up the keyboard and down again and Scrope's attention was gone with it, far into the realms of music where grubby King Mammon held no sway. Carey bit his tongue on several unwise retorts and strode to the door.

"Um...Robin?"

"Yes, my lord?"

"Ah...Thomas the Merchant Hetherington is reliable and not too...um...exorbitant. A penny in the shilling, mainly."

"Per month?" Carey's tone was undeniably sarcastic, but Scrope only coughed.

"Er...no. Per quarter."

Carey shut the heavy door behind him with exaggerated care and the gossamer notes faded into the darkness of the spiral staircase.

"Did ye tell him of the guns?" Dodd asked in the dusky courtyard, after Carey had ordered him curtly to make ready for a journey to Dumfries.

"Good God, no. How on earth could I explain how I knew?"

"We're going into Scotland." Dodd stared into the middle distance, looking gloomy. "Ay. Tonight?"

"No, no. Tomorrow. There's a couple of things I need to do first and I need a good night's sleep."

"We're going into Scotland in braid daylight?" Dodd was shocked and horrified.

Despite his money-worries, Carey grinned at him. "Yes," he said. "Why not? We're not planning to lift any livestock, are we?"

"Nay, sir, but..."

"Not that you've ever done any reiving in that area yourself, have you, Sergeant?" Dodd's neck reddened immediately. I really shouldn't tease him, Carey thought to himself, it's not fair.

"Er…nay, sir, but…"

"So there wouldn't be any fear of you meeting any enemies, would there?"

"Well, there would, sir, if ye follow me. There's the Johnstones for one, and what'll we do if we meet up with Wee Colin Elliot again?"

Carey gave him a cold blue stare. "Smile sweetly and bid him good day. We're going to Court, not to a God-damned battle. Make sure you're in your best jack and your helmet is polished."

Dodd nodded sadly and went to check on his tack. It was clear he would infinitely have preferred a battle.

# monday 10th july 1592, early morning

Carey's sister refused to let Barnabus travel with them, which was deeply annoying since it meant Carey would have to do without a manservant at the Scottish court. Still, Barnabus was clearly very unwell, looking yellow, feverish and tightlipped. Philadelphia had put him back to bed in the little sickroom next to her stillroom with a brazier burning sweet herbs and a pile of blankets to help the fever. Carey, who had miraculously avoided ever catching a dose himself, hoped devoutly that he would stay lucky: Barnabus had been adenoidally eloquent on the trouble he had passing water and a number of intimate medical details that Carey could have done without. Philadelphia had also been firm on the subject of money.

"I haven't a penny," she sighed, busily stirring a steaming little pot over a dish of hot coals on her stillroom table. Putty-coloured and unnaturally still in the sickroom's other bed, Walter Ridley snored heavily in the background. "I can't even afford to buy embroidery silks, thanks to you and that big lolloping horse of yours," she added accusingly. "And my lord's no help; he says I should have known better than to wager on anything with Sir Simon Musgrave, let alone horse-races. Why don't you take Thunder with you and sell him at the Scottish court? King James likes good horseflesh, and he's probably a bit short at the moment, what with the raid on Falkland Palace and everything."

Carey looked at her with annoyance, because he hadn't thought of that himself.

"Isn't it illegal to trade horses into Scotland?"

Philadelphia sniffed. "Don't be silly, Robin, that law's for peasants and their hobbies, not proper tournament chargers."

It would be a wrench to sell Thunder. George, Earl of Cumberland had offered him forty pounds for the animal before he left London, and he had been too sentimental to take it. Besides, at the time he had just wheedled a loan out of the Queen and was feeling rich. But there was no denying that Thunder was eating his head off in Carlisle, was too big-boned and heavy for Border-riding and was very unlikely to win him any tournaments at the moment. He might make something in covering fees but not enough to earn his keep.

"Hm," Carey said, thinking it over. "Perhaps it would be worth taking him. But in any case, I need travelling money now and some for bribing the Scots courtiers as well."

Philadelphia shrugged and stopped mixing the tisane she was making for Barnabus. "Well then, you'll have to hock some rings, Robin, I'm sorry." She cautiously sipped the brown liquid in the pot over her chafing dish with a silver spoon and shuddered. She began carefully decanting it into a silver goblet through a muslin strainer.

"What's in that?"

"Hm? Oh, wild lettuce, camomile, dried rosehips. That kind of thing. It should make him a bit less sore, but I'm afraid if Barnabus is going to go on catching the clap every year, he'll need to see a surgeon. Have a word with him about it when he's better."

And so Carey delayed their departure for an hour while he did his business with Hetherington. This gave Dodd time to find his brother and tell him he was going into Scotland with them. Both Dodds were appalled at the thought of only themselves and Sim's Will Croser crossing the land between Carlisle and Dumfries with the Courtier, who was plainly insane and tired of life, and the Graham water-bailiff who was not to be trusted.

"It's no' the going there I'm so worried about," Red Sandy said, chewing a bit off his fingernail. "It's the coming back. D'ye mind that raid a few years ago where the Johnstones jumped us by Gretna?"

"Ay," said Dodd, who had a scar on his leg for a souvenir. "We could take every man in the garrison wi' us and still not be more than halfway safe."

"He's mad," said Red Sandy, positively. "Run woodwild."

"Are ye coming or no'?"

Red Sandy sighed heavily and bit down on his thumbnail. "Ay, of course I am, brother. God help us."

Sim's Will Croser was a stocky and phlegmatic man who saddled up without complaint as if he were doing no more than taking a dispatch to Newcastle. Carey had left orders that they were to bring a week's supply of hard-tack and horse fodder with them, and so they also had to load up four pack ponies with food and a fifth with blankets and a bag that clanked when shaken.

Carey chose that moment to come striding into the yard, followed by the English Graham water-bailiff. Dodd noticed that the Courtier was broader by the thickness of a money belt around his middle under his jack and black velvet doublet and that he had two rings fewer on his long fingers. "Are we running a raid intae the fair Highlands?" Red Sandy wondered, shaking his head at the preparations. Carey smiled at him.

"Plagues of locusts and looting Tartar hordes have nothing on a Court for stripping a place bare," he said. "And that's only the English court I'm thinking about; God alone knows what King James's gentle followers are doing to Dumfries."

He went over to the stables and led out Thunder, who was already tacked up, hitched him to the big horse called Sorrel that was Carey's normal Border mount. Thunder whickered in protest at the indignity of being led, and pulled at the reins as Carey swung into the saddle.

He led them at a brisk pace out of the crowded town, nodding to some of the local gentry he had met at the old Lord's funeral, and headed north towards the Border. They would have about five miles of the southern end of the Debateable Land to cross in order to go over the Border and Carey obviously needed to do it as quickly as possible, before word could get to any broken men about Thunder and their packponies.

He was in a hurry but to Dodd's surprise, Carey did not immediately take the route across the Esk and past Solway Field that led mostly directly to the Dumfries road. Instead, after a conversation with the Graham water-bailiff, he turned aside to Lanercost, until he came to the little huddle of huts where Long George's family lived. The half-tanned hide across the entrance of the living hut still hung down unwelcomingly, although there was movement within. There was also a fresh grave a little way from the place, under an apple tree. Dodd looked at it and wondered nervously about ghosts.

Carey dismounted, went over and knocked on the wattle wall and poked his head around the leather, immediately to start coughing at the smell of woodsmoke and porridge. All the four children he had seen before were piled up asleep like puppies in the bundle of bracken and skins and blankets where Long George had died and Goodwife Little was stirring at the pot hanging over the central fire.

To Goody Little the Deputy's sudden appearance like that was a nightmare come true again, and she shrieked softly at the horned appearance of his morion before recognising the face.

"Cuddy," she shouted. "Get up and stir the pot."

The boy fell blinking out of bed, scratching himself under his shirt and shambled obediently over to the pot. Goodwife Little wiped her hands on her apron and came to the Deputy, where she curtseyed.

"Ay, sir?" she said, looking up at him, her hard thin face steely with hope firmly squashed and sat upon so it could not sour on disappointment.

"May I come in, Goodwife?"

She gestured and Carey stepped around the hide.

"Long George was owed sixty shillings and sevenpence back pay, of which I have fifteen shillings and sevenpence here." Goody Little took breath to speak but subsided when Carey raised his hand, palm towards her. "I have also arranged a pension which is only threepence a day, but which I have the word of the Lord Warden will be paid on any day of the month that you choose to collect it. You may collect the rest of his back pay at the same time, in instalments, or as a lump sum, and you must present yourself in person with this paper here at the Carlisle Keep."

Goody Little had gone pale and put her hand against the wall. She smelled sourly female and as well-smoked as a bacon haunch, and as far as Carey could make out she had no breasts and no hips to speak of.

Was she going to faint, blast her? "Goodwife? Are you well?"

"Yes, sir," she whispered. "Only I was...I was relieved. I can pay Richie Graham what we owe him now, ye follow. I hadnae expected to see ye again, sir."

Carey said nothing for a moment. He took her scrawny rough hand between his two long-fingered hard ones.

"Goodwife, this will not affect your pension, but I greatly desire to know the answer. It could help avenge your husband."

She looked at him warily.

"What were Long George and his kin up to on the Wednesday before he was hurt? Don't tell me lies: if it's over dangerous for you to tell me, then I won't press it, but please, it would help me. What was he doing?"

"Why, sir?" she asked shrewdly. "Why is it so important to you to know?"

"He got a gun in payment for it, right? A pistol?"

After a moment she nodded at him.

"Well, Goodwife, whoever it was gave him the weapon was the man that killed him. That pistol was faulty: it burst in his hand when he fired it the second time, and that was how he came to lose his life."

Her mouth opened slightly and her eyes narrowed. She was not a fool, Carey could see, only very wary and weary also.

"Are all of the guns bad?" she asked. "All the guns that was in the armoury?"

Carefully, not revealing what she had let slip, Carey nodded.

Goodwife Little thought for a moment longer while Carey held his breath because he desperately wanted to cough. "My man was out wi' his uncle and cousins," she said finally. "Taking a load of guns from carts and loading them on a string of packponies."

"And, I suppose," said Carey quietly, "putting another load of guns into the carts that went on to Carlisle?"

Goodwife Little nodded.

"Where did the exchange take place?"

"East of here, in the Middle March, at a meeting place. I dinna ken where."

"Please, Goody, I will not say where I got the information, but where did the guns come from?"

She laughed a little. "Where all trouble comes, fra ower the Border, where else?"

Carey nodded, released her hand, gave her the purse he was carrying and the paper, then bowed in return to her curtsey and pushed his way out of the tiny smoky little hellhole. He was coughing and wheezing as he got back on his horse and when he wiped his face with his handkerchief he found a pale brown dinge on it.

"Christ," he remarked to no one in particular. "How can anyone live in a place like that?"

"It's no' sae bad, sir," sniffed Dodd, offended once again. "Ye stop crying and coughing in a week and then they're snugger than a tower, believe me."

"Thank you, Dodd," said Carey, hawking and spitting mightily. "I'll try and remember it." He put in his heels and led them at a fast trot back to the path, without looking back.

◇◇◇

"So tell me about the guns," the Courtier said conversationally to Henry Dodd as they turned their horses' heads west and northwards.

"The guns, sir?"

"Yes, Sergeant. The guns in the armoury. What is it that everybody else knows about them and I don't?"

Dodd's face had taken on a stolidly stupid expression.

"I'm sorry, sir…"

"What I'd really like to know is what makes the armoury clerkship worth fifty pounds, since it seems that's what Lowther and his cousin Ridley managed to bilk me out of. It can't simply be a matter of selling all the guns as quickly as you can: even on the Border someone would notice, surely."

There was the faintest flicker of Dodd's eyelid.

"For Christ's sake, Dodd, have pity."

Dodd coughed.

"Well, sir, ye see, ye can loan the handguns out for a regular fee with a little care—and a deposit, of course—and get more in the long run than ye would by selling them."

Carey greeted this with a shout of laughter. "By God, that's ingenious. I hope the clerks at the Tower never get to hear of it, the Spaniards would end up better armed with our ordnance than we are. So generally when there was an inspection, the guns would all be there?"

"Ay, sir. It fair queered Atkinson's pitch, you rousting the place out without warning like that."

"Did Scrope get a cut?"

"I dinna ken, sir," said Dodd carefully. "But ye see, it had the benefit that the surnames would kill more of each others' men wi' the guns and save us the bother."

"I wonder if that sort of thing goes on in Berwick. I must tell my brother."

"I dinna ken, sir," said Dodd again, having heard some of the stories about Sir John Carey.

Carey caught his tone. "Oh, I see," he said cynically. "So I'm the only innocent who doesn't know about it."

Dodd grunted and thought it more tactful not to answer.

"What about the risk that the surnames would be better armed in a fight than the garrison?"

"Wi' Lowther leading the trods, sir?"

"No. Plainly the situation wouldn't arise. I tell you, Sergeant, I'm not bloody surprised this March is gone to rack and ruin and there's been no justice out of Liddesdale for sixteen years."

"Rack and ruin, sir?"

Carey turned his horse and waved an arm expansively.

"Look at it, Sergeant. Look at that."

It was only a huddle of burned cottages and a broken down pele-tower, plus some overgrown fields. Hardly surprising, so close to the predatory Grahams of Esk and the assorted wild men of the Debateable Land. Dodd thought the place might have been Routledge lands once.

"Ay, sir?"

"It's tragic. This is beautiful country, rich, fertile, wonderful for livestock, and there's more waste ground than field, more forest than pasture. And what do you see? Pele-towers and such for the robbers to live in, or burned-out places like that. How can anyone till the ground or plant hedges or orchards or anything useful if they never know from one day to the next if they're going to be burned out of house and home?"

Dodd looked at the burned huts. Like Long George's children, he had lived in places like that in his youth, they weren't so bad, usually warm and dry if you built them right. And why would anyone want to plant an orchard, with all the trouble that was, when a cow would give you milk inside three years and mainly feed herself?

"And this thing about blackrent, it's a scandal and a disgrace."

Dodd stared at him. Blackrent was traditional. Carey made an impatient gesture.

"You're only supposed to pay one lot of rent, Dodd, to your actual landlord, plus tithes to the church, of course," he said. "You shouldn't be paying another lot of rents to a bunch of thieving ruffians to stop them raiding you."

"Well, it's worth it if they protect you," protested Dodd.

"Do you pay blackrent, Dodd?"

"Ay, of course I do. I dinna need to pay off the Armstrongs and I willna pay the bloody Elliots nor Lowther neither, but I pay Graham of Brackenhill like everyone else and I pay a bit to the Nixons and the Kerrs to keep them sweet."

"Did you know it's against the law to pay it? Did you know you could hang for paying it?"

Dodd was speechless. His jaw dropped.

"Who in the hell made that law?" he demanded when he could speak again. "Some bloody Southerner, I'll be bound."

"So who pays you blackrent in turn, Dodd?"

"Naebody."

Carey's eyebrows did their little leap.

"It's no crime to take blackrent," he said sourly. "Only pay it. And yes, it was a bloody Southerner made that law, and he was an idiot."

"Well, it's no' precisely blackrent, see ye," Dodd began to explain. "But some of the Routledges give me a bit and what the wife collects on my behalf I dinna ken and…"

"Oh, never mind. Look over there. Do those look like hobbies to you?"

Dodd looked and saw to his relief that the horses were on English Graham land. The water-bailiff was at the back of their small party and hadn't noticed Carey's interest.

"Nay, sir, they do not." Let Bangtail's dad talk his way out of this.

"Six of them, and very nice they are too, if a little short of food."

"Och, them fancy French horses eat their heads off…" Dodd began and stopped. "…Or so I've heard."

"Hmm." Carey looked sideways at him and Dodd wondered what it was about Carey that caused Dodd's own tongue to become so loose. He made his face go blank and stared severely at the foreign horses trotting about in the field ahead of them.

Carey did nothing much about the horses: simply pulled out a leather notebook and a pen and little bottle of ink and scribbled down the descriptions of each one of the horses in the field, resting the book on his saddle bow. They carried on, noting eight more horses of suspiciously fine breeding in lands owned by Musgraves and Carletons.

At last, to Henry Dodd's relief, Carey picked up his heels a bit as they approached the Border country itself. They crossed at the Longtown ford and then covered the five miles of Debateable Land at a good clip. They took the horse-smugglers' path by the old battlefield and followed it into the Johnstone lands north of Gretna, where Carey had them slow down to bate the horses.

We have thirty-five miles to ride to Dumfries before night, Dodd thought sourly, through some of the wildest robber country in the world, and hardly a man with us, just a bloody Graham water-bailiff and a Deputy Warden who thinks he's immune to bullets.

To Dodd's mind, Carey rode like a man going to a wedding with a cess of two hundred behind him. He took his time, never doing more than a canter, and stared around with interest at what he called the lie of the land, which looked like rocks and hills to Dodd, asked the few people in the villages they passed through what surname they were and generally behaved as if he was somewhere in soft and silly Yorkshire, where no one was likely to attack him at all.

When Dodd tactfully tried to reason with him, he got nowhere.

"Dodd, Dodd," Carey said with that tinge of tolerant amusement in his voice that Dodd found intensely irritating, "nobody is going to attack us at this time of all times. King James is on the Border with three thousand men and he would just love to suck up to the Queen by hanging anyone who attacked me."

Ye think ye're very important, Courtier, thought Dodd, but heroically didn't say. Has it crossed your mind that there are broken men all over the place here and not a one of them that gives a year-old cowpat for King James and all his men? He glanced across at the leathery water-bailiff, with the telltale long bony Graham face and cold grey eyes. He was riding along on his tough little pony looking as if he was half-asleep. No help from there.

"Ay, sir," said Dodd, still trying to rotate his head on his neck like an owl. "I'm verra glad to hear it. Will we be there by nightfall at this pace, sir?"

He paused, stark horror chilling his blood like winter. "And what's that, sir?"

There was movement in the distance, the characteristic purposeful movement of a man riding towards them at speed. They sat and watched for a few seconds and then Carey was quietly loading his dags, and Red Sandy and Sim's Will Croser drawing their swords. Dodd spun his horse about, staring suspiciously at the farmlands and waste ground about them. Nothing. The land was empty save for the inevitable women weeding gardens and harvesting peas. Only there was the lone horseman riding like the clappers.

Man? He seemed small and light, and there was a smear of gold above his face, beneath his dark woollen cap.

"Och," said the Graham water-bailiff, visibly relaxing. "I ken who that is." He shook his head and tutted.

"Well?" said Carey impatiently.

"That wild boy, Young Hutchin."

It was. As the figure came closer he resolved into Young Hutchin, wearing the black livery he had worn for Scrope's funeral, bending low over his hobby's neck and riding like one demented.

As he came up to them at last, he reined in and grinned. "Do you have a message for me?" Carey demanded, tension showing in his voice. Young Hutchin looked surprised.

"Nay, sir. Your lady sister said I wis to serve ye for page if I could catch up to ye, sir. That's why I'm here."

The boy had a very guileless blue stare and for a moment even Dodd believed him.

"You're lying," said Carey with emphasis. "My sister would no more send you to be my page at King James's court than parade ten naked virgins mounted on milkwhite mares through the Debateable Land at night."

Hutchin's face fell slightly. "She did so," he muttered. "I'm to be yer page."

"She did not. Go back to Carlisle."

"Ah willna."

"Young Hutchin," said Carey through his teeth. "I have enough to do without nursemaiding you through the Scotch court. Go back to Carlisle."

"Ye canna make me."

"I can tan your impudent arse for you, if you don't do as you're damned well told!" roared Carey.

The water-bailiff tutted and rode forward. "Sir," he murmured modestly. "A word wi' ye."

"Yes, what is it, Mr Graham?"

"The lad's my cousin's child and he's three parts gone to the bad already."

"Do you want King James's court to complete the job?"

"Ye canna make him go back if he doesnae want to. He'll only ride out o' sight and then trail us intae Dumfries alone."

Carey growled under his breath. "Are you telling me I have to take him as my page and under my protection or risk him coming to Dumfries on his own anyway?"

"Ay, sir. That's the size of it."

"God damn it to hell and perdition. What the Devil possessed you, Young Hutchin? I don't need a bloody page."

"Ye do sir, at court. Ye canna be at court without a servant to attend ye. What would the Scottish lords think?"

"Who gives a damn what the Scottish lords think? And anyway, that's not why you came."

Hutchin grinned knowingly. "Nay, sir. I had a fancy to see the Scotch court for maself."

Carey stared at him narrow-eyed for a moment, as if trying to size up exactly how much he understood of the world. Eventually he shrugged.

"On your own head be it," he said. "I don't want you and if you've a particle of sense you'll turn around and head back to Carlisle."

Young Hutchin sat and waited Carey out. Carefully, the Courtier discharged his dags into the air, causing Young Hutchin's horse to pirouette and rear. If Carey thought that would make Young Hutchin think twice, he was mistaken: the lad was a Borderer born and bred and had heard gunfire since babyhood. He waited until Carey had gestured his small party onwards with an impatient hand, and fell in at the back looking as meek and prim as a maiden. Although if what Dodd had heard about the Scottish court was true, one of Carey's fanciful virgins on horseback would have been safer there.

They ate late of the food they had brought with them by the side of the track in Annan, after being refused point blank when they offered to buy anything the womenfolk happened to have around. The women claimed bitterly that there was not a scrap of food left anywhere since the King's harbingers had been through and they had seen nothing but forest berries and fresh peas for two days. The water-bailiff was known there and got some guarded nods.

The afternoon passed wearily for Dodd in the long complex climb up and through low hills and bogs to Dumfries. Carey was enjoying himself again. Some of the way he was whistling one of the repetitive complicated ditties he and his brother-in-law seemed to set such store by, to Dodd's mystification. What was the point of a song that had no story? Finally Dodd rode a little ahead, to get away from the wheedling little tune. The countryside gave him a bad feeling in his gut all the way: true, he was legal this time, and riding with the water-bailiff. It didn't help. Every time previously that he had passed into Scotland, except for the occasional message to Edinburgh when he was a lad, had been at dead of night and very very quietly. He did know the area somewhat, different though it looked in daylight, although the Johnstones and the Maxwells were both a little spry to be stealing cows off too regularly. A few years back there had been some pickings when the two surnames had been at each other's throats. They were quiet at the moment and Dodd wondered gloomily what they were brewing. There were plentiful signs of devastation about: broken walls, burnt cottages, even a roofless pele-tower here and there, many fields going out of cultivation. The Courtier seemed less morally outraged by it, though, presumably because the sufferers were only Scots.

Nearer Dumfries there was less waste, more fertile farmed land, but still it looked bad. Some of the farmers had taken their harvest in early, no doubt to take advantage of the King's Court. But that meant the oats and wheat that was left over would be subject to rot later on. Oh, there was a famine brewing for next year and no mistake: first Bothwell and his men and then this, the Court and the Scottish army. Nowhere in the world could hope to feed so many people so suddenly and not suffer. Not to mention the horses. Dodd thought he would mention it to his wife, so she would keep any surplus from their harvest and not sell it.

## monday 10th july 1592, evening

They came into Dumfries at the southwesternmost end of the town, on the path from Bankend that splashed through the Goosedub bogs by the Catstrand burn, past the evil green of the Watslacks on their right before passing into the town itself at the Kirkgate Port. Dumfries had no walls. It was amply defended by being built on a soggy bend of the River Nith with river on two sides and bog on the other two.

To Dodd and Young Hutchin the town was a howling maze of chaos, full of people with strange ways of speaking and strange cuts and patterns to their jacks. The water-bailiff said he would go and stay with a woman of the town that he happened to know and disappeared among the beer-drinking crowds before either Carey or Dodd could find out where. Carey shrugged and began threading through the eternal evening twilight of July, patiently asking in his fluent Scots at the three inns and five alehouses if anyone had room for them. Mostly the Dumfries citizens laughed in his face and Dodd began to wonder if cobbles were as bad to sleep on as they looked. Typically, as the sky darkened a roof of cloud formed and it was coming on to rain a fine mizzle. Tents had ominously mushroomed in the Market Place itself, huddles of pavilions pitched between the Tolbooth and the Fish Cross, and rows of better quality, some of them painted and coloured with badges, behind the Mercat Cross. Crowds of men streamed in and out of the best house they had seen in Dumfries, a large solid stone building with pillared arches at its ground floor entrance, and more were sheltering under them, richly dressed and leaning against the stone or playing dice like men who were used to waiting.

Carey dismounted and led his horse to one group, spoke softly and handed over some coins. The Dodd brothers, Sim's Will Croser and Young Hutchin watched hopefully until they saw the sneers.

Carey came back to them shaking his head.

"Sir?" asked Dodd, mentally girding his loins for a night in the open.

"I am reliably informed that the lad might have some chance of lodging," Carey replied drily, "but none of us do." If Young Hutchin understood what the Courtier meant by that, he gave no sign of it.

"If we go out of town a little way there might be a dry place we could light a fire…" Dodd said, preparing to make the best of it and hoping Carey would not sleep a wink on the hard cold ground.

Carey smiled. "One more place to try."

They trailed back through the crowds and tents and horses, picking their way over the dung that already lay in heaps at street corners, to one of the smaller inns at the corner of Cavart's Vennel.

Again Carey dismounted and spoke to one of the men lolling by the door picking his teeth, handed over some more money. They waited while the ponies behind stamped their feet tiredly, and ugly-looking men in jacks passed by eyeing the supplies and livestock. Dodd eyed them right back.

At last the servingman came back, shrugged and gestured. Carey smiled, led them forwards under the low arch, where men were already settled down for the night, bundled up in their cloaks with a little fire in a corner, and into the inn's tiny yard. It was clogged with horses, tethered in rows and looked after by harassed grooms.

"Red Sandy, Sim's Will and Hutchin, take care of the horses," Carey ordered. "Unload the packs, pile them up and have a man guarding them at all times, no matter what happens. I'm going to see the old Warden."

Sir John Carmichael was finishing a late supper in the tiny common room, seated at the head of one of the trestle tables, with his followers packed tight on the benches. He had his court clothes on which made him look incongruously gaudy in gold and red brocade, and a broad smile on his face.

"God's blood," he boomed as Carey walked in, followed by Dodd. "It's Mr Carey."

Carey smiled and made his bow, which Sir John returned.

"I'm Sir Robert now, my lord Warden," he said. "And my father sends his best regards."

"Ay, and how is he? How's his gout? Och, sit ye down, and Jimmy, will ye go ben and fetch vittles for the Deputy. Ay, that's fine, shove up, lads, make room."

Dodd had never been so close to so many Scots in his life unless he was killing them, and certainly not in their own land. He sat down gingerly on the bench where a space appeared and wondered if there was any hope at all of getting out if they turned nasty. Carey perched on the end next to Carmichael and smiled.

"And also either his congratulations or his commiserations, depending on your mood, at your resignation from the Office of West March Warden," Carey continued in the complicated way he could command without a tremor.

"Congratulations?" shouted Carmichael, his round red face beaming. "I wis never sae glad to get shot of an office in my life. D'ye ken what the King pays? Ain hundred pound Scots, that's all, and I spend more than that on horsefeed in a season."

Carmichael had a vigorous tufting of white hair all over his head, and broad capable hands, and his face had an almost childlike straightforwardness about it.

Carey winced sympathetically. "I had heard tell the place was ruination for anyone but a magnate," he said.

"Ay, it's the truth. And not a hope of justice fra the scurvy English either," Carmichael added with a fake glower. "Ye're Deputy Warden now under Scrope, I hear. How d'ye find it?"

"More complex than I expected," Carey answered. "And harder work."

"They do say peddling gie's a man a terrible thirst," said Carmichael with a grin. Carey had the grace to grin back and accept a horn mug filled with beer. To his surprise, Dodd was given one as well. The beer was sour. "By God, that was a good tale I heard about you at Netherby. Jock o' the Peartree held prisoner in his own brother's tower…Nae doubt that's when Bothwell's ruffians found out about the horses at Falkland."

"It was. I can't think how I let it slip out."

Carmichael barked a laugh. "Ye did me an ill turn there, ye ken, lad. My cousin Willie Carmichael of Reidmire at Gretna's in an awful taking about a black horse that was stolen that night and he reckons Willie Johnstone of Kirkhill's got it." Carey raised his brows and said nothing. "See, the horse is the devil of a fine racer, though he's only a two year old, he'll bear away the bells at every meet he goes to next year if Cousin Willie can get him back and he's writing me letters every week giving me grief about it like an auld Edinburgh wifie. I've written to Scrope about it, but can ye do aught for me?"

"I'll try," said Carey. "You know what it's like with horses."

"Och, ye canna tell me anything about it. I mind the time some Dodds hit us for our stables, once, stripped out the lot of them."

"Did they?" said Carey neutrally, not looking at the Sergeant. "What did they get?"

"Och, it was a while back, a fair few years now, but they were nice horses—there was Penny, and Crown, and Farthing and Shilling…"

Dodd buried his nose in his beer. Was the old Warden teasing him?

"Dodds and English Armstrongs it was, a nice clean job of it too. We never got them back nor a penny of compensation."

Carey coughed. "I'm very sorry to hear of it, Sir John. I'm afraid I can't help you with them, but I'll see what I can do about your cousin Willie's black horse. What's it called?"

"Blackie, I expect," said Carmichael. "The man's got nae imagination." He tossed a chicken leg at a pile of dogs in the corner which promptly dissolved into a growling fight. "Meantime, what can I do for ye, Sir Robert?"

"Tell me about your successor as Warden."

"Lord Maxwell." Carmichael nodded and smoothed out his white moustache. "He's clever and he's got something in the wind."

"Against the Johnstones?"

"Of course. Who else? He was uncommon willing to be made Warden, which means he'll use his Wardenry against Johnstone, and he's rich and he's cunning. I dinna like the man myself, ye ken, but he's a good soldier."

"Catholic too, I understand."

"Ay, and that's another matter. Ye may mind the trouble he caused hereabouts in the Armada year?"

"Didn't the King arrest him for backing the Spanish?"

"Ay, and executed a couple of dozen of his kin."

Carey whistled. "And he's going to be made the new Lord Warden?"

Carmichael shrugged. "The King's a very forgiving prince when he wants."

"Must be."

"Ay, well, Maxwell's been in Spain and France and all over, brought home some fancy foreign tastes. A while back he had his ain personal wine merchant fra foreign parts, and his ain personal wine merchant's wifie as well." Carey raised his eyebrows quizzically and Carmichael barked with laughter. "Ye wait till ye see her, lad. She's moved on fra the Maxwell now, dropped him like an auld glove once the Earl of Mar showed an interest in her. Even the King tolerates her and God knows, he's no love o' women nor foreigners."

"Spanish?" asked Carey.

Carmichael shook his head. "Italians."

"How very cosmopolitan of the Maxwell." Carmichael snorted and finished his beer. "Tell me, my lord Warden," Carey went on, "any Germans about the Court at the moment?"

This produced an interesting result. Carmichael drew back and went still.

"What d'ye know of him?"

"I saw him arrested by the Earl of Mar." Carey described the sinister encounter, which had been coloured over for Dodd and almost obscured by the wounding of Long George.

"Well, I dinna ken meself, because I've not been in Edinburgh inside a year, but I think he was an alchemist. I think he was going to make the King a Philosopher's Stone or gold or some such, in Jedburgh, and it all went wrong. He made an enemy of the King and that's an ill thing to do, mark my words."

"What happened to him?"

"I heard, he got the Boot to learn him better manners and then the King handed him over to some Hanse merchanters from Lubeck who hanged him for some bill he'd fouled over in Germany."

Carey sighed. "Damn," he said. "I wanted to talk to him."

Carmichael shrugged.

"How about his Majesty the King, God bless him?" Carey continued after a moment. "Do you know what he's planning to do with his army?"

"Hit Liddesdale and burn a lot of towers, nae doubt," said Carmichael comfortably. "He's got blood in his eye for the Grahams and nae mistake, he blames them entirely for the raid and he says they're all enchanters and witches like the Earl of Bothwell for the way they could carry off so many horses from so far away."

"They're highly experienced raiders…" said Carey.

Carmichael smiled. "Don't tell him," he said. "Ye'll make him worse."

"And the Italians?"

"Who knows?" Carmichael belched softly into his napkin and wiped his moustache. "Now then, Sir Robert, how're ye for a place to lay your head the night?"

Carey shook his head. "Worse than the Holy Family on tax night in Bethlehem."

"How many have ye got?"

"Myself, Sergeant Dodd here, two men and a boy."

Carmichael's eyebrows drew together. "A boy?"

Carey spread his hands helplessly. "The bloody child followed me half way here on some half-witted whim of his own, and rather than have him come into Dumfries by himself and take his chances, I let him join me."

Carmichael harrumphed and shook his head. "Ay, well."

"We've our own supplies though."

"Hmn. Let's take a look at them."

Carmichael came to his feet, followed politely by Carey and picked his way round the benches and men, went through into the yard. There Sim's Will and Red Sandy had found a clear patch of ground where they had hobbled the ponies in a circle and put Thunder and the packs in the middle. Hutchin had his doublet off and was rubbing the animals down at a frenetic speed.

Carmichael spotted Thunder instantly, and was naturally transfixed. Other horsemen in the yard, some of them worryingly well-dressed and armed, were standing eyeing the animal too. Carmichael smiled with the pure childlike pleasure of a Borderer faced with prime stock.

"Now there's a handsome beast," he said to Carey. Carey nodded noncommittally.

"My tournament charger, Thunder. I brought him in case there was any tilting."

Carmichael evidently didn't believe this. "Ay," he said knowingly, pushing between the hobbies to pat Thunder's nose and feel his legs. Dodd instantly bristled at the sight of a Scot sizing up one of their horses, but Carey seemed relaxed. Carmichael slapped the high arched neck lovingly.

"By God, this one puts Blackie in his place. Would ye be interested in selling him?"

Carey looked indifferent. "I hadn't considered it, my lord Warden," he lied. "I wouldn't have thought anyone at this Court could afford him."

Carmichael's smile stiffened slightly. "Och, I don't know about that," he said. "It's only we dinna choose to throw our money awa'. Would ye be open to offers?"

Carey examined his fingernails. "That would depend on what they were," he said.

Carmichael's smile relaxed to naturalness again. "Ay," he said. "Nae doubt. Well, Sir Robert, if ye'll have yer men bring the packs intae the inn we can all budge up and find space for ye this night at least. Would ye mind a pallet on the floor, if I put ye in wi' my steward?"

"Not in the least, my lord. Half an hour ago I was bracing myself for cobbles."

"Och," said Carmichael. "They'd be soft enough by now, what wi' all the animals in town. Would ye credit the place?"

"Oh, I've seen worse, my lord. Far far worse."

"Ay, the Queen's progresses are said to be a marvel to behold."

"That's one way of putting it."

# tuesday 11th july 1592, dawn

Dodd slept extremely badly that night, his head on one of the packs, a knife in his hand and one of the horse-tethers in the other, under a canvas awning. The night was warm enough but the noise of drinking and fighting in the town never stopped and it seemed that every time he shut his eyes he was in the middle of some horrible nightmare in which he was a mouse in a den of cats, all speaking broad Scots. The Courtier was inside on a straw pallet, bundled into his cloak and no doubt giving grief to Carmichael's steward with his snores. That was some satisfaction.

Bleary-eyed and itchy with ferocious Scotch vermin at dawn, Dodd relieved his brother to try and snatch an extra hour, and began feeding and watering the horses. Young Hutchin was curled up among the packs still asleep; Dodd had excused him standing a watch on the grounds that he was one of the valuables they were guarding.

Noises and lights inside the inn announced that Carmichael was no stranger to brutally early rising. The Courtier appeared in the doorway, also scratching like an old hound, and went to wash his face in a bucket of water.

"Morning, Sergeant," he said cheerily as he went past combing his hair, and Dodd grunted at him.

They ate a good breakfast of bread and ale and then left Red Sandy and Sim's Will with the packs to go and visit Lord Maxwell in his town house at the other end of Dumfries. Carey took Thunder as his mount, which seemed a further piece of complacent lunacy to Dodd, and Young Hutchin rode one of the packponies.

The market-place was heaving like a ten-day-old corpse. The reason was easy to see: drawn up in a circle around the Mercat Cross were wagons and handcarts full of food, round loaves of rye and oat bread, round cheeses of varying levels of decrepitude and serving men crowding up to buy from the barkers sitting on the wagons. Dodd recognised a JP stamped on the cheeses and pointed it out to Carey who seemed to find it funny. If King James's court was eating rations originally intended for the Carlisle garrison (and rejected on grounds of age), that was fine by Dodd.

The press of people was so tight, it was hard to get their horses to push through, so Dodd and Young Hutchin dismounted and led them forward. Carey stayed mounted for the better vantage point. Then, just as they came to the schoolhouse on the corner of Friar's Vennel, empty of schoolboys but filled with men, Carey saw something that made him stop and turn his horse's head away and to the right.

Dodd followed his stare and saw the tall severely-dressed woman in her grey riding habit and white lacy falling band, riding pillion behind a groom among the crowds by one of the wagons. He struggled to keep up with Carey who was shouldering Thunder through the close-packed obdurate Scotsmen. Just as Carey almost reached her, she touched the groom's shoulder, their horse stopped, and the groom dismounted to hand her down. Dodd wondered if she was pregnant, because there was something oddly stiff in the way she moved.

"Lady Widdrington, Lady Widdrington," called out Carey with a boyish laugh of excitement, sliding from his horse and ducking around the animal to follow her. "My lady, I…"

She paused just long enough to look over her shoulder at him. The long grave face coloured up and the grey eyes sparkled, but she shook her head severely and turned her back on him. Carey stopped in mid-bow with a guilty expression.

"Bugger," said Dodd.

Facing Carey now was a wide balding Englishman in a magnificent black velvet suit and furred gown. He had corrugated ears and a long sharp nose. Carey straightened up quickly.

"What business do you have with my wife, Sir Robert?" demanded Sir Henry Widdrington in a very ugly tone of voice.

For once in his life it was clear Carey couldn't think of anything to say. Dodd loosened his sword and pushed through the crowd: in his experience, elderly English headmen with the gout never went anywhere without their men and they were in lawless Scotland now. Carey seemed to have remembered it too: his hand was also on his swordhilt.

Sir Henry Widdrington limped up close to Carey and pushed him in the chest with a knobbly finger. Instinctively the crowd widened around them.

"I have forbidden my wife—*my wife*, Sir Robert—to have any further conversation with you under any circumstances at all."

Yes, thought Dodd, he does have backing: there's that spotty Widdrington boy over by the inn gate and four more I don't like the look of in the crowd behind the Deputy, and what about those two over by the horses…Why the hell didn't we bring the patrol, at least, poor silly men though they are, we're almost naked in this pack of Scotsmen and thieves. He began to sweat and look for good ways out of the marketplace.

Carey was still silent which seemed to enrage Widdrington.

"I know, ye see," he hissed, still poking Carey in the chest. "I know what ye were at when I made the mistake of letting her go to London in the Armada year, you and your pandering sister between ye."

Och God, groaned Dodd inwardly, knowing how Carey loved his sister and spotting another knot of six men at their ease just within the courtyard. Carey however gave the impression of being struck to stone, with only his eyes too bright a blue for a statue.

"…and as for Netherby…" Rage made Widdrington quiver and gulp air. "What did ye give her for the loan of my horses, eh,

Carey? How did ye persuade the bitch, eh?" Poke, poke went the finger. "Eh? *Eh?*"

Carey's face was a mask of contempt.

"You know your lady wife very little, Sir Henry," he said, in a soft icy voice. "She has too much honour for your grubby suspicious little mind. As Christ is my witness, there has never been anything improper between us."

Sir Henry Widdrington spat copiously on Carey's boots.

Dodd was directly behind Carey when this happened. Knowingly risking his life, he held Carey's right elbow and whispered urgently, "Dinna hit him, sir, he's got backing."

Carey's face was masklike and remote. Sir Henry seemed to be waiting for something, watching them both closely.

"Hit him?" Carey repeated coldly and clearly. "I only hit my equals or my superiors, Dodd. I would never strike a poor senile gouty old man, that has the breeding of a London trull and the manners of a Dutch pig."

Well, it was nice to see the way he turned his back on Widdrington, insolence in every line of him, and remount Thunder. Perhaps having Thunder prance a showy curvette was taking defiance a little far, but it at least cleared the area around them slightly so that Dodd and Young Hutchin could mount as well. Carey led the way to the Town Head where Maxwell's house was. Dodd showed his teeth at Widdrington who was bright red and gobbling with fury, and followed him. Still, his back itched ferociously right up to the gate of the magnificent stone-built fortified town house that the Dumfries men called Maxwell's Castle. It continued to itch while Carey talked to the men standing guard at the gate and passed over the usual bribes, and went on itching even as they passed through into the small courtyard. That too was packed tight, though here all the men were either in livery or wearing Maxwell or Herries jacks and no lack of family resemblance either. As usual Thunder drew a chorus of covetous looks and some quietly appraising talk. Carey beckoned that Dodd was to follow him.

Back still pricking like a hedgehog's, Dodd gave Young Hutchin his horn with orders to wind it if one of the scurvy Scots so much as laid a finger on anything of theirs. Young Hutchin grinned and touched his forelock.

The servingman was leading them through the crowded hall and out the back past the kitchens into a long low modern building tethered to the castle like a barge. Dodd followed Carey in through the door and blinked in the morning light coming through the high windows.

The shock of the caliver blast almost by his ear nearly caused Dodd to leap under the table. Even Carey jumped like a skittish horse, whisked round and half drew his sword.

Loud laughter made Dodd's ears burn and he turned to snarl at whoever had frightened them. A blurred glimpse of an elaborate padded black and red slashed doublet and a wonderfully feathered velvet hat made him bite back his indignation. It was the tall man who had fired a caliver at a target surrounded by sandbags at the other end of the bowling alley. The barrel was smoking as he blew away the powder remnants from the pan.

"Whae's after ye and what did ye reive?" asked the man, still laughing. "Ye baith jumped like frogs at a cat."

Carey took in the magnificent clothes, dropped his sword back in its scabbard and managed a fairly good laugh and shallow bow in return.

"We did, sir," he said in Scots. "Ye have the better of us. I am Sir Robert Carey, Deputy Warden of Carlisle, and I am in search of the honourable Lord Maxwell, newly made Lord Warden of this March. Would ye ken where we could find him?"

"Ay, ye're looking at him."

Carey did a further, splendid court bow, the gradations of which Dodd was just beginning to appreciate, and took out of his belt pouch the exquisitely penned and sealed letter that Scrope had dictated and Richard Bell written the night before.

"I am sent to bring congratulations to you, my lord, from my Lord Scrope, Warden of the English West March, with the hopes of a meeting soon to discuss justice upon the Border and in Liddesdale."

Maxwell was a tall well-made man with dark straight hair and beard and hazel eyes under a pair of eyebrows that ran right across his face like a scrivener's mark.

"Well," said Maxwell, handing the letter to a smaller, subfusc man behind him in a plain blue stuff gown. "I'm honoured at the rank of the messenger, Sir Robert." He tilted a finger at the clerk.

The clerk coughed hard, unrolled the paper and began to read in a nasal drone that Scrope greeted his brother officer of the peace right lovingly and made no doubt that now justice would be done impartially and immediately upon the Borders and out of Liddesdale with such an excellent and noble lord...And so on and so forth. Dodd understood about half of it, despite it being seemingly written in English, but no doubt that was the lawyers' part in the writing of it.

Meanwhile Maxwell was cleaning and reloading his caliver. Carey watched, looked at the target which already had a hole in it not far from the bull's eye. Then as Maxwell settled the stock into his shoulder, squinted along the barrel and prepared to squeeze the trigger and bring the match down into the powderpan, he suddenly stepped forward with a cry and pinched out the glowing slowmatch end with his gloved hand. There was a flurry as Maxwell pulled away from him and Carey cursed, flapping his hand as the leather smouldered.

"What the hell d'ye think ye're playing at?" thundered Maxwell, outraged. Carey reached over to one of the wine goblets standing on the table behind Maxwell and doused his fingers in the wine.

"I'm very sorry, my lord," he said, swirling them about and wincing. "But that caliver's faulty."

"It is no'," roared Maxwell. "It's brand new."

"If you fire it again, it will burst in your hand," Carey said stolidly, stripping off his gloves and examining his fingers.

"It willna."

"It will. I'll bet a hundred pounds on it."

"It's a new weapon fra...Ain hundred pounds?"

The Courtier hasn't got a hundred pounds, Dodd thought; as far as I know he hasn't got ten pounds at the moment, bar the travelling money.

Maxwell's eyes had lit up at the thought of the bet.

"On the next firing?"

"The next firing. If you've fired it once already."

"Ay, that's what had ye jumping about and pulling out yer blade."

"True. Nevertheless."

"Ain hundred pounds? English or Scots?"

Carey shrugged. "English, of course," he said, with the irritatingly self-satisfied air that Dodd had noticed he also wore when he was playing primero. Betting in English money had just raised the stakes by a factor of ten. Each Scots pound was worth only two shillings thanks to repeated debauchings of his money's silver content by the impoverished Scottish King. "If you've got it, my lord," he added, sealing his fate as far as Dodd was concerned.

Maxwell drew himself up and beckoned a servant over. Unlike Sir John Carmichael, he was a powerful magnate with ample funds from legal rents, blackrent and various other criminal activities. The servant went scurrying off and came back with a bulging leather purse. Maxwell counted out the money in good English silver.

"What about ye?" he asked insolently. "Have ye got it?"

Carey took off his largest ring, the one with a ruby the size of his finger nail in the middle of it and thumped it down on the table.

"I think that's worth about a hundred and fifty pounds, English," he said with fine courtierly negligence. "The Queen of England gave it to me."

Maxwell smiled wolfishly, picked up the ring and examined it closely. Like most noblemen he was a good judge of jewels. He smiled again and put Carey's ring back on the table where Dodd mentally bade it farewell.

They tied the caliver to one of the benches with rope, cleared the bowling alley of all hangers-on, servingmen and children. Lord Maxwell refilled the caliver with a full charge—though Carey offered to permit a two-thirds charge, so confident was he. At last Maxwell leaned over from behind the upturned table to put the slowmatch to the pan.

Dodd was already squatting down behind the table with his fingers in his ears. There was a different timbre to the cracking boom of the gun and the patter of metal hitting the wood in front of him. He thought he saw a bit of the stock go sailing up onto the roof. It had a cross scratched in it, which finally made sense of the Courtier's actions.

Maxwell stood up to look at the remains of the caliver and the hollow it had made in the bench, with a face gone paper white.

"Holy Mother Mary," he whispered. "Will ye look at it."

Carey stood, picked up his ring. "My lord?" His hand hovered over the Maxwell side of the bet.

Maxwell was still examining the remains of his new gun, while servingmen went running for stronger drink than early-morning beer and like Lord Maxwell some of them crossed themselves. Their lord looked up at Carey abstractedly. Maxwell was still pale as a winding sheet, a sheen of sweat on his nose as his imagination caught up with him, and small blame to him, thought Dodd. Carey had just saved at least his arm, perhaps his eyes and probably his life.

"Ay," he said in a shaky voice. "Ay, take it, it's yours, Sir Robert. Jesus Christ. Will ye look at it. Jesus."

Carey swept up the money with a happy grin, poured it back in the purse and hung it on a thong round his neck under his shirt. He waved over one of the servingmen who had been peering bulging-eyed at the remains of the gun. One piece of barrel was stuck firmly in a beam, gone as deep as an arrow.

"Aqua vitae for my Lord Maxwell," he ordered. He had found the goblet of wine and was swirling his scorched fingers in it again.

A servant in Maxwell livery brought the aqua vitae which Maxwell and Carey both tossed off like water. The Maxwell then came over to Carey and solemnly gave him his right hand.

They shook on it, and Maxwell clapped Carey on the shoulder. "That's one in the eye for the Johnstones," he said triumphantly. "Cunning bastards."

"My lord?" asked Carey cautiously.

"Ye'll eat wi' us, of course. And yer Sergeant and yer men?"

"I've only got a boy who's with the horses at the moment. The others are with Sir John Carmichael," Carey explained innocently, to Dodd's horror.

"Ye brought nae men wi' ye?" asked Maxwell, puzzled at the idea of riding anywhere with fewer than twenty men behind him, and quite right too, thought Dodd, it was indecent.

"The bare minimum, my lord. Short of an English army complete with horse and ordnance it seemed safer to rely on good faith. Sir John has been most hospitable."

"Och, no," said Maxwell. "He's resigning the day and I'm Warden now. Ye're my guest, Sir Robert, my friend and guest. Ye'll sleep here tonight, by God. That was well done wi' the slowmatch, man. Is yer hand sore? Will I get the surgeon to it?"

Carey was examining the blisters and blowing on them before dipping them back into the wine to cool them.

"No, it's only scorched."

"How did ye ken sae fair the gun was bad?"

"I have a feel for weapons, my lord," lied Carey gravely. "And there are a number of faulty firearms somewhere around the Border at the moment."

"Where from?" Maxwell demanded, his eyes narrowed suspiciously again.

Carey shrugged. "I'd give a good deal to know that myself. They're not English make, nor Scots I think. One of my men was killed by one a couple of days ago."

Maxwell was staring at Carey. "Killed?"

"Blew his hand off and he died of it."

The Maxwell's jaw set. Carey was looking at the blisters on his fingers again while Dodd stared at the painted walls of the bowling alley and thought of Long George showing him the gun when they waited to go out on patrol, and how he had been envious at the man's good luck. Carey smiled at Lord Maxwell.

"Perhaps the Italians know something about it?" he ventured.

"Nay...I doubt it. Jesus," swore Maxwell again. "Jesus Christ. I wonder..."

Carey sauntered to the silver plates of tidbits laid out on the table for Maxwell's refreshment, took a small flaky pie and bit into it.

"A number of them?" repeated Maxwell.

"Yes, my lord."

"All bad like that?"

"Some of them worse. Some burst on the first firing."

"How d'ye know?"

Carey swallowed, drank some wine, winced and coughed. "A couple of them came into my…er…possession and Sergeant Dodd did the same good deed for me that I did for you, my lord. I took another apart and there's no doubt of it: the forge-welding's faulty."

"Jesus Christ," said Maxwell monotonously. He was twiddling his moustache around his fingers and tapping his fingers nervously on his empty cup. "But they've the Tower mark on them?"

Dodd was having difficulty keeping a straight face and by the grave impassivity of his demeanour, so was Carey. He shrugged.

"It's a famous mark and I'm sure it's no more difficult to forge than any other."

"A number of them?"

"A couple of hundred, my lord. I hope you've not been persuaded to buy any weapons for which you do not know the provenance."

The unctuous concern in Carey's voice almost had Dodd exploding like a gun. So that was the way, was it? The Maxwell and Lowther between them had raided the Carlisle armoury at some trouble and expense and were now the proud possessors of a heap of scrap iron. Now that was poetical, if you liked. That could restore a man's faith in God's impartial providence.

Suddenly the Maxwell waved to one of his liverymen and when the servant ran over, spoke low and urgently into the man's ear. The servant whitened, and sprinted off in the direction of the stables.

There was something indefinably different about Carey as he allowed one of the Maxwell women to salve his fingers, a deference that Dodd had not seen before. He smiled a lot and peppered his conversation with 'my lords', owned himself greatly impressed with the size and appointments of the new bowling alley, and asked flattering questions about the way Maxwell had had his fortified house made strong. Ay, thought Dodd, finally enlightened, this is the Courtier we're seeing. He didn't like it. Frankly he found it embarrassing, watching Carey lavishly butter up a Scotch nobleman, and dull, which was worse.

Dodd finally caught Carey's eye, who raised his brows at him. Dodd coughed.

"Only I was thinkin' of going and seeing how Young Hutchin was getting along wi' the horses and all, sir," he said awkwardly.

"Good idea, Sergeant," said Carey easily. "See if you can get yourselves some refreshments while you're at it."

Dodd nodded his head, trying to hide his fury at being treated like some servant, turned on his heel and marched out.

The horses, Thunder in particular, were not in the courtyard. One of the men hanging around finally told Dodd that they'd been taken to the stables. Dodd hurried to the stables, checked every stall and found his horse and Hutchin's pony, but no sign of the black charger and no sign of Hutchin either.

Dodd caught a groom as he rushed past with a bucket of feed in each hand.

"The big black stallion that was here with the blond lad," he said. "Where are they?"

The groom shrugged. "I dinna ken."

Dodd didn't let go. "I think ye do," he hissed. "Or I think ye'd better guess."

The groom looked at Dodd's hand on his arm. "And who the hell are ye?" he wanted to know.

For a moment Dodd was on the brink of saying he was Sergeant Henry Dodd of Gilsland, which in those parts would have put the fat well and truly in the fire, but thought better of it. "I'm with the Deputy Warden of the English West March. The beast's his own, and he's presently sitting at my lord Maxwell's table and talking about guns. D'ye want me to fetch him and say ye've let his tournament charger be reived under the neb of my lord Maxwell? Eh?"

The groom paused. "A courtier came to the blond lad and asked him if he'd show the animal to my lord Spynie."

Dodd's eyes narrowed. "And he went? Just like that? I dinna think so. Ye come wi' me and we'll talk to yer headman…"

The groom coughed. "Well, the courtier gave the lad some money for it, not to make a fuss."

"Och, God. Put the buckets down, man, and come wi' me."

Reluctantly, the groom obeyed.

Carey, Maxwell and some of Maxwell's cousins were in the great hall of the Castle, at table under the war banners, eating a haggis with bashed neeps, some baked pheasants and a boiled chicken.

"What's the matter, Dodd?" asked Carey, catching Dodd's expression and then seeing the struggling groom.

Dodd glowered with satisfaction at being proved right so quickly. "According to this man, Young Hutchin's gone off with one of Lord Spynie's men and taken Thunder to show him. Little bastard. Nae doubt of it, the lad's planning to sell Thunder for ye, pocket the cash and run for it to the Debateable Land. That one wants his hide tanned for him."

Carey put down his spoon with a worried frown.

"Gone off? When?"

Dodd shrugged again.

"Damn." Carey was up off the bench and reaching for his swordbelt.

"Ay," Dodd said with mournful satisfaction. "Put a Graham in charge of a prime piece of horseflesh like your bonny Thunder and what d'ye expect, it's putting the wolf in charge of the sheepfold, that's what it is for sure…"

"For God's sake, Dodd, stop blethering; it's not the bloody horse I'm worried about, it's the boy."

"What does he look like?" asked Maxwell.

"Blond, blue eyes."

Maxwell laughed coarsely. "Well, he'll thank ye for it once his arse heals up. They'll pay him well enough."

"Can I borrow a few of your men, my lord?"

Maxwell's face became serious. "Och, why bother? He's only a boy and a Graham to boot."

Carey didn't seem particularly surprised at this rebuff. He smiled sweetly at Maxwell. "Never mind the men, my lord. Where do you think they might have gone with him?"

"Och, wherever. Spynie's with the King, down by the market place in the Mayor's bonny house with the arches. I heard tell his friends were lodging in the Red Boar beside it, that has the hole in the wall, but what's the hurry…"

Carey was already striding through the hall. Over his shoulder he called, "My lord, if you want to borrow one of my dags for the shooting competition, I'll have to find Thunder first because they're in a case on his back."

Maxwell had his mouth full and was still chewing, with a comical expression of annoyance.

Dodd followed Carey through the crowds as he marched down the muddy street to the Red Boar, looking uncommonly grim. With some effort Dodd caught up with him just under the painted sign and asked, "Will I fetch Red Sandy and Sim's Will, sir?"

Carey paused, opened his mouth to answer and stopped.

There was the sound of shouting and a boy's shrieking of insults, suddenly muffled, from the upstairs private room. Carey put his head back and listened. Dodd heard a soprano yell of "Liddesdale!" followed by a couple of dull thuds, a crash as furniture went over, a deep-voiced cry of pain and more thuds and crashes.

"No time, damn it," said Carey. Some large lads were sitting stolidly by the inn door, playing dice and ignoring the commotion. Carey passed by them boldly, set his foot into the lattices on the wall, tested it for strength and before the lads could do more than stare, was climbing up to the first floor like a monkey on a stick. Dodd watched with his mouth open, as did the diceplayers. Carey kicked open the double window that the sounds were coming from, and disappeared inside. His broad Scots roar echoed down the street.

"Get away from that boy, you God-rotted sodomites!"

There was a confused babble of voices, followed by the crack of a fist on somebody's flesh and a dull thud, no doubt of a boot landing somewhere soft.

Dodd was already amongst the diceplayers, sword in one hand, dagger in the other. The lad who was just scooping up dice unwisely tried to draw his sword and Dodd booted him in the face. The only other one who seemed interested in a fight became suddenly less interested when Dodd put the point of his sword against his neck and grinned.

There was some nasty work going on upstairs as crashes and the clattering of plate reverberated, but there was nothing Dodd could do about it except what he was doing. If Carey got himself killed in a sordid brawl over a pageboy, it would do no more than serve him right for not bringing enough henchmen with him to Dumfries. Still holding the diceplayers at bay with sword and dagger. Dodd cautiously toed open the inn door. The commonroom was full of men, caught in mid-move, staring at him and beyond him. Dodd wondered what they could see at his back but didn't dare take his eyes off the diceplayers long enough to look.

Almost to Dodd's disappointment, there was the crash of an upstairs door flung open and footsteps. Carey appeared at the top of the stairs with a scarlet and dishevelled Young Hutchin in front of him. He came down sideways, with his sword holding a brightly dressed young man at bay. Young Hutchin had his dagger in his hand as well and had the squint-eyed look of a Graham about to kill something.

"Out to me, Hutchin," Dodd called. It seemed Carey had managed to avoid bloodying his sword and seeing this was King James's court and these were some of King James's best-liked hangers-on from the glamour of their clothes, that might be a good thing to continue. Hutchin stumbled forwards, ducked by the staring diceplayer still on the verge of death from Dodd's sword, and stood behind Dodd with his chest heaving and his mouth working.

Carey backed out to the door, silently daring the company to attack him. It wasn't at all that the young courtiers following him down the stairs or the liverymen in the commonroom were cowards; it was only that Carey looked as if he positively hoped they'd try an attack so that he could kill them. Nobody wanted to be the first to take on a lunatic Englishman, they were all waiting for someone else to try it first. It showed you the sad corruption of the court, Dodd felt; most Scotsmen he had ever met would have taken the both of them without even thinking about it. Dodd kicked the nearest diceplayer's kneecaps hard enough so he fell backwards and they both came away and into the street.

Maxwell was standing there with fifteen of his men, shaking his head and grinning. For the first time in his life Dodd found himself warming to a Scot. Another Maxwell came hurrying out of the little vennel by the side of the inn, leading the big black horse almost as wide as the passage. Carey caught sight of this all in the one moment and started to laugh.

"Ay, it's true what I heard," said Maxwell. "Ye're an education and an entertainment, Sir Robert."

Carey bowed with a flourishing salute of his sword.

A handsome young man in gorgeous padded purple and green brocade was leaning out of the window with spittle on his lips.

"King James'll hear of this, ye bastard Englishman! I'll hae ye strung up for treason..."

Both Carey's knuckles were grazed. He sucked the left one and looked up at this and his face darkened with instant rage.

"Come anywhere near me or mine again, my lord Spynie," he bellowed, "and I'll cut off your miserable little prick and stuff it down your neck."

A gaggle of women were tutting behind Dodd, an interested crowd was forming.

"Ye dinna sceer me..." sneered the young man, although he had recoiled a little, no doubt from the sheer volume of noise.

"And then I'll stick you on a pole and shoot at you like a popinjay," finished Carey, calming down enough to be witty.

"King James will..."

"Isn't the King's bed enough for you, my lord?" Carey asked in a voice that drawled insinuatingly. "Do you want fresher meat than His Majesty's? I'm sure he'd be very interested to hear it." With a theatrical turn, Carey tutted and shook his head sadly. Lord Spynie flushed and he pulled his head back in again.

The crowd laughed knowingly and some of them began haranguing the young men about the door for the court's sinfulness in the sight of the Lord. Some of them were well-educated enough to begin quoting Leviticus at length. Carey sheathed his sword, turned and strode back in the direction of Maxwell's Castle, with the Lord Maxwell on his left, Thunder being led by Young Hutchin on his right and Maxwell henchmen in an almost reassuring bunch around them. Dodd tagged along, still keeping a weather eye open for Scotch ambushes and wondering whether it would still be possible to get out of town unscathed now Carey had put the King's favourite against him. Probably not. Which would be better? Rejoin Red Sandy and Sim's Will with Sir John Carmichael, or send for them both to come and take refuge with the new Lord Warden? Better stick with the new, now Carmichael had no official power. On the other hand, could Maxwell be trusted?

They had no trouble coming to Maxwell's Castle, overflowing with Maxwell's cousins and Herries kin as well. In the courtyard, Maxwell exclaimed over the beauty of Thunder and felt his legs and looked in his mouth, all the while Carey solemnly denied that he was interested in selling the beast at all.

Hutchin held the horse's bridle as if it was a mooring in a storm and said nothing. When Maxwell had gone back into the hall, Carey looked at the boy and raised his eyebrows.

"The man said he was fra the King and give me a shilling to come and show Thunder for him," Hutchin answered in a sullen mutter. "How should I ken what they wanted?"

Dodd waited for Carey to shout at Hutchin, tell him what a fool he was for believing any man with a tale like that, perhaps give him a beating for being so gullible. Hutchin's face was still working with rage and humiliation. He had gripped his dagger so tight in his hand. Dodd could see blood on his palms, coming in half-moons from where his nails had bitten.

"Scum," said Carey to Young Hutchin gravely. "They're scum. There's dregs like that at every court but there are more here because the King…The King is soft on his followers."

Tactfully put, Dodd thought.

"They try it with every unprotected boy they find and they'll do the same with every girl and the reason why is that they're evil bastard scum and they think they'll get away with it."

Hutchin was still shaking with rage.

"I'll mind them," he managed to whisper. "I'll mind every one o' their faces."

"You do that, Young Hutchin," said Carey. "I'll look forward to hearing the tale of how you kill them all when you're grown."

"I marked one of them this time," said Hutchin fiercely. "I hope he dies screamin' o' the rot."

"So do I," said Carey. "Go and see what's to eat in the kitchens and then stay close to us. If you have trouble again, give your family warcry…What is it?"

"L-Liddesdale."

Carey smiled wryly. "I'll come to it and so will Dodd. Off you go now."

Dodd's mouth was open with outrage. When Hutchin had trotted off, he gasped, "But sir, will ye no' thump him for nearly losing ye the horse?"

Carey laughed softly. "Lord, Dodd, what could I do to him that would be worse?"

"But he'll no' respect ye…"

"Oh, the hell with the bloody horse, Dodd, there's no chance Spynie could keep Thunder, any more than Maxwell could. And I think the boy will be more careful now."

"Sir, how did ye guess so fine what they were after?"

"Come on, Dodd, you know I've been at King James's court before? Though I have to say it wasn't this bad then."

Dodd shut his gaping mouth before he said something he would regret. Wild speculation and surmise began to crowd through his mind. He managed to nod stolidly.

"Ay," he said. "Will I go and fetch Sim's Will and my brother now?"

Carey considered this. "No," he answered. "Not on your own, not yet. I'll get my lord Warden to send one of his servants with a letter to Carmichael and a couple of his men as backup."

Dodd nodded approvingly at this. The two of them took Thunder round to the stables and settled him in the best stall which had been cleared by Maxwell's head groom. Carey unstrapped the dag-cases and slung them on his shoulder.

"More shooting, sir?" Dodd asked sadly.

"My lord wants to win the shooting match and I promised him the loan of my dags for it, though I think he'd be better off with a longer barrel. Come on. You can have a few shots too, if you like."

"No thank ye, sir," said Dodd with dignity. "I dinna care for firearms."

They sat down again to eat with Lord Maxwell who had polished off much of the haggis and half the chicken, Carey waving Dodd to a seat on the bench next to him. Mollified as to his dignity,

Dodd took the rest of the haggis, though it wasn't as good as the ones his wife made when they had done some successful raiding.

"Boy keep his maidenhead then?" asked Maxwell casually.

"Just about."

"I could have warned you not to bring a lad that pretty here." Carey sighed.

"I know, my lord."

Maxwell swilled down some more of the terrible wine. "Ye ken what it's like," he said. "Lord Spynie's friends and relations reckon they can do as they please, and mainly they can…"

"On her last progress, the Queen hanged a man that was caught raping a girl—after a fair trial, of course."

Maxwell nodded. "The King should do it too, but Spynie begs him and the King always gives in. Any road, who knows; most of the time, the girls are willing enough for a ring or a couple of shillings. It's the boys I feel sorry for."

The talk wandered on in a desultory way until it came back, remarkably enough, to the topic of the mysterious German.

"No one knows," said Maxwell flatly. "I heard he was a mining engineer from the Black Forest and he was to find the King a rich gold mine at Jedburgh and work it for him, by a new and Hermetic system for seeking out metals in the earth, but the mine collapsed and the King hanged him for lying about his knowledge."

Carey nodded wisely at this.

"I heard he was from Augsburg," he said.

"Nay, the Black Forest, I'm certain of it."

"What was his name?"

Maxwell made a small moue of ignorance and shook his head. "I never saw him, only heard tell of him." He poured himself some more of the wine, sipped, seemed to notice the taste for the first time and spat it out into the rushes. "Jesus Christ, this stuff is shite."

Carey looked sympathetic again. "I had heard that you had found a decent wine merchant to supply you with…"

Maxwell's face darkened with anger. "I found a slimy bastard of an Italian catamite, that's what I found, Sir Robert, him and his wife together."

The depth of sympathy in Carey's face was masterly.

"Oh?" he said.

Maxwell grunted. "Brought them into Scotland, introduced them to the Court and what thanks do I get for it? None. Bonnetti's bringing in French and Italian wine by the tun for His Highness and do I get a drop of it? I do not. As for his whore of a wife..." Maxwell spat into the rushes again. "If I didnae ken very well it's not likely, I'd say she was in the King's bed and Queen Anne should watch out." He drank some more of his inferior wine and made a face. "Mind, she's nothing so special there either, for all her looks."

"You've...er..."

Maxwell shrugged elaborately. "Ye ken what these Southern bitches are like, Sir Robert. Allus on heat. But I dinna care to eat another man's leavings, if ye understand me."

Carey nodded, completely straight-faced, while Dodd hurriedly buried his nose in his beermug.

"She might be slipping out of favour wi' the King as well," Maxwell added, "seeing she came making up to me a couple o' days since. I soon settled her, though. Bitch."

He stared up at his family's battle trophies with an expression of gloomy reminiscence. There was a short awkward silence. Carey broke it.

"And how is the King finding Dumfries?" he asked.

Maxwell shrugged. "His Highness says he likes roughing it in the best house in town, after mine, but he wouldna stay here with me for all the assurances I gave him. He said he doesnae like castles much, for all he wouldnae be surprised by Bothwell here with me as he was at Falkland and Holyrood as well."

"No," agreed Carey in a tactful voice.

"At least he said he's coming to my banquet tomorrow, though, after he's been hunting."

"Mm. Where is he hunting?"

"Five miles west of Dumfries, over by Craigmore Hill. My gamekeepers and huntsmen have been finding game for him all week, and we'll beat the drive tomorrow."

"Mm."

"Of course, we canna use guns in the hunting, the King doesnae like them."

"Of course. Will this be a private hunt or..."

Maxwell laughed at Carey's tact. "Och, God, ye can come along if ye want, everyone else will. The King's always in a good mood after a hunt, ye canna pick a better time to ask him for something."

Carey smiled back. "Splendid," he said. "I wonder if he'll remember me."

"And then there's my banquet. It's a masked ball and he said last time I spoke to him, he'll be here incognito and seduce all the ladies. Good God," Maxwell added with distaste, "who does he think he's fooling?"

Carey said nothing to that. He spent an hour after the meal showing Maxwell how to wind up the fancy lock of one of his dags and arguing with him over the right charge and how much it threw to the left. Maxwell was enchanted by a firearm not completely crippled by rain and further one where you did not have the bother of hiding the bright end of a slowmatch if you were lying in wait in some covert. Carey and he had a long technical discussion on the rival merits of wheel-locks and snaphaunces compared with matchlocks, but as the Maxwell pointed out, when you were talking about a fight, the key was numbers and anything more complicated than a matchlock was fiendishly expensive. The thought of the Maxwell clan armed with weapons like that made Dodd shudder, but Carey didn't seem to see it. On the other hand, the Courtier's fancy dags missed fire often enough for Dodd to feel that if you had to use the infernal things, perhaps you were better off with ones you were more sure might work in a tight spot.

The bowling alley reverberated to the booms from the gun while Maxwell got its measure, and then all of them went out to the pasture on the other side of the river where the earthbank and targets had been set up. The King was not there, though an awning with a cloth of estate and carven chair had been set up ready for him. He was only a little less frightened of guns than he was of knives and would not come out until the contest was over and the football match ready to begin. The legend was that his unnatural fear of weapons had come about while he was still in his mother's belly: Mary Queen of Scots had been six months pregnant with him when her husband Lord Darnley and the Scottish barons of the day had dragged her advisor and musician David Riccio from her presence at gunpoint and stabbed him to death in the next room. Or it could have been the shock of seeing his foster father bleed to death from stab wounds when the King was five years of age. Whatever the reason, King James was seriously handicapped as King of Scotland by being probably the least martial man in his entire kingdom. On the other hand he was at least still alive after twenty seven years on the throne, a rare boast for a Stuart.

Dodd stood with Carey as the various lords who had come out with their followers to provide James with his army, stood forward one at a time to show off their prowess at shooting. For the archery they shot at a popinjay: not a real parrot, being too expensive for the burghers of Dumfries, but a bunch of feathers on a high stick, that wobbled in the soft wind. It was a far harder mark than the targets set up against an earthbank ready for the musketry competition.

Carey watched with attention and then said to Dodd quietly, "If you want to recoup your horse-racing losses…"

"I cannae," said Dodd gloomily. "The wife has all that was left."

"I thought you managed to give her the slip at the muster?"

"Her brothers found me afterwards in Bessie's once we'd gone back up to the Keep and she wouldna take no for an answer."

Carey tutted sympathetically.

"Ay," said Dodd. "She even took the money I had back for my new helmet and said she'd pay it herself or we'd end up in debt to the armourer."

"Very disrespectful of her."

"Ay," moaned Dodd. "And I'll be getting an earful of it every time I see her no matter what I do. I'd beat her for it, I surely would, sir, but the trouble is it wouldnae make her any better and there'd be some disaster come of it after."

The last time Dodd had tried to assert his authority with his wife he had wound up in ward at Jedburgh as a pledge for one of her brothers' good behaviour and spent three months in the gaol there because the bastard had seen fit to disappear immediately after. Dodd still wasn't sure how it had come about, but he had no intention of making the experiment to find the connection. Besides she was fully capable of putting a pillow over his face while he

slept if he offended her badly enough and she'd never burn for the
crime of petty treason because Kinmont Willie would take her in
as his favourite niece, no matter what she did. That thought alone
had kept Dodd remarkably chaste while he did his duty at Carlisle
and his wife spent most of her time running Gilsland. Still no
bairn though, which was a pity. There was no wealth like a string
of sons.

Applause and ironical cheers distracted him from his normal
worries. The archery contest had been won by a Gowrie. Now the
gun shooting contest began and it seemed as if Carey had been
busy laying bets. The laird Johnstone shot first and did reasonably
well; Maxwell stepped forward and managed to put his first shot
in the bull. Then a tall broadshouldered young Englishman with
a face as spotty as a plum pudding stepped out. Carey groaned.

"Damnation," he said to Dodd. "It's Henry Widdrington the
younger. I hadn't realised he was in it or I'd have put all my money
on him."

"Good, is he?" asked Dodd with gloomy satisfaction that Carey
was going to get a set down. Of course, Carey was craning his
neck, looking about in the crowd: no sign of Lady Widdrington
or her husband, thank God, thought Dodd, though Carey was
disappointed.

"Too good, and he has a decent gun as well."

"Who's the lad standing by him?"

"His brother Roger, I think."

They watched the competition in an atmosphere of deepening
dismay, shared by the rest of the crowd who disliked watching an
Englishman beat a Scot at any martial exercise. To scattered
applause and some booing, young Henry Widdrington easily bore
away the bell which was presented by the King's foster-brother
and erstwhile guardian, the Earl of Mar.

Carey sighed deeply, counted about twenty pounds out of his
purse and went off to pay his debts. He wound up in the knot of
men congratulating Widdrington on his shooting, and when Dodd
wandered over nosily to find out what they were about, discovered
that Carey was being persuaded to come into the football match
and steadfastly refusing.

The King arrived at that point, announced by appalling trumpet playing, surrounded by a crowd of brilliantly dressed men and riding on a white horse from which he dismounted ungracefully and stumped to his chair. Lord Spynie was there, a little back from the main bunch about the King, talking intently with the wide balding figure of Sir Henry Widdrington. Elizabeth paced stately at her husband's side, curtseyed poker-backed to the King and took up a place nearby. Spynie laughed at some comment of Widdrington's, then went and stood by a stool beside the carven chair.

Dodd stole a look at Carey's face as he watched Lady Widdrington. Unguarded by charm or mockery, for a moment the Courtier's heart was nakedly visible there as his eyes burned the air between him and the woman. It was the face of a starving man gazing at a banquet.

Dodd elbowed the Courtier gently. "Sir," he growled. "If I was Sir Henry, I'd shoot ye for no more than the look of your face."

Carey blinked at him, evidently not all there. Dodd tried again.

"Sir Robert," he said, gruff with annoyance at feeling sorry for the silly man. "Ye'll do her more harm if ye stare like that."

For a moment the blue glare was ferociously hostile and then Carey coloured up and looked at the ground. He cleared his throat.

"Er…yes, you're right. Quite right."

Watching the way he settled himself, it was exactly like watching a mummer put on a mask. Dear Lord, thought Dodd, he's caught a midsummer madness to be sure. Carey was moving again, to the background noise of the Dumfries town crier announcing the King's pleasure at the football match to be held and making a hash of it.

When the sheep-like bleating had finished, Carey moved up to the awning, swept his hat off, muttered quickly to the town crier and genuflected on one knee to the King. Sweat shining on his face the town crier shouted something incomprehensible about Sir Ronald Starey, Deputy Warden of the English West March.

King James squinted his eyes suspiciously for a moment as he looked down on the Courtier and then his face cleared and lightened with a surprisingly pleasant smile as he spoke. Against his will, Dodd was impressed: it seemed the King of Scots did know Carey and was willing to acknowledge him. Carey held out the other letter he had brought from Carlisle. The King took it and read it with heavy-lidded boredom and let Carey stay there with one knee in the damp grass for a considerable time while he sat and talked to Lord Spynie and the Earl of Mar on his other side about the contents. Eventually the King nodded his head affably and said a few words. Carey rose to his feet, backed away, bowed again.

This time Dodd watched Lady Widdrington. She looked once at Carey, when his attention was on the King, and for a moment, if Dodd had been Sir Henry, he would have shot her too. Then her lips compressed and she stared into the middle distance instead.

Carey arrived, busy undoing the many buttons and points of his fine black velvet doublet. He unbuckled his belts and shrugged it off his shoulders, handing it to Young Hutchin.

"I wouldn't lay any bets on this match," he said conversationally to Dodd as he rebelted his hose, rolled up his shirtsleeves and undid the ties of his small ruff, which ended coiled in his hat. "Not with the number of Johnstones on the one side and Maxwells on the other."

"Ye're not going to play at the football, are you, sir?" asked Dodd, appalled at this further evidence of the Deputy's insanity.

"Well, I can hardly refuse when the King asked me to, now can I? Even if he told me to play for the Johnstones, since they're a man short."

"Have ye played at the football?"

Carey's eyes were cold and surprised. "What do you take me for, Dodd? Of course I have, and in Scotland too. The King likes watching football. He has a notion that it promotes friendliness and reconciliation."

"Friendliness and reconciliation?" Dodd repeated hollowly, remembering some football games he had played.

"That's right."

"Och, God."

Carey nonchalantly handed over to Dodd what was left of his winnings from Maxwell, which felt as if it amounted to some eighty pounds or so and was much more money than Dodd had ever met in one place in his life before. Wild thoughts came to him of slipping away from the match and riding like hell for Gilsland to give it to his wife and calm her down, but Dodd was not daft. He slung the purse round his own neck and felt martyred.

Dodd looked across at the young laird Johnstone who was disaccoutring with his men. The Lord Maxwell was stripping off as well. Silks, velvets and brocades piled one on top of the other, producing two anonymous herds of men in shirts, hose and boots, who glowered at each other across a grassy chasm of competitive rivalry and family ill-feeling. Carey spoke briefly to Maxwell, who laughed and shrugged. Then he sauntered over and joined the other lot.

Dodd shook his head and stepped back with the crowd. Young Hutchin was sitting up on a fence. The Earl of Mar stood on a small hillock in the middle of the field and announced that the holes dug at each end of the pasture were the goals and no man was to touch the ball with his hands or run with it under his arm. And further no weapons of any kind were to be used or even brought on the pitch.

King James smiled kindly from his carved seat, said a few words about playing in a Godly and respectable way, raised a white handkerchief. Lord Spynie threw the ball into the middle of the crowd of men, the handkerchief dropped and the game began.

Elizabeth Widdrington stood beside her husband near Lord Spynie and stared at the field full of desperately struggling football players, trying not to squint in order to focus on one particular man among them. She could feel her husband simmering with spleen beside her, waiting for her to make some slip he could punish her for. She prayed automatically for strength, but could not help thinking that it was very unfair of God to put Robin Carey across her path so persistently when it hurt her heart to look at him and know she could never speak to him again. Her husband had decreed it and backed his orders with the threat, which she had no doubt he was capable of carrying out, that he would personally geld Carey if she disobeyed. She would have obeyed him in any case, naturally, since that was her duty, or she thought she would, but...She trembled for Robin's impetuosity, his odd contradictory nature:

he could plan and organise as wisely as an old soldier or the Queen of England herself, and then suddenly he would take some wild notion and throw himself into the middle of hair-raising risks with blithe self-confidence and trust in his luck. She loved him for it but she was certain that Sir Henry could use his daring to outmanoeuvre and destroy him very easily. And even though she felt as if a stone was hanging from her heartstrings in the middle of her chest at the thought of never talking to him or smiling at him, there was some comfort at least in his still being alive, whole, running like a deer over the rough grass with the ball at his feet, his elbows flying and his face alight with laughter at the pack of Maxwells behind him.

Christ have mercy, she could not take her eyes off him.

Sir Henry's fingers bit into her arm. "Enjoying the match, wife?"

She could feel her cheeks reddening, but she managed to look gravely down at her grizzled husband. Remotely she wondered if her life would have been easier if she had been of a more womanly height: it had been the source of the first contention between them, the simple fact that she was taller.

"No, my lord," she said evenly. "It has always seemed to me much like watching a herd of noisy cows lumbering from one end of the field to the other."

Sir Henry snorted and peered at her, looking for deceit. There was none; how could she enjoy the match? What if Robin was hurt or killed?

"Do you want to go back to our lodgings?"

She thought for a moment, what her answer should be. The words were kind and solicitous, but the tone of voice was ugly. She ducked her head humbly.

"Whatever you wish, my lord," she said eventually, taking refuge in pliancy. It didn't mollify him. His fingers bit deeper, hurting her. He might be short, but her husband was very strong for all his ill-health and his gout.

"Ye can stay," he hissed. "Stay and watch. And keep your countenance, bitch."

She curtseyed to him and said, "Yes, my lord." The stone hanging from her heart swayed and chilled. He was planning something ugly, and he wanted her to see. Oh, my God, Robin, take care, be careful...Lord Jesus, look after him, guard him...

The courtiers were enjoying themselves, cheering on either the Johnstones or the Maxwells, depending on their affinities and their wagers. There was a blurring in Elizabeth's eyes and she stared at the field in a general way, trying not to focus on Carey. The herd of two-legged cattle thundered past them again, shouting confusedly. Occasionally a faster runner than the others would burst from the ruck and run in one direction or the other with the ball bobbing at his feet and then generally two or three of the other side would launch themselves at him, punch him or wrestle him down, the ball would run free and a yelling shouting heap of men would struggle for possession until somebody else burst from the ruck and the process began again, leaving the occasional body prone on the broken sod behind them. She couldn't help but catch sight of Carey every so often, generally kicking the ball away from him to James Johnstone and on one occasion leaping in, fists flying, to a more than usually vicious contention for the ball near one of the goal-holes.

She couldn't warn him. She could only watch helplessly and pray.

When it did happen the thing was so confused she had no clear idea how. One moment the ball was in the air and Carey was in the centre of a pyramid of men all trying to leap and head it one way or the other. The next moment, the ball was in play down the other end of the field and Carey was lying on his side with his knees up to his chest, writhing silently. She saw Sergeant Dodd and the rather beautiful fair-haired Graham boy run out from the crowd and bend over him solicitously, then help him off slung between their shoulders, his face still working and his legs not seeming able to support him.

Sir Henry trod heavily on her foot and combined both a satisfied grin and a scowl.

"I said, keep your countenance, wife."

Elizabeth looked down at him and for a moment felt strangely remote from him and herself, as if she was staring down at an ugly squat creature from some mountain peak. If she had had any kind of weapon in her hand at the time, she would have killed him and burned for it gladly. Sir Henry seemed to recognise her hatred, paused, perhaps even recoiled a little.

She could no longer see Carey, who seemed to be sitting by the fence with people round him. She had seen no blood when he was helped off the field, but she knew enough not to put reliance on that. Please God, let him not be hurt badly.

"Did ye hear me, bitch?"

She looked back at her husband, the man she had been so determined to serve dutifully as a good wife when the match had been arranged ten years before, the man she had tried so very hard to please because God required it of her. Quite suddenly, like a lute string tuned too far, her loathing broke and transmuted itself into cold, indifferent distaste.

"Yes, my lord," she said, not bothering to hide her weariness of him and his posturing.

"I paid one o' the Johnstones to grab his bollocks," said Sir Henry. "That'll learn him to keep his gun in its case."

"Did you, my lord?" she said tonelessly. Sir Henry's eyes narrowed. "I suppose you got Lord Spynie to convince the King to have him play?"

"What are friends for?"

"Yes, my lord." She turned slightly away and swallowed a yawn—from nervousness, not boredom, but Sir Henry didn't know that and she could feel the anger vibrate in him again. He told her to keep her countenance, but in fact he wanted her to break down and weep and beg him to have mercy. She had even tried it years before, but she never made the mistake of repeating experiments that failed. He sneered at her sometimes for being as stiff-necked as a man, and she thought bitterly that no man would stand for what she stood for, no, not a galley slave in the French navy. No man would have to.

He will beat me again tonight, she thought, still distant from herself, her body gathering and shrinking inside her clothes with well-learned fear, her mind strangely unmoved. Perhaps she was at last getting used to it.

Instead of bowing her head as she usually did, consciously trying to placate him, she turned and looked in Carey's direction though she couldn't see him since he was still sitting on a rock. What was the point of trying to placate someone who enjoyed beating her? She carried on looking, ignoring the fingers bruising her arm and shifting her feet to avoid Sir Henry's, until she saw Carey standing, still pale, still coughing, but not obviously dying. He was shaking his head.

This is a stupid thing to do, she thought to herself; I don't even like football.

"My lord, I am feeling a little faint with the heat," she said to her husband in a voice loud enough to be heard by the other courtiers nearby. "By your leave, I'll go back to our lodgings now as you so kindly suggested."

She knew the King would have no interest at all in the few women attending him, unlike Queen Elizabeth. She also knew that now she had seen what Sir Henry had brought her to see, he would be less insistent.

Sir Henry looked briefly pleased at having made an impression and then hissed, "Ye can stay and watch till the end."

She curtseyed gravely to him, as if he had said yes. "My lord is very kind."

Without pausing, she turned and curtseyed to the King in his carven chair and then walked away over the Brig Port and back into Dumfries. Obedience to Sir Henry had never made any difference as far as she could see, so she would try pleasing herself for a change. Besides, she wanted to get some sleep before the evening. Behind her the football match continued with much shouting.

## wednesday 12th july 1592, dawn

Carey had slept very badly, partly because his balls were sore. In the long run, though, he had been well out of the football match which had descended into a pitched brawl at the end amid such confusion that nobody could tell which side had won. The King had been very displeased. The other reason for wakefulness was the fact that the truckle bed Lord Maxwell's servants had found him was alive with fleas and six inches too short for his legs which dangled off the end even though he lay diagonally. On waking up he found that one of Maxwell's enormous Irish wolfhounds had curled up next to him at some time during the night and could thus explain the strange hairiness of the dream women he had met in his sleep.

"Good morning, bedfellow," he said politely. The wolfhound panted, yawned and slobbered a vast tongue lovingly over his face. There was shouting in the next room, something about a surgeon. It seemed Lord Maxwell was already awake. He came in, drinking his morning beer while he put on his jack.

"The King's gone fra the town for the hunt already," he said without preamble as Carey swung his legs over the bed and sat up scratching and wiping dog drool off with his shirtsleeve. "I'm riding out to join him, if ye care to come?"

"I said I would, my lord," Carey answered after a moment as he put on his hose.

Dodd appeared in his usual foul dawn mood, Red Sandy and Sim's Will at his back, but there was no sign of Young Hutchin.

"Not again," said Carey. "Did you see anything that…?"

"He slipped off when he woke, said he wanted to find his cousins and to tell ye not to be afeared for him, he willnae fall for it twice."

"Bloody Grahams," muttered Carey as he put on his doublet and began buttoning the front. "Will it be safe to leave our packponies and remounts here, my Lord Maxwell?"

Lord Maxwell was already on his way down the stairs, irritable about something. He gestured.

"They'll be as safe as mine own. Are ye coming?"

Carey hurried to pull his boots on and follow the new lord Warden down to the courtyard, still rubbing his face and wishing he could shave. The wolfhound came padding softly after him, shaking herself occasionally. There was no doubt about it, Maxwell was in a temper and was looking at him with suspicion under those sooty eyebrows of his. What had Carey heard when he woke, something about a surgeon? Ah. Inspiration suddenly flowered.

"The guns," he said aloud.

"Guns?" asked Maxwell, eyes like slits.

"The two hundred-odd mixed calivers and pistols you have in Lochmaben, along with ammunition and priming powder," Carey enlarged coolly. "If you like, I'll inspect them for you and tell you if they're bad or not."

It wasn't how he had planned to find out for certain whether Maxwell had the guns from the Carlisle armoury, but springing it on him that way certainly got an answer. Maxwell was bug-eyed with surprise.

"How did ye ken…?"

Carey sighed. "Somebody bought them," he said. "And you have the money."

Maxwell leaned over the trestle table set up to feed the men, and cut a piece of cheese. "Why should I want so many guns?" he asked with a failed attempt at being casual.

Carey laughed. "To wipe out the Johnstones, of course, my lord, once King James has gone back to Edinburgh."

Maxwell sniffed and examined his fingernails elaborately. His other hand drummed a beat on the table.

"How do ye know?"

"I didn't know for sure, my lord," Carey admitted, breaking open a penny loaf and throwing some crumbs to the doves from the cote on the roof who had come out cautiously in hopes of food. "Only, any man would like to end a feud in his favour if he could."

Maxwell started examining the other fingernails now, while his right hand began stroking at his dagger hilt. Oh, not again, Dodd groaned inwardly. He had been too outraged at Carey's question to speak, why can the bloody Courtier never let be? We're in the Maxwell's own townhouse and he's March Warden forbye…

But Carey was grinning, sitting carefully down on a bench, leaning back and plunking his boots on the table with a heavy double thud.

"I don't care what you do to the Johnstones, my lord," he said, waving his bread. "It's none of my concern, because it's Scottish West March business entirely and the Johnstones are a thorn in our side as well. I'm only interested in guns."

"And ye'd know if ye saw them whether they were faulty or not?"

"Yes," said Carey simply. "And if somebody's already been hurt by one, don't you think that would be wise, before you take on the Johnstones?"

Maxwell stared at him for a moment longer, calculating. "My cousin," he answered obliquely, "was blinded last night and may not live the week. When can you check them?"

"At your lordship's convenience, after I've seen the King."

The King of Scotland was hunting the deer. In the distance, he could hear the hounds at full cry and the beaters behind them with their drums and trumpets and clappers and in between the beating of hooves on the ground as the game the foresters had found in the days preceding were driven inexorably down through the valley to where the court waited, bows strung at the ready. Occasionally the King liked to stalk a single noble beast, perhaps a hart of twelve points, the King of the Forest, with only the help of a couple of lymer-dogs and foresters, spending perhaps a day or more to waylay the animal and take his life personally with a crossbow. Certainly that was the hunting which gave him the greatest personal satisfaction and he knew he was good at it, being as patient and cunning as a ghillie, but this was business. His court needed venison in quantity, which unfortunately eliminated finesse.

Their hides had been well-built and disguised with brush. Each of the nobles had their best-liked weapon, whether longbow, crossbow or lance. Some had boar spears in case some wild boar should have been put up. None had firearms, mainly because of the damage they did to the skins and also to reduce wastage in beaters. And it was well known King James didn't like them.

The dawn was exquisite: pale peach and gold at the eastern horizon shading to royal blue overhead, and the nearer forest was quiet with anticipation, a breeze blowing which carried all the scents of greenery and earth, unreproduceable no matter how many perfumes you mixed. Only the sounds of the drive coming nearer gave tension, the lift and overhang of a wave before it broke...

The game burst milling from the forest: red deer and roe and fallow, all ages and sexes. The King took aim at the best animal: a stag of ten, shot it with a bolt through the neck, reached out his hand and was given another loaded crossbow in exchange for the discharged one and shot it again directly under the chin. The whup and twang of longbows and crossbows filled the air with a music that delighted the King's ear, and beasts lurched and fell as they slowed and turned, leaped about in panic. King James laughed with pleasure at the sight: here was a true glory—to meet the bounty of the wild and conquer it.

With two men behind him rewinding his bows, the King had shot four of the deer by the time the forest's harvest was lying down and flopping about, save a couple of wiser or luckier does who had jumped past the hides and disappeared into the undergrowth behind.

Sweating foresters began the work of turning the carcases on their sides. King James stepped from behind his hide and marched up to the stag he had killed first. He took the long heavy hunting knife from the gamewarden, who had been warned to be on bended knee, and waited impatiently for the musicians who were hidden off to one side to begin playing. He had heard that the Queen of England always unmade the first deer to the sweet strains of music.

One of the musicians popped his head up from the foliage, ruining the effect of faery music that had been planned. The musician's velvet cap was askew.

"Your Highness, one of the deer fell on George Beaton's viol."

King James waved the hunting knife. "Get on with it," he growled.

"Ay, sire."

After a couple more moments, frenetic sawing began from the bushes, with pipes and drums at variance and the strings all at venture. King James sighed deeply, bent to make the first cut. Although he stabbed at the furry throat gingerly, a red tide burst out of the animal's nostrils and washed over his boots, ruining his red pompoms.

King James dropped the knife in the mud and stepped stickily away from the small lake of blood. He sighed again. What was the saying? Make a silk purse of a sow's ear? God knew it sometimes seemed to him that he had a better chance of making a lady's veil of a sow's pigbed than imitating the English court, but they had to learn ceremony, these mad battle-crazy nobles of his, or they would humiliate him when the old bitch in London died and he came into his own.

While the butchery was carried out in front of the hides and some of the professional huntsmen took lymers and crossbows to track down the deer that had been wounded but not killed in the confusion, King James remounted his white horse. It had been a successful drive and the court was now supplied with much of the meat it needed in Dumfries. He smiled and waved his hand at dear Alexander Lord Spynie's compliments and then, for all his good temper, became grave again. A long fellow with odd hair in a nicely London-cut black velvet doublet was approaching, limping slightly as he threaded between the horses and the boasting nobles. He was carrying a goblet and a white towel. Well, were they learning at last?

The long fellow doffed his hat, genuflected gracefully twice and then after ceremoniously tasting the wine in the King's sight and wiping the goblet's lip with the towel, held it up to him so he only had to bend down and take it.

King James did so and finally recognised the man properly.

"Sir Robert Carey again, is it not?" he said as he drank. Spices hid the fact that the wine was as bad as all the wine in Godforsaken Dumfries, except for what he himself had brought. Yes, Carey was at Court, he remembered now, though as always his memory of the previous afternoon was somewhat wine-blurred. Carey had played well in the football match until the eye-watering foul that put him out of it. Even James had felt the urge to cross his legs.

"Are ye quite recovered now, Sir Robert?" he asked solicitously. "No ill-effects, I hope."

"No, Your Majesty. I don't think so."

"I think the best remedy would be a piece of steak," James went on ruminatively. "Externally rather than internally, ye follow. And an infusion of comfrey with perhaps a few ounces of blood from the arm."

"Your Majesty is most kind in your concern. I tried the steak last night and it certainly…helped."

James smiled at Carey. Lacking it conspicuously himself, he had always found a strange fascination about male beauty: a wonder and a miracle in the way big bones and hard muscles produced something powerful and cleanly exciting, utterly different from the cloying softness and vapidity of women. Carey, at the age of twenty-three when King James had first seen him in Walsingham's ambassadorial train, had truly been beautiful, with sophistication and fluent French from his recent stay in Paris, and the glorious arrogance of youth. James had been a few years younger in years, a few centuries older in experience and had delighted in him. Poor d'Aubigny would have approved James's tall base-born cousin as well, but by that time poor d'Aubigny had been thrown out of Scotland by the Ruthven Raiders and was dead. After Walsingham went south again, King James had sent several warm letters and spent considerable time trying to persuade the Queen of England and Carey's father, Lord Hunsdon, to let Carey come back to the Scottish court for a longer stay. Unfortunately, the old lord had blocked him for some reason and James had turned to find other friends for his loneliness. Carey had carried some messages to Edinburgh for the Queen of England, had even been the man rash enough to bring the news of Mary Queen of Scots' execution—not that James had let him set foot in Scotland that time. Now, many years after their first meeting, Carey was back once more. His shoulders had broadened as you would expect of the son of one of King Henry VIII's byblows. But he had lost none of his charm and, from the look of him, none of his arrogance either.

King James felt the heat rising in him again, decided to prolong the conversation.

"And what did ye think to the sport, Sir Robert?"

"I marked a kingly shot at the highest ranked deer present," said Sir Robert smoothly. "Was it Your Majesty's?"

Ay, it was lovely the way the English could flatter. Carey had been at Queen Elizabeth's court for ten years, the best school of courtesy in the world. Still, it *had* been a good shot. King James allowed himself to preen a little.

"I think it was. I had the benefit of a clean view."

"In the best run of hunts, a man may always miss if his hand be not steady," said Sir Robert. "I saw Your Majesty kill at least five."

"Is a King but a man?" James asked, wondering if philosophy would make the Englishman sweat at all. No; he was smiling. "In the sight of God we are all but men," said he. "But in the sight of men, I believe that a king must be, as it were, a god." James was enjoying this immensely. He finished the wine. "Did ye have a particular god in mind, Sir Robert?"

Carey hesitated not at all, which confirmed King James's suspicion that he was rerunning a good workmanlike arselick that had already seen service up Queen Elizabeth's metaphorical petticoats.

"Apollo sprang to mind, Your Majesty."

"Not Diana, mistress of the hunt?"

Carey almost grinned, but not quite. "No, Your Majesty, saving your grace's pardon, I would reserve the figure of the pale virgin of the moon for my liege and Queen, Your Majesty's good cousin."

"And so I should hope. Well, Apollo will do for the present." It was nice that Carey remembered the courtly games and masques they had played years ago, with King James taking the role of Apollo the Sun God and much ribaldry on the subject of that Virgin Moon as well.

Having emptied the goblet, King James made a move to hand it back, but Carey stepped away and spread his hands gracefully.

"How dare mere mortal lips touch that which has refreshed the Sun God?" he said with a fine rhetoric. Over behind his left shoulder in the pressing knot of courtiers, James heard someone mutter that if every fucking Englishman was as prosy as this one, it was no fucking wonder their Queen could never be brought to decide on anything.

King James sighed again, and examined the silver goblet, which was nicely chased and inlaid with enamel and a couple of reasonable garnets. There was no question but that his court could do with some polish.

"Ay," he said. "It's a mite melted round about the rim. I'll keep it and have my silversmith mend it for me."

"Your Majesty, may I ask a boon?" added Carey, once more with his knee crunching in the leaf-litter. No doubt all the fucking Englishmen would have terrible rheumatism of the kneejoints with all the bending and scraping they must do at the Queen's court, continued the commentary behind the King.

"Ay, what can I do for ye, Sir Robert?"

"Would Your Majesty favour me with a few minutes of your time?"

So he wanted audience and knew how to ask for it prettily. Lord, it was a lot easier on the nerves than some of the earls about the King who tended to march up to him and begin haranguing him at the least opportunity. And perhaps...who knew? Perhaps they could be friends? Or more? King James positively beamed at his cousin.

"Ay, of course, Sir Robert. It would be a pleasure. This afternoon, I think, when I have refreshed myself after the hunting."

"Your Majesty does me the greatest conceivable honour."

"Ay, nae doubt of it. Farewell, Sir Robert."

King James rode off with his goblet tucked into his saddlebag, chuckling to himself and wondering idly was Carey still as much of an innocent as he had been? Surely not. Lord Spynie was riding close by, but casting looks like daggers over his shoulder at Carey. Well, it was always a pleasure to see a well-looking man with a bit of polish and a nice smooth tongue on him, it reminded him of poor d'Aubigny in a way that none of the ruffianly heathens and sour-faced Godlovers that generally surrounded him could ever do. Certainly not Spynie, whose polish was thinly applied and increasingly gimcrack.

The King began to look forward to the afternoon's audience.

Young Hutchin had spent the morning finding the house of the Graham water-bailiff's woman, in the unhealthy part of town near the Kirk Gate. His curiosity to see the court had completely left him, but he had a more urgent desire now. In the little wooden house he had discovered the water-bailiff, well settled in and dandling a baby on his knee while a plump girl laughed and stirred a pottage on the fire. Round the table were two other cousins of his, and his Uncle Jimmy.

There was some ribald cheering when he came in and his cousin Robert asked if he was planning to join the court and if he thought

King James would like him too. Uncle Jimmy cuffed his son's ear and asked if it was true what he had heard, that the Deputy Warden had gone after him alone with his sword.

Beetroot at the thought of the story getting back to his father, Young Hutchin nodded.

"He shouldnae have let ye come here," opined cousin John, who was the elder and took his responsibilities seriously.

An innate sense of fairness forced Hutchin to explain. "I came after him meself and I wouldnae go back to Carlisle though he told me to," he said. "Ye cannae blame the Deputy for the mither."

Uncle Jimmy grunted. "D'ye want us to do anything?" he asked.

Hutchin thought about this for a while. It was a serious matter. If he said the word, he could be sure that every man in the room at the Red Boar would have a price on his head and the whole Graham surname after his blood. It was a warming thought, that, but would it be as satisfying as seeing them die himself?

"Nay," he said at last. "I'll kill them all meself when I'm grown. I can wait."

Uncle Jimmy exchanged looks with the water-bailiff who nodded approvingly.

"That's right, lad," said Uncle Jimmy. "Allus do the job yerself if ye can, and be sure it's done the way ye want it. And what's the Deputy doing here anyway?"

"He's looking for the guns that were reived out of Carlisle Keep on Sunday, for one thing," Young Hutchin told him. Uncle Jimmy laughed shortly. Everyone knew what had happened to them, except the Deputy of course. "And he keeps asking after a German he saw arrested on the Border the Saturday as well, wants to talk to him."

"Why?" asked Uncle Jimmy.

Young Hutchin frowned. "How would I know?" he said. "He might want to make friends. Can ye keep an eye out for him?"

The other Grahams sighed deeply. "That's ticklish, Young Hutchin," said his other cousin. "What if this German doesnae want to meet the Deputy?"

Young Hutchin shrugged. "I think he'll be as bitten by curiosity as any other man," he said. "Would ye not at least go to gawk, Cousin Robert, if ye were not at the horn, that is?"

Cousin Robert snorted.

Not one of the Grahams, other than Young Hutchin and the water-bailiff, was legally there, because at least one of the stated reasons for the King being in Dumfries was to harry the evil clan of Graham, that had lifted so many of his best horses, off the face of the earth. The evil clan knew this perfectly well and were anxious to hear about it when the King finally decided what to do with his army.

So there were the Johnstones who were old friends and with the town as packed as it was, a few extra louring ruffians in worn jacks were hardly noticeable. Uncle Jimmy and his sons promised to look out for the German, and gave Hutchin news of his father and his Uncle Richard of Brackenhill, who were finding that people were even slower with their blackrent payments than usual. According to Uncle Jimmy, Richie of Brackenhill blamed the new Deputy Warden who was shaking everything up so well, and wanted Hutchin's estimate of what it would cost to pay him off and how he should be approached.

Hutchin blew out his cheeks and drank some of the mild ale poured by the water bailiff's woman. She had pretty brown hair and a lovely pair of tits to her; Hutchin found his attention wandered every time she passed, and when she sat herself down on a stool to feed the babe, it was all he could do not to state. God knew, it was older men and weans had all the fun. None of the maids he met would let him so much as squeeze their paps.

"Young Hutchin?" pressed Uncle Jimmy, looking amused. "How much for the Deputy's bribe?"

"It's hard to tell," Hutchin said slowly. "I dinnae think he thinks like other men."

"Och nonsense," growled Uncle Jimmy. "Every man has his price."

"Ay, but I dinna think it's money he wants."

"What d'ye mean?" demanded cousin Robert. "O' course he wants money, what man doesnae?"

"Land? Cattle? Women?"

"Nothing so simple, see ye, Uncle Jimmy," said Hutchin. "Ay, he wants something, but I dinna ken for sure what it is."

"When ye find out, will ye pass the word to your Uncle Richie, Hutchin? God knows, it's why we paid to put ye in the Keep in the first place."

"Of course." Hutchin was offended. "I know that. But it's no' so simple as I thought. It's…well, he doesnae treat me like ye'd expect, and he doesnae think like a Borderer. I'm no relation of his at all, but there it was, he came after me."

Surprisingly, Uncle Jimmy nodded. "Your Uncle Jock o' the Peartree was saying something alike the other day. He's as puzzled as ye are. But dinna forget, Carey's got his price, same as any man. All ye need to do is find out what it is and we'll do the rest."

Hutchin smiled. "Whatever it is, it'll be high. Have ye seen the velvets and silks he wears and the way he treats 'em?"

Uncle Jimmy laughed. "Och, we'll even pay his tailor's bills for him, if he wants. Uncle Richie's a businessman, no' a headcase like Kinmont Willie."

Belly packed tight with a hot pottage and more ale Young Hutchin said goodbye to his relatives and started back up the Soutergate towards the Townhead and Maxwell's Castle. He felt very proud of himself for never mentioning the water-bailiff's rather older wife that he had left in Carlisle.

As he picked his way between the heaps of dung and the men playing dice and drinking at every corner, he realised that someone was keeping pace with him. Narrow-eyed with new suspicion, he looked sideways as he drew his dagger, saw a stocky youth a little older than himself, but well-dressed in a wool suit and wearing a sword, though not obviously a courtier. His face seemed a little familiar, but Hutchin couldn't place it.

"Good afternoon," said the youth cheerfully. "Are you Hutchin Graham?"

"Who wants to know?" demanded Hutchin, backing to the wall and looking around for ambushes.

The youth took his cap off politely. "Roger Widdrington, second son of Sir Henry," he said, and then added, "Lady Widdrington sent me."

Young Hutchin relaxed slightly. He could hear easily enough that this Roger Widdrington was no Scot, but did indeed come from the East March.

"Ay," he said. "I'm Hutchin Graham."

"Sir Robert Carey's pageboy?"

"Ay. What about it?"

Roger Widdrington moved closer, ignoring Hutchin's dagger, so that they were under the overhang of an armourer's shop. "Ye know that my Lady Elizabeth has been forbidden to speak to the Deputy?"

Hutchin nodded. He had carried the letter, but had not been able to read it. However, it was easy enough to guess what it said from the Deputy's reaction to it.

"Well," said Roger Widdrington with a knowing grin, "my stepmother still likes to hear about him. Will ye tell me anything you can about him while he's in Dumfries?"

"The Deputy doesnae take me into his confidence much."

Roger Widdrington nodded wisely. "Whatever you can tell me," he said. "And my lady will pay you of course, sixpence for each item of information."

Hutchin nodded cannily. That made sense and Lady Widdrington was a sensible woman. God knew, he sometimes thought the Deputy needed a nursemaid to keep him out of trouble.

"Ay," he said. "I can do that."

"What can you tell me now?"

"Not much. I havenae seen him since last night, for I left the Castle before him this morning."

"How are his balls?"

Hutchin suppressed a grin. "Not bad, not bad at all, considering some bastard tried to swing on them, though he doesnae ken who, it being too close and too quick. He didnae need the surgeon, though Dodd was all for sending for one, but the Deputy said most of the surgeons he knew were ainly interested in what they could cut off, and that wasnae what he had in mind."

Roger Widdrington laughed. "I'll tell her he's better," he said, and handed Hutchin a silver English sixpence as proof of his integrity.

"Meet me here tomorrow at noon," said Roger Widdrington. "Can you do that?"

"I reckon I can."

"Excellent. Oh, and don't tell the Deputy about this—Lady Widdington doesn't want him worrying about what might happen to her if Sir Henry finds out."

"Ay," said Young Hutchin, well pleased with himself, pulled at his cap and went on up to Maxwell's Castle.

King James had finished his repast, mainly of brutally tough venison, and was well into the Tuscan wine when the English Deputy Warden was announced. Beaming happily he rose to greet the man and found him down on one knee again.

"Up, up," cried King James. "By God, I had rather look ye in the eye, than down on ye, Sir Robert. Will ye sit by me and take some wine? Good. Rob, my dear, fetch up some of the white Rhenish and some cakes for my good friend here."

King James watched his page trot off dutifully and sighed a little. At that age they were delightful; so fresh-faced and rounded, but King James was a man of principle and had promised himself he would have nothing to do with children. Poor d'Aubigny had been clear in his contempt for those who did and besides, as he had also said in his delightful trilling French voice, how could one tell that they would not suddenly erupt with spots or become gangling and bony? Beauty was all to d'Aubigny, beauty and elegance, things in precious short supply in Scotland.

King James turned back to Carey and smiled. "It's such a pleasure to meet someone newly from the English court," he said. "Can ye tell me aught of my esteemed cousin, Her Majesty Queen Elizabeth?"

Carey, who was extremely tall once off his knees, had sat down at once when invited to, tactfully upon a low folding stool by the King's great carven armchair. He spoke at length about the Queen, from which King James gathered that the old bitch was still as pawky and impossible as ever; that she was spending money like water upon the war in the Netherlands and the miserable fighting against the Wild Irish led by O'Neill in the bogs of Ireland; that if James's annual subsidy was actually delivered he should be grateful for it, since there was no chance whatever of an increase—a sad piece of news to King James, but not unexpected.

"Och, it's a fact, Sir Robert," he said sadly. "There is nothing more stupid than a war. If I have a hope for the…for the future, it is that I may one day become a means of peace between England and Spain."

Sir Robert took this extraordinary sentiment like a man. Not a flicker of surprise did his face betray; instead he managed to bow from a sitting position and say "Her Majesty is often heard to say the same thing: that the war was never of her making and that she fought against it with all she had and for as long as she could, but that at the last you cannot make peace with one who is determined to fight."

"Ay," said the King. "That's true as well and well I know it."

"What Her Majesty deplores most of all is the waste of gold to pay for weapons. She says it is like a great bottomless pit, and if you tip in cartloads of gold, still you never hear them so much as tinkle."

King James smiled at the figure, but felt he could improve it. "Or the mouth of an ever hungry monster, a cockatrice or a basilisk, perhaps."

"It's not surprising," continued Carey. "For weapons are expensive, above all firearms."

"So they are, so they are," agreed King James affably as the young Robert came trotting back with a silver flagon and two silver goblets. The wine was better than most of the stuff swilling around Dumfries, but still not up to its surroundings, and Carey had some work to swallow it. King James was more used to the rotgut that the Hanseatic merchants had been unloading on thirsty Scotland until the Bonnettis arrived, and knocked his own drink back easily.

"We had a strange accident in Carlisle upon the Sunday," said Carey after a moment's pause. "A number of newly delivered firearms were stolen out of our very armoury while we were at muster in readiness to assist you."

"Never?" said King James. "Well, I am sorry to hear it, Sir Robert, sorry indeed. Such dishonesty…"

"It was thought that they might have come to Scotland, perhaps brought by an ill-affected noble?"

"Och no, to be sure, they'll have been auctioned all over the Debateable Land by now," said King James. "The surnames might well be a wee bit concerned with myself in the district to do justice and the hanging trees all ready with ropes. It's not to be wondered at that they might try a thing like that to arm themselves better against me. Not that it will do any good."

"And then there was the rumour of a Spanish agent at Your Majesty's court."

"Never," said King James very positively. "Now why would we do a silly thing like that, harbouring an enemy of England, considering the manifold kindnesses and generosities to us of our most beloved cousin, the Queen of England."

"Not, of course, with Your Majesty's knowledge," said Carey, managing to sound very shocked, slipping from his stool to go on one knee again. "Such a thought had never crossed my mind. It struck me, however, that some among your nobles might have...designs and desires to change the religion of this land, or something worse, and the Spanish agent might be a part of it."

"Och, never look so sad, man, and get off yer poor worn out knee again. That's better. Have some more wine. Nay, any Spaniard at the court, and I'd have had word of him from my lords here all at daggers drawn, quarrelling for his gold." He smiled wisely at Carey who smiled back.

"Of course, Your Majesty, I was a poor fool to think otherwise."

"Ay, well, we'll say no more on it. And when I go into the Debateable Land to winkle out Bothwell, that black-hearted witch of a man, I'll keep a good eye out for your weapons, never fear."

"Yes, Your Majesty. If I might venture a little more on the subject: for God's sake, do not try any that you might capture, for they are all faulty and burst on firing. You may tell one of the faulty guns by a cross scratched on the underside of the stock."

King James nodded. "I shall bear it in mind," he said. "But personally I do not care for the crack and report of firearms no more than for the clash of knives or swords. Ye may have noted how most of the beasts we hunted this morning were slain by arrows or bolts or the action of dogs. So I'll be in no danger from yer badly-welded pistols, have nae fear."

"I am very happy to hear it," said Carey after a tiny pause. "Your Majesty's life is, of course, infinitely precious, not only in Scotland, but also in England."

Hm, thought King James, is this some message from the Cecils, I wonder? Do they see danger somewhere? I wonder where?

Gently he probed Carey, but thought that in fact the man was as he seemed: concerned at the lost guns from Carlisle and with the rumoured Spanish agent, but he had left London in the middle of June and was already a little behind with the court news. Also it transpired that he was one of the Earl of Essex's faction, rather than with the Cecils, which showed he was disappointingly short-sighted.

Surely it couldn't be much longer to wait, thought James as they discussed the merits of hunting par force de chiens as opposed to using beaters; surely the old battle axe would die soon. But it seemed that she was like the Sphinx: full of riddles and immortal, her health depressingly good apart from being occasionally troubled by a sore on her leg.

King James was sinking the wine as quickly as he usually did, with Rob already gone down to the butler for a refill. One of the clerks would be in soon with administrative papers for him to sign and letters to write: he knew he was getting a little tipsy when he slopped some of the wine down his doublet and laughed. Ever the courtier, Sir Robert fetched one of the linen towels off the rack by the fireplace and proffered the end to wipe up the spillage—something that would never even have occurred to Rob or the Earl of Mar or any one of his overdressed hangers-on.

James was full of goodwill and caught Carey's wrist with his hand as he came close.

"Will ye speak French to me?" he asked. "I dinna speak it well mesen, but the sound of it always thrills my heart."

"Avec grand plaisir. Alas, Your Majesty, my accent is not what it once was and I have forgotten much," said Carey in that language. On an affectionate impulse, James kissed his cheek which was so near and so inviting. Only a kiss.

It was a mistake. Carey permitted the familiarity but no more. James felt the tension in him: damn the cold-hearted bloody English, they all bridled at a touch from him as if he was diseased.

"Ye used to remind me so much of d'Aubigny, ye know," James said thickly, hoping as he looked into Carey's handsome face that the man was either easily overawed or as sophisticated as he seemed. "Ye still have very much his style, Robin."

Carey smiled carefully. "Perhaps from the French court," he said, in Scottish this time. "My father wanted me to learn Latin as well as French, but alas I was a bad student and spent most of my time pursuing sinful women." Yes, there was a distinct, if tactful accent on the 'women'. Another man still in thrall to the she-serpent then. "My ignorance is entirely my own fault."

James let go of Carey's arm and drank down what was left of his wine. "My tutor George Buchanan warned me that the wages of sin is death," he said, wondering whether to be angry at the rebuff or simply sad, and also whether it would be worth having Carey to supper privately and filling him full of aqua vitae. He had known it work sometimes, with the ambitious, although that of course also contained the seed of heartache, in that the love could never be pure. How he longed for the clarity of the love and partnership between Achilles and Patroclus, or Alexander and Hephaistion. And David and Jonathan: it had been a revelation to him when he read how their love surpassed that of women, for how could the ancestor of Christ be guilty? Their love was never condemned in the Bible as was David's adultery with Bathsheba.

"Mr Buchanan was right, of course," said Carey softly, not looking at James, his face impossible to read. "We are all sinners and all of us die."

"Even godlike kings?" sneered King James.

"Your Majesty knows the answer to that better than I do."

"And queens? What about queens, eh? When do they die?" I am getting drunk, thought King James. That was a tactless question. Carey bridled only a little.

"When Death comes for them."

"Has she bribed him, or what?"

Carey smiled, the blue eyes intense as chips of aquamarine. "If that were possible, she surely would, but as you know, she would prefer to hold him rather with the promise of a bribe and a flood of sweet words."

King James laughed at the satire. Carey was sitting down on his stool again, meekly, as if James had never touched his hand, nor kissed his face. It was a pity, a pity: he had lovely shoulders and although his hair was odd, most of the curls black but the roots reddish brown, he had the long Boleyn face and the Tudor hooded bright blue eyes, and he had the smoothness and culture that d'Aubigny had shown King James when he was a raw lad of sixteen. The King's face clouded: affection and sophistication had been heady things to discover for the first time in his hard-driven scholarly life. He looked on the time he had spent with d'Aubigny as a brief respite in Paradise, before the bastard nobles had kidnapped their King in the Ruthven Raid, with their usual lack of respect, and forced him to send d'Aubigny away. Not content with that they had then almost certainly poisoned the Frenchman. One day, thought King James, one day I'll have satisfaction on all of them for it.

"Speak some French to me again," he said, watching Rob refill his goblet and Carey's. But it wasn't boys he wanted, unlike Spynie and his friends, it was men with good bodies and good minds: true companions as the Greeks had been, without the mucky dim-witted clinginess and greedy softness of women. Lord God, how Queen Anne his wife bored him with her pawing and treble complaints.

"Je parle tres mal la belle langue," said Carey, the brand of his Englishness striking through all the music of French. It was like hearing a spinet played by someone in gauntlets and King James sighed again. What was it about the French language that had the power to bewitch him so? The first time he had heard d'Aubigny speak with the rolled rrs so different in Scots and the lilting cadences, he had been moved almost to tears with longing. Perhaps it had been witchcraft...No, the witches were all Scottish like the Earl of Bothwell. D'Aubigny had simply been...d'Aubigny, and this large, proud and beautiful Englishman was nothing of the kind.

There had been a knock at the door some time before and now the secretary and the clerk stood there waiting with sour impatience. Carey had opened the door for them: well, it wasn't James's fault if Carey couldn't see what Buchanan had beaten into the boy-King so well: that, like the wicked French mermaid Queen Mary his mother, women were darkness and dirt combined, the true root of sin, and an ever-present danger to every man's soul, the invariable tools of the Devil. Poor Carey, to be in thrall to such creatures…Never mind. Perhaps a quiet supper some other time, perhaps the promise of advancement when King James came into his own: the English were the greediest nation on earth, everyone knew that.

King James gestured imperiously to dismiss Sir Robert, who once more genuflected and kissed the royal hand, the contact of skins dry and without content. The clerk and the secretary exchanged glances when they saw their king's squint-eyed look, and the secretary reordered the papers he was holding. Dammit, he could drink if he wanted to, he was the King.

Carey backed off, bowed at the door, stepped back another three paces out of sight and then turned and left. King James sighed, tears of self-pity pricking at his eyes: one day he would find someone like d'Aubigny again, one day it would happen. He was the King, and he tried to be a good king and bring peace and justice to his thrawn dangerous uncharming people; surely God would relent again and let him taste love.

Dodd came on Carey washing his hands and face in well-water and drinking aqua vitae by the gulp. He was already a little drunk, Dodd saw, which was no surprise if he had just had audience with the King of Scots, and he was also wound up tight, almost quivering with tension.

"Did the King have anything to say about the guns?" asked Dodd, who knew what Carey had been hoping for.

Carey grunted, shook his head, looked about for a towel, saw that the courtyard of Maxwell's town house had no such things, and wiped his hands on his hose.

"Any luck with the German or the Italians?" he demanded harshly.

Dodd shook his head in turn. "I dinnae think the German can still be alive," he said positively, wishing he knew why the foreigners were important. "I've been up and down this bloody nest of Scots and not a hide nor a hair of him is there anywhere. Signor Bonnetti is supplying His Majesty with wine, but ye knew that already. How's the King?"

At least I didn't nearly puke in his lap this time, thought Carey gloomily, but Jesus, it was close. What is it about me that makes

him like me so? I don't look anything like Lord Spynie, thank
God. The aqua vitae burned pleasantly in his throat and he poured
Dodd some, as well as more for himself. Dodd, he saw, was full of
morbid curiosity about his audience and clearly fighting the
impulse to ask nosy questions.

"Drunk when I left him, drunk and maudlin," snapped Carey.
"Come on, let's go out and ask some more questions."

They spent the rest of the afternoon on Irish Street, starting at
one end and going into every armourer's and gunsmith they could
see.

As it turned out, the first one was typical. "Nay, sir, I canna
undertake yer order," said the master gunsmith, with his broad
hands folded behind his leather apron and a bedlam of bellows,
furnace, hammering and screeling metal behind him.

"Not even if I pay you forty shillings sterling for each pistol
and fifty shillings for the calivers?" pressed Carey, holding one of
the sample wares from the front of the shop and looking at it
narrowly.

"Nay, sir, it's impossible," said the master gunsmith firmly. "Not
if ye was to pay double the amount, I couldnae do it. Not before
Lammastide next."

"How about by Michaelmas?"

The master gunsmith sucked his teeth. "I tellt ye, it's
impossible," he said, "I'm no' dickering for a price, sir, I could get
what I asked, but I canna make enough guns for the orders on my
books as it is."

"What's the problem?"

"See ye, sir, we allus have full order books, because in Dumfries
we make the best weapons in the world, and my shop here makes
the best, the finest weapons in a' of Dumfries. I have none but
journeymen makers, here, not a part of yer gun will be made by a
'prentice, and the lock will be made by meself or my son-in-law
that's a master gunsmith as well. My guns shoot true, they dinna
misfire, and they never blow up in yer hand. I've turned down
bigger orders than yourn fra the Papists, because I canna fill them."

"Could you not take on extra men?" Carey asked.

The master gunsmith's red face took on a purple hue. "What?
Untrained? Cack-handed fools that canna tell one end of the stock

fra the other? No, sir. And ye'll not thank me if I did, for the
weapons they made would be as like to kill ye as yer enemy. We
make the finest weapons in the world here and…"

"I thought Augsburg had good weaponsmiths," said Carey
provocatively.

The master gunsmith spat magnificently. "Sir," he said. "I'll
thank ye to leave my shop. I'll have nae talk of German
mountebanks in this place, ye might sour the metal. Go to
Jedburgh for yer weapons if ye've a mind to, but begone from
here. Out."

Carey went meekly enough, rubbing his lower lip with his
thumb and looking pleased. He tried two more shops, the second
of which was full of the choking indescribable stench of the flesh
being burnt off horse hooves in a dry cauldron, so that the hooves
themselves could be used to case-harden the gun-parts. They
retreated from the place in some disorder and stopped at a small
alehouse to drink aqua vitae to clean their throats. Carey sent Red
Sandy Dodd on with Sim's Will Croser to carry on the questioning.
Dodd stayed with him.

"Sir," he said tactfully. "What do ye plan to pay for the new
weapons with?"

Carey spread his hands. "Consider the lilies of the field," he
orated. "They toil not, neither do they spin."

"Sir?"

"I only want to know if the Dumfries armourers could fill an
order like that and it seems they can't. Which is interesting."

"Oh?"

"Interesting but not surprising."

"Ay, sir."

"Do you know what I'm talking about, Dodd?"

"Ay, sir. Ye've the Maxwells and the Johnstones glowering at
each other, all wanting guns. Ye've the Armstrongs, the Bells, the
Carlisles and the Irvines wanting to protect themselves fra the
Maxwells and the Johnstones, and each other, not to mention the
Douglases and the Crichtons hereabouts. Ye've Bothwell buying
armaments, and ye've King James's army in town, also wanting
armaments and ye've the Irish rebels over the water and they want
guns too."

"And us," added Carey softly. "One lot of good Tower-made weapons lost on the road from Newcastle, swapped for deathtraps, and one lot of deathtraps reived out of the Carlisle armoury under our noses. And where did they go, Dodd? Answer me that."

"I thought Maxwell had'em."

"He's got the deathtraps, Sergeant, not the good weapons. Two hundred mixed calivers and pistols don't disappear into thin air; somebody has them."

"Bothwell?" wondered Dodd.

"God forbid. But whoever it was made the exchange is the man who murdered poor Long George."

"Ay," said Dodd. "That's a fact."

"Besides, I want them back. Some of them had snaphaunce locks and I want them back."

"Can the King not help ye, sir?" Dodd knew he was pushing it a little, seeing how upset the Deputy had been ever since his audience. Carey's face darkened instantly, and he finished his aqua vitae in a single gulp.

"Oh, bugger the King."

"Ay, sir." Dodd kept his face absolutely straight, which was just as well for Carey glared at him suspiciously.

Luckily Red Sandy and Sim's Will returned at that point to tell them that for all the multitude of gunsmiths in Dumfries, there was not a single one that could fill their order. They went back to Maxwell's Castle in awkward silence, Carey striding ahead with an expression of thunder on his face.

Hutchin turned out to be in Maxwell's stables, assiduously turning Thunder's black coat to damask.

"I should have brung some ribbons to plait his mane with, sir," said the boy sorrowfully. "I couldnae find a haberdasher's that had any the day, so I cannae make him as fine as the ither horses that'll be in the masqueing."

Carey grunted and ordered Hutchin to wash his hands and come and brush his doublet and hose with rosepowder. Hutchin looked surprised but went meekly enough to the pump. Dodd followed him to wash his own hands and face. He had never before seen the Deputy in such an ill temper.

"What the Devil's got intae the Deputy?" Hutchin wanted to know. Dodd shrugged.

"The King must have said something to upset him."

"What could it be?"

"Well, I…"

"None of your bloody business, Dodd," snapped Carey's voice behind them. "I don't suppose either of you knows how to shave a man?"

They shook their heads.

"Hutchin, run down to the kitchens and fetch me some hot water. Boiling, mind. Dodd, did you bring your best suit as I told you?"

"I'm wearing it, sir," said Dodd with some dignity.

"Jesus Christ, it's homespun."

"Ay, sir. My wife's finest."

"You're the Land Sergeant of Gilsland. Can't you afford anything better?"

He's drunk, Dodd reminded himself at this insult. "Happen I could, sir," Dodd said coldly. "But it's no' what I choose to spend my money on."

Carey's blue eyes examined him minutely for a moment. "Get it brushed down and I'll lend you my smallest ruff."

"Am I to attend ye at this Court masque, sir?"

"All of you are. Red Sandy and Sim's Will can stay outside with the horses, but I want you and Hutchin attending me inside."

"Ye'll have to forgive me, sir," said Dodd still very much on his dignity, "I've no' been to Court, like yourself, sir."

"You can learn. If Barnabus could, you can."

"Ay, sir," said Dodd, blank-faced. "Will I take my sword?"

Carey got the message at last, that Dodd was no servingman to order about, but a freeholder and a land-sergeant with as much right to bear a sword as Carey or Lord Scrope. He paused and his face relaxed slightly.

"Yes, dammit, take your sword and try to look respectable."

"I shall look like what I am, sir," said Dodd, with frigid dignity.

For an hour there was a whirlwind of shaving and combing hair, powdering and brushing of velvet, checking of ruffs and polishing of boots and blades. It finally dawned on Dodd, as Carey stood in a clean shirt, critically examining his black velvet suit, that one of the things eating the Courtier was the fact that he wasn't able to dress fine enough for a Court feast. For a moment Dodd almost laughed to see a man as put out by his lack of brocade and gold embroidery as any maid short of ribbons. He swallowed his amusement hastily, quite certain the Courtier wouldn't see it that way.

By the time they were ready strains of music were coming up from Maxwell's hall and Maxwell and Herries horsemen were assembling in the courtyard with torches. Looking down on it from the turret room next to Maxwell's solar, where Carey had a truckle bed, you could tell that this was no raid from the ribbons and ornaments on the horses and the splendour of some of the clothes. You could also tell from the way they lined up and sorted themselves out that raiding was more usual to them than masqueing.

He followed Carey down the winding stairs and found Red Sandy, Sim's Will and Hutchin Graham waiting with the horses, polished and smart and shining so he was quite proud of them, really. The Courtier inspected them with narrow eyes and nodded curtly, before going off to talk about precedence with the Lord Maxwell. He came back wearing a black velvet mask on his face which did nothing to disguise him but did make him look ridiculous, in Dodd's opinion.

The masked cavalcade streamed out of the gate of Maxwell's Castle and down through the market place of Dumfries where the townsfolk stood shading their eyes from the golden evening to see them.

They waited outside the townhouse where the King was staying for half an hour before the cavalcade of Scottish courtiers and lords and ladies came glittering from the gate to mount the horses waiting in rows. For the first time, Dodd saw womenfolk among them and was shocked: they were wearing the height of French fashion, most of them, their hair shining with jewels and their silken bodices begging for lungfever with the acreage they left bare, their faces decorated into birds of paradise with their own delicate jewelled and feathered masks. Even Lord Spynie helped a woman to her horse, which must have been his wife, and amongst the crowd, Dodd spotted Sir Henry and Lady Elizabeth Widdrington, though she was wearing English fashion that made her more decent. Both of them were masked, Sir Henry expansive with bonhomie and solicitously helping her to her pillion seat behind him. She did not look well, Dodd thought, her face pale and tired under the velvet, with her lips clamped in a tight disapproving line. He stole a glance at Carey but Carey was busy keeping a skittish Thunder under control in his reasonably honourable place behind and to the right of the Lord Maxwell.

They rode in stately fashion down from the Mercat Cross, past the town lock-up and the Tolbooth, past the Fish Cross until they could hear the watermill on the Millburn. Then they turned right and came back again up Irish Street to the Townhead while speeches were made at intervals and the musicians in a wagon clattering and squelching along behind, played music from the French court.

By the time they got back to Maxwell's Castle the long summer evening was worn away and the sky in the west gone to purple satin. The horses lined up stamping in the courtyard, far too many of them with all the attendants as well, and the higher folk separated themselves to go into Maxwell's hall.

Carey beckoned Dodd and Hutchin to him and they went in to the feast after Lord Maxwell and his attendants.

Dodd had seen feasting before but not on this scale, and not with this kind of food, most of which he did not recognise at all. Dodd found a seneschal placing him well below the salt with distant Maxwell cousins, while Hutchin was ordered to stand behind Carey like the other pageboys, to fill his goblet, pass his napkin and hold the water for him to wash his hands between courses. Carey was on the top table, not far from the King, exerting himself to be pleasant and taking very little from the silver- and gold-plated dishes that passed him. He had a plump, comfortable woman on his right to whom he spoke gravely; she seemed to enjoy the conversation well enough. Sir Henry wasn't as close to the salt as Carey, not being there in any official capacity and not having any tincture of royalty in his veins either. He looked irritable now, under his velvet mask, as if he found Carey's higher placing than himself a calculated insult, rather than the normal effect of precedence.

The noise was bedlamite, for no one stopped to listen to the musicians and the King under his cloth of estate was visibly rolling drunk. Dodd watched with disapproval.

Even below the salt the bread was white and the meats soused in sauces full of herbs and wine and garlic, stuffed with strange mixtures heavy with spices. Dodd ate very little, and only what he could identify with certainty, but the beer was good enough and he drank that.

At last trumpets blasted out. The King stood, the company at the top table stood and moved out of the hall, filtering through the passageway towards Maxwell's bowling alley.

"Where are we going?" Dodd asked himself and was answered by the Herries man that had been on his left.

"There's more food there."

"More?" He was shocked. "Good God, is the King no' full yet?"

And it was true; at one end of the bowling alley were more tables covered in white cloths and strangely carved and glittering glass dishes, with creams and jellies and brightly coloured and gilded gingerbreads gleaming like jewels under the high banks of candles. Amongst them went the womenfolk and courtiers, with little dishes made of sugar plate, picking and selecting from the red and green and pink jellies and comfits, like butterflies among flowers.

Dodd stood by the tapestry-covered wall and watched with the other henchmen. Somewhere they seemed to have lost the King and some of the courtiers and he supposed they were having their own even more extravagant sweetmeats somewhere else.

But then there came a blasting of trumpets and a strumming of harps so loud Dodd jumped and put his hand on his sword. Into the bowling alley came a kind of chariot, painted and gilded, pulled by men clad in strange clothes, and in it, with a gilded wreath on his head and some kind of gold breastplate on his chest, was King James. He was laughing and nearly fell out when the chariot jerked to a stop. One of the attending lords, wearing an extraordinary helmet with plumes on the top, made a speech in rhyme which seemed to be talking about Alexander the Great and some magical fountain. Dodd noticed that King James had his arm wrapped round Lord Spynie who was in the chariot with him, also decked out in a fake silver breastplate.

The chariot paraded up and down the bowling alley, stopping every so often for another of the courtiers to make a speech in rhyming Scots, or for the womenfolk to dance in a way which somehow combined the stately and the lewd. No doubt it was all very cultured and courteous, though Dodd had rarely been so bored in his life: why could they not listen to a gleeman singing the old tale of Chevy Chase or making the backs of their necks prickle with the song of the Twa Corbies? What was the point of all the prosing about Alexander the Great, whoever the hell he was? Or have the women dance a little more: that was good to look on, though King James seemed more interested in cuddling up to Lord Spynie, God forgive him. Carey seemed to enjoy it greatly: he laughed with the other courtiers at some of the verses and clapped when the King replied. Hutchin, who was still standing behind him, seemed on the point of falling asleep.

At last the King got down from his chariot, which was wheeled away again, and helped himself to jellies and creams from a separate table. And then, just as Dodd was beginning to hope the thing was finished and they could go home to their beds, all the bright company followed the King back through the passageways into Maxwell's hall.

His servants had been busy clearing the tables and benches away, leaving the newly swept boards lit by torches and candles hanging from the great carved black beams of the roof. The musicians were up in the gallery and when the King waved his hand, they began to play a strenuous galliard.

Dodd had no intention of making a fool of himself by dancing measures he had never learned, which was a pity because at last the women came into their own. They formed up, talking and laughing, and flapping their fans in the stunning heat from the lights, while the men paraded in front of them like cock pheasants.

And there was Carey, a long streak of melancholy in black velvet slashed with taffeta, bouncing and kicking in the men's volta, gallant and attentive to his partner in the galliard, stately as a bishop in the pavane. By some subtle method invisible to Dodd he managed to dance several times with the peach of the ladies' company, a dark woman with alabaster skin, black hair in ringlets snooded with garnets, a perky little mask made of crimson feathers and a crimson velvet gown to match, whose bodice must surely have been stuck on with glue, because otherwise, Dodd could not understand how it stayed where it was.

Carey was talking to her all the time as he danced and whatever he was saying seemed to please her, because she laughed and tapped him playfully with her fan. When the dance ended, she allowed him to escort her to a bench at the side of the room. Carey looked around impatiently for Hutchin, but his expression softened when he saw the boy on a stool by the door, fast asleep. He beckoned Dodd over.

"Sergeant," he said quietly. "Will you do me the favour of fetching a plate of sweetmeats for Signora Bonnetti, and some wine?"

For a moment Dodd bridled at being treated like a servant again, but then he thought that if he was making up to a pretty woman like the Signora, he might not want to leave her alone for someone else to find either.

Coming back with a sugar plate piled with suckets and a goblet of wine, he gave it to Carey and then stood nearby, trying to eavesdrop on how you talked to a court-woman.

He grew no wiser because Carey was speaking French at a great rate and in a caressing tone of voice. The Signora answered him with little inclinations of her head and popped suckets in her mouth greedily. Smiling she pulled Carey's head down near hers and fed him a sweetmeat and they both laughed in a way which was instantly comprehensible in any language in the world.

How does he do it, Dodd wondered enviously; how the hell does he draw the womenfolk like that?

He looked about the hall for the Widdringtons and found them, Elizabeth sitting wearily on one of the benches although she had not danced, and Sir Henry standing, rocking on his toes with his hands behind his back. Carey's performance with the Italian woman was easy for him to see, although it didn't seem to be pleasing him. Sir Henry bent down to Elizabeth and spoke to her, nodded in their direction. Elizabeth looked briefly, shut her eyes and said nothing. Sir Henry's fist bunched, but his son came back from dancing a pavane and sat beside Elizabeth. He had the painfully careful movements of a boy who had broken a lot of furniture before he got used to his size, and it was touching how protectively he sat between his stepmother and his father. When he saw what Carey was up to, his spotted features frowned heavily.

Carey had more than one audience for his courtship of Signora Bonnetti. The King himself seemed interested in it, which surprised Dodd, for between kissing Lord Spynie on the cheek and applauding the dancers, occasional regal glances would come in Carey's direction and then sweep away again. If Carey noticed all the attention, he didn't show it.

I wonder where the Signora's husband is, Dodd thought, but he saw nobody else among all the courtiers in Maxwell's hall who seemed foreign.

As it happened, Carey was asking the Signora precisely that, to be rewarded by an arch look from under the crimson feathers on her face and a wrinkling of her nose.

"He has a flux," explained Signora Bonnetti in her lilting Italianate French. "He was much too ill to come feasting for he cannot be more than five steps away from a close stool."

"Poor gentleman," said Carey with fake concern. "But how generous to allow his wife to come dancing and gladden this northern fastness with the fire of her beauty."

Signora Bonnetti giggled. "He has a woman to attend him," she said. "And I am the worst of nurses."

"I can't believe it."

Signora Bonnetti tapped Carey's arm with her fan. "But I am, sir. I am angry and furious with anyone who is sick."

"And when you are sick?"

"I am never sick, save when with child. And then I am angry and furious with myself. To be sick is to be dull and squalid, isn't it? And full of sorrow and self-pity; oh, Lord God, the pain, oh, my dear, my guts, oh God, fetch the pot...arrgh."

Carey laughed. "And I cannot believe you are a mother?"

"But I am, and two of them still live, thank the Virgin. They are at home with my family in my beautiful Rome."

"Such devotion to follow your husband to the cold and barbaric north, Signora."

"Sir, you are the first Scot I have met who admits to being a barbarian."

"I am not a Scot, Signora; I am English and we are a little less barbaric because more southerly."

"English. Well! I would never have guessed. Why are you here?" Carey told her and watched a fleeting instant of calculation cross her face under the feathers. Her manner instantly changed from a pleasurable flirtation into something much more focused and intent. He smiled in response, a smile which was an invitation to conspiracy, and she smiled back, slowly, the feathers nodding and tapping her smooth pale cheeks, a light dusting of glitter in the valley between her breasts catching the torchlight in the roofbeams.

She tapped him with her jewelled fan again. "Shall we dance again, Monsieur le Deputé?" she said, and he bowed and led her into the rows of lords and ladies waiting for the first chord in the music.

To dance with the Signora was a delight: she was small and her feet in their crimson silk slippers moved like thistledown. Briefly, like a man feeling a sore tooth with his tongue, Carey wished he could dance with Elizabeth Widdrington instead, but that was utterly impossible with her jealous bastard of a husband standing guard over her. He had never before known the obsession with a woman that he felt for Elizabeth and he disliked it thoroughly. He felt perpetually confused and at war with himself, wanting to take the simplest route, march over to where she sat, pale, composed and frankly dowdy in her high-necked velvet gown, punch her loathsome consort in the nose and sweep her away with him. What he would do with her then made the material of all the sleeping and waking dreams that pestered him and frayed his temper. But none of it was possible. Elizabeth herself, with her stern sense of propriety, could and would prevent him. He could hardly see her without creating elaborate internal flights of fancy in which he tore off her clothes and took her gasping against a wall, and yet he also knew that he could not bear to hurt her and would stop if she so much as frowned. It was all too complicated for him.

If I press my suit to the Italian lady, thought the calculating courtier within him, it may ease Sir Henry's suspicions. It might even convince the King I am not what he thinks me and perhaps...perhaps, who knows?—Signora Bonnetti might not be quite so staunch in defence of her honour?

The music of the pavane stopped and he realised he had gone through all its figures without even registering them. Signora Bonnetti curtseyed low to him and he bowed and they waited for the next dance.

Another volta, and Carey found himself grinning impudently at her. There were ways and ways to find out. He pranced and spun through the opening jig, and held her hand lightly while she responded with the women's footwork. With his index finger he gently stroked the hollow of her palm as she danced. She laughed and spun, her skirts billowing, came neatly into his arms and in the beat and a half when he was placing his hands to lift, he made his move. In the volta the man was supposed to grip the bottom edges of the woman's stays, front and back, to lift and spin her as she leaped. His hands disguised by crimson satin, Carey put them in two quite different places, causing the Signora to gasp and flush. He lifted her anyway as she jumped, and she spun neatly and came back to him again. He was braced for her to slap him, or stand on his toe or even accidentally on purpose dig her fan handle into his privates—all of them counter-moves he had known court-ladies make before. She didn't, only leaned against him as he caught her, and whispered, "Gently, my dear, I am not made of marble."

"Nor am I," he whispered back, as he placed his hands exactly where they had been before. "See what you do to me."

She jumped as he lifted, spun, jumped again and laughed when he steadied her in an equally scandalous manner.

The dance separated them into their own figures and Carey concentrated on lifting the solidly built lady who came into his arms as the partners changed without rupturing himself or hurting his back. His whole body was alive with the dance and the music, he felt like thistledown himself and his feet flung themselves through the complicated steps without any need for his conscious direction. He could look across the expanse of whirling courtiers and find Signora Bonnetti watching him. Perhaps? Please God, he prayed profanely, thinking about Catholic countries where the possibilities were so pleasingly endless and forgiveable.

At last the dance brought her back, whirling breathlessly into his arms and once again he held her delectably tight arse instead of her stays and flipped her up. Although he believed he had done it properly, he thought he must have mistaken the balance. She came down heavily and seemed to twist her ankle. Immediately contrite he held her up and as the measure finished, he supported her to the bench at the side of the hall.

"Signora, I am sorry," he said. "How embarrassing for you to have such a clumsy partner..."

"Yes," she said, not looking at all annoyed with him. "My ankle is sore and I am very hot indeed. Please take me into the garden to cool myself."

He held his arm out to her and she wove her hand into the crook of the elbow and squeezed eloquently. "Monsieur le Deputé, you are very gallant."

"Signora Bonnetti, you are very beautiful, but too formal. Will you not call me Robin, as the Queen of England does?"

Another squeeze and the brush of her hip against his told him she was pleased.

"Why then, Robin, you may call me Emilia as my husband does—though he is no longer so gallant, alas."

Carey bowed his head. "How can I help paying court to Emilia, the fairest jewel in Scotland?" Hackneyed, he knew; whatever had happened to his tongue?

She tossed her head and limped assiduously as he led her out towards the bowling alley, past the crowd of lords and ladies predating on the delicacies of the banquet, and through the door into the garden, where their feet crunched on gravel paths between herb beds and her ankle seemed much better already. She led him through hedges into a rose garden, from the scent, and sat them both down on a stone bench.

"For the crime of hurting my ankle with your wickedness," said Emilia Bonnetti in a whisper, "you must now forfeit a kiss." She proffered her cheek and shut her eyes.

Just for a moment, uncharacteristically, Carey hesitated. Somewhere inside him came a plaintive cry, protesting that this was the wrong woman, that what he needed to do was go back into the hall, kill Sir Henry Widdrington and bring Elizabeth out to the rose garden instead…And then the unregenerate old Adam arose and pointed out that wrong or not, this was *a* woman and an extremely juicy one at that and…God knew, he needed a woman.

She was still holding up her cheek to be kissed. He bent towards her, touched her very gently with his lips below the feather fringe of her mask, then took her shoulders and turned her so that her mouth came under his. Then he kissed her properly.

After that there was another, more ancient dance than the volta, only marginally complicated by her farthingale and his padded hose, which ended inevitably with her sitting astride his lap giggling as he bucked and gasped into the white-hot little death and bit her quite carefully on her creamy shoulder, just below the line of her gown.

She squeaked, nibbled his ear and lifted the hand that was under his doublet and shirt to tweak his nipple. They stayed like that for a while.

"We should go back," she whispered, and sighed.

"Just a minute, Emilia my heart," he temporised, happier than he had been in months, sliding his hands under her thighs again. God, they were beautiful to feel; why did women hide their beautiful plump smooth arses under acres of silk and linen, it was a miraculous treasure that they kept there and he wanted more…

She squeaked again, differently, and laughed. "Mon Dieu," she said flatteringly. "I had heard Englishmen were cold-hearted."

"Not me," he managed to pant, his heart building up to a gallop once more, Jesus God, it had been so long…"Kiss me."

"Tut tut. At least it's true that Englishmen are greedy…" She was thoughtful, or her top half was, while her rump rocked gently to and fro and made him feel he was going to burst again.

"I admit it," he muttered. "I admit it, I'm greedy, only kiss me again."

She slid her arms out of the front of his doublet and held him round the neck so he could do it more thoroughly. She twisted her fingers in his hair and grasped in a way that would normally have hurt him while he directed her honeypot and let himself quite slowly drown in it. This time both of them cried out dangerously in the empty rose garden, and Carey crushed her against his chest as her faced relaxed like a baby's.

The night had darkened while they were dancing, and now the first few spots of rain began to fall. Emilia Bonnetti gasped with dismay as the specks of cold touched her neck and shoulders and lifted her head.

"Blessed Virgin, my gown will be ruined," she cried in Italian, hopping off him to his own near ruin and rummaging under the silks to rearrange her underskirts. Carey thought wistfully about taking a nap, but he didn't want his black velvet to spot and run either. He stood with a few creaks and winces as the hardness of the bench told on him at last, and made himself decent. She used the edge of a petticoat to wipe her facepaint off his face, an intimacy that made them both smile, and they trotted down the path back to the bowling alley and the torches.

A few steps from the door, Emilia began limping again.

"Am I respectable?" she asked, looking him over critically before they joined the surprising throng of dalliers in the garden.

Carey bowed with more than usual extravagance. "Positively virginal," he said, naughtily. "But you were limping on the other foot before."

She wrinkled her nose at him. "*You* have done your doublet buttons up unevenly," she told him, turning to go in.

"Wait. When can we meet again?"

"I am lodging with my husband at the sign of the Thistle near the Fish Cross, very expensive and not at all clean. Will you come and attend me there tomorrow morning, Robin, and entertain me? I shall be very bored and in a bad mood, I'm afraid."

"With the greatest possible pleasure, ma belle."

She went in ahead of him, looking plump and pleased with herself, straightening her mask. He waited for a count of thirty and followed her, still happily glowing.

The King was on the point of going to bed, barely held up by Lord Spynie who was not much better off, hiccupping and laughing at the invisible jokes of alcohol. It was an odd thing to see a monarch so drunk he could hardly stand, Carey thought. The mere idea of the Queen of England so unguarded smacked of sacrilege. The company stood and bowed or curtseyed as the trumpets blew discordantly, while King James with his surrounding company withdrew to take horse back to the Mayor's house.

The Signora went with the courtiers, studiously and cautiously ignoring him. He took care not to do more than glance at her, thinking fondly about stroking the secret places between her thighs and...

Elizabeth Widdrington was staring at him, looking as if she was reading his mind. Guilt and a schoolboy sullenness brought the blood into his face involuntarily. Black velvet masks made for an exciting and illusory anonymity, but it was also harder to read people's expressions. He hoped she couldn't see him flush, he couldn't work out what she was thinking at all, if she could tell, if she minded (of course she minded). She linked hands distantly with her rightful husband, turned and left, young Henry yawning at her other shoulder.

Just for a moment he felt truculent. Am I supposed to spend my life yearning after her like some goddamned troubadour, he thought rebelliously. I'll marry her the instant Sir Henry's safely buried, but until then, what am I supposed to do? Live like a goddamned Papist monk? It didn't matter. Sadness and weariness set in and more than ever he wished it had been Elizabeth straddling his crotch in the rose garden, Elizabeth moaning and collapsing against him at last, Elizabeth telling him to do his doublet buttons up straight...He sighed and went over to where Dodd was sitting on a bench near the curled-up and sleeping Hutchin, nibbling at some shards of sugar plate.

Dodd's miserable face cheered him up a little, it was so full of the plainest envy.

"What now, sir?" asked Dodd, dolefully.

"Bed. Let's wake the boy, I'm not carrying him up those stairs."

Hutchin was not easy to wake and smelled of wine fumes. He was a fast learner, Carey thought with amusement; he had already learned the pageboy's trick of toping a quick mouthful out of every drink he poured for his master. Carey himself was much less drunk than he had been earlier and Dodd looked exactly the same as always.

"Did you enjoy the feast, Sergeant?" he asked.

Dodd shook his head. "Is that what ye do at court, sir?" he asked. "All the time?"

"Pretty much." Though it was interesting to contemplate what King James's court at Westminster would be like if the King was habitually drunk in the evenings.

"It wouldna suit me, sir."

"You can get used to it."

"Ay, sir," said Dodd, disapproving and noncommittal. "Nae doubt."

## thursday 13th july 1592, morning

Dodd was still in a bad mood the next morning, along with every single man in Maxwell's entire cess. Finding the hall where he had slept before so packed with men rolled in their cloaks that it was hard to pick your way among them, he, his brother and Sim's Will had dossed down in the stable next to Thunder. He neither knew nor cared where the Deputy Warden had slept since he thought the man deserved to sleep on the floor, and Young Hutchin had curled up by the hall fire in a pile of pageboys all sleeping like puppies. It was very different from what he had imagined about court life. And what were they doing, still there anyway?

Carey came striding into the stable the next morning, a whole hideous hour before sunrise, looking fresh and not at all hungover. He was wearing his jack and morion. Behind him was a red-eyed silent Hutchin and outside in the courtyard there was a brisk feeding and watering and saddling of horses.

"What now?" moaned Dodd, leaning up on his elbow and picking straw out of his hair. Beyond the stable door he could see that it was spitting a fine mizzle.

"My lord Maxwell is very anxious for us to ride out to Lochmaben and inspect his guns," said Carey cheerfully. "Good God, what's wrong with you, Dodd? You didn't drink much yesterday."

"Och," said Red Sandy, sitting up and scratching, "he's allus like this, he hates mornings. Always has. Will ye be wanting us too, sir?"

"No. I want you and Sim's Will to go and do some drinking on my behalf."

Red Sandy brightened up at that.

"Ay, sir."

"I want you to spend time with the men around town, buy a few drinks, and see if you can catch any hint of a sudden influx of good firearms anywhere. Just listen for rumours, or envious complaints and take good note of who's talking and who they're talking about. That clear?"

Red Sandy was on his feet and so was Sim's Will, both looking much encouraged. Sim's Will nodded and went out to see who had taken their feed bucket, while Red Sandy brushed down two of the hobbies and put their saddles on.

Carey handed over several pounds in assorted Scots money to Red Sandy while Dodd sat up and fumbled for his boots.

"Do you think you could do that work for me without getting roaring drunk or into any fights with the Scots?" Carey asked. Red Sandy was offended.

"Ay, o' course, sir."

"Young Hutchin, you have to stay either with me or Red Sandy. Which do you prefer?"

Young Hutchin swallowed stickily and looked at the ground.

"I'd prefer to stay with Red Sandy, sir," he said. "Ah...the Maxwells are at feud wi' the Grahams, sir; Dumfries is well enough with the King here and all but it might be better for me not to go to Lochmaben."

Carey lifted his eyebrows at the boy. "Is there any Border family your relations are not at feud with?" he asked.

Hutchin looked offended. "Ay, sir, we're no' feuding with the Armstrongs or the Johnstones, nor never have."

"And that's all? Has it never occurred to your uncles that merrily feuding with every surname that offends you in any way might not be a good long-term policy, especially if you have the King of Scotland after your blood as well?"

Hutchin looked blank. "What else can we do, sir?" he asked.

"Be like the Routledges, every man's prey?"

Carey sighed. "Stay with Red Sandy and Sim's Will and try to keep out of trouble."

"Ay, sir."

◇◇◇

Lord Maxwell looked no happier than any of his relatives or attendants, and seemed to have cooled towards Carey as well. They broke their fast hurriedly on stale manchet bread and ale, and then followed him out of the Lochmaben Gate of Dumfries and northeast along the road to his castle. They struck off the road after about four miles, into a tangle of hills and burns, until they met with a number of angry looking Maxwells, gathered about three battered wagons whose wheels bit deep into the soft forest track. Lord Maxwell's steward came forward and spoke urgently into his ear, at which Lord Maxwell's face became even grimmer.

He waved at the wagons.

"There ye are, Sir Robert," he said. "See what ye can make of them."

"Are we not going into the castle?" Dodd questioned under his breath.

"It seems my lord Warden wants to be able to deny the weapons are anything to do with him," Carey answered softly. "Count your blessings, he's not going to be a happy man."

Carey slid from his horse, squelched over to the nearest wagon and climbed onto the board next to the driver. He pulled out a caliver or two, turned them upside down, grunted and threw them back. The last one he examined more carefully and then shook his head.

"Well?" demanded Maxwell impatiently.

"They're all faulty," said Carey simply. "The barrels are all badly welded, the lock parts have not been case-hardened and some of them are cracked already. If you use these in battle, my lord, your enemies will laugh themselves silly."

"One of my cousins has been blinded by one and another man had his hand hurt."

"There you are then, my lord. If you like we could prove a couple."

"Ay," said Maxwell, rubbing his thumb on the clenched muscles in his cheek. "Do so."

Although he knew as well as Dodd that it was unnecessary, Carey went through the motions, rigged a caliver to a tree stump and spattered it all over the clearing.

There was a kind of contented sigh from the Maxwells standing about. Carey left the wagon, came back to his horse and mounted up again in tactful silence. They waited, finding the paths all blocked by Maxwells.

The tension rose, broken by wood-doves currling at each other through the trees and anxious alarm calls from the jackdaws.

Finally Maxwell flung down his tall-crowned hat and roared, "God damn it! Bastard Englishmen, bastards and traitors every one, by God..."

He swung suddenly on Carey and at the motion the Maxwell lances seemed to lean inward towards the Deputy Warden and Sergeant Dodd. "And what d'ye ken of this, eh, Sir Robert? Sitting there so smarmy and clever and telling me I canna do what I plan because the guns are nae good..."

"Would you have preferred me to keep silent and let you use them against the Johnstones, my lord?" asked Carey levelly. "I could have done that."

Ay, thought Dodd viciously, wondering how many of the lances were aimed at his back, and why didn't you, you interfering fool?

"Ye're in it wi' Scrope and Lowther and the Johnstones, aren't ye, aren't ye?" yelled Maxwell, forcing his horse over close to Carey and leaning in his face. "And a clever plot it was too, to gi' the advantage to the pack of muirthering Johnstones."

"Nothing to do with me, my lord," said Carey steadily.

"Lord Scrope's yer warden, ye'd do what he tellt ye."

"I might," allowed Carey. "If he had mentioned this to me, of course. In which case I would hardly have come here with you, would I? But I don't think it was him."

"And who was it then?"

"From whom did you buy the guns, my lord? Ask yourself that and then ask who did you the favour of stopping you firing one of them."

Oh, thought Dodd as a great light dawned on him. So that's what the interfering fool's about, is he? Well, well. It took most of his self-control not to let a wicked grin spread itself all over his

face. That night spent tediously marking all the guns in the
armoury with an x before we even knew there was anything wrong
with them, it was time well-spent. And now we've found them
again and we can go home.

Maxwell's face was working. He seemed to be thinking and
calming down.

"Ye came to find these, did ye no'?" he said at last.

Carey shrugged. "I knew we had lost the guns during the muster
on Sunday, and I knew someone must have put a big enough price
on them for…someone to want to take the money and embarrass
Scrope at the same time." Noticeably he did not mention the
previous theft on the road from Newcastle, when the Tower-made
guns had been swapped for the deathtraps now owned by Maxwell.

"The bastard," breathed Maxwell repetitiously. "God damn his
guts."

"Amen," answered Carey piously.

"I paid good money for this pile of scrap iron."

Carey tutted. "Who to, my lord?" he asked casually.

Maxwell's lowering face suddenly became cunning. "I canna
tell ye that, Sir Robert."

Carey sighed at this sudden niceness. "No, of course not," he
agreed. "Will you say what you paid?"

"Twenty-five shillings a gun, English, and we were to send them
back once we'd had the use of them."

Up went Carey's eyebrows at this unexpected titbit. "Really?"
he said slowly. "Is that so?"

"The usual arrangement, ye ken, only we wanted more of them.
And for longer. Sir Ri…He was to find them at Lammastide in an
old pele-tower near Langholm, ye follow."

"Ah yes, I understand. And take the credit for it. Hmm. Well,
what will you do with them now, my lord?"

"Throw 'em in a bog."

"Don't do that, my lord."

"Will ye take them back then?"

Carey smiled thinly. "I don't think so, my lord. But will you
keep them here for a couple of days?"

"Why?"

Carey looked opaque and tapped his fingers on his saddle horn.
"Just in case, my lord, just in case. You never know what might
happen."

Maxwell grunted sullenly. "What am I to dae about the
Johnstones?" he demanded to know.

"Entirely your affair, my lord. But if I were you, I'd let them
sweat until you're ready."

"And stay bloody Warden all that time?"

Carey made a self-deprecating half-bow from the saddle. "It
might not be so bad," he suggested. "Perhaps you and my lord
Scrope could even agree on a Day of Truce and clear up some of
the bills that have been accumulating for the past sixteen years."

Maxwell glowered at him. "Good God, whatever for?"

"For peace, my lord. For the rule of law."

The sneer on Maxwell's handsome features was magnificently
comprehensive. "While I've my men at my back, I'll make my ain
laws and my ain peace."

Carey said nothing. Maxwell was silent for a time which seemed
very long to Dodd's stretched nerves. Carey sat patiently, seeming
intent on the stitching of his riding gloves, the growth of the nearest
tree.

Maxwell jerked his horse round and came close to him.

"Well?" he demanded.

"What can I do for you, my lord?" said Carey softly.

"I want my money back."

"What?"

"Ay." Maxwell leaned on his saddle horn and spat words. "The
Deputy Warden of Carlisle sold me a pile of scrap-iron that half-
killed my cousin, and I want my money back."

"Not this Deputy Warden," said Carey.

Maxwell shrugged. "Who cares. Ye get me my money back. I
want it and it's mine."

"From Lowther?"

"I never said that. From whoever. D'ye understand me?"

There was something almost amusing about one of the richest
lords in the Scottish West March demanding his money back like
an Edinburgh wife waving a bad fish at a stallholder, almost but
not quite. The fact that the whole thing was ludicrously irrational

and unjust hardly mattered when they were surrounded by Maxwell's kinsmen and Maxwell himself looked like a primed caliver ready to go off at any minute. Dodd began praying fervently. Please God, let the Courtier keep a civil tongue in his head, please God...

"I'll do my best, my lord," Carey said, prim as a maiden.

"Ye'd better."

Maxwell turned his horse foaming back towards the wagon and shouted orders, then whipped the beast to a canter in the direction of the road to Dumfries. Perforce, Carey and Dodd rode with them, less escorted than guarded now.

They returned quickly to Maxwell's townhouse, recipients of a double-edged hospitality. Carey strode into the stall where Thunder stood stamping and tossing his head impatiently and found Hutchin there already.

When the boy turned to greet him, they saw a magnificent black eye, a bust lip and pure rage.

"Oh, Lord," said Carey, wearily stripping off his gloves. "What happened? Did Lord Spynie..."

The boy spat. "Red Sandy and Sim's Will got intae a fight."

"How?"

"Wee Colin Elliot was in the Black Bear wi' some of his kin and when Red Sandy come in, Wee Colin asked him if he'd lost any sheep lately and Red Sandy went for him. An' they're both in the town lock-up now. It wasnae my fault," finished Hutchin self-righteously.

"Who's in the lock-up? Wee Colin as well?"

"Nay, sir. Just Red Sandy and Sim's Will, of course."

Carey glared at Dodd as if it was his fault his brother was an idiot.

"That's all I bloody need," said Carey. "Come on, we'll go and see them."

They were stopped at the gate to Maxwell's Castle by a stern-faced Herries.

"Ye canna all go out," he said to Carey. "My lord Maxwell says one of ye must stay here."

"As a hostage," said the Courtier, coldly.

"Ay, if ye wantae put it that way."

Carey looked at Dodd and Hutchin, calculating. "Then it's you, Dodd, I'm sorry. I'll see what I can do to bail your brother."

Dodd wanted to protest at being left in the middle of a heaving mass of Maxwells, but could see there was no point. It was better for Carey to have freedom of action since he at least had some friends among the Scots. Hutchin was a bit young to play the hostage and a Graham furthermore. It had to be him. He nodded gloomily.

"Ay," he said. "I'll be wi' the horses."

Carey hurried down the street, Hutchin trotting at his heels, until he came to the small round lock-up by the Tolbooth. As expected, it was packed full of brawlers, half of them still drunk, and it took a while for Sim's Will to struggle out of the crowd and peer through the little barred window.

"Well?" said Carey, furious at this complication.

"Ah…Sorry, sir," said Sim's Will, looking very sheepish. He was battered, though not too badly, considering the idiocy of taking on a pack of Elliots on their own ground.

"How's Red Sandy?"

"No' so bad. He lost a tooth but he found it again, and he's put it back now and his nose stopped bleeding a while ago," Sim's Will said.

"Tell me how the fight started."

Sim's Will recounted a very pathetic tale in which Wee Colin Elliot had snarled scandalous and wounding insults about Red Sandy and Sim's Will, impugning their birth, breeding, courage and wives. To this unprovoked attack Sim's Will and Red Sandy had responded with mild reproach, until the evil Wee Colin had sunk so low as to attack the sacred honour of the Deputy Warden, at which point, driven beyond endurance, Red Sandy had tapped him lightly, almost playfully, on the nose and…

Carey rolled his eyes. "Red Sandy hit Wee Colin Elliot first."

In a manner of speaking, allowed Sim's Will, you could say that, although the way Wee Colin Elliot had been ranting you could see it was only a matter of seconds before…

"I don't suppose you found out anything of use before that, did you?" Carey asked.

Sim's Will Croser's face was blank for a moment before, rather guiltily, recollection returned. "Ah. No, sir," he said.

"No rumour of somebody suddenly having quite a lot of guns where before they had none?"

"Nay, sir. Nothing like that. And we did ask before we met…"

"Wee Colin Elliot. God's truth. Well, you can tell Red Sandy I'll do what I can to bail you out of there, but since the matter's ultimately a decision for the Lord Warden of this March, I don't know how long it will take."

"Ay, but is that not Lord Maxwell?" said Sim's Will. "Red Sandy said ye're friends wi' him."

"Well, I was. I'll see what I can do."

An attempt to talk to the King at the Mayor's house produced the information that His Majesty was out inspecting some of his cavalry and likely to go hunting after that.

And so Carey found himself heading for the alehouse known as The Thistle, as crowded as any of the others with the King's attendants and minor lords. The common room was a bedlam of arguing, dicing and drinking and as no one stopped him, he and Hutchin quietly went and climbed the stairs to the next floor. Four doors off a narrow landing faced him and after listening for a moment, he tried the one on his right. No answer, so he tried the next one and heard Signora Bonnetti's voice answer, "Chi é? Who is?"

"C'est moi, Emilia," said Carey, trying the latch and finding the door bolted.

A moment later it opened a crack and Carey stepped through, firmly stopping Hutchin with a hand on the chest.

"Sit at the top of the stairs and shout if someone tries to come in," said Carey and Young Hutchin grinned with understanding beyond his years. "And if I catch you listening or peeping at the latch-hole, I'll leather you, understand?"

"Ay, sir," said Hutchin.

In fact, Hutchin managed to restrain his curiosity for nearly twenty minutes until the muffled noises coming through the door told him he was safe enough. He put his eye to the latch-hole and was rewarded by the sight of two pairs of legs on a bed playing the old game of the two-backed beast. For all his efforts at squinting and seeing through wood, he could see nothing else and had to use his imagination. Fortunately he had more than most.

The red feather mask had flattered Signora Emilia Bonnetti because it had hidden the fine tracery of lines around her magnificent dark eyes. Carey no longer doubted that she had borne children, for she had the marks of it on her belly and her deliciously dark and pointed nipples. He didn't care. He had always preferred older married women for dalliance and not simply because, at the Queen's Court in London, to meddle with the virgin Maids of Honour was to risk the Queen's fury and a ruinous stay in the Tower. His first woman had been a much older and more experienced French lady in Paris, and he had never got over his awed pleasure at finding the truth in the saying that women burned hotter the older they got.

Now he lay full length in the little half-curtained bed and watched sleepy-eyed as Emilia, full of vigour and mischief, poured him wine and chatted to him in French and Italian mixed.

It seemed he could do her some great service, if he chose. Ah, he thought, we're coming to the point at last now. Ten years before he might have been disappointed that sheer desire for him had not been Emilia's motive after all. No more. He had long ago decided that women rarely had fewer than four different motives for anything they did.

He took the goblet of wine and drank as Emilia pulled a white smock over her head and disappeared briefly, still talking.

At first he wasn't certain he had heard right. "I beg your pardon?"

"I want to buy firearms," repeated the Signora. "You know, guns." She said the word in English to be sure he could understand.

Mind working furiously, he watched her and waited for her to explain herself.

"Signor Bonnetti has a commission to buy at least twelve dozen calivers and twelve dozen pistols, with perhaps more later. It has been very difficult, we came to Dumfries full of hope to buy them here where so many are made, but now we find that so many are used here as well the gunsmiths are fat and lazy, and they will not sell to us."

"Who are the guns for?"

She shrugged her creamy shoulders and made a moue of disdain. "I do not know; for the Netherlanders perhaps, or the Swedes. Even the French Huguenots might want them; Signor Bonnetti has not told me."

She's lying, Carey thought to himself, every one of those people have better sources nearer home than Dumfries.

"Have you any money to pay for them?"

"We have gold and banker's drafts," she said. "But none will take them. Or they will take them, but they will give us nothing but promises in exchange. Where can I find guns to buy, Robin chéri, so that I may leave this cold and uncivilized place and go back to my beautiful Roma?" She sat next to him on the bed and put her head down on his chest. "We have sold all the wine, but we cannot leave without the guns, and we are both miserable."

"Why are you asking me?" Carey wondered, twiddling his fingers in her black ringlets. "Why do you think I have guns?"

"Well, the Scots all say it. If you canna get guns here, they say, try the Deputy Warden of Carlisle. And then they laugh."

Carey smiled and stroked her cheek. "Hmm," he said. "And why do they laugh?"

She shrugged and sat up, tidying her hair with a busy pulling out and pushing in of hairpins. "Because many of them have very beautiful firearms from Carlisle and are proud of it. The laird Johnstone has many of the finest Tower-made, which is why my lord Maxwell is so worried."

"Have you tried asking Maxwell?"

Her face screwed up with distaste. "He was the first one I tried and he said he might be able to help me in a little while, but he is untrue and a liar and he will not speak to me any more. The laird Johnstone says he needs his guns against the Maxwells. The Earl of Mar has been very kind..."

"Lucky Earl of Mar."

She sniffed. "But he is only trying to delay me because I think he takes money from the English. And the King, of course, is not very approachable and the Queen has no influence with him.

Huntly is in too much disgrace and poor beautiful Moray is dead. I have no one to turn to."

"Poor darling," said Carey not entirely listening to her sad tale. He gave her an inquiring squeeze. She disentwined his arms and frowned at him.

"You must get up and dress," she scolded. "You have already been here a very long time."

"But if I find you some guns, I will never see you again," Carey protested, putting his hand to his brow sorrowfully. Emilia prodded him in a sensitive spot without warning and made him gasp.

"You might. But if I have not guns in the next few weeks, the Signor and I shall be ruined and so you will never see us more at all."

"And if I can find you a few guns?"

"We will pay you perhaps forty shillings each for them."

Carey stared hard at her as she busied herself pulling on her stays. He was thinking and calculating and wondering how far he could trust his luck this time. Imperiously she ordered him to help her with her backlaces, and he obediently did the office of a lady's maid, with a few additions of his own invention. Unfortunately, she was no longer in the mood and they didn't work. The complex layers went over her inexorably, one after the other, and when she was fully dressed and pinning on her cap, she turned on him and frowned again.

"And you are still disgraceful, why will you not put your shirt on?"

"Hope," he said with mock despair and a lewd gesture.

She gave him his shirt and hose crushingly. "No, Monsieur le Deputé, I think not."

"And if I can find you some guns?"

Now she smiled. "Who knows?"

He laughed. "If I get you the guns you need, I'll want more than kisses in recompense."

"A ten per centum finder's fee?"

"Twenty."

"Fifteen."

"Done," Carey said happily, drinking to it.

"Now you must meet my husband."

◇◇◇

Giovanni Bonnetti was in a sorrowful state as he sat casting up his accounts. He was a small lightly built, swarthy man with a curled up waxed beard and moustache and very dark bright eyes. Three shirts and a knitted waistcoat under his fashionable orange and black taffeta doublet could not keep out the dank cold of the miserable joke that the Scots called summer. His legs were a perpetual mass of goose-pimples under his elegant black hose and, while the uproar in his bowels had calmed somewhat, he was not a well man. Cursed inefficient northerners, none of them knew what proper plumbing was.

And furthermore he had a stifling head-cold which caused his nose to drip all the time and a sore throat and hardly any of the illiterate savages of Scotland could speak Italian and many of them only spoke halting French with a nasal drawl that would have disgraced a Fleming. A generation ago they had been better cultured, when their alliance with France was strong and they had the wisdom of Mother Church to guide them. The foul heresy of Protestantism had sealed them up in their poor little country to stew in their own juices. And the King was no better than his nobles, though he at least had Italian and French.

But the worst of it, the absolute worst, was that here he was in Dumfries, the centre of gunmaking for the whole of Scotland, being placed in the area of highest demand, and nobody would sell him any handguns, not pistols, nor calivers, nor arquebuses. He might as well have been in London trying to buy munitions from the Tower. The locals looked at him and denied point blank that they owned any guns, ever had owned any guns, even knew what guns were. The gunsmiths he could persuade to talk to him in the first place said their order books were full for the next six months and they could barely keep up with demand. It had seemed such a fine idea from Antwerp. He would make use of his wife's scandalous liaison with the Lord Maxwell to make contact with the Scottish Court. They would both travel to Scotland with Maxwell and there buy weapons and ammunition to ship on to the Irish rebels and thus help to destroy the Earl of Essex, Elizabeth's general in Ireland. Perhaps with good weapons for the Irish thrown in the balance, he might be the means of dislodging the heretical English grip on Ireland completely. And Ireland, as the Queen of England and the King of Spain both knew very well, was the back door into England. His elaborate and painfully written proposal had gone through the many layers of Spanish bureaucrats and officials and finally returned with the tiny mincing script of the King of Spain in the top righthand corner: fiat, let this be done.

Their children had not exactly been taken in ward, only the officials had made it clear that they would come to Antwerp and remain there, as security for Philip II's investment. Giovanni had triumphantly taken his Medici bank drafts and converted some into gold to defray his expenses and buy wine as samples. He had taken ship with his minx of a wife and her noble Scottish bandit of a lover, closing his eyes firmly to her antics and solacing himself with one of his maids, all within the last few months.

And now here he was, on the verge of the biggest coup of his life, and nobody would sell him guns. The King was no help, insisted that he hadn't enough firearms himself, though he bought and drank every drop of the wine Bonnetti had brought as his cover-story: the powder he had been promised at a swingeing price would, no doubt, be bad and his time was running out before the autumn gales closed the seas between Scotland and Ireland. Also the wine that the Scottish nobility drank was appalling. If he could only pull off his coup, he might indeed set up as a vintner, supplying the barbarians with something a little better. He drank some more, the cloves and nutmeg completely failing to hide the fact that it had been pressed from the last sweepings of third-rate Gascony vineyards, watered, adulterated and brought in foul leaky barrels.

There was a knock at the door of the miserable back room of the alehouse he had rented as a makeshift office to take orders for wine.

"Prego," said Bonnetti, gulping down the rest of his vinegar.

His wife appeared at the door with a man behind her, though not, unfortunately, the Lord Maxwell. He had been furious with her when she had quarrelled with her Scottish lover; her wilfulness had brought their whole enterprise in danger. He had known what she was doing to find another contact and it made him no happier.

This one was a new barbarian, elegantly dressed in black, with dyed hair. Extremely tall, even for the Scots, and with the national tendency to loom menacingly.

"Bonjour, monsieur," said the barbarian in excellent French, making the merest fraction of a bow. "I'm very pleased to make your acquaintance."

"Votre nom, monsieur?"

"Sir Robert Carey, Deputy Warden of Carlisle."

Every ounce of self-control Bonnetti possessed was needed to stop him from leaping out of his seat and jumping from the window. He stared and croaked for a moment with his heart thumping and his hand behind the table, stroking the hilt of the little knife he had strapped to his wrist for emergencies. Meanwhile his wife smiled sweetly and triumphantly at him, and modestly withdrew. The Englishman stood at ease with his left hand tilting the pommel of his sword and his right propped on his fashionable paned hose. He said nothing, simply smiled and waited for Bonnetti to recover. As Bonnetti became capable of thought again, he realised he had actually heard something of the Careys from his brother in London: the nearest thing to Princes of the Blood Royal that the feeble Tudor line possessed, much favoured cousins of the Queen. This particular one he had not come across by name, but the fact that he was Deputy Warden of the English West March was bad enough. Nothing of their mission could possibly be accomplished if the infernal English knew about it: they might not have been able to stop him buying weapons in Scotland, but they could and would send ships to prevent him transporting them to Ireland.

"Please, don't be afraid," continued the Englishman softly. "I came because I heard you were interested in buying firearms."

Deny it? No, the man was too sure of himself. No doubt his little whore of a wife had been blabbing.

"I might be," Bonnetti admitted cagily. "Please sit down."

The Englishman sat on the chair for potential customers, stretched out his long legs and crossed them at the ankle.

"Excellent," said Carey. "I have eighteen dozen handguns, mainly calivers with some pistols, that I might be willing to sell to you. If you happen to be buying."

It must be a trap. This was too extraordinary. An English official selling him weapons to fight the English in Ireland? It was certainly a trap.

"I am not buying weapons," said Bonnetti. "I am not even interested in weapons. I am here to negotiate for the sale of Italian wine with the Scottish court."

"Oh," said the Englishman, without a trace of discomfiture. "Have you any samples? I might be interested in buying some myself."

"The Scottish court has drunk them all."

Carey grinned. "Isn't that a surprise? Well, Signor Bonnetti, I'm sorry to hear you aren't interested in my suggestion, since the Signora was quite sure you would be. You must know that nobody in Dumfries or anywhere in Scotland will sell weapons to you because you are a Papist and a foreigner. The King of Scotland will very soon lose patience with you, take your money anyway and probably you will end up with a dagger in your back. Never mind. Not my affair. Good day to you."

"One moment," said Bonnetti. "You are an English official. What you are doing is therefore treason."

"Treason?" said the man blankly. "I understood the weapons are to take into Sweden. Why would selling you weapons meant for the Swedes be treason?"

Bonnetti's head was spinning, but at least it was clear that his wife had not gossiped about where the weapons were intended to go. He heard the threat in what Carey said about the King; no doubt the English Deputy had men who could put daggers into backbones, just as much as the King of Scots.

And the English were the most avaricious and unprincipled nation on earth, everyone knew that. Perhaps the offer was a genuine one. Perhaps the Englishman would take his money one way or the other. Perhaps there was even something in what he said.

Bonnetti coughed, blew his nose. "What kind of weapons would these be?" he asked. "And how much would you want for them?"

The price was outrageous. Carey wanted sixty shillings each for the weapons. Argue as he might, Bonnetti could not get him below fifty, in gold and bankers' drafts, half in advance and half on delivery, plus a sum of money he delicately referred to as a finder's fee. On the other hand, now Bonnetti had had time to get his breath back, there might be a great benefit in buying the weapons off a Carey, even at an inflated price. By blood, he was close to the Queen; blackmail might well make him very useful. In fact, as a coup for gaining control of one of the Queen's closest relatives, this weapons dealing could be only the beginning of a glorious new career for Bonnetti. His brother had dabbled a little in espionage: Giovanni was not at all sure precisely what had happened, but he suspected that Walsingham, the Queen's spymaster, had caught him and turned him. This would be a much greater triumph, a fitting revenge. And he did have the money for it.

With typical barbarian lack of finesse, Carey insisted on half his fifteen per cent bribe in advance, in gold, as well as a banker's draft for half the price of the guns. If he had not been desperate, Bonnetti would never have agreed, but he had no choice, as the Englishman blandly pointed out. Without some good faith from him, Carey had no reason to take any risks to help him.

## thursday 13th july 1592, noon

Roger Widdrington had been sitting at the crowded alehouse waiting for the tow-headed Graham boy to meet him for at least an hour and a half. The boy finally appeared, at the trot, looking flushed and excited and in a tearing hurry.

"I canna stay long, Sir Robert sent me out for a pie and I must be back. Ye can tell her ladyship that Sir Robert's got to make friends with my lord Maxwell again, to fetch Red Sandy and Sim's Will out of gaol, and so he's gonnae buy a big load of guns off him. He's going out to Lochmaben to get them."

"Where is he getting the money from?" Roger Widdrington asked.

"I wouldnae ken that," said Hutchin.

"Did he bring it with him?"

"Nay, he couldn't have, he had to pawn some rings for travelling money, or so Red Sandy said. He's got it here in Dumfries but who knows how?"

"Anything to do with the Italian woman he's been paying court to?"

Hutchin's face became so craftily noncommittal, Roger almost laughed.

"I wouldnae ken. Any road, I must go. Will ye tell my lady that she mustnae put too much on the Italian woman, he couldnae help it for she all but flung herself at his head."

Roger nodded gravely, not trusting himself to speak, and paid the boy a shilling. He had heard different but there was no reason to argue. He watched Hutchin Graham hurry away to find a pie-seller and as soon as he was safely out of sight, he went back to report to his father.

◇◇◇

Signor Bonnetti fully expected the Deputy Warden never to reappear again, but to his astonishment he was back within the hour, slightly flushed and looking very pleased with himself.

"They are in wagons in the forest, five miles northeast of Dumfries," he explained. "Would you like to come and inspect them, Signor Bonnetti?"

Bonnetti had the feeling of being watched as he rode on the mean little soft-footed long-coated mare behind Carey and his young golden-haired pageboy. His heart had not yet stilled its thumping: the Englishman could simply be inveigling him out to the forest the better to put a knife in him, though the King's protection might possibly help him...No, not in a forest. But if what this cousin of the Queen of England said was right, then Giovanni Bonnetti had done what he had set out to do and might even see Rome again by the end of the year. Assuming the shipment to Ireland went well...

The wagons full of armaments were in a clearing under guard by some Scots wearing their native padded jacks—miserably poor as they were, they could not afford breastplates. Carey was in a jocular mood: he made some incomprehensible comment as he handed over a letter and a ring as identification to one of the thugs who greeted them and the man laughed shortly.

Giovanni examined the guns. They seemed well enough, but then you never knew unless you fired one.

"Fire this one for me, monsieur," he said to Carey in French.

"What about the noise?"

Giovanni shrugged. "I will certainly not buy any weapons without seeing at least one of them fired first."

Carey bowed, loaded and primed the caliver with long fingers that seemed slightly clumsy about it, borrowed slowmatch from one of the men and lit the gun's match. It hissed, lighting his face eerily from below.

"What shall I shoot?" he asked.

"The knot in the middle of that oak over there."

Carey smiled a little tightly, raised the caliver to his shoulder, brought it down and fired.

Giovanni went to inspect the hole left by the bullet while Carey cleaned the gun. The long fingers were shaking again, which reassured Giovanni: it was right and proper for a man probably committing high treason out of greed to be nervous.

"Good," he said, coming back. "It fires a little to the left, I see."

"Perhaps my aim was off."

"You are modest, monsieur."

Giovanni took the caliver, which was still hot, examined the pan and the barrel and then nodded.

"The shape of the stock is unusual," he said. "Almost a German fashion."

"I understand that some Germans work for the Dumfries armourers," said Carey.

"And this is from Dumfries?"

"Indirectly."

Giovanni waited for further explanation on the guns' provenance and got none.

"Well, monsieur," said Carey politely. "Are you satisfied, or shall I fire another?"

Giovanni went over to the wagon, pulled out a pistol, looked it over and put it back. He did the same with a number of the other weapons. They seemed well enough.

"No," he said. "I am satisfied."

In fact, although he was pulling out guns and looking at them, flicking the locks and squinting down the barrels, in his relief Bonnetti was thinking far ahead, about the next stage. He would have the weapons greased and packed in winebarrels for the journey on barges down the River Nith to Glencaple where he had a small ship lying ready. Given God's grace (which surely would be forthcoming for such a noble cause) he would cross the narrow sea to Ireland in two stages, stopping off at the Isle of Man. Providing he met no English or Irish or Scots pirates, and the weather was calm and the ship sprang no leaks, he might be back in a month or so, God willing.

Carey confirmed the legendary reputation of the English for avarice in the way he dickered over the hiring fee for the wagons to take the guns into Dumfries. The Lord Maxwell was even willing to furnish guards and men to help load the weapons on barges, again for a fee. It would have to be done that night, Carey said, for there were no guarantees and the King himself might well decide to confiscate the weapons if he heard what was happening, since he had need of them too. At last it was all agreed and Giovanni was the proud possessor of eighteen dozen assorted guns which he could now send to the O'Neill in Ireland. He felt quite light-headed with the relief of it. And he also had a valuable lever to use against the noble English official who had sold him the weapons: as the Englishman mounted up and rode away, Giovanni was already framing the letters he would send to his brother in London and to the King of Spain in his palace at San Lorenzo and thinking about how he would return to this miserable northern country next year and begin to apply a little pressure. Dodd was still awake in a corner of Maxwell's hall when Carey finally returned, although it was well past sunset and he was yawning fit to crack his jaw. He had spent an uncomfortable and tense day cooped up in the crowded house, finding that whatever he did and wherever he went, two large Maxwell cousins went with him. At any moment he expected an order to be given and himself hustled into some small cell and the door locked. It would almost be a relief, he tried to convince himself, because then at least he would know where he stood. But he knew too much about the accidents that could happen to any man held hostage by a Border lord, and he knew as well that there was nothing he could do to help himself. He had to rely on Carey finding some way to mollify Lord Maxwell and pay him off, and for the life of him he didn't see how that was possible.

In the end, he had taken refuge from being followed and watched by sitting in a corner of the hall, next to Maxwell's plateboard set with gold and silver dishes, put his feet up on the bench and started whittling a toy out of a piece of firewood.

As it happened, Carey came in with Lord Maxwell himself, both of them laughing uproariously over some joke and Maxwell at least quite drunk. There was much backslapping and bonhomie: Dodd wondered if the Courtier could tell how false it sounded, but he looked drunk as well. Maxwell disappeared through the door into his parlour, shouting for meat and drink.

Dodd examined the little fighting bear he had nearly finished and kept his feet on the bench. Carey came over to him, humming a court tune, while Hutchin trailed yawning over to the fire, kicked himself a space amongst the pageboys and curled up into sleep like a puppy.

"Well?" asked Dodd grimly.

"My lord Maxwell is quite happy now," said Carey with a bright smile, checking the silver jugs next to Dodd. He found some aqua vitae in one and drank it straight down.

"Whit about Red Sandy and Sim's Will?"

"They can stay the night in the lock-up to teach them sense but my lord Maxwell says he'll bail them tomorrow morning and we can leave whenever we want."

Well, it sounded promising, if you could trust a Scottish baron, which personally Dodd didn't believe possible.

"How did ye do it, sir?"

"Acted as an honest broker and found a buyer for Maxwell's scrap iron."

"Who?"

Carey smiled and tapped his nose like a southern coney-catcher.

"Ahah."

By God, he's full of himself, thought Dodd, and what poor unfortunate bastard did he persuade to buy the damned things? The Johnstones? The King?

"Ye didnae sell them to the Johnstones?" Dodd asked in dismay. They had to pass through Johnstone land to get home and he could imagine the vengefulness of that clan if a few of their number had had their hands blown off.

Carey tutted at him and sat down beside him on the bench. "No, of course not. In any case, I think it's the laird Johnstone that made the original swap for the Tower weapons. I've heard he's well-armed which is what panicked Maxwell into stripping Carlisle bare."

"Nay, I dinnae think so, sir." Dodd was shaking his head as he thought it through. "The Johnstones have been well-armed for a month or more. That's why Maxwell hasnae taken them on yet."

"It's what I heard, anyway. You can rest easy, the guns won't be staying in Scotland or England to plague us." He laughed and drank some more Scottish aqua vitae. "They've gone to the best people for them and I've made enough on the deal to pay you and the men next month."

What the hell did he mean by that? Who could he...The Italian lady? He'd sold wagonloads of firearms to a Papist? Good God, he couldn't be such a fool. Surely? Yes, he could, came the despairing thought, because when you put Carey under pressure, there was no telling what he might suddenly decide to do.

"Are ye drunk, sir?" asked Dodd pointedly. "Because if ye arenae, ye're plainly tired of life and it'd be a kindness to put a dagger in ye."

"Lord, Sergeant, what's your problem? You've come over all prim."

"Prim, sir, is it? Ye've just sold the entire load of Carlisle's weapons tae the Italian wine merchant that any fool can see must be working for the King of Spain and..."

"What the hell do you think we were going to do with them? Take them back to Carlisle? Use them?"

It was disgraceful. "And which poor creature did ye get to fire one of the bloody things?"

"Me."

Dodd shook his head and finished the last of the beer. "Ye're mad, sir," he told Carey flatly. "Ye think ye're being ower clever, but ye're no'. Ye cannae deal weapons wi' a foreigner like that, especially not a Papist, it's treason. And why did my lord Maxwell not deal with 'em direct, eh?"

"Didn't have time to think of it. He only knew the weapons were bad this morning."

"Time enough, I'd say. He was the one brung the foreigners here to Scotland, he could have done the deal hisself and not lost any of the gold to ye. Did ye think he's too stupid? Nay, he's too clever..."

"I don't remember asking your opinion, Sergeant." Carey's voice was cold, perhaps a little slurred. How much booze had he put down his throat in the twenty-four hours or more since his interview with the King of Scotland? It wasn't that he was reeling or even unsteady, only he must be more affected by it than he seemed, to have pulled a mad dangerous trick like this one, full of the ugly scent of treason and trickery.

"Ay, sir," said Dodd. "Nor ye didnae, but if I see a man riding full pelt for a cliff edge, I wouldnae be human if I didnae call out to him."

Carey was rechecking the jugs, and doomed to disappointment. "Oh, rubbish, Sergeant. I thought you'd be more grateful to me for rescuing your idiot brother from gaol and you from being a hostage. Where else was I going to get the money to calm Lord Maxwell down? Rob the King's bloody treasury?" Carey grinned again. He was irrepressibly and ludicrously pleased with his own cleverness. "Mind you," he added. "That's a thought, isn't it? I'll bet His Majesty's got his funds in a chest under his bed at the Mayor's house guarded by naught bar a couple of bumboys."

Dodd for one did not see why he had to sit there and watch the Courtier preen. With sudden decision he removed his boots from the bench, put away his nearly-formed chunk of firewood and stood up. "I'm for my bed," he said. "I cannae keep court hours. Goodnight to ye, sir."

"Goodnight, Sergeant," said Carey.

"Are we tae go back to Carlisle the morrow?"

"No, Sergeant, we haven't finished yet."

"And why the hell not?"

"Don't take that tone with me, Sergeant. I appreciate you disapprove of what I've done and frankly I don't care. But you can talk to me civilly or not at all."

Dodd grunted. He struggled for self-control because as often happened, the loquacious little devil inside him was in a good mind to give the Courtier a mouthful and see how he liked it. But Dodd had paid thirty pounds English for the Sergeantship and he knew his wife wanted the investment back: the truth was, he was more afraid of his woman than he was inclined to give the Deputy a punch in the mouth, a fact which made him feel even more tired than he already was.

"Why have we no' finished, sir?" Dodd said after a moment, with heavy politeness.

"We haven't retrieved the true Carlisle handguns from the Johnstones yet, Sergeant, the ones the Queen really sent us from the Tower armouries, and we're not going until we do. Goodnight to you."

## friday 14th july 1592, before dawn

If Sir Henry Widdrington had ever been priest-hunting with one of Sir Francis Walsingham's men, things would have gone very differently, Carey often thought afterwards. Unlike the priest-finders, the Widdringtons had not properly scouted their target nor forewarned their helpers.

It was the shouting and ruddy light of torches in the black of the night that propelled Young Hutchin Graham out of his sleep by the fire. He ran to the window and squinted through stained glass to look out into the yard. The Maxwell guards were arguing with a square-shaped gentleman, hatted and ruffed and standing outlined in the open postern gate. There was a flash of white paper; the ominous phrase *In the King's name* floated to Hutchin's ears. Lord Maxwell himself and two of his cousins hurried through the dim hall, fully dressed and armed, to meet the men at the gate.

It suddenly occurred to Hutchin that he might have been a little too trusting of Roger Widdrington.

"Och, God, no," he moaned, turned and sprinted through the parlour and up the spiral stairs to Lord Maxwell's solar and through from there into the anteroom that had been given to Carey. The two enormous wolfhounds that he was sharing it with woke up and growled at him, and Carey himself sat up, blinking.

"What is it?"

"Sir, sir, I'm sorry, I thought it was Lady Widdrington, not Sir Henry."

"What? What are you blabbering about? And what the Devil's that noise?"

Hutchin swallowed hard and fought for control. "It's Sir Henry Widdrington, Deputy. He's got a Royal Warrant to arrest someone."

There was the sound of the gate bolts being opened.

Noticeably, Carey didn't ask who the warrant was for. His eyes narrowed to chips of ice.

"You've been passing information about my doings."

"Ay, sir," Hutchin confessed miserably. "To Roger Widdrington. I thought it was for my lady. That's what he said."

Carey was out of bed now, peering through the narrow window into the yard where Sir Henry and a large number of men were marching across between the horses and men camping out there, towards the hall door.

"You halfwitted romantic twat," said Carey, feeling under his shirt and unbuckling a moneybelt. "Pull up your doublet and shirt."

Mouth open, Hutchin did as he was told. Carey strapped it onto him, where it went round twice.

"Och, it's heavy, sir," said Young Hutchin Graham, waking up rather more and now beginning to take on a canny expression.

"It's gold and a banker's draft."

"Christ."

"Don't swear. Come with me."

Carey led the boy out into Maxwell's solar where there was a trapdoor let into the ceiling. He hauled a linen chest underneath, stood on it, opened the bolts, shoved back the trapdoor and then boosted Young Hutchin up into the dark spaces above.

"What's happening, sir?" Young Hutchin asked, kneeling at the edge of the hole. "Where does this go?"

"There'll be an escape route via the roof, no doubt. I never heard of a Border lord yet that didn't have one. Use it."

"What about ye, sir?"

"Thanks to you, I think I'm about to be arrested by the King of Scotland."

"But can ye not come with me?"

"Use your head, Hutchin. This is Maxwell's bolthole. It's me they're after, and if I'm not here, his lordship will know where I've gone and they'll catch both of us. Whereas nobody's interested in you."

"Och, Jesus, sir. Will they hang ye?"

"Certainly not. Being of noble blood, I've a right to ask for beheading. Here, catch this ring."

"Whit d'ye want me tae do, sir?"

"You've a choice, haven't you? You could go to Dodd if he's still at liberty, or try and see Lady Elizabeth Widdrington, herself, in person this time and not through intermediaries. Show her the ring and ask for her help. She might even give it."

"Or?"

"Or you could pelt off to your cousins and run for the Debateable Land with the gold that's in that belt. Which might be safer for you in the short term."

Young Hutchin said nothing.

Young Hutchin silently scrabbled at the heavy trap and put it back in its hole. Carey scrubbed the fingermarks off with his shirtsleeve, jumped down, pushed the chest back against the wall, kicked the rucked-up rushes about a bit and ran back to his anteroom, shutting and bolting the door behind him while the dogs milled around him looking puzzled, and the tramp of boots echoed on the spiral stair. First one and then both of the wolfhounds began to bark and growl menacingly, standing to face the door with their hackles up and their teeth bared. Carey patted them both affectionately. If he had wanted to make a fight of it, they would have given their lives for him, but he saw no point in that.

There's nothing like a bolted door to please a searcher, old Mr Phelippes had told him once, it is so exactly the kind of thing one is looking for. Also the bolt gave Carey time to pull on his hose and boots, before the end of it cracked out of the doorjamb to the multiple kicking. He faced Sir Henry Widdrington and about five other Widdringtons with his sword in his hand. The wolfhounds began baying like the Wild Hunt.

"What in the name of God is going on?" he demanded over the noise.

Sir Henry Widdrington had a loaded wheellock dag in one hand and an official-looking paper in the other. He hobbled forwards a few paces on his swollen gouty feet, his face turned to a gargoyle's by the torches and deep personal satisfaction. Like a town crier he read out the terms of the warrant in a booming tone.

From behind him Lord Maxwell called his dogs to him and they stopped barking, looked very puzzled, whined sadly at Carey and padded out to their master. Maxwell then, rather pointedly, left.

All was perfectly legal: the King of Scotland had made out a warrant for the arrest on a charge of high treason and trafficking with enemies of the realms of both Scotland and England (nice touch) of one Sir Robert Carey.

"Let me see the seal," said Carey.

"You're not suggesting, I hope, that I would forge the King's Warrant?" said Sir Henry.

"Lord above, Sir Henry, I wouldn't put anything past you." Carey was still holding out his left hand for the warrant, his sword en garde between them. Sir Henry reddened and swelled like a frog, then shrugged and gave it to him, the dag's muzzle not moving an inch from the direction of Carey's heart. Carey wondered how much insolence it would take from him for the weapon to go off unexpectedly and shoot him dead. Also the seal was genuine.

Carey handed back the warrant and laid his sword down on the truckle bed. He was immediately grabbed by four of Widdrington's henchmen and his arms twisted painfully up behind his back, which started to make him angry as well as afraid.

"I've surrendered to you, Sir Henry," he managed to say through his teeth. "There's no need for this."

Sir Henry answered with a punch in Carey's belly which almost had him spewing up the sour remains of the aqua vitae he had drunk earlier.

"Ye chose the wrong man to put the horns on, boy," hissed Sir Henry in his ear as he tried to straighten up. "Any more lip from ye an' I'll send ye to the King with your tackle mashed to pulp."

Carey didn't answer because he hadn't got the breath. Somebody was putting wooden manacles on his wrists behind him, some kind of primitive portable stocks.

They propelled him downstairs and through the parlour where Maxwell was standing with his men, watching impassively. Over his shoulder, Carey called to him, "I don't know what I've done to deserve this from you, my lord Warden."

Maxwell shrugged and looked away, which was not worth the further fist in the gut administered by Sir Henry.

Widdrington's keeping away from my face, Carey thought, when he could think again, which means he's been ordered to bring me in unharmed. That's good. Or is it? Perhaps King James just wants a fresh field for his interrogators to start work on. No, they're not that subtle.

It was hard to keep his feet as they shoved him along, through the hall, through the courtyard now filled with sleepy watchers, and out into the Town Head. One of the Widdringtons held him up when he missed his footing on the cobbles and would have sprawled full length. Carey caught a glimpse of looming breadth and heroic spottiness and recognised young Henry, Widdrington's eldest son. Henry was wearing a steady flush and a sullen expression and kept his head turned away from Carey's as he helped him.

They were hustling him on foot down towards the Mercat Cross and the town lock-up, but that was not where they were going. Instead, before they reached it, Sir Henry and his men turned and went under the arcades of the Mayor's house, through the side door and into the broad kitchen. There a baker was firing his oven and woodmen beginning the work of relighting the fires on the hearths for cooking, while the older scullery boys still slept near the heat and the flagstones gleamed from washing by the yawning younger ones.

Next to the massive table in the centre, under the hams and strings of onions dangling from the roof, Carey tried to slow down, turn, demand to know what the hell was going on here. Somebody, not young Henry, grabbed his shirt and shoved him forwards, causing him to skid on the wet stones and land on his side, which winded him once more. Until his eyes unblurred it was confusing: a whirl of flames from the main hearth and the bread-oven, and men with hard faces, but at least nobody had kicked him while he was on the ground. He got his feet under him and stood up with some difficulty.

"Keep yer mouth shut," hissed Sir Henry Widdrington, dag at the ready once more.

And yet, Carey still had the feeling that this was cautious handling: certainly they had not been so gentle with the German. Once more he was grabbed by the shoulders and hurried across the kitchen and into a dark passageway. Yes, there was a sense of furtiveness and hurry, definitely. Surely this was far less official than it appeared? Or why use an English gentleman for the dirty work? King James might be short of loyal soldiers, but any one of his nobles would have been highly delighted to arrest and ill-treat an English official.

They went down stairs echoing with the clatter of boots and his own heavy breathing, into another narrow corridor that smelled headily of wine. A massive iron-bound door was unlocked, swung briefly open and somebody, Sir Henry no doubt, booted him into the opening. He stumbled on the slippery bits of straw on the floor and barked his shoulder as he rammed into the opposite wall. The door slammed shut immediately to a clashing of keys and bolts, leaving him in a darkness that put him in doubt whether his eyes were open or shut. The smell of wine permeated everything, so strong it made his head reel almost at once, though there was another less pleasant smell mixed in with it.

Carey set his back against the wall he had hit and caught his breath. For a while all he could hear was the beating of his own heart and the air in his own throat. Then gradually his nose told him what the other smell was: there was someone else in the wine cellar, someone who had been there for some time. For a moment he was afraid it was a corpse and then he made out the other man's harsh breathing.

"Who's there?" he asked tentatively.

A kind of moan, nothing more.

"Well, where are you?"

This time, a kind of grunt. How badly injured was he? Had the other man been tortured? Or was he a plant of the kind that Walsingham had used to get information from Catholics in prison?

Wishing he had the use of his hands, Carey began shuffling cautiously across the wine cellar from one wall to the other, trying to learn its geography. The huge wine tuns were in a row by the furthest wall, with smaller barrels set at random on the floor, lying in wait so he could stub his toes and bark his shins on them. Sawdust and straw on the floor to soak up spillage, cool dampness and that maddening Dionysian smell. At last his feet struck something soft and he squatted down. More incomprehensible muttering. What the Devil was wrong with the man?

On impulse Carey tried the few words of High Dutch that he knew: "Wie sind sie?"

Silence and then the sound of soft sobbing. "Oh, Christ," said Carey, suddenly understanding almost everything. "You're the German—what was it—you're Hans Schmidt? Das ist Ihre Name, ja?"

"Jawohl."

"What the hell did they do to you?"

A high whining, choked with sobs.

For a while, Carey was too sickened and depressed to do more than sit uncomfortably on the damp straw beside the German. Somewhere at the back of his mind a large and complicated structure was forming to explain all that had been going on, but what he was mainly conscious of was the fact that the chill of the wine cellar was cutting through his shirt and giving him goosepimples, he was already dizzy from the fumes, his stomach hurt and so did his shoulder, and that whatever was left of the man beside him was weeping its heart out.

"All right," said Carey awkwardly at last, as if talking to a horse gone lame. "All right now. Ich…er…ich help sie."

Sniffling, coughing, thick swallowing, well, there was at least enough of the German's pride for him to try and get a grip on himself. And this was no plant: none of that kind of crew were good enough actors. Carey deliberately pulled his thoughts away from what might have happened to the unfortunate foreigner. He couldn't find out anyway, with his hands bolted behind him. The rough wooden shackle hanging on his wristbones was already causing his fingers to prickle and tingle painfully.

"All right," he said pointlessly again. "I'm Sir Robert Carey, Deputy Warden of Carlisle. It seems we share an enemy. I want to talk to you. Ich will mit sie sprache."

There was something a little like a bitter laugh. "Nonsense," Carey snapped. "If it's too hard to talk, just grunt. Give one grunt for yes, two grunts for no and three for I don't know. Eins fur ja, swei fur nein, drei fur ich kenne nicht. Ja?"

"Ja."

So far, so good, thought Carey, shifting his back up against the wall again and trying to get his legs comfortable. He wished with all his heart he spoke more German, or the German more English. Though from the mushy sounds next to him he suspected the man was having to talk out of a mouthful of broken teeth. "Now, do you understand French? Sprechen sie Franzosich?"

"Oui. Meilleur qu'anglais."

"Thank God," said Carey, mentally switching gears into that language. "Alors, parlons nous."

◇◇◇

Young Hutchin sat in Maxwell's loft with his arms wrapped round his knees and watched the rats watching him in the light squeezing up through the ceiling boards from the candles and lanterns below. The cold heavy belt wrapped round his waist was warming up. In his imagination he saw the gold there, thick heavy roundels of it, straight from Spain, stamped with letters he could not read and, no doubt, a few with bite marks in them. He had seen gold when his father had had a good raid, he knew what it looked like and what it could buy.

Below him and to the right there were bangs and thumps and talk. Sir Henry and his men were searching Carey's sleeping place for the gold, but although Hutchin could feel his heart beating hard and slow, he was less afraid than excited. Hiding from searchers was something he had done many times after thieving; it was only a matter of staying still and silent. He had already taken the precaution of putting one of the main roof beams between himself and the trapdoor, in case someone should come up for a look, treading softly and carefully over the narrow boards while Carey argued with Sir Henry below. He could see an escape route where the slates were loose on one side. Picturing the building in his mind, he thought it was at a point on the roof where there was a way down to the roof of the bowling alley and from there to the ground. Or he could go down through the trapdoor when the men below had given up and gone. After that, once out of Maxwell's Castle—there were horses aplenty in the town, or he could find his cousins on foot, an unremarked boy among dozens in Dumfries. And then...

Young Hutchin shook his head with exasperation. The Courtier had somehow caught him neatly in a trap of words and loyalty. What had he said, after outlining precisely the things Hutchin could do? He had said the choice was Hutchin's. No hint there of which he should choose, only the bald stating of it. And yet, Young Hutchin knew perfectly well that the Deputy Warden would be hoping he would find Dodd or Lady Widdrington and get him out of whatever dungeon the Scottish King had thrown him in. What could they do? Ransom him perhaps with the gold around Hutchin's middle. Jesus, what a waste of a fortune.

Hutchin bit his lip, weighing up his choices. If he ran off, he was as good as killing the Deputy, or worse. He had heard the words of the warrant through the ceiling boards, the ugly frightening phrase 'high treason'. Sir Henry Widdrington had read it out loudly enough. They did worse than hang you for high treason, he knew, though he had never seen it done. They hanged you first, then they took you down while you were still alive, cut off your cods and burned them in your face and slit your belly and pulled out your guts and then cut you in four bits like a woman making a chicken stew. He had heard tell that if the hangman wasn't bribed beforehand, he'd let you down before you were more than a little blue and then...Hutchin had seen hangings and more than his share of men dying, but his imagination balked at this. It was true, he had a morbid curiosity to see it done at least once, and envied the apprentice boys in Edinburgh who had more of a chance, but not to the Courtier. He liked the Courtier, soft southerner though he was, and after all, Carey had come after Hutchin when he had been inveigled away from the stables by the young man in tawny taffeta. Carey had appeared at the upstairs window like an avenging angel, while Hutchin was fighting and dodging for his life, had climbed through, punched one of the men and kicked another, giving Hutchin the chance to bite the other man holding him and head-butt a fourth. That had been a good fight, though Hutchin personally would have liked to see Carey's sword bloodied instead of merely used as a threat.

Never mind, the fact was he had been there as if he were an uncle or an elder brother or something, not just a southern courtier. And Young Hutchin had repaid him by spying for his enemy, Sir Henry Widdrington. That annoyed Hutchin profoundly. He had been taken like a wean by Roger Widdrington, he had naively believed the tale about Lady Widdrington, *him*—Hutchin Graham, most promising son of the canniest surname on the Border. It was infuriating and shaming. And hardly a word had Carey said to curse him for it, though he was facing arrest by the very man he had no doubt horned, and plainly due to Hutchin's treason. And now Young Hutchin had the means of freeing him. Or not.

God damn it, thought Hutchin, they were still turning over Carey's room, what the Devil's taking them so long? Do they not know how to find good loot in a room? Stupid bastards. He started to pick his teeth with his fingernail. Perhaps he'd be here all night. Perhaps by the time they had finished, the King's men would have broken Carey's long legs in the Boot and put him out of hope of ever walking again. Perhaps after a session with Scottish torturers, he would prefer to die, even by hanging, drawing and quartering?

Young Hutchin was getting tired of thinking. He realised that at last the thumps and bangs had stopped. Still moving cautiously, he picked his way through rat droppings and ancient clothes chests to the loose slates and pulled a few out. There was a gutter that seemed firm enough. The curve of the roof hid him from the yard where

Widdrington's men were gathering. With painful slowness he eeled his way out through the small hole and lay full length on the roof, gripping with the toes of his boots and his fingers. He inched his way down until his foot met the edge of the leads, and he could rest his weight on it a little and go sideways to the place where the roof of the bowling alley joined the main building. Although this was a fortified town house, there was no roof platform here for standing siege, only some crenellations and elaborate chimneys, more for show than for use, and a nuisance to climb over.

The bowling alley roof was newer and had no crenellations. At least it was at a flatter pitch and by lying full length and gripping the ridge with his arms at full stretch he could inch himself along and so gain the change from shingle to thatch where the stables began. Arm muscles bulging at the extra weight round his middle, Hutchin let himself down off the bowling alley roof by means of the gutter, watching the pinnings creak and pop. He dropped onto the thatch before the whole lot could come away. The thatch was rotten and he actually went part way through, his feet dangling sickeningly in space, his hands grabbing at one of the cross-ties. A couple of horses whinnied and snorted below.

"Och, the hell with it," Young Hutchin said to himself, knowing the stables were only one storey high, and he let go of the cross-tie and let himself slide through and rolled into the thick straw between two alarmed horses. Brushing straw and reeds off himself he calmed the animals down, patting them and swearing at them gently under his breath, until he felt the iron prod of a sword in his back and stopped dead.

"Stealing horses again, eh, Young Hutchin?"

"Sergeant Dodd," said Young Hutchin, his stomach lurching back from his throat with relief.

"Ay. And ye woke me up, ye little bastard."

The sound of a yawn followed this, so Hutchin cautiously turned about. Sergeant Dodd had bits of straw in his hair and his eyes full of sleep. The hand not holding a sword was scratching fleabites on his stomach and his foul temper in the mornings was legendary.

"It's a pity the men in the yard didnae do the like then," Hutchin said in a triumphant hiss. "Sir Henry Widdrington just came with a Royal Warrant and arrested the Deputy Warden."

The sword didn't move, but Dodd blinked slightly. He moved to one of the half doors, still keeping his sword pointed at Hutchin, opened it a fraction and looked out. He was just in time to see the last Widdringtons leave the yard and the Maxwells on guard shut the gate behind them.

"What was the charge?" asked Dodd after a moment's pause.

"High treason and...er...trafficking with enemies."

Dodd whitened and looked out into the empty yard again.

"I told him," he muttered. "I told the fool."

"Ye mean it's true?" asked Hutchin, impressed. "Is the bill foul then?"

"Near enough."

"Jesus. What shall we do, Sergeant?"

Dodd appeared to be thinking while he stared at Hutchin. Hutchin hoped very much that the Sergeant wouldn't notice the thickening round his middle.

"Well, we canna rescue the Courtier this time by calling out the Dodds or even the Grahams," he said with finality. "This is official business. Who was it came to arrest him?"

"Sir Henry Widdrington and his kin."

"Was it now? That's odd."

Hutchin Graham nodded. "And they were in an awful hurry and it didn't sound like they knocked him about much."

"How did you get away?"

"The Courtier put me up under the roof through the trapdoor when he heard them and gave me this to take to Lady Widdrington." Hutchin showed him the ring on his thumb which he had been admiring for the size of its red stone and the letters of some kind carved in it. "Is it a ruby, d'ye think?"

"Ay, no doubt."

"What are the letters?"

"RC for Robert Carey," answered Dodd at once, impressing Young Hutchin for the first time with his clerkly knowledge. "Did he give ye anything else?" Dodd asked casually. Hutchin shook his head. "They've got it then," he said sadly.

"Got what?" asked Hutchin with artful ignorance.

"Nothing to concern ye, lad. Come on."

"Where to?"

"Out of here first, and out of the town too. I dinna want to end up in the Dumfries hole with the Courtier."

Hutchin shook his head. "I'm for going to Lady Widdrington," he heard himself say. "That's what the Courtier wanted me to do, and that's what I'll do."

"Ye'll come with me, lad."

"Where are you going?"

Dodd thought for a moment. "If the Maxwells are agin ye, who's most like to back ye?" he asked rhetorically. Hutchin nodded. It made sense to try the Johnstones. "Do you know a good way out of this place? Is there a garden gate?"

Hutchin thought about this professionally. "I heard tell from one of the other boys there's a way by the new bowling alley, that Maxwell had built from the old monastery stone. The wall there's nobbut the monastery wall and they werenae too choosy how they treated it."

Dodd nodded. "If I can make it back to Carlisle, we'll get the Warden to write to the King and see if we can ransom him out of there."

Hutchin's face twisted. "That's nae good," he said. "Once it goes to the Warden, then he's done for one way or the other, for the Queen will hear of it."

Dodd had put on his jack and his helmet, giving him the familiar comforting silhouette of a fighting man, though the quilting on the leather was different from the Graham pattern. Now he was busy bundling up the shape of a man in the corner where he had been sleeping, out of straw and his cloak.

"Lad," said Dodd gravely, almost kindly, "we cannae spring the Courtier out of the King's prison."

"Why not? Ye saved him from my uncle when he was trapped on Netherby tower."

"That was different. Your uncle's one thing, the King's another."

"I dinnae see why," said Hutchin stubbornly. "They're both men that have other men to do their bidding, only the King's got more."

"That's enough, Young Hutchin. We canna rescue the Courtier again because...Anyway, what can a woman do about it?"

"He wanted me to take the ring to Lady Widdrington, so he must think she can do something. And that..." said Hutchin virtuously, the decision somehow made for him by Dodd's opposition, "...is what I'll do, come ye or any man agin me."

He slipped under the horse's belly and whisked to the rear door that led to the midden heap. Sword still in his hand, Dodd didn't try to stop him, so Hutchin checked that the backyard was clear and the Maxwells were watching outwards, and then turned again to the Sergeant with an impish grin.

"He gets in a powerful lot of trouble, doesn't he?" he said. "For a Deputy Warden."

"Ay."

# friday 14th july 1592, dawn

Elizabeth Widdrington always woke well before dawn to rise in the darkness and say her prayers. In the tiny Dumfries alehouse where they were lodging, it was easier for her to do it: firstly her husband had been out much of the night and had not been there to disturb her sleep with his snoring and moaning and occasional ineffectual fumbling. Secondly the new belting he had given her on top of the old ones the night before had kept her from sleeping very well in any case.

Fastening her stays was always the hardest part, as she pulled the laces up tight and the whalebone bit into the welts and bruises, but once that was done they paradoxically gave her support and armour. None of her clothes fastened fashionably at the back, since she did not like to be dependent on a lady's maid, and so it was the work of a few minutes to tie on her bumroll, step into her kirtle and hook up the side of her bodice. She had changed the sleeves the night before and half-pinned her best embroidered stomacher to it and so once her cap was on her head she was respectable enough to meet the King if necessary.

She knelt to pray, composing her mind, firmly putting out of it her swallowed fury at her husband since it was, after all, according to all authority, his right to beat her if she displeased him, just as he could beat his horses. She worked to concentrate on the love and mercy of Our Lord Jesus Christ.

After a few minutes she said the Lord's Prayer and stood up: it was hopeless and always happened. She couldn't keep her mind on anything higher than the top of Robert Carey's head. Since the age of seventeen she had been married to Sir Henry, happy as the fourth, gawky and dowryless Trevannion daughter to travel on the promise of marriage from the lushness of Cornwall to the bare bones of the north. Everything had been arranged through the Lord Chamberlain, Lord Hunsdon, as a kindness to one of his wife's many kin. She had gone knowing perfectly well that her husband-to-be was gouty and in his fifties but determined to do her best to be a good wife to him, as God required of her. She had tried, failed and kept trying because there was no alternative. And then, seven miserable years later in 1587 the youngest son of that same Lord Hunsdon had spent weeks at Widdrington, waiting to be allowed to enter Scotland with his letter from the Queen of England which tried to explain to King James how Mary Queen of Scots had so unfortunately come to be executed. Robin had ridden south again at last, the message delivered by proxy, and she had wept bitter tears in her wet larder, where she could blame it on brine and onions. And then there had been the nervous plotting with her friend, his sister Philadelphia Scrope, so she could travel down to London the next year, the Armada year of 1588, and the year that shone golden in her memory, with Robert Carey the bright alarming jewel at its centre. But she had kept her honour, just. Only by the narrowest squeak of scruples on several occasions, true, but she had kept it.

Four years later she was still as much of a fool as ever, still burned to her core by nothing more than a glimpse of him caught as she dismounted in the street. She had accepted punishment from her husband for her loan to Robin of his horses the previous month, accepted it because ordained by God. But to be beaten for no more than a look, accused unjustly of cuckolding her husband and nothing she said believed...

I am wasting my time, she thought, trying to be firm. Besides, Robin has very properly abandoned his suit to me, look at how he was paying court to Signora Bonnetti...

Her stomach suddenly knotted up with bile and misery. How could he so publicly abandon me, he did not even try to speak to me at the dance the day before yesterday? (Ridiculous, of course he wouldn't, Sir Henry was standing guard over me.) How could he dance with the vulgar little Italian in her whore's crimson gown? (Whyever should he not, since he could not dance with me?) How could he disappear into the garden with her and what had he done there...(What business is it of mine, what he did, and do I really want to know?) How *could* he, the bastard, *how could he*...?

I will go for a walk outside, Elizabeth Widdrington said to herself, and escape this ridiculous vapouring. Anyone would think I was a maid of fifteen. I will not allow myself to hate Robin Carey for doing exactly as I told him to in my letter (*bastard!*).

She slipped her pattens on her feet and ducked out of the little alehouse. It had been very crowded with her husband's kin, various cousins and tenants but now the place seemed half-empty. Her step-son Henry was lying asleep on one of the tables with his cloak huddled up round his ears, his pebbled face endearingly relaxed. He seemed to get broader every time she looked at him: his father's squareness reproduced but almost doubled in size. Roger was nowhere to be seen. Because she was looking for sadness, she found more there. She had brought them up as well as she could and now they were growing away from her, abandoning her for their father's influence.

Stop that, she commanded herself and walked briskly down the wynd that led behind the alehouse, past a couple of tents filled with more of King James's soldiers, past three drunks lying clutching each other in the gutter, whether in affection or some half-hearted battle, past the jakes and the chickens and the pigpen and the shed where the goat was being milked, into the other wynd and back down the other side of the alehouse. Inside she still found no sign of her husband or half his men and climbed the stairs.

A boy was sitting swinging his legs on the sagging trucklebed she had been using, a rather handsome boy with cornflower blue eyes and a tangled greasy mop of straight blond hair, the beginnings of adult bone lengthening his jaw already. Despite his magnificent black eye, she recognised him at once.

"Is it Young…Young Hutchin?"

The boy stood up, made a sketchy bow and handed over a small piece of jewellery. It was a man's signet ring with a great red stone in the centre, carved…Robert Carey had shown it to her at court.

The scene burst into her mind's eye, the Queen's Privy Garden at Westminster in 1588, the clipped box hedges and the wooden seat under the walnut tree, Robin peacock-bright in turquoise taffeta and black velvet, the day before he rode south with George Cumberland to sneak aboard the English fleet and go to fight the Spanish. "If ever you see this away from my hand," he had said in the overly dramatic style of the court, "then I am in trouble and need your help. Do not fail, my lady, I will need you to storm and take the Tower of London, for the Queen will have thrown me into gaol for loving you better than I love her." She had laughed at him, but she had also shown him the small handfasting ring with the diamond in the middle that had been her sole legacy from her mother, and told him the same thing. That had been one of her narrower escapes from dishonour, she had rashly let him kiss her that time.

So she took the ring, her heart beating slow and hard. She examined it carefully for blood or any other sign of having been cut from a dead hand, sat down on the bed with it clasped over her thumb and looked at Young Hutchin.

"What's happened to him?" she asked as calmly as she could.

He told her the tale quite well, with not too many diversions and only a small amount of exaggeration about how he had climbed from a roof. So that was what her husband had been up to all night. She made Young Hutchin go through the whole thing again, listening carefully for alterations. Young Hutchin mentioned handguns; she made him tell her about them and more of her husband's activities became clear to her. The rage she had stopped up for so long, which had killed her appetite and kept her dry-eyed through all her husband's accusations and brutality, suddenly flowered forth in a cold torrent. She sat silent, letting it take possession of her, using it to form a plan.

"Sir Henry and Lord Spynie are old allies," she said at last. "Sir Henry knew Alexander Lindsay's father years before he was born.

Take it from me, Young Hutchin, King James knew nothing of this outrage."

She dug in her chest and found paper and a pencase, which she opened and scrabbled out pens and ink. She waited for a moment for her hands to stop shaking and her thoughts to settle. Although she was only a woman, she had influence if she chose to use it. Her husband was not the only one with friends at the Scottish court. She began with a letter begging urgent audience with the King.

"Take this to the Earl of Mar," she said, folding the first letter and sealing it with wax from the candle. "Where is Sergeant Dodd?"

Young Hutchin spat expressively. "Run fra the town, mistress, I hope. He said he'd try the Johnstones."

"Good. When you have delivered the first letter, come back to me here. Don't speak to any of the Widdringtons except me, do you understand?"

"Ay, mistress. Will all this writing free the Deputy?"

"It might. Off you go."

The lad whisked out of the door and pelted down the stairs. Elizabeth took up her pen again, though her hand was starting to ache and wrote another letter to Melville, King James's chancellor, who had stayed in Edinburgh. They were old friends for she had fostered his son at Widdrington for a year, at a time when Scotland was too hot for him and he had been afraid of his child being used against him. In it she set down a precise account of what she guessed or knew about her husband and his activities, which she folded up, sealed and put crackling under her stays. Then she went downstairs again, face calm as she could make it. The few other men who had been sleeping there had woken and gone out to see to the horses. Her step-son had also woken up at last, and was sitting on his table, scratching and yawning and gloomily fingering yet another spectacular spot that had flowered on his nose in the night.

"Good morning, Henry," she said sedately.

Henry coughed and winced: blood-shot eyes told her the rest of the tale.

"Who gave you so much to drink?"

The young jaw stuck out and the adam's apple bobbed. "Nobody," he said truculently. "Sir Henry's still at the Red Boar."

Elizabeth's eyes narrowed. "What do you know about the arrest of Sir Robert Carey?"

He looked away sullenly, his ears red and his feet twining together as they dangled off the table. Elizabeth went to the almost empty beer barrel, pushed aside the scrawny creature trying pathetically to clean up spillages with a revolting mop and tilted it to get the last of the beer out into a leather mug.

"Drink that," commanded Elizabeth.

"I'll puke."

"You will not," said his stepmother drily. "You'll find it has a miraculous effect. Go on."

With an effort Henry drank, coughed again, wiped his mouth where the incipient fur on his top lip caught the drops and put the mug down.

"Go on, tell me."

"Well, I had to do it, didn't I? He's my father, isn't he?"

Elizabeth said nothing. Henry sighed.

"Sir Henry rousted us all out about midnight or one o'clock, said he had clear evidence Sir Robert was trafficking guns with the Italian wine merchant."

"And how did he find out?"

"Roger got the tale from his pageboy."

"On the pretext that I wanted to know?"

Henry nodded.

"Go on. I shall speak to Roger later."

"And Sir Henry said Lord Maxwell had confirmed it and was very annoyed because he said Carey had cheated him on the deal. So we went up to the Mayor's house with him, with father I mean, and waited about a bit and then father came down again with my Lord Spynie and the warrant. We went back to Maxwell's Castle and Lord Maxwell let us in and we kicked Sir Robert's door down and there he was with his sword in his hand and his hose and boots on, wanting to know what we wanted."

"Did he fight?"

"No. Once he'd seen the Privy Seal on the warrant and the signature, he surrendered."

"What did he say about it? Did he say he was innocent?"

"He didn't get the chance."

"How badly was he beaten?"

Henry coughed and looked away again. "Not badly," he muttered. "I've had worse."

Elizabeth nodded thoughtfully. "And where is he now?"

"We took him back to the Mayor's house again, to the wine cellar. Aside from the Dumfries gaol, which is full, it's the only lock-up they've got here."

"Where did your father go?"

"He's off with Lord Spynie and his friends."

"So you came here and drank yourself asleep, instead of telling me."

"Father made me swear not to tell you."

"Oh, *did* he?"

Clearly Henry did not understand the significance of that, but it lightened Elizabeth's heart. If Sir Henry didn't want her to know something that he knew would cause her pain, then there was an excellent reason for it. She could think of only one good enough.

"Smarten yourself up, Henry," she said with a wintry smile. "Or at least comb your hair. Then find the steward. When I've talked to him we're going to see the King."

◇◇◇

Walking alone at dawn into the rough encampment of Johnstones in the part of Dumfries south of Fish Cross, Dodd had not been recognised at once. This was a relief to him since he still had a number of kine and sheep at Gilsland that had once belonged to various Johnstone families. When he insisted that he had important information about the Maxwells that he would give to the laird only, they brought him through the tents to the best one, which had been brightly painted and carried two flags.

The laird was breaking his fast on bread and beer. He was a bony gangling young man with a shock of wiry brown hair and his face prematurely lined with responsibility. His great grandfather, the famous Johnny Johnstone, had been able to put two thousand fighting men in the saddle on the hour's notice, but the King of those days had taken exception to such power being wielded by a subject. Johnny Johnstone had been inveigled into the King's presence on a promise of safeconduct and summarily hanged. Now the power of the Johnstones was much less and their bitter enemies the Maxwells were stronger than them.

"Your name?" asked the laird.

Dodd took a deep breath and folded his arms. "Henry Dodd, Land-Sergeant of Gilsland."

Johnstone's brown eyes narrowed and his jaw set.

"Ay."

"I'm here with Sir Robert Carey, Deputy Warden of the English West March."

"Mphm. Last I heard, ye were staying with the Maxwell."

"That's why I've come to ye, sir," said Dodd. "Maxwell's got the Deputy Warden arrested on a trumped-up charge."

"Well, ye shouldnae've trusted him, should ye?"

"You're right, sir," said Dodd bitterly. "But Sir Robert wouldnae listen to me."

There was a very brief cynical smile. The Johnstone finished his beer.

"And?"

"Did ye know that the Maxwell recently bought at least two hundred firearms, powder and ammunition off Sir Richard Lowther in Carlisle?"

Johnstone wiped his mouth fastidiously. "I had heard something about it. What of it?"

"Would it interest ye to know more about the guns?"

"It might."

Dodd stood there with his arms folded and his whole spine prickling, and waited.

Johnstone smiled briefly again. "What d'ye want for the information?"

"Your support, sir. Your protection against Maxwell for myself and Sir Robert. Your counsel."

Johnstone took his time thinking about this, looking Dodd up and down. He had a fair amount to consider, to be fair to him. What Dodd was offering, unauthorised and unstated, was a possible alliance between the Johnstones and the Wardenry of Carlisle. It wasn't merely a matter of information.

"Hm."

It all depended on whether the laird had any of the daring of his great grandfather. He would be taking a chance on Dodd's faith, and the faith of Sir Robert, although Dodd thought he would also be quite grateful for the information as well, once he had it. But there again, the laird could then discard Dodd and Sir Robert if he chose: they were both taking a chance on faith.

Johnstone stared into space for a moment. "Very well," he said without preamble. "Ye have my backing agin the Maxwells for you and your Deputy Warden, and my counsel for what that's worth."

So easily? Dodd was still suspicious. But there was nothing else he could do: he simply had to hope that the laird was a man of his word, unlike Lord Maxwell.

He coughed. "The Maxwell's weapons are all bad, worse than useless. They explode on the second firing. Maxwell knows this now and he's got rid of them, but his men have practically no guns as a result."

Johnstone was sitting utterly still. "Ye're sure of this?"

"On my honour, sir."

Johnstone held his gaze for a long moment more. Then he banged his folding table with the flat of his hand and jumped to his feet. "By God," he laughed. "Let's have them."

After that, Dodd was almost forgotten as Johnstone strode from his tent trailing a flurry of orders and the camp began to stir and buzz like a kicked beeskep. Dodd knew he had just broken the strained peace between the two surnames and rekindled what amounted to open civil war in the Scottish West March. It was extremely satisfactory.

◇◇◇

Carey had been in prison before. Paris had been expensive and in the end his creditors had caught him and thrown him in gaol until his father could send him funds and a scorching letter through the English ambassador. At the time he had been in the depths of misery, cooped up in a filthy crowded communal cell and away from his fascinating Duchesse (who, he found out later, had tired of him in any case). But it had only lasted a couple of weeks and he had not been chained nor in darkness.

He tried to do something about his hands, flexing them and trying to shift the wooden manacles, which made his shoulders cramp and his fingers buzz with pins and needles. He had found out all he needed to know from the German, whatever he was really called—Hans Schmidt was clearly not his name—through a painful process of question and answer, guesswork and elimination. He had been merciless in his quest for hard facts and the exhausted man now slept, moaning softly every so often. Perhaps it would have been sensible to sleep as well, but he couldn't, not with the stink of wine and pain in his nostrils, and the overwhelming pit of fear in his bowels.

He thought back to what he had done, wondering if he had made a mistake. Perhaps...perhaps he had acted hastily, dealing on his own initiative with the Italian. Perhaps he should have talked to the King first. But the King had either lied about the guns or genuinely not known what was going on. And the opportunity had been there to be seized, with no time for careful letters to London. Naturally he would file a report back to Burghley when it was all over, but...He had not expected to be arrested. He had not expected Young Hutchin to be so willing to spy for the Widdringtons. Perhaps his greatest mistake had been prancing back to Maxwell's Castle so blithely, trusting Maxwell at all. But he had done what the Maxwell wanted, he had gotten the man his money back and Lord Maxwell had been full of gratitude and favour. Seemingly. Damn him to hell.

He had been caught rather easily. Perhaps he should have fought: but that would have given Sir Henry the excuse he needed to shoot. And what was his legal position anyway—arrested on a false warrant for a crime of which he was in fact guilty? Technically.

Gloomily he thought it would make no difference anyway: possession was nine-tenths of the law and King James would no doubt wink at the fact that he had probably not actually seen the warrant himself.

Carey tried hard to stop his mind from running on to the further consequences: the grave letters back and forth from Edinburgh to London while he and the German rotted in

Dumfries. Almost certainly, the Queen would insist on his extradition for questioning by Sir Robert Cecil's experts, like Topcliffe. Oh, Jesus Christ.

Carey swallowed hard, terror taking on a new and even uglier dimension. Queen Elizabeth was a Tudor and took any hint of betrayal extremely seriously indeed. She also took it personally. The fact that she had liked him would make that worse, not better.

He simply could not stay still and his backside was freezing and numb from the stone-flagged floor anyway. He struggled to his feet, causing the German to groan protestingly, stamped and swayed on the spot in the darkness, like a horse in its stall, hunching his shoulders and ducking his head and trying to get some feeling back in his hands.

Another appalling thought hit him. Perhaps Hutchin had not been coney-catched by Roger Widdrington. Perhaps Lady Widdrington had indeed been the one paying him for information; perhaps Carey's chasing after the pretty little Signora had turned Elizabeth utterly against him. Perhaps she had bought back her husband's favour by giving her would-be lover up to the wolves. No. Surely not. She would never...She might. Who could tell how any woman's mind worked? Even though it had been nothing but a light-hearted dalliance he could hardly be expected to turn down, she might be unreasonably jealous, she might be angry enough. In which case his sending Hutchin to her was worse than useless...

He was standing like that, quite close to mindless panic, vaguely wondering how it was possible for him to be sweating while he was also shivering, when the door rattled and creaked open. He had to blink and squint from the light of lanterns. The German didn't because his eyes were too swollen. In fact his whole face was a horrible foreboding, like an obscene cushion, pounded until it was barely human. No wonder the poor bastard had had difficulty speaking. His arms had been chained to a bolt above his head, his fingers were also grotesquely swollen and black, as was his right foot and ankle. Carey looked away from him.

Sir Henry again, three henchmen at his back, Lord Spynie at his side. Lord Spynie was at the head of a different group of three men, luridly brocaded and padded as were all King James's courtiers. Had none of them heard of good taste?

Spynie looked extremely pleased with himself, but also a little furtive. Carey wondered again if he had really been arrested by the King's warrant, or did Spynie have access to some legally trained clerks and the Privy Seal of the Kingdom? Given James's sloppiness with his favourites, surely it was possible? Lord Spynie came up close to him, sneered something he couldn't quite catch in Scots and spat messily in his face. Rage boiled in Carey, it was all he could do to keep from childishly spitting back.

Two Widdringtons gripped him under the arms while one of Spynie's men dragged a little stool into the middle of the wine cellar floor, next to a barrel on its end. On the barrel top, as on a table, another courtier with a puffy eye ceremoniously placed a bunch of small things made of metal.

Carey recognised the courtiers. Two of them still bore the marks of his fist, and one had Hutchin's toothprints in his arm. They all crowded the little space of the wine cellar and fogged it with their breath and heat, and the smoke from their torches and lanterns.

"Good morning, gentlemen," said Carey, his mouth completely dry and his stomach gone into a hard knot of recognition. Those were thumbscrews lying on the barrel top.

"Why are his legs free?" demanded Lord Spynie.

"We havenae brought legirons," said a courtier. "Shall I fetch some?"

"No," said Spynie. "Use his." He pointed at the German still slumped against the wall. A key was produced, and the chains holding him to the ring in the wall were unlocked, allowing him to crumble down into a lying position at last. He lay still as a corpse, hardly breathing.

One of the Widdringtons who had brought him here took the irons and knelt to lock them round Carey's ankles.

"Sit down, traitor," said Lord Spynie.

Carey looked at him, knowing dozens like him at the Queen's court. Alexander Lindsay, Lord Spynie was a young man, around twenty years old, and already beginning to lose the freshness of his beauty. He had a young man's cockiness and sensitivity to slights, and he had acquired a taste for power as the King's minion.

Now he knew he was losing it, although he was not intelligent enough to know why. But he was hiding his uncertainty. Carey could read it there, in the way he stood, the way his hand gripped his swordhilt, just as if Spynie was bidding up his cards in a primero game. Instinctively Carey felt it was true: this was unofficial, a favourite taking revenge, not King's men about the King's business.

"I appeal to Caesar," Carey said softly, pointedly not sitting.

"What?"

"I want to see the King."

Sir Henry backhanded him across the mouth, having to reach up to do it.

"I'll want satisfaction for that, Widdrington," Carey said to him, anger at last beginning to fill up the cold terrified spaces inside.

Sir Henry sneered at him. "Satisfaction? You're getting above yourself, boy. Tell us what we want to know and we might recommend a merciful beheading to the King."

"If your warrant came from my cousin the King, then he is the one I will talk to," Carey said coldly and distinctly, hoping they could not hear how his tongue had turned to wool. "If it did not, then you have no right to hold me and I demand to be released."

Spynie stepped up close. "Do you know who I am?" he demanded rhetorically.

Carey smiled. "Your fame is legendary even at the Queen's Court," he said, sucking blood from the split in his lip. "You are the King's catamite."

Spynie drew his dagger and brought it up slowly under Carey's chin, pricking him slightly.

"Sit down," whispered Spynie.

"I can't," Carey said reasonably. "Your dagger's in the way."

Spynie took the dagger away, pointed it at Carey's eye.

"Sit down."

"Why? You can talk to me just as well if I'm standing. Take me to the King."

"Where's the Spaniard gone?" demanded Sir Henry suddenly.

Carey shrugged. "I've no idea," he said. "And as my lord Spynie knows perfectly well, he's an Italian."

"You admit talking to him then?"

"Of course. One of my functions as Deputy Warden is to discover what foreign plots are being made against Her Majesty the Queen."

"How much did ye sell him the guns for?"

"What guns?"

Spynie lost patience and grabbed the front of his shirt. "Where's the gold?"

"What gold?"

"The gold Bonnetti gave you for the guns?"

"It surprises me," Carey said looking down at Spynie's grip, "that you think he had any money left at all, after being at the Scottish court for as long as he had. The bribes to all of you gentlemen must have been costing him a fortune. Take me to the King."

"What were you doing in the forest this afternoon?" gravelled Sir Henry.

"Hunting. Take me to the King."

"Where's the fucking gold?" shouted Lord Spynie. "You got it from him, I ken very well ye did, so what did ye do with it?"

"Take me to the King and I'll tell him."

Spynie finally lost control and started hitting him across the face with the jewelled pommel of the dagger. As if that were the signal for all pretence at civilisation to disappear, there was a flurry of blows and hands grabbing him, his arms were twisted up behind his back until he thought they would break. By sheer weight of numbers they made him sit on the stool and they forced his head down until his cheek rested on the barrel-top. It smelled of aqua vitae. Cold metal slipped down over the thumb and first two fingers of his left hand behind him and tightened. He went on struggling uselessly, blind with panic, not feeling it when they hit him.

Then somebody was tightening the things on his hands until shooting pains ran up his arms, until he knew beyond doubt that his fingers would break if they tightened any further and then they did and more pain scudded through his hand. It was astonishing how much pressure it took to break a bone. There was more metal slipping onto the fingers and thumb of his right hand, tightening, biting, until his palms contracted reflexively and he shut his eyes and gasped.

"Now," hissed Lord Spynie. "Ye've one more chance. Half a turn more and your fingers will break and ye'll never hold a sword nor shoot a gun again. Where's the gold?"

"Take me to…my cousin the King."

Spynie banged Carey's head down on the table, bruising the place where Jock of the Peartree had cracked his cheekbone the month before.

"The King doesnae ken ye're here. It's me and my friends, naebody else. I'll give ye ten minutes to think about it."

Carey had stopped struggling. He did think about it, despite the shrieking from the trapped nerves in his fingers, and he decided he had nothing whatever to lose by keeping silent until he had to talk. If Young Hutchin had indeed gone to Lady Widdrington it would give her time to act, if she wished, and if he had not, it would give the boy a chance to get into the Debateable Land, away from Spynie and his friends, which would be some satisfaction at least. God help me, thought Carey, how long can I hold out?

He turned his head so his forehead was resting on the table and tried to marshal his strength for the next step. It came sooner than he expected, which was no doubt intentional. The half turn was made on the forefinger of his left hand, with a vicious sideways jerk, and the bone broke. He couldn't help it, he cried out. The next finger took a full turn before it went. He jerked and gasped again but there were too many people holding him down. Saliva flooded his mouth, his stomach was too empty to puke. No wonder Long George had wept when his pistol burst.

"Where's the gold?"

"Fuck off."

They were going to break the fingers of his right hand. Never to hold a sword again, never to fight…

He closed his eyes and took a deep breath, held it, so he wouldn't scream when the next finger broke, he was on the edge of screaming already…

For a moment he thought he had, a long drawn-out roar of despair and rage. The men holding him let go momentarily and he caught a glimpse of someone charging at Lord Spynie, a shambling hobbling creature with a monstrous face, flailing his way through the courtiers, launching himself at Lord Spynie with a magnificent headbutt, blood flowering on Spynie's astonished, affronted face. Carey half-stood, cheering the German on and had his feet swept from under him so he slammed over onto his side, causing a stabbing pain through his ribs, and lost himself in whitehot agony when his hands hit the floor. Someone trod on him, he was helpless with his feet tangled in chains, somebody else kicked him and then the mêlée opened out and he saw the German falling, threshing like a gaffed fish with a dagger in his throat.

Spynie was dabbing at his nose with a lace-edged handkerchief and breathing hard. He stepped back from the kill and the German's body was rolled over, out of the way, next to the wine barrels. Mentally Carey saluted the man.

"Pick him up," Spynie hissed.

Carey was hauled upright again, forced to sit on the stool again, his head shoved down again. It didn't seem possible, they were going to do it and his gorge rose. Once more he held his breath and tried to get ready.

There was a clatter and a creak behind him which he couldn't identify.

"Lord Spynie," came a new voice, wintry and measured. "Sir Henry Widdrington, release that man."

It was the voice of King James's foster-brother, the Earl of Mar. A pause, then the men holding Carey down let go. Very very carefully he let out his breath, lifted his head off the barrel-end and looked straight up at the Earl. For the moment he couldn't stand, he wasn't sure of his legs. The Earl's face was hieratic and stern, but neither sympathetic nor surprised.

"I want to see my cousin the King," Carey whispered.

"Ay," said the Earl of Mar and jerked his chin at one of the courtiers in unspoken and imperious command.

After a moment's hesitation, and with no gentleness, the man unlocked the wooden manacles from Carey's wrists so he could bring his hands round and rest the agony of metal on his lap.

He was not surprised to find he was shaking, astonished that there was no blood. The Earl of Mar was bending in front of him, unscrewing the thumbscrews which made his swollen fingers hurt worse than they had before, leaving livid pressure marks behind. He had to bow his head and stop breathing again while Mar took them off the broken ones. Mar saw the swelling and bruising, the unnatural bend, and took time to glare at Spynie, before taking out his handkerchief.

"I'll bind these two to the third for the moment," he said. "Can ye hold still while I do it?"

"Yes," said Carey remembering Long George. When Mar had finished he stood up, cautiously. He was lightheaded, the pain in all but his broken fingers was beginning to change to a dull throbbing and for some reason, he was desperately thirsty.

"You'll come wi' me," said the Earl of Mar. "The King wants to see ye."

He couldn't help it: he gave a triumphant grin to Lord Spynie and Sir Henry Widdrington, both of whom were looking stunned and afraid. His sudden joy wasn't only because he had kept the use of his right hand; it was because of what the Earl of Mar's intervention told him about Elizabeth.

He came joltingly back down to earth when he moved to follow Mar and the chains on his ankles almost tripped him up.

"Like this, my lord Earl?" he asked falteringly.

Mar looked him consideringly up and down. "Ay," he said.

"But…"

"The King said he wanted tae see ye. Naebody said anything about releasing ye."

Carey was about to argue, but then stopped himself. He rested his broken hand carefully on the better one and told himself worse things could easily be happening to him than having to clank in chains through the Scottish court in nothing but his filthy shirt and hose, with a bloody face and no hat on his head. It was no good. The humiliation of it on top of everything else made him feel sick with rage, until he could hardly lift his feet enough to follow the Earl.

Lord Spynie moved to follow them out, but the Earl of Mar stopped him.

"You and Sir Henry are under arrest, my lord," said the Earl. "Ye can bide here together until His Highness is ready for ye." And he shut and locked the wine cellar door in their faces.

That Carey was also still under arrest was made clear by the Earl of Mar's men in their morions and jacks, carrying polearms like the Yeomen of the Guard at the Tower, who were waiting to surround him at the top of the stairs. He went with them, for the first time in his life wishing he were not so tall. He wanted to hunch down so they could hide him, but forced himself to stand up straight and concentrate on moving his feet so the chain didn't trip him up. The stairs were hard to manage, he had to pause every so often to get his balance and his breath back. Once he did trip, but the guards waited for him and although he saw faces he had known, they didn't seem to recognise him, perhaps because of the blood and dirt he was wearing.

At the door to the King's Presence chamber, Carey stopped, balking completely. The Earl of Mar turned and glared at him.

"What is it?"

"Let me wipe my face, at least," begged Carey. "I cannot see His Majesty like..."

There was a dour look of amusement around Mar's mouth. "Och, never ye mind what ye look like," he said gruffly. "He's no' sae pernickity as yer ain mistress."

"But, my lord..."

The Earl of Mar tutted like an old nurse and banged on the door. A young page with one oddly ragged ear opened it to them and blinked at the apparition without expression. The guards left him at the door and stood there, not to attention, but simply waiting in case they were needed.

In they tramped, Carey more acutely embarrassed than he could have imagined: every minute of training during his ten years' service at Queen Elizabeth's court told him that it was not far off blasphemy to appear in front of royalty in such a bedraggled state. Without the assured armour of well-cut clothes and a good turn-out he felt as tongue-tied and confused as any country lummox. Her Majesty would have been throwing slippers and vases at the smell of him by now.

Something deeper inside him suddenly rebelled at his own ridiculous shyness, anger rising at his craven fear of disapproval by someone who was, whatever God had made him, still only a man.

The man in question, who could sentence him to a number of different unpleasant deaths, was standing by a table, stripping off his gloves, with wine stains down one side of his padded black and gold brocade doublet. He was watching Carey gravely, consideringly.

Realising he was standing there like a post, Carey made to genuflect, remembered in the nick of time that he had chains on his ankles and went down clumsily on both knees in the rushes, jarring his hands.

"Sir Robert, I'm sorry to see ye like this."

He was expected to respond. How? What would work with Queen Elizabeth might annoy King James and vice versa. On the other hand he would never ever have been brought so easily into the Queen's presence after a charge of treason had been made. Even in a letter, abject contrition would have been the only course. But this was not a brilliant, nervy, vain and elderly woman, this was a King three years younger than himself, who would almost certainly be King of England one day. King James might be unaccountable, with odd tastes, but he was at least a man.

"Your Majesty, I'm sorry to *be* like this," Carey said, trying for a glint of wry humour.

"Ay," said King James. "No doubt ye are. What the Devil's happened to your hands?"

Carey looked down at them. The Earl of Mar's handkerchief splint hid his broken fingers which had settled down to a steady drumbeat throbbing, but the others were swollen and the ones that had felt the thumbscrews were going purple. His last remaining gold ring on his little finger was almost hidden by puffed flesh.

"My Lord Spynie was impatient to hear his tale," explained the Earl of Mar.

King James's eyes narrowed. "He's nae right to torture one of the Queen's appointed officials, let alone my ain cousin, does he no' ken that? Why did ye let them take ye, Sir Robert, I had ye down for a man of parts?"

"My Lord Spynie and Sir Henry Widdrington said they had a Royal Warrant. It had your signature on it. Naturally, in Your

Majesty's own realm I had no choice but to surrender." He omitted the detail of being outnumbered and outgunned.

King James made an odd sniff and snort through his nostrils. "A Warrant?" he said. "With the Privy Seal?"

Carey nodded. "Yes, Your Majesty. And your signature."

The King turned to the Earl of Mar.

"He's no' to have access to the Seal nor the signing stamp any more," he said, "if this is how he uses it."

The Earl of Mar's face took on a patient expression.

"Ay, Your Highness."

"And take the gyves off the man's legs. He's never going to attack me with his hands in that condition."

Mar beckoned to one of the guards, who came over and took the chains off Carey's ankles. He was not invited to stand, and so he didn't. No matter, he had knelt for hours at a time while attending on the Queen in one of her moods.

King James went to the carved chair placed under the embroidered cloth of estate and sat down, ignoring the large goblet of wine standing on a table by his hand. His face had somehow become sharper, more canny.

"Now then, Sir Robert. What was it ye were so determined to keep fra my lord Spynie?"

"Your Majesty, may I begin the tale at its right beginning?"

The King nodded. "Take your time."

Where the hell to start? Carey took a deep breath, and began with the German in the forest and Long George's pistol exploding.

An hour later he had finished, his throat beginning to get infernally dry and croaky. King James had interrupted only to ask an occasional sharp question. Running out of voice, his knees beginning to ache and his left hand turned into a pulsing mass of misery, Carey finally brought himself into Lord Spynie's clutches and left the tale there.

"Ye say the German's down in the winecellar now?"

"His corpse is, Your Majesty."

"Hmm. And ye say the false guns ye sold to Signor Bonnetti explode at the second firing?"

"Yes, Your Majesty."

King James started to laugh. He laughed immoderately, leaning back in his chair, hanging one leg over the arm and hooting.

"Och," he said, coming to an end at last. "Och, that's beautiful, Sir Robert, it's a work of artistry, it surely is. Ay. Well, my lord Earl, what d'ye think?"

The Earl of Mar was stroking his beard. "I think we can believe him, Your Highness."

King James leaned forward, suddenly serious. "What did ye get for them and where did ye put it?"

Carey's gut congealed again. "That was what my Lord Spynie was so anxious to know."

"Ay. So am I."

Carey coughed, smiled apologetically, spread his throbbing hands. "I gave it to a friend of mine, but I don't know where he's gone."

The atmosphere had cooled considerably. "When did ye give it?"

"When I heard Sir Henry coming and realised he had a warrant."

"Mf. This friend o' yourn, did he ken it was gold he was carrying?"

"Yes, Your Majesty."

King James looked regretful. "Ay well, nae doubt of it, he's ower the Border by now."

"He might be."

"And ye say ye're still in search of the right guns for Carlisle, the ones that came fra the Tower o' London?"

"If I can find where Spynie's got them hidden, Your Majesty."

The King was still half-astraddle the chair, gazing out of the portable glazed window, occasionally sipping from his wine goblet. Carey stayed where he was, his face itchily stiff with dried blood, weariness weighting every limb, and his throat cracked down to a whisper. God, for some beer and a bowl of water to wash in.

After what seemed a very long time, King James seemed to come to a decision. He swung his short bandy legs to the floor and stood up.

"My lord Earl," he said, "have Sir Robert taken to the tapestried chamber upstairs, give him the means to clean himself and a surgeon brought to him, and find him some clothes. When he's eaten and drunk his fill, bring him back to us."

"Your Majesty is most merciful," said Carey humbly, wondering if this would give the King's men time to comb the streets for Young Hutchin. King James's eyes narrowed.

"Ay," he snapped. "Merciful maybe, but I'm no' daft and if I find out any of this is a lie, ye'll be begging me to gie ye back to Lord Spynie before the day is out."

Carey bowed his head. None of it was a lie, he had told strictly the truth, but he had certainly not included any of the things he had learned or guessed from what the German told him. He wasn't daft either.

He got himself to his feet after the King had rolled from the room, looked at the Earl of Mar and waited. The procession reformed itself. He needed all his concentration to stay on his feet since his brain was spinning with weariness and tension, and he had to keep his head high in case anyone he knew should recognise him.

Elizabeth Widdrington was waiting with Young Hutchin Graham and her stepson Henry in an anteroom when they saw the Earl of Mar and the guards go by. She recognised Robin only by his height and the way he moved: his face was a mask of blood with an unhealthy grey tinge underneath. Her first emotion was sheer breathtaking joy that he was alive and could still walk. She stood and followed quietly behind, no longer caring what happened to her afterwards. It was not beyond the bounds of possibility that Sir Henry would kill her if he got out of this. The King had told her he would be arrested along with Lord Spynie. It was more than likely that he would try to take her down to destruction with him, if he could.

They took Carey to one of the upper rooms, and the key turned in the lock, she could hear it clearly. She waited on one of the narrow landings until the Earl of Mar came by and then she stepped in front of him and curtseyed. He blinked down at her.

"Ay," he said. "Lady Widdrington."

"My lord," she said. Her voice stopped in her throat. What was she going to ask him? To see Carey? For what reason that wasn't concerned with her unruly heart? And if he let her? What price her honour then? Would she make all Sir Henry's accusations and suspicions true?

"Hrmhrm," said the Earl of Mar, old enough to read her sudden dumbness. "If it's Carey, ye're after, he's still under arrest, but the King's more pleased wi' him than angry, and I'm to call the surgeon."

Her heart thundered stupidly; she had seen him walking, why panic? But still her voice shook.

"Is...he...is he badly hurt?"

"Nay," said the Earl kindly enough. "He'll need splints on a couple of his fingers for a few weeks and his thumbs will be sore enough for a while, but he's no' half so bad as he looks."

She nodded silently, enraged with her husband for hurting Robin, perversely also furious with Robin for making it so easy for him. She wanted even more to see him, was hoping the Earl of Mar would ask a question that made it possible for her to ask, and also hoping that he would not.

Her second prayer was answered, he did not. He made a courteous bow to her, which she returned, and when she had stood aside he carried on down the stairs, leaving two of his men on guard by the door.

She went back to where Henry was waiting at the foot of the stairs.

"Well?" he asked. "Did you see him?"

If she spoke she would certainly weep. What was wrong with her? His hands would get better, given the chance. She shook her head, tilting her face so that the unshed tears would stay in her eyes, led the way brusquely back to the anteroom, where she waited to find out what would become of her husband and if she would have another audience with the King.

"Was he..." Henry began, stopped himself and began again as he hulked along beside her. "Did they...er..."

"Torture him?" Her voice came out metallic in her determination not to break down. "I think they had started but the Earl of Mar reached them in time."

Henry clearly had many more questions to ask, but couldn't bring himself to ask any of them. Instead he nodded, dropped his hand from her arm.

"Lady Widdrington." It was the Earl of Mar's voice again, austere and somehow colder than it had been.

She turned and curtseyed.

"His Highness the King asks if you will consent to tend to Sir Robert Carey," said the Earl, "since it appears the surgeon is drunk."

For a moment she stood there stupidly. Should she risk it? But what the King asked, even in Scotland, was a command. She could hardly say no.

"Of course, my lord," she said gravely.

"Your stepson and page must stay here."

Henry stepped back beside Young Hutchin, looking nervous. He was still too gawky to be entirely happy at being on his own, surrounded by the nobility of Scotland. She must send him to London soon, so he could get some polish. The roguish Young Hutchin Graham looked far more poised and at home than he did.

Once more she followed the Earl of Mar, through the over-crowded rooms of the best house in Dumfries, full of nobles dressed in French fashions or sober dark suits, and their multiple armed hangers-on, up the stairs, between the guards in the narrow second storey passage lined with rooms, and the Earl unlocked the door again.

"My lord," she said. "I may need bandages and salves and the like."

"Knock on the door and call through what you need," said the Earl stiffly. "It will be brought."

The door opened: it was an irregularly-shaped room, very small, with a bed in it and a table, and unexpectedly bright tapestries on all the walls, full of complex erotic doings of the Olympian gods, swans and bulls and cupbearers and the like. The light streamed in through a small window. Carey was standing by the table, trying ineffectually to wash his face in a bowl of water. He straightened up at the first sound of their coming in, and he stood there now, a comical expression of horror and dismay under the water and blood on his face. Lord Above, he was embarrassed, his face was flushed. Elizabeth swallowed the tender smile that would have offended him mortally. Why were men so vain?

She stood and looked at him for a moment until she could speak without a tremor and then turned sharply to the Earl.

"My lord, I want two bowls of water, one hot, one cold with comfrey or lovage in it, and at least four clean white linen cloths. I want any comfrey ointment you might have in the place, I want a good store of clean bandages and a clean shirt and hose for him and…"

"I'll see it done, my lady," said the Earl of Mar, his face masklike.

"I may also need splints: send in at least four withies, about this thick and so long and a knife to cut them with."

"No knife."

"My lord, please don't be ridiculous. I will be responsible for the knife."

"Hrmhrm."

"Do you have laudanum in the house?"

"I dinna ken."

"If you have, I would like some. You say the bonesetter's drunk?"

"The surgeon. Ay."

"Well, I shall do my best, my lord."

She marched into the room, heard the door shut and lock behind her and could have kicked herself for forgetting to ask for an older lady to act as chaperon. Well, no matter, she had done enough already to enrage her husband: merely confirming all his suspicions might even cheer him up.

The silly goose had tucked his hands behind his back. His shirt, which was one of Philadelphia's making, she saw, was in a revolting mess, stained to ruination with mud, blood, sweat, and something pink, and torn in several places. His hose were black and so less obviously disgraceful, but still disgusting. He smiled crookedly at her because his mouth had swollen, though much of the blood had come from his nose and some cuts on his forehead and cheeks.

"Have mercy, my lady," he said trying for rueful charm. "Don't be angry with me."

She simply could not think what to say to him, since what she wanted to do was run to him and hold him tight and kiss him and then slap him as hard as she could. Instead she walked to the bowl of water, looked at it for a moment, carried it to the tiny window and carefully tipped it out. Dirty water splattered its way down the roofs below. The silence between them was very awkward.

Somebody knocked on the door: one of the guards opened it, and two boys came in, each carrying a bowl of water and a man followed them with his arms piled high.

"The hot water on the table," she snapped. "Cold water on the floor. Where is the comfrey that should be in the water?"

"The Earl says we havenae got none."

"Very sloppy. Do you have splints?"

The man produced several withies, some too wide, and a very small but sharp knife and put it on the table. Elizabeth took the clothes, cloths and bandages from him and laid them out on the bed.

"Out," she snapped. "And tell the Earl I want a woman to come in here with me, to protect my reputation."

"Ay, my lady," said the man, hiding a grin. If she had been at home, Elizabeth would have cuffed his ears for the knowingness of it.

"You, wait," she said imperiously as the boys trotted out again. "So I do not get my hands dirty, would you please take Sir Robert's boots off him? Take them away and get them cleaned."

For a moment the man looked mutinous, then as Carey sat still smiling on the bed and stuck out a foot, he did as he was told, walking out with them held well away from his smart cramoisy suit. The door locked behind him.

"Stay there," Elizabeth ordered Carey, who made a wry face and also did as he was told, sitting meekly on the edge of the bed with its half-tester above him.

She took one of the white cloths and wrapped it round her waist for an apron so as not to spoil the expensive grey wool of her kirtle, took another cloth, dipped it in the hot water and began dabbing carefully at his face in silence. When that was clean at last, she came close and examined the cuts on his head.

"Where's Hutchin?" he whispered at once.

"Downstairs with Young Henry. I thought it better to keep an eye on him."

Carey smiled in obvious relief, making her wonder what was so important about the boy.

"That's good. Where's Dodd?"

"I believe he's gone to the Johnstones."

"Hm."

"And what made these cuts?" she demanded.

"A dagger's jewelled pommel, wielded by an enraged minion."

She sniffed. "None of them are bad, I'll leave them as they are. There's blood on the side of your shirt," she added. "What happened there?"

Carey looked down in surprise. "Oh," he said. "I took a cut there a week ago and I suppose it must have opened again. I'd forgotten all about it."

"Did Philadelphia bandage it?"

"Yes, after she sewed it up."

"Have you changed the bandage since then or had the stitches out?"

"Er...no."

She put her fists on her hips. "Is it hurting, throbbing?"

"Not much. Mostly it itches."

"Show me your hands."

He didn't want to, he put them further behind his back. Elizabeth tapped her foot and glared at him and so he brought them out again and let them rest on his thighs, palms up.

"Thumbscrews?"

"Yes."

"Turn them over."

He did, wincing slightly. At the moment, they were no longer such beautiful hands, Elizabeth thought, forcing herself to be dispassionate; they looked as if they had been slammed in several doors. Very gently she examined the right hand.

"I think you'll lose the thumbnail anyway, and perhaps the two fingernails as well, although there is something I can do about that. Are they broken?"

Carey was looking at them as well as if seeing them properly for the first time.

"I don't think so," he said absently. "I think they're just bruised. I can move them."

Elizabeth pointed at the fingers still splinted together. "These two are broken."

"Yes."

"My husband, no doubt."

"And Lord Spynie."

"I expect despicable behaviour from Lord Spynie."

Carey looked up at her woefully, the expression in his blue eyes exactly like a little boy who has fallen out of a tree he was forbidden to climb. Damn him, she wanted to kiss him again.

"Are you very angry with me, sweetheart?"

Honestly, why was it he could melt her so easily? She took a deep breath and told him the truth.

"I am extremely angry," she said. "With my husband, with Spynie and with you."

She straightened up and went to look around the various bottles that the boy had brought. There was an elderly bottle marked 'Comfrey bonesetting ointment' half full of something that smelled just about useable. The bottle marked laudanum had some sticky substance at the bottom and nothing else.

"There's no laudanum," she said to herself in dismay.

"Oh."

"Can you take your own shirt off, or will I do it for you?"

"If you undo the ties, my lady."

She did so, not looking in his face, nursing her anger so she could be cold enough to help him properly. He struggled the shirt over his head and dropped it on the floor, and she kicked it into a corner. It was not the first time she had seen him stripped to the waist. She remembered nursing him alongside Philadelphia when he came back from Tilbury in a litter after fighting the Armada, not wounded, but completely off his head with a raging gaol-fever caught aboard ship. Against all the advice of the doctors they had fought to cool him down. That had been easier than this was going to be, because it was comforting for him to be sponged, even in his delirium. Still, she tried not to look at him too much because it unsettled her, and made her long to run her hands down the muscles of his shoulders and back...

She put the bowl of hot water on the floor by the bed and cold water on the table.

"Put your hands in the cold water," she said.

"Why?"

"To bring down the swelling."

She went to the door and shouted through it: "Bring me a crewel needle, embroidery snips and eyebrow tweezers and aqua vitae. And food and mild ale." There was an answering shout. Carey was looking distinctly nervous when she came back to him, but he had his hands in the water.

The bandage around his side was stained and smelled. She used the small knife to cut it off him and hot water to soak it away from his wound. The wound itself was not bad at all, mostly healed, only one end had opened again and exuded a trickle of blood and white fluid. The skin around Philadelphia's neat silk stitches was red and angry and Elizabeth tightened her lips with annoyance at the congenital carelessness of men.

There was a knock at the door again, and a page slid round it. He was carrying a small hussif and a leather bottle. He scooted across the floor, put them down on the table by the bowl and scooted out again. Elizabeth wondered what was scaring everyone so much and sat down beside Carey.

With the eyebrow tweezers and embroidery snips she took out the stitches that were actually causing trouble now the rest of the wound had healed. She cleaned the part that had bled and bandaged it all carefully again.

Carey sat in silence, not even wincing. He seemed to be far away, in a kind of daze. She took the withies, measured them, trimmed and cut them to size.

"Now," she said, mentally girding her loins, "I'm going to cut off that bit of rag holding your fingers together."

"It's the Earl of Mar's handkerchief."

"I'll buy him a new one. Take your left hand out of the water, and put it on my lap." After a moment's hesitation, he did. Very carefully she cut the cloth with the small knife. As the fingers came free, Carey sucked in his breath and held it.

The splints and bandages were beside her on the bed. She started by patting his swollen hand dry and examining the thumb, which was bruised, but not broken. There were marks and bruises around his wrists but nothing that needed attention.

"Let me tell you a story," she said, taking his forefinger and feeling it carefully. The swelling was down a little and she could feel the greenstick fracture inside the flesh. It would have needed no more than a splint only someone had twisted it sideways. "About two weeks ago, while I was still in Carlisle, my husband called out most of his kin at Widdrington and rode due west to the Border." She knew Carey was watching her face intently, trying to ignore what she was doing to his hand. "Probably at Reidswire in the Middle March he met his friends from the Scottish court, come south from Jedburgh, and took command of a string of heavy-laden packponies, carrying handguns. Then he rode south and east again and, according to my steward, he met Sir Simon Musgrave and the arms convoy on the Newcastle Road at night. Sir Simon is an old friend of my husband's, they collect blackrent off each other's tenants. There they exchanged one set of guns for another."

He was interested now, listening properly. She held his forearm tightly under her arm, took his forefinger, pulled and stretched it straight, ignoring the jerk and his startled "Aahh", until she felt the ends of bone grate into place. Quickly, she put the splint up against it and bandaged it on.

"How do you feel?" she asked. "Dizzy?"

His face had gone paper white, but he shook his head.

"Warn me next time," he said, panting a little.

"Very well." The next one would be harder, being the long middle finger. She took it and started stroking it again. This was more of a crushing fracture, badly out of place. Well, all she could do was her best.

"Try not to clench your hand," she said. "Ready?"

He nodded, watching anxiously.

"Robin," she said. "Look over at the tapestry, over there."

He did, fixing his eyes on a place where the heavy folds swung gently as if in an invisible breeze. She took the finger, gripped his arm tight against her stays and set the bone into place. It took longer this time to get it to her satisfaction and splint it to the other withy, and at the end she had sweat running down under her smock and stinging the grazes there. Carey was green and clammy, eyes tightshut. She smeared ointment on, splinted the three fingers together, took the little bottle off the table, tasted it to make sure of what it was, and gave it to him.

"Not too much," she warned, watching his adam's apple bob. "I haven't finished yet."

"What the hell else is there to do?"

"I can make your other fingers feel better if I release the pressure of the blood under the nails."

He was cradling his left hand against his chest and swaying slightly.

"How?" he asked, not looking at her.

"By making a hole in the nails."

"Oh, Christ. Are you working for Lord Spynie?"

He meant it as a joke, though it was a very poor one. She tried to smile and failed. She was not enjoying this, although she might have thought she would, given the stupid man's cavortings with Signora Bonnetti.

"It doesn't hurt so much," she managed to say. "My mother did it for me when I caught my hand in a linen chest lid."

Now he was offended for some reason. "Get on with it then," he growled.

She got the strongest needle out of the hussif case, sharpened it on the carborundum and slipped the cobbler's handstall on. There was a candle and tinderbox by the little fireplace. She lit the candle and heated up the end of the needle. The blood that came out from under his thumbs was sullen and dark, so she thought he would keep those nails, but when she drilled through into the nailbed of his right forefinger, the blood spurted up into her face and Carey yelped.

She mopped herself with her makeshift apron, pressed to make sure it was all out and attacked the final one, leaning well away. There was pressure under that one as well. She cleaned them both up, once more fighting the distraction of his body. At last she bade him put just his right hand in the cold water again and wrapped a compress round the thumb of his left hand.

"Are you finished?" he asked.

"Yes," she said. "I'll make you a sling when you're dressed, but I see no point in bandaging your right hand when the bruising doesn't need it. You can take it out of the water when it stops throbbing. What you need now is to sleep."

He shook his head, as much to clear it as to dismiss the notion. "What's the rest of your tale? Who helped make the transfer on the Border? Was it the Littles? And why did they give guns in payment to the Littles who helped them?"

"I don't know what you're talking about."

Carey explained about Long George and his new pistol and Elizabeth shrugged cynically. "I have no doubt that Long George simply stole one. What else do you expect?"

"All right. So the Scottish weapons are now on the Newcastle wagons and coming into Carlisle with Sir Simon. What happened to the English weapons?"

"Apparently my husband took them north again to Reidswire where he handed them over to Lord Spynie's men."

Carey sighed and tilted his head back. "Of course, where else? Put like that, it's bloody obvious."

"What is?"

"Everything. Who has our guns, where the bad ones came from, why they were swapped, who killed Long George."

"Well, I'm glad somebody understands what's been happening," said Elizabeth tartly.

He grinned at her, ridiculously pleased with himself again, and kissed her smackingly on the lips.

"You are a woman beyond pearls and beyond price," he told her, putting his arms around her with great care. "I love you and I will never never chase Italian seductresses again."

She tried to hang onto her anger, but she couldn't. "Don't make promises you can't keep," she muttered and he laughed softly.

"Was that tale about your husband what you told the King, to get me out? About the swapping of the firearms?"

"I told him more than that," she snapped, still unwilling to be mollified. "I told him what you did last month to stop Bothwell's attempt at kidnapping him. Anyway, all I needed to do was tell him what Spynie was up to. You know the King likes you."

Carey shrugged, then grinned, tightened his arms around her bearlike. She could feel his heart beating against hers.

"Magnificent, beautiful, capable woman," he whispered. "Come back to Carlisle with me. Leave your old pig of a husband, come live with me and be my love."

For a moment she struggled with temptation, more amused than offended by his rapid recovery. He found her mouth, began kissing her intently. Why not, she thought, why not? I've taken my punishment for it, why shouldn't I take the pleasure? She was letting him overwhelm her, she didn't care that she had the taste of the blood from his lip in her mouth, that he smelled of blood and sweat and surprisingly of wine...And then one of the splints on his fingers jarred on one of the raw places on her back and they both winced away together. He was puzzled, she was suddenly enraged with herself and him.

"No, no, no," she snapped, jumping up and straightening her cap with shaking fingers. "How can you want me to break my marriage vows that I made in the sight of God?" The words sounded pompous and false because they were false; she knew she would have broken any vow in the world if she could have done it without destroying him.

His face was nakedly distressed. "Because I am so afraid," he said, quite softly. "I'm...I'm afraid that Sir Henry will kill you or break you before he dies. And I love you."

Infuriatingly, the door unlocked, opened and two boys and a manservant processed in carrying food: a cockaleekie soup, bread, cheese and some heels of pies, plus a large flagon of mild ale. The manservant stretched his eyes a little, to see her standing beside a half-naked man, even if she was fully dressed.

"Now," she said, turning to the Scot as businesslike as she could manage, considering that she was trembling and close to tears. "What's your name?"

"Archie Hamilton, ma'am."

"Well, Archie, do you think you could act as Sir Robert's valet de chambre?"

A short pause and then, "Ay, ma'am, I could."

"Excellent. Clear the table, lay the food. I shall leave while you help him to dress. Be very careful of his hands."

She walked out with the boys carrying the bowls of dirty water, waited in the little passageway and fought to get control of herself. At last Archie re-emerged and she went in again, quickly made a sling for his arm. They had laid the table for two and she sat herself down again at the other end of the bed, so the table was between them, and dipped some bread in the soup.

Carey was in a plain black wool suit of good quality though a little small for him, with a plain shirt and falling band, a short-crowned black felt hat on his head. He was still pale and moved his left arm as little as possible, but somehow, despite it all, he was in good spirits. He ate and drank as if he were not facing another dangerous interview with the King of Scotland. Elizabeth could only nibble and sip.

"What's wrong, my lady?" he said. "This is good; it's from the King's table, I think. Are you very offended with me?"

She shook her head, but she could see he had thought up something amorous and courtly to say by way of apology and further invitation.

"If I burn with love..." he began and she interrupted him brusquely.

"You're still a prisoner," she said. "I can't think how to get you out."

He smiled, winced and touched his lip, drank his ale very carefully. Sometimes he was so easy to read: there went the courtly phrases back into the cupboard in his mind marked 'For soothing offended females (young)'.

"Never you worry about it," he said, switching to irritating cheeriness. "I know the King and he's a decent man. It's hardly treason to sell your enemy eighteen dozen booby traps."

"Who were they for?"

"The Wild Irish, I expect, poor sods."

"Don't you feel sorry for them?"

"Yes. I also feel sorry for Bonnetti if he hangs around in Ireland long enough for them to find out what he's brought. I'll ask the King to make sure he gets away with them."

"And the real guns?"

Carey's eyes were dancing, though he was careful not to smile again.

"We'll see what we can do."

They finished their meal, talking amiably and distantly about young Henry and his awkwardness, and the Grahams. Robin said nothing more about Elizabeth leaving her husband and coming to live with him. It was impossible anyway, and always had been. If news of any such behaviour came to the Queen's ears, which it would, she would strip Carey of his office and call in all the loans she had made him. He would be bankrupt, on the run from his creditors and with no prospect of ever being able to satisfy them because the Queen would never allow him back at court again. Frankly, unless he turned raider, they would starve.

When they had finished, Carey wandered to the locked door, kicked it and shouted out for the Earl of Mar. It opened and the Earl was standing there, his face as austere as before.

"Ye'll be wanting to see His Highness again."

"If he wants to see me, my lord."

"Ay, he's cleared an hour for ye."

"Excellent. And thank him for sending Lady Widdrington to tend to me, she is unparalleled as a nurse and far better than any drunken surgeon."

"Hmf. Ay."

"My lord Earl," said Elizabeth. "May I ask what's happening to my husband?"

The Earl sniffed. "That's for the King to decide, seeing he's under arrest."

"And Lord Spynie?"

Another much longer sniff. "Ay, well," said the Earl. "The King's verra fond of him, ye ken."

"Yes," she said with freezing politeness. "So it seems. Sir Robert, what would you suggest I do now? May I serve you further or should I tend to my husband?"

"Tend to your husband by all means, my lady," Carey said very gravely. "I am greatly beholden to you."

She curtseyed, he bowed. She walked away from him, refusing to look back, refusing to think of anything but dealing with her husband.

"Lady Widdrington." She stopped and turned, felt a touch from him on her shoulder where it was most tender and automatically shied away. Carey was there, smiling at her.

"May I have my ring back?"

She blushed, embarrassed to have forgotten, wondering at the sudden hardness in his eyes. She fished the ring out of her purse under her kirtle and put it into his hand. He fumbled it onto his undamaged little finger, bowed once more and turned back to the patiently waiting Earl and his escort.

The King of Scotland had often enjoyed the use of the secret watching places he had ordered built into many of his castles. Through holes cunningly hidden by the swirling patterns of tapestries brought from France, he found the truth of many who swore they loved him and learned many things to his advantage about his nobles. It was something of a quest for him: he never stopped hoping for one man who could genuinely love him as d'Aubigny had, in despite of his Kingship, not because of it. And like a boy picking at a scab, he generally got more pain than satisfaction from his curiosity.

At the Mayor's house in Dumfries he had lacked such conveniences. But in the little rooms on the third storey there had been a few with interconnecting doors and it had not been difficult to set up some with tapestries hung to hide those doors. Thus he need only leave his room quietly, nip up the back stairs and into the next door chamber to the one where he had told Mar to put Carey. Sitting at his ease, with the connecting door open, he had quietly eavesdropped on Carey and his ladylove, as he had before on Lord Spynie and on some of his pages and others of the Border nobility. Some might have found it undignified in a monarch: James held that nothing a monarch did could be undignified, since his dignity came from God's appointment.

This time, as he descended the narrow backstairs and stepped to his own suite of rooms, he wasn't sure whether to be disappointed or pleased. That Carey turned out to be a lecherous sinner was not a surprise to him; that Lady Widdrington was a virtuous wife astounded him. He was saddened that Carey was clearly a hopeless prospect for his own bed, but he did not want to make the mistake with him that he had as a younger and more impatient King with the Earl of Bothwell. And Carey had called him 'a decent man'. It was a casual appraisal, something James had been taught to think of almost as blasphemous, but the accolade pleased him oddly because it was spoken innocently, in private and could not be self-interested. And further, it seemed that both of them were honest. Yes, there was disappointment that his suspicions were wrong; but on the other hand, honest men and women were not common in his life, they had all the charm of rarity.

He was sitting at the head of a long table, reading tedious papers, when Carey at last made his appearance in the chamber, having been kept waiting for a while outside. He paced in, genuflected twice and then the third time stayed down on one knee looking up at the King and waiting for him to speak. King James watched him for a while, searching for signs of guilt or uneasiness. He was nervous and paler than was natural for him, his arm in a sling, but he was vastly more self-possessed than the bedraggled battered creature that the King had seen in the morning.

"Well, Sir Robert, how are ye now?" he asked jovially.

"Very much better, thank you, Your Majesty."

"We have made sundry investigations into your case," the King pronounced, "and we are quite satisfied that there was no treason by you, either committed or intended, to this realm or that of our dear cousin of England. And we are further of the opinion that ye should be congratulated and no' condemned for your dealings with the Spanish agent in the guise of an Italian wine merchant that some of our nobles were harbouring unknown to us."

Carey's head was bowed.

"We have therefore ordered that all charges be dropped and your good self released from the Warrant."

Carey cleared his throat, looked up. "I am exceedingly grateful to Your Majesty for your mercy and justice." Was there still a hint of wariness in the voice? Did the Englishman think there might be a price for it? Well, there would be, though not the one he feared. King James smiled.

"Well now, so that's out o' the way. Off your knees, man, I'm tired of looking down on ye. This isnae the English court here." Carey stood, watching him.

King James tipped his chair back and put his boots comfortably on the tedious papers in front of him.

"Oh, Sir Robert," he said, "would ye fetch me the wine on the sideboard there?"

Carey did so gracefully, though with some difficulty, without the offended hunch of the shoulders that King James often got from one of his own subjects. On occasion he was even read a lecture by one of the more Calvinistically inclined about the evils of drink. It would be so much more restful to rule the English; he was looking forward to it greatly, if the Queen would only oblige him by dying soon and if the Cecils could bring off a smooth succession for him.

Carey was standing still again after refilling his goblet, silently, a couple of paces from him. On the other hand, it was very hard to know what the English were thinking. Sometimes James suspected that with them, the greater the flattery, the worse the contempt. Buchanan had said that the lot of them were dyed in the wool hypocrites, as well as being greedy and ambitious. Well, well, it would be interesting at least.

"It's a question of armaments, is it no'?" he said affably. "Ye canna tell the Queen that ye lost the weapons she sent ye and ye canna do without them." He paused. "It seems," he said slowly, "that I have a fair quantity of armament myself, more than I had thought. Lord Spynie was in charge of purveying my army's handguns, and it seems he did a better job than I expected."

Carey's eyes were narrowed down to bright blue slits. "Indeed, Your Majesty."

"Bonnetti is in the midst of lading his…ah…his purchases into his ship. He is still not aware of any…problems." King James beamed. "I gave him some gunpowder I'd no use for."

"Your Majesty is most kind."

King James let out a shout of laughter. "I am that. Now," he said again. "I'm no' an unreasonable man. I see ye're in a difficult position with the armaments and I would like to put a proposal to ye."

Carey's eyebrows went up.

"Oh?" he said.

"Ay, I would. I…we would like to sell ye our…spare weapons for the price of twenty shillings a gun, it being wholesale, as it were."

Carey's face was completely unreadable. There was a short silence.

"I should hate to make a similar mistake to Lord Maxwell's," he said cautiously at last.

King James nodded vigorously. "Of course ye can check them over, fire them off a few times, take them apart if ye like. Ye'll find they're right enough: most of them have the Tower maker's mark on them which was a surprise to me."

Carey nodded, face completely straight. "Of course," he murmured. "May I ask if Your Majesty has sufficient weapons to defend yourself against Bothwell?"

"It's kind o' ye to be concerned for us, Sir Robert," said the King. "But we have decided there is no need to burn Liddesdale since the headmen there have come in and composed with us so loyally. Richie Graham of Brackenhill has made a handsome payment, for instance. And we have it on excellent authority that Bothwell has gone to the Highlands. We had always rather make peace than war, as ye know. Besides, it often strikes us that when ye give a man a weapon ye dinna always ken what he'll use it for."

If Carey disapproved of this reversal of policy, there was no sign of it in his face. He tilted his head politely, though he seemed very depressed about something.

"Now," said King James, who hated to see any man so sad. "I would have wanted to talk to ye in any case, Sir Robert, even without all this trouble."

"Your Majesty does me too much honour," said Carey, mechanically, as if he were thinking about something else.

"Not a bit of it," said King James, leaning forward to pat the man's shoulder. "It's the horse."

"The horse?"

"Ay. That big black beast o' yours."

"Thunder?"

"That's the one. Now it seems to me ye'll hardly be doing much tilting whilst ye're Deputy Warden, and he's the finest charger I've seen in a long weary while, myself. What would you say to selling him to me for, say, half the gold finder's fee ye got from the Italian, at the same time as you sign over to me all the bank drafts in payment for the guns. Eh?"

Carey paused and then spoke carefully. "Let me be sure I've understood Your Majesty. You will give me the guns Lord Spynie reived from the Newcastle convoy to Carlisle…"

"I never said they were the same, only that they were originally from the Tower of London."

"Of course, Your Majesty. You will give me your spare guns, release my men Red Sandy Dodd and Sim's Will Croser from the Dumfries lock-up, give me all my gear back including my pair of dags…"

"They're waiting for ye downstairs," put in the King helpfully.

"…in exchange for Thunder, several hundred pounds English of banker's drafts and half my liquid cash."

"Only half."

"Your Majesty, I am overwhelmed."

"Is it a done deal?" asked King James.

"If the weapons have not been tampered with by…any ill-affected persons, then yes, Your Majesty, it is a deal."

"Excellent," beamed King James. "Have some wine, Sir Robert. Oh, and what would ye like me to do with Sir Henry Widdrington?"

Carey compressed his lips together and looked down.

"May I think about it, Your Majesty?"

"Ye can, but not for long. He's an Englishman, given leave to enter the realm, I must charge him and have him extradited or let him go. An' I'm no' so certain what the charge should be, neither."

In fact this was another of King James's games. He liked to tempt people; as usual he had already decided to release Sir Henry since it would save him a mountain of tedious letter-writing to the Marshal of Berwick, but he was interested to see what kind of revenge Carey would want.

He met the bright blue eyes and wondered uneasily if Carey had somehow penetrated his game. Carey still had his lips tight shut. At last he spoke.

"If you still have him here, Your Majesty, I want to talk to him in private."

"Why?"

"I am afraid for his wife. I know she was the one who came to you with the information on her husband's doings, and he may…be angry with her for her betrayal."

And small blame to him, thought King James, a typical woman to do such a thing.

"Is she your mistress?" King James asked nosily.

Carey's face went red like a little boy's. At first the King thought it was embarrassment, but then he realised that Carey was pale skinned enough to go red with anger as well. Perhaps he had been a little tactless.

"No, Your Majesty," Carey said quietly enough, and then smiled tightly. "Though not for want of my trying."

"Ay well," said the King comfortably. "They're odd creatures, sure enough. I dinna understand my Queen at all and it's not as if she's been over-educated and addled her poor brains, she seems naturally perverse."

Carey coughed and smiled more naturally. "Lady Widdrington is a woman of very strong character," he said. "If I could make her my wife, I would be the happiest man in the Kingdom."

"Oh ay?" said the King, sorry to hear it and wondering if Carey was about to ask him to do away with his rival somehow.

"Although to be honest," Carey continued, "what I would like is to petition Your Gracious Majesty to string her husband up and make an end of him, unfortunately I am completely certain that if I did, she would marry any man in the world except me."

King James shook his head sympathetically. "There's no pleasing them, is there?" he said. "Ay well, I'm glad ye didna ask me to do it because I canna string him up in any case, our cousin the Queen would be highly offended if I took such liberties with any of her subjects."

He caught Carey's narrow look: that was as close as a King could come to an apology and he was glad that Carey had taken the hint.

"It would be a shame," Carey said obligingly, "if Her Majesty were to be disturbed with any of these...er...problems."

"It would," agreed the King heartily.

"Such a thing would only be necessary if there was a further...er...problem with the guns. Or if my Lady Widdrington were to die unexpectedly for any reason whatever."

King James sniffed in irritation at this piece of barefaced cheek, justified though it was. "We are quite sure that the guns are as they should be."

"Lady Widdrington?"

"*I'll* speak with Sir Henry, if ye like. He'll understand where his true interests lie."

"Of course, Your Majesty. There is also the practical problem of getting the guns back to Carlisle, since I brought hardly any men with me. And as I said, two of them are in the Dumfries lock-up for fighting."

The King waved a hand. "Speak to the Earl of Mar and we'll bail your men and find ye an escort. Can ye lay your hands on the money?"

"I think so, Your Majesty," said Carey resignedly, no doubt thinking of what the funds could have bought him if he had managed to keep them. "I hope so." Still, you've no cause for complaint, Sir Robert, thought the King comfortably; I could have taken the lot of it for all the trouble you've caused me.

"Speak to the Earl of Mar to fetch your gear. Ye can make the exchange today if ye move quickly."

## fRIÐay 14th July 1592, afteRnoon

Sir John Carmichael had only just heard the latest gossip about the doings at the King's court when the subject of it breezed into the alehouse in the late afternoon, free, armed and with his left hand bandaged and in a sling. At his heels trotted his Graham pageboy. Sir John was not quite sure how to treat the hero of such melodramatic stories but, for the sake of his father, led him into a private room and sent for wine.

It turned out that all Carey wanted to do was borrow the services of a trustworthy clerk and dictate an exact account of what had been going on in Dumfries and Carlisle over the past couple of weeks, particularly in relation to no less than two loads of mixed calivers and pistols which seemed to have had the most exciting time of all.

By the end of it, Sir John was calling for more wine and damning Lord Spynie's eyes and limbs impartially. He was particularly shocked at the idea of a gentleman and cousin of the Queen being tortured by some jumped-up lad of a favourite as if he were a bloody peasant. Carey agreed with him, read over the fair copy and then took a pen in his purple fingers and painfully wrote a further paragraph in a numerical cipher, topping and tailing the whole with the conventional phrases of a son to his father. Sir John privately doubted that Sir Robert was in fact as humbly obedient to Lord Hunsdon, the absentee Warden of the East March, as he professed to be or indeed should have been.

"My father's in London," Carey said. "Would you make sure this reaches him without going near either Lord Scrope or Sir John Forster, nor even my brother in Berwick?"

Sir John Carmichael nodded sympathetically.

"Will he show it to the Queen?"

"Only if I die...er...unexpectedly in office, or that's what I told him to do."

"Mphm. Ye'll stay the night here, of course, since ye can hardly go back to Maxwell."

Carey coughed. "Hardly. Thank you. Now, Sir John, I wonder if I could ask you another favour?"

"Ye can always ask and I can always listen."

"I talked to Sir Henry Widdrington before I left the Court and the King promised to hold him for me until tomorrow evening, but I have a packtrain of armaments to get back to Carlisle. Even if I leave before dawn that won't give me much of a start."

"Ay," agreed Carmichael, having got there long before him. "I canna lend you men, but I can give ye some information. Someone stirred up the Johnstones this morning: the laird and his kin moved out of Dumfries in a body. My esteemed successor went hammering out of town in the direction of Lochmaben shortly after, wi' every one of his men."

Carey frowned.

"The Maxwells and Johnstones are massing for battle?"

Sir John tipped his head. "Maxwell blames you."

"Oh, Christ. What the hell has he got against me?" demanded Carey, clearly not feeling as blithely confident as he looked. "I saved his life."

"Och, but that was days ago," said Carmichael. "Wi' the like of him, it's a hundred years back. And he wants your guns."

"To wipe out the Johnstones?"

"Ay. See ye, the Johnstones had just taken delivery of a surprising number of guns fra Carlisle, through the usual…er… system, ye ken, when ye arrived in the north and made yer surprise inspection of the Armoury. After that, they got to keep them and that had Maxwell awfy worried, so he put in a large bid to Thomas the Merchant Hetherington to get some for himself, which went, I believe, through your ain predecessor in office, Sir Richard Lowther."

"Why can't any of these idiots buy guns in Dumfries?" asked Carey wearily. "Why does Carlisle have to supply their every want?"

Carmichael shrugged. "It's cheaper, mostly, the Dumfries armourers are very pricey men, and slow if ye want a lot in a hurry, and o' course it's more fun that way. Now, ye may have saved Maxwell's life, but ye also diddled him out of a fortune and spoiled his plan for catching the Johnstones unawares, which he resents and so…"

Carey knuckled at his eyes and then shook his head.

"And I haven't even kept the bloody money. What about the King? I've got twenty lancers from him already to see me through the Debateable Land. Would he give me more troops as protection, do you think?"

"Ay, the King," said Carmichael carefully. "They do say he kens an awful lot more than he lets on."

Carey looked straight at him, considering. "Yes," he said. "That's what I thought."

## saturday 15th july 1592, dawn

When dawn came up the next day Carey and his packtrain were already heading eastwards into its bronze light, with a royal escort of twenty lancers and a Royal Warrant in Carey's belt pouch commanding safeconduct for him to the Border. Young Hutchin was not at his side, having been sent ahead with an urgent message on the fastest pony Carey could find.

He was not at all his usual self that morning. He already felt weary and a night of poor sleep made fitful by the throbbing pain in his hands had not helped. He was nervous because he knew perfectly well he could not even hold a sword, let alone wield it, and if he tried to shoot one of his dags, he would drop it. It was hateful to be so weak and defenceless, and the knowledge of his incapacity shortened his temper even further and filled him with ugly suspicions. He was quite sure that many of the lancers escorting his convoy were privately wondering just how annoyed their King would be if they simply stole some of the weapons and slipped back to their families. He very much doubted if they would lift a finger for him if the Maxwells showed up.

*When* the Maxwells showed up, he corrected himself, because they were guaranteed to do so. Lord Maxwell was a Border baron, descended from a long line of successful robbers; what he wanted, generally speaking, he took. And Carey was alone apart from the battered and subdued Red Sandy and Sim's Will, and made very nearly helpless by Lord Spynie.

He kicked his horse to a canter alongside the line of patiently plodding ponies, up to their leader which was being ridden by a dourfaced Scottish drover.

"Is this the fastest pace you can take?" he demanded of the man.

The drover stared at him for a moment, then spat into a tussock of grass.

"Ay," he said. "There's thirty-five mile to cover. Ye canna do it in less than two days and if ye have no fresh beasts waiting at Annan, ye canna do it at all wi' out care, the way they're laden."

That was unanswerable. Carey harumphed impatiently and rode a little ahead where he had put the least-villainous looking of King James's inadequate troops. No wonder the King didn't want to take them into Liddesdale on a foray. Then he rode back to the rear of the train to take a look at the others there. He was wasting time and effort, he knew. The ponies plodded on in their infuriatingly patient way and all he had to do was look at their tails and pray silently.

It was almost a relief to him as they climbed on what passed for a path along the sides of the hills, when he began to see armed men notching the skyline to their left and heard the plovers being put up in the distance.

"Here they come, sir," said Red Sandy, loosening his sword and taking a firm grip on his lance.

"Do you know who they are?" he demanded.

"Ay," said Sim's Will. "By the look of their jacks, they're Maxwells."

"God damn it," muttered Carey. "Where the hell is Dodd?"

"Ah'm here, sir."

"Not you, Red Sandy; your brother."

Red Sandy looked puzzled and Carey stood in his stirrups and looked around. Ahead of them on the road was the golden flash of sun on a polished breastplate and the flourish of feathers in a hat.

Carey pressed his horse to a canter again. "Keep going no matter what happens," he snarled at the chief drover as he passed.

Lord Maxwell's saturnine face was aggravatingly relaxed as Carey approached.

"Good day to ye, Sir Robert," he called out.

"Good day, my lord," said Carey, tipping his hat with the very barest minimum of civility.

"We'll escort ye to Lochmaben now."

For a moment Carey thought of a variety of responses, ranging from the reproachful to the courteous. In the end he ditched them all in favour of honesty.

"In a pig's arse, my lord."

This was not how Maxwell was accustomed to being addressed. He blinked and his heavy eyebrows came down.

"What?"

"I said, in a pig's arse, my lord," repeated Carey with the distinctness usually reserved for the imbecilic or deaf.

"I'll have my guns one way or the other, Carey."

"To begin with, my lord, they are not your guns, they are guns belonging to the Queen's Majesty of England."

"They're mine now," said Maxwell with a shrug.

"No," said Carey. "They're not."

"Ye're not in yer ain March now, Carey. If ye give me no trouble, I'll let you and yer men go free without even asking ransom."

The sound of a single gun firing boomed out like the crack of doom in the quiet hills and danced between them. Carey looked over to his right and saw the distant lanky figure of Sergeant Dodd standing on a low ridge to the south of the road, with a smoking caliver. He lowered it, handed it to the Johnstone standing beside him who began the process of swabbing and reloading, and took another caliver that also had its match lit, blew carefully on the end to make it hot and took painstaking aim at Lord Maxwell.

Maxwell knew that breastplates do not stop bullets and that where one Johnstone was visible there were likely to be plenty more. He darkened with fury.

Carey worked hard to keep his relief from showing on his face. He had known that Dodd and the laird Johnstone were both too experienced to show themselves before their enemies had done so, but he hadn't been sure they would be there at all.

"Now, my lord, unless you want a fight with the Johnstones over the packtrain in which the Johnstones have guns and you have not you'll let us go on to Carlisle in peace."

Maxwell's face twisted. "Is that what ye think? D'ye believe the laird Johnstone will let your precious packtrain into Annan and ever let it out again?"

"Nobody in Scotland is getting possession of these weapons," said Carey through his teeth, "though at the moment I am more inclined to trust the laird Johnstone whom I have never met than I am to trust you, my lord."

Maxwell sneered.

"But," Carey continued, "in the interests of peace on the Border and the amicable co-operation of the two Wardenries, I am willing to allow this arrangement. You and the laird Johnstone may accompany me to the Border itself along with your men to be sure that neither one of you lays hands on the guns."

"Ye're in no condition to dictate terms."

"I believe I am, my lord. Think where I must have got these guns from. Think who's sitting in Dumfries with an army."

"The King couldnae take Lochmaben."

"He could if we lent him our cannon from Carlisle."

"Well, ye've the Johnstones and the King to protect ye. Are ye not man enough to protect yourself?"

Perhaps it was just as well Carey couldn't hold a sword at that moment. Maxwell's gesture made his imputation clear enough.

"Take it or leave it," said Carey when he could trust himself to speak, settled down in the saddle and stared at Maxwell.

He was never sure afterwards why Maxwell blinked first. Perhaps it was the ominous distant hiss of slowmatches from the hillside where the Johnstones were watching, or perhaps it was the drovers bringing the ponies up and past them as if neither side were there. Maxwell had not been Warden of the Scottish West March very long, perhaps he was uncertain enough of what King James might really do to be willing to wait for a better time to take on the Johnstones.

Never did a packtrain have a more puissant escort. All the long road into Annan, all the long night while Carey, Dodd and the King's lancers stood guard in watches over the guns, and all the next day, the Johnstones and Maxwells watched balefully over the weapons that could tip the balance so lethally between them.

As they watched the ponies splash over the Longtown ford into England at last and start south on the old Roman road, Carey growled at Hutchin.

"If your relatives turn up now, I'm taking you hostage."

Young Hutchin grinned at him. "Ay, my Uncle Jimmy thought about it," he said disarmingly. "It's very tempting after all."

"And?"

"I persuaded them not to."

"Indeed."

"We've the King after us wi' blood in his eye for the Falkland raid, after all. We dinna want mither wi' the Queen as well."

"Oh? That sounds very statesmanlike."

"Ay. And our friends the Johnstones shared the guns they got to keep after ye turned over the Armoury, and besides we wouldnae want to mix it with the Maxwells without all our men here."

"Astonishing. Borderers thinking before they fight."

"Ay, sir. We're learning."

The two surnames watched glowering from the other side of the Esk to be sure that neither one of them made a sudden attack.

The ponies passed the ford and plodded on for the last eight miles of their journey, leaving them far behind. For the first time in his life, Carey felt quite weak with relief that there was not going to be a fight.

## sunday 16th july 1592, evening

Lord Scrope, Warden of the English West March, was of course delighted to see Carey return from his trip to Scotland at the head of a pack train laden with guns, all of Tower-make, all of precisely the pattern that the Queen issued to the north, with only about ten missing. It was worrying to see he had somehow injured his left hand, which was bandaged and in a sling, and also from the evidence of his face he had been in at least one fistfight. Sergeant Dodd, Red Sandy and Sim's Will Croser were looking uncharacteristically subdued, while a lad who had been missing from Carlisle had evidently tagged along with Carey unasked, and got into a fight as well. Heroically, Scrope suppressed his questions until they had dealt with the weapons. Those were stowed in the Armoury again while Richard Bell took a record of exactly what was there, Carey locked the door with a flourish and a suppressed wince and then turned to Scrope.

"Um…" said Scrope, bursting with curiosity to know what had happened to him. "Your report?"

"To you, verbally, my lord," said Carey. "Now."

That was worrying. They returned to Scrope's dining-room cum council chamber and Carey sat down in one of the chairs with a sigh and blinked at him.

"Will you call for beer, my lord?"

"Of course."

They waited, Carey tipping his head back against the chair and shutting his eyes. When the beer came, Carey reached out to take the nearest tankard and noticed he still had his gauntlet on. With his teeth he stripped the glove off. Scrope stared at his hand which was mottled purple and red, and missing two fingernails.

"Good God, man, what happened to your…?"

"Thumbscrews," said Carey shortly and drank most of his beer. "I'll give you my interpretation of events as I go along, shall I, my lord?"

Scrope nodded, clearly finding it hard to look at his damaged fingers. Carey didn't blame him. The empurpled nailbeds made him feel queasy in a way that a much worse wound would not.

Carey blinked again at the florid hunters on the tapestry hanging behind Scrope's head, marshalling his thoughts with great effort. At last he spoke again in a flat tired voice.

"Well, my lord, in my humble opinion we were dealing not only with two loads of firearms, but also with two separate plots. One load of firearms came from the Tower of London and was stolen on the road from Newcastle. The second load was swapped for them to hide the theft. They were the ones that ended up in our Armoury and every single weapon was faulty.

"The first plot concerns Lord Spynie. He had been given the power to procure the King of Scotland's handguns, but like most army contractors he spent much of the money on other things and was then in a quandary to buy the weapons he needed. Luckily there was a German in Edinburgh, newly arrived from Augsburg where they also make weapons, who offered to supply him the guns at a cut price. All would have been well if the German had in fact been a master gunsmith as he claimed, because to be honest, my lord, the German weapons are usually better than ours. Unfortunately he was not a master, nor even a journeyman. He had been expelled from a Hanseatic gunsmithing guild for shoddy workmanship and fraud. Spynie didn't know this, or didn't care, and accepted the deal happily.

"The German, going by the name of Hans Schmidt, set up a gun foundry in Jedburgh where he simply turned out the guns as quickly as he could with untrained labour. I don't believe he bothered to caseharden the lock parts and the forge-welding and beating out of the barrels was so badly done, they were bound to crack at the first firing and explode at the second.

"Spynie had paid for them, taken delivery of them, when he found out—no doubt, the same way we did—that they were no better than scrap metal. Also the German had disappeared, the King's procurement money was spent, and Spynie couldn't make the weapons useable. The problem became more acute after Bothwell's raid on Falkland Palace, when the King called out his levies for a justice raid."

"But didn't he find his runaway German? You told me you had witnessed his arrest..."

"Yes. Schmidt was hiding with a woman who sold him to Spynie once he ran out of money—I'm afraid he was as bad a fraudster as he was a gunsmith."

"Bloody man deserves to hang, for the maiming and deaths he caused."

Carey shut his eyes again. "He's dead," he said shortly. After a moment he carried on.

"So then Spynie gets wind of our new delivery of weapons from London and with a little help from his English friends—most notably Sir Simon Musgrave, Sir Henry Widdrington and his kin, and the family of Littles—he carries out a daring swap a day or two out of Carlisle. He gets the good Tower weapons; we get the ones the German sold him and put them into our Armoury. Purely incidentally, while helping to swap the weapons over, Long George Little steals himself a new pistol. Which explodes in his hand when he's on night patrol with me."

Scrope had steepled his fingers and was looking through them like a child at a frightening sight.

"Clear so far?" prompted Carey.

"Eh? Oh, yes, very clear. A model of clarity, my dear Robin. Would you prefer to continue with this tomorrow, after you've had some sleep. You can have had none at all last night—you must be exhausted."

"I am tired," Carey admitted in a wintry voice. "But I prefer to make my report while it's fresh in my mind."

Scrope inclined his head politely.

"Now we must switch to another plot. Quite separately, Lord Maxwell was very anxious to lay hands on a good supply of firearms to continue and, he hoped, finish his feud with the Johnstones. He needed them because the Johnstones appear to be very well-armed, again with guns corruptly acquired from the Carlisle Armoury."

"I wish one lot or the other would win," interrupted Scrope wistfully. "It would cut in half the amount of trouble from the West."

"Maxwell made contact with Sir Richard Lowther and asked for the longterm hire of the weapons in the Armoury, on the usual illegal and damnably corrupt terms. Not in any way realising that the guns were faulty—in fact they hadn't arrived at this point— Sir Richard agreed."

Scrope nodded.

"But with me around and his pet Armoury clerk, Jemmy Atkinson, dead, he realised the old system could no longer work. At the same time, he wanted Maxwell's money. And so Lowther arranged to break into the Armoury while we were at the muster and steal the guns out of Carlisle. The plan was he would eventually 'find' them again once Maxwell had finished off the last Johnstone and no longer needed them. While he was about it, I wouldn't be at all surprised if he had found clear evidence that it was I stole 'em."

Scrope let out a humourless little "Heh, heh, heh." Then he added anxiously, "Unfortunately you have no proof it was Lowther who organised the theft."

"No, my lord, I haven't. There's nothing you could call proof for any of this."

Scrope tutted.

Carey paused, editing his story. Would it be wise to tell Scrope he had broken into the Armoury the night before the guns were stolen, marked them and borrowed two for target practice. Scrope would quite probably be finicky about that and also about why Carey hadn't told him. No, there was no point.

"At any rate, the bad guns went to Lord Maxwell and nobody knew there was anything wrong with them." Carey's expression changed to disgust. "That man has the luck of the Devil. If I hadn't happened to be in Dumfries and saw that the gun he was using looked like Long George's, we'd be shot of one major Border nuisance."

Scrope nodded, poured aqua vitae into his tankard and sipped. "Never mind," he said comfortingly. "You weren't to know, after all."

Matters were getting a bit delicate here. Carey decided to skate over some of the details.

"The long and the short of it is, my lord, that Maxwell was highly offended with me when I told him his new guns were all faulty. As a result of his treachery and Sir Henry Widdrington's, I was arrested by Lord Spynie on a trumped-up charge of treason."

"Ah," said Scrope sympathetically. "The thumbscrews."

"Yes. Fortunately, I have friends at the Scottish court who told the King what had happened and His Majesty was pleased to release me as soon as I had explained myself."

"How very lucky for you," said Scrope neutrally. Carey did not respond to his unspoken question.

"Yes. His Majesty was also munificent enough to return to me in recompense the guns that Spynie had stolen from our arms convoy and provide me with an escort to bring them to Carlisle."

"How extremely…er…munificent. And that's the story, is it?"

"Yes, my lord," said Carey.

"The full story?"

All of it that I'm prepared to tell you, Tom Scrope, Carey thought to himself. Too tired to talk he simply nodded.

"How much of this should we pass on to the Queen?"

"None," Carey answered instantly.

Scrope's face broke into a childlike smile of pure relief.

"Absolutely. I quite agree, my dear Robin, Her Majesty shouldn't be troubled with any of these little difficulties at all."

"That's what I said to King James."

"Splendid, splendid," said Scrope, leaning over to pat Carey's arm and then, after thinking better of it, his knee. "His Majesty's very wise and so are you. Discretion, clearly, is in order here."

"Yes."

"Right. Well. You'll be wanting to get to your bed, I expect. Barnabus is waiting for you in your chamber. We'll house and feed your escort and the ponies and send them back in a couple of days. Where's Thunder, by the way?"

"Oh," said Carey distantly, stumbling over another reason to feel depressed, "I sold him to the King."

"Excellent," beamed his inane brother-in-law. "Dreadfully expensive to feed and far too good for this part of the world. He'll be much happier in the King's stables. Did you…er…get enough for him?"

"Yes, my lord, I can pay the men next month." He hoped Dodd still had his winnings from the bet with Maxwell that he had given him to look after. Even without that, he thought he could make shift.

Scrope leaned over and aggravatingly patted his knee again. "You're a miracle-worker, Robin," he said. "Absolutely extraordinary."

Never had the spiral stair up to his chambers at the top of the Queen Mary Tower seemed so long. He actually had to stop halfway up with his better hand on the stone central spine to catch his breath and wait for his head to stop spinning.

The door of his chamber was open wide with Barnabus getting the fire going and Philadelphia standing there, hands on hips, imperiously overseeing. Carey paused again on the threshold, wondering how much more he could deal with before he fell over.

Philadelphia turned, saw him and ran to him, then skidded to a halt and frowned severely at him. With uncharacteristic gentleness, she folded her arms around him. God, thought Carey, I must look bloody terrible.

However bad he looked, he felt worse. He went and sat on the bed, which had yet another new counterpane on it. Philadelphia sent Barnabus away and then sat down next to him.

"I heard," she whispered. "I heard it all from Hutchin and Dodd. Let me see."

"For God's sake, Philly, I…"

"Oh, shut up." She picked up his right hand, examined it with her lip caught in her teeth, then took his splinted left hand. "This is Elizabeth Widdrington's work."

"Yes," said Carey, trying to remove it from her grasp. "And it hurt like hell when she did it, so don't undo it…*Aagh*! Christ *Jesus*, woman, what the hell do you think you're…"

"I only pressed the ends of your fingers to make sure you still have feeling in them."

"Well, I do."

"Don't growl at me like father, numbness is the first sign of gangrene."

"Philly, I've had about as much nursing as I can take."

"Then you won't want the spiced wine I brought you with laudanum in it to help you sleep."

"No, I…"

"And you won't want to hear what I found out about my lord Scrope."

Pure curiosity helped to clear his bleary head. He blinked at her questioningly.

"Scrope knew all about it, about swapping our proper guns for the faulty ones on the Newcastle road. And I'll bet he knew of Lowther's little scheme to steal the faulty ones out of our Armoury too."

"How do you know that?" he asked. "When did you find out?"

Philadelphia sniffed eloquently.

"When I read King James's letter about it to Scrope, the night after you left for Scotland. He had it in that stupid secret drawer in his desk which I check every so often to make sure he isn't doing anything idiotic like dealing with Spanish agents and the like."

She looked at him with kittenish satisfaction at knowing something he didn't, and her face fell. "Oh," she said. "You knew?"

Carey shook his head. "I suspected," he said. "Who arranges the bearfight?" he said. "The bear or the bearwarden? No, it had to be King James operating through Lord Spynie. I remember the Earl of Mar said that the King wanted the German, that night when we saw them capture him in the forest."

Philly nodded vigorously. "They had it all cooked up between them. Scrope kept quiet about the guns being swapped, King James could use our firearms to settle matters with the Debateable Land, and then he would return the guns to us. They only used the bad guns as dummies because you were about, causing trouble. It wasn't exactly official, but the King did pay my lord a consideration."

"A consideration," said Carey bleakly. "Philly, Scrope's lands yield three thousand pounds a year."

"Oh they do, but we spend an awful lot."

"So then what about Lowther…"

"I expect Scrope thought he had nothing to lose and plenty to gain by letting Lowther steal the bad guns. Maxwell might be badly weakened by the guns exploding in people's hands, he might even lose a big battle with the Johnstones as a result, which would sort him out and even up the balance in the Scottish West March."

"He might have died himself."

"Yes, true. And of course, if he didn't, he would be very annoyed with Lowther for selling him bad weapons, so Lowther would be weakened as well."

"So why in God's name did Scrope send me into Scotland without telling me any of this so I could protect myself?"

Philly smiled crookedly at him. "The silly idiot doesn't trust anyone and he didn't think you'd work it out. And I couldn't send Young Hutchin to you because the silly boy had disappeared. Scrope knew you'd want to go. You were the mechanism for King James to return the good guns to us in the end."

Carey laughed a little hollowly. "So I've been rooked," he said.

"You knew all this, didn't you?" Philly said intently. "Or you guessed?"

Carey nodded and rubbed the heel of his right palm into his eyes, yawning mightily. "I guessed," he said. "I guessed because of the way Scrope kept me away from the firearms; not at the time, unfortunately, but later, on the way back. Oh God, Philly, why does everything have to be so complicated?"

"Well," said Philly judiciously, "I suppose to Scrope it wasn't a lot different from King James borrowing our cannon to reduce some noble's fortress, which he does occasionally; it was just on a private basis, instead of officially."

"Yes. That wasn't what I meant."

"He didn't know Lord Spynie would do that to you."

"No. Did he know Sir Henry Widdrington would be there, trying to curry favour with King James in readiness for when the Queen dies?"

Philadelphia shrugged. "I don't think so. And you were eager enough to go and curry favour too."

"So I was."

"How's Elizabeth?"

"Her husband beat her black and blue for lending me his horses last month, and I think he beat her again after she dared to look at me across a street in Dumfries," said Carey bleakly.

Philadelphia nodded, unsurprised. "She told me she thought he might," she said. "About the horses, I mean. I'm not surprised he did it again either. For all his gout, he's very jealous of her."

"How long does it take an old man to die of the gout?"

"Too long."

Neither of them said anything for a while. At last, mercifully without a word, she undid his doublet buttons and laces for him, gave him the goblet of spiced wine and kissed him on the cheek when he had drunk some.

"I'll send Barnabus in to see to you," she said.

"Philly," Carey's voice was remote. "You don't think he'll kill her, do you?"

She considered gravely. "He might. But there's no point challenging him to a duel because he'd be bound to appoint a champion, so the whole thing would be a waste of time."

Carey smiled wanly. "I thought of that. When I talked to him in Dumfries, after King James had arrested him, I told him that whatever way he hurt his wife, I would infallibly do the same to him twice over and be damned to my honour."

"Well, you'd have to catch him first and beat off his surname, but I don't think he will kill her. He's old and he's sick and he needs her to nurse him when he's having an attack. In a way, I feel sorry for him despite what he does to Elizabeth."

"I don't," said Carey.

Philly smiled. "Sleep well, my dear," she said and shut the door softly.

By the time Barnabus went in to help him undress, he was snoring.

To receive a free catalog of other Poisoned Pen Press titles, please contact us in one of the following ways:

Phone: 1-800-421-3976
Facsimile: 1-480-949-1707
Email: info@poisonedpenpress.com
Website: www.poisonedpenpress.com

Poisoned Pen Press
6962 E. First Ave. Ste 103
Scottsdale, AZ 85251